The Ring

·THE·

Ring

DANIEL KEYS MORAN

BASED ON A SCREENPLAY BY

William Stewart and Joanne Nelsen

A Foundation Book
Doubleday

NEW YORK   LONDON   TORONTO   SYDNEY   AUCKLAND

A Foundation Book
Published by Doubleday, a division of
Bantam Doubleday Dell Publishing Group, Inc.,
666 Fifth Avenue, New York, New York 10103

Foundation, Doubleday, and the portrayal of the letter F
are trademarks of Doubleday, a division of
Bantam Doubleday Dell Publishing Group, Inc.

Library of Congress Cataloging-in-Publication Data
Moran, Daniel Keys.
The ring/by Daniel Keys Moran; based on a screenplay
by William Stewart and Joanne Nelsen.
p.   cm.
I. Stewart, William (William Layton), 1941–   . II. Nelsen,
Joanne. III. Ring (Motion Picture) IV. Title.
PS3563.0764R5   1988   88-10902
813'.54—dc19   CIP
ISBN 0-385-24816-4

Designed by Ann Gold

All Rights Reserved
Printed in the United States of America
October 1988
First Edition

For Amy Stout, who is basically a doll.

The Ring

The Ring

. . . the rush and roar soon took musical shape within my brain as the chord of E flat major, surging incessantly in broken chords: these declared themselves as melodic figurations of increasing motion, yet the pure triad of E flat major never changed, but seemed by its steady persistence to impart infinite significance to the element in which I was sinking. I awoke from my half-sleep in terror, feeling as though the waves were rushing high above my head. I at once recognized that the orchestral prelude to *The Rhinegold*, which for a long time I must have carried about within me, had at last come to being in me: and I quickly understood the very essence of my own nature: the stream of life was not to flow to me from without, but from within.

—Richard Wagner

The Children

The Year 3018 After the Fire

In these, the Later Days of the Earth, Spring comes less quickly than in the youth of the world, and flees sooner. Trees grow tall, untended oak and ash and walnut, along the banks of the great river Almandar, and bring forth their leaves as the air warms to the brief approaching summer. One huge patch of giant redwood spreads slowly to the north of the Valley. Silence lies over what was once called the Valley of the Rulers; from the north of the Valley, where the Great Dam keeps out the encroaching water of the One Ocean; silence, down the hills and steppes across which Almandar flows. Silence reigns in the buildings that are left standing now, eons after man left Earth to the Dolphins. Gentle winds stir blossoms of cherry and hyacinth, wild white orchids and the scarlet roses that are called Solan's Blood.

Birds break the silence now and again as Spring progresses, robins and crows and bluebirds, fat pigeons, and seagulls by the thousands. Once a shrike blunders into the airspace over the Valley, and weapons left dormant for thousands of turns about the sun flare into life. Lasers designed to shear metal make short work of feathers and hollow bone, and the bird falls with a single, almost human scream. The Dolphins observe this from the waterlocks that overlook the Valley and chuckle their pleasure to one another, for the shrikes are strong, fell creatures that have dragged more than one Dolphin across the surface of the waves to a nearby grounding, and made a meal of it.

Larger animals than birds pad quietly through the forests that have grown to fill the Valley. Polar bears, less furred than the old breed

3

from which they are descended, are the foremost carnivores across the length of the Valley. Herds of maverick horses run wild, and deer; beavers work along the river Almandar's length, and trout and catfish and rainbow willies flash beneath its surface. The genegineered treebunnies, with their grasping forehands, scamper through the tree-tops, their passage contested only by the languid, almost disinterested descendants of the cats who kept company with both Rulers and Workers in eons past.

North and east the Valley of the Rulers is ringed by the One Ocean, kept at its distance by force fields and the Great Dam; to the south and west rise the mountains. The Valley itself is not small; once there were eighty towns and villages spread across its length, from the foot of the mountains to the Great Dam which holds back the sea. At the north end of the Valley is the lake T'Pau, which is fed by water filtered from the Ocean, and from which flows the river Almandar.

One with a penchant for the cynical—one such as, say, the flame-haired Loga, Lord of Light, who has seen more wars than friendships; he of many vices, who rediscovered poker, craps, and rock and roll—one such as he might be tempted to point out the resemblance between the Valley of the Rulers and the Eden of one of man's early religions.

It is unlikely, of course, that such a comparison shall be made.

The Valley is empty, and has been so for long and long.

Spring wears away.

"Forget I even mentioned Eden, forget I even brought up the concept of Paradise, will *that* make you happy? Does it *matter* that the Creator T'Pau was a devout Christian? In the wisdom of your five years you have struck upon the answer: probably not."

Their shadows mingled with the shadows of the forest. The twelve children, following the tall adult down the path among the overarching trees, hurried. They were normal children; in their childhood they were all that was left of the childhood of the human race. With the advent of adulthood they would take on powers and duties the likes of which no human of an earlier day could have envisioned, would metamorphose in a change more striking and no less fundamental than that of a butterfly from a caterpillar.

But that would be later; they were, for now, only children.

Dressed all in green and black, the curled red hair flowing down across his shoulders, the adult did not pause for them. His steps were even and measured, as though he might walk straight around the world without slowing if the fancy took him.

Despite the shortness of their breath, the children threw questions at him with the zeal of inquisitors. At first his manner had intimidated them, but only for a short time. For most of them this was their first time visiting Earth; for most of them it would also be their last. Some of their questions the adult answered, and told them of bears and why bears were carnivores, of the Ice Times and the Floods which had followed the first and largest of the Fire Wars, and of the Dolphins and the treaty that had given them the water-covered planet so strangely misnamed Earth. Some questions he ignored, and so they did not learn of the laser weapons that protected most of the Valley, nor of the genegineered red silkies and shriken which were produced during the later stages of the Fire Wars.

In response to one question he said, "You should have gone before we left."

They came at length to a vast field, kilometers across, a clearing where no trees grew, and no flowers. Wild grass filled it across its length, green and brown beneath the bright sun. The river called the Killing Creek, flowing down to join the great river Almandar, bordered it on one side, and the forest on the other. Standing at the edge of the trees, they could see, if they looked south and east into the rising foothills of the Black Mountains, the distant, glowing crystal spires of the city of Parliament.

The adult did not look toward Parliament. His gaze roved out across the empty field. "It happened here," he said, so quietly that the children must strain to hear him. "Solan fell here, and our hopes for peace. . . ."

He stood so, silently, lost in memory, until the children behind him began to stir, and one, a girl of some eight years, with more bravery or less sense than the others, said, "Loga? May we see Parliament?"

The man said nothing. A brilliant band of light gathered itself in around them, momentarily outshining the sun itself.

They were gone.

THE RING

They appeared in the Hall of Mirrors.

Their images bounced away from them, hundreds of tall, blue-eyed Logas, thousands upon thousands of children. It was a choice Loga had made for effect; as a result he waited patiently as the children exclaimed in wonder at their surroundings, and tried to walk through the mirrors to see what was on the other side. At length, without word, he turned away from them and strode off down the length of the Hall.

The children made haste behind him, before the real Loga vanished into his mirrored reflections.

They stumbled out into the Chamber of Parliament with shocking abruptness. One moment they had been in the Hall of Mirrors; an instant later they were not, and there was no doorway to be seen. That alone did not startle the children, for there were such Gates at home as well, though they were always well marked and did not vanish at the other end.

But the Chamber of Parliament was not what they had expected.

Oh, they had audited descriptions of it, to be sure, and seen holos, but that was not sufficient to prepare them for the sheer grand spectacle of it.

The structure itself was laid in an open clearing hundreds of meters across, nestled high in the Black Mountains. An ancient landpad, its once-brilliant landing markers covered with the dirt of ages, was, with the Chamber of Parliament itself, all there was to be found in that clearing.

None of that, to be sure, startled them at all.

But . . . the ceiling hung full fifteen meters above them, sculpted gold and silver, without any physical structure supporting it. The walls rose eight meters around most of the perimeter of the Chamber, to the south and east and west, and then dropped to touch the floor at the north end, so that the entire north quadrant was open to the air. From any seat within the Chamber one could look down, north, and see the ancient landpad, and beyond it, the entirety of the Valley. Rows of seats rose in a tier around the center of the Chamber, enoꞏ ꞏh seats to accommodate hundreds at once. Dusty white marble covered most of the Chamber. A single spire of black marble, with gleaming veins of gold, thrust up two meters south of the exact northernmost point of the Chamber, the podium from which the Rulers of Earth had addressed one another on formal occasions.

"This is where the Rulers had meetings," said Loga. The expression on his face was unreadable; the index finger of the glove on his right hand was gray from the thick layer of dust he had traced off of the surface of the podium. "Here they tried to bring everyone together—Cain and Maston, Warriors and Workers, and the Giants . . ."

The boy who had questioned Loga about his reference to Eden, a grave-faced five-year-old named Innelieu, said, "How do you know, Loga?"

"Hmm?" Loga looked over at the boy absently. "How do I know? It does not matter."

The child refused to be turned away from his question. "Were you there?"

Loga considered the question. At length he said slowly, "There was a man named Loga, and he was there, yes. But that was a long time ago, and things were very much different, then, than they are now." He turned his back on them and looked back out over the Valley. Someday he would have to stop making this trip, give the burden over to another. The children needed it, needed to touch the soil from which their people had sprung, to breathe the air of the planet that Loga still thought of as home.

But perhaps Loga was not the one to bring them. Perhaps he would wait a couple of decades and load the job down on one such as Innelieu, for whom the beauty of Earth would be unmixed with the pain of memory.

"Will you tell us about it?"

Amazing, thought Loga, *after all these years, a question I have never been asked before.* He had no intention of telling any of them anything about the childhood of their race, about the horrors that the Rulers and the Workers and the Giants had inflicted upon each other. They were far too young. . . .

He heard his own voice coming from somewhere else, the words moving out of him in a calm and measured fashion.

"A long time ago people warred upon one another. They fought, children, poorly and without sufficient skill to destroy those whom they thought their enemies, only enough skill to harm those enemies and leave them free to seek vengeance, in a circle from which there seemed no end. It started because the Workers wanted freedom, and the Giants, who were working for the Rulers . . . no," he said, and his voice carried strongly, almost harshly, "it started because they wanted control . . ." His voice broke in the middle of the sentence, and he became aware of the trembling of his hands, and crossed his arms across his chest to hide their lack of steadiness. "Fools they were, all of them, they fought over the Light as though it were something outside them, as though it were a weapon or a tool, never once before the end stopped fighting—and that is not the way to go from the dark to the Light."

His bright blue eyes staring out sightlessly over the length of the Valley of the Rulers, the Lord of Light named Loga told for the only time in his life, as though it were a vast weight being lifted from his shoulders, the true story of Cain and Loden, Senta and Solan, and yes, the truth behind the legend that was Orion of Eastmarch.

PART ONE

The Diamond of the Day

The Theft

The Year 1284 After the Fire

Beneath the rolling hills of Eastmarch the starship took shape over the space of a decade. In the huge Caverns at the east end of the Valley, technicians designed and built and tested, flew the ship and redesigned it, ran stress analysis tests on it, crashed it and rebuilt it again.

The subwave motor they could not even test; they did not know enough about how it functioned. As near as the engineers could estimate, the engine was reliable for—perhaps—four or five subspace Drops. They could not even attempt a Drop as a test, for that would use up one of the precious few problematical Drops left to the engine.

There was only one such engine in all the Caverns.

One morning, early in Winter Quarter 1284 A.T.F., a tall man with chalk-white skin sought entrance to the presence of his master. The man's name was Kavad. He was, to the folk of the Valley—Rulers and Workers alike—a barbarian from beyond the Glowing Desert, one of the pale, silver-eyed ken Selvren. If he did not act the role of a barbarian, perhaps it was simply because he was quite old, and well versed in the ways of the civilized world. Most of his adult life had been spent in the service of a man whom even Kavad's mother had found formidable.

He knocked at the door to Cain's suite of quarters, once, sharply. The guards in front of his master's door—one of them ken Selvren, like Kavad—did not even seem to notice him; they would near as soon have questioned Cain himself. Cain's bath servant was sleeping with a blanket and pillow beside the door.

The soft, musical voice was muffled only somewhat by the door between them.

"Enter."

Kavad pushed through the door. The first room in the five that composed his master's quarters was nearly dark; it often was, and it did not bother Kavad. His night sight was better than Cain's, better than that of any Worker; better, he suspected, than that of the genegineered Rulers. Cain was seated in the exact geometric center of the room, among the soft rugs of deer fur and the cushions of white sunsilk; sitting cross-legged with his spine straight, hands resting upon his knees. Dim glowfloats bounced restlessly in the air behind Cain, sent his shadow wavering out toward Kavad in grotesque shapes. Quietly, he spoke.

"Good morning, Kavad."

Kavad inclined his head slightly; his lord had never required more of him than that. Had he been required to bend his knee as the Workers were used to doing for their masters, he could not have remained in Cain's service. Thirty-seven years now Kavad had spent in that service. Their roles were clearly defined, and Kavad was deeply satisfied with them. Cain was his lord, and Kavad was his servant; and if they were also friends, nonetheless the first relationship took precedence over the latter.

"Good morning, my lord."

"What have you for me, Kavad?"

"My lord, the shipwrights have informed me that the ship is ready, as ready as it will ever be."

Cain's head moved in what Kavad thought a nod. "Have you learned anything new regarding the plans of the Rulers? *Something* is happening at Parliament . . . I can feel it."

"My lord, I regret, we have learned nothing new."

In the darkness Cain's features were not clear. Kavad thought he might, perhaps, have smiled. "So. But the ship is ready." He clapped his hands together, sharply, once. His bath servant appeared in the doorway almost instantly. "Bring me my flight suit," he instructed. The bath servant, a young girl whose name Kavad could never recall, ran past Kavad, into the next room.

The quiet sounds of clothing being prepared reached them.

"Ten years of peace," said Cain. As always, the voice was smooth, almost lyrical; Kavad had often thought that his master might have made a fine singer, though he had never heard Cain raise his voice so. "Ten years of truce with the Rulers, and twenty years of war with them before they would grant that; and a thousand years of slavery before even that.

"Now, Kavad," he said, "we will *win*."

It lacked better than an hour before sunrise.

In a flight suit of ancient design and recent construction, the tall, black-haired, dark-eyed man who was Cain of Eastmarch walked alone through the dimly lit corridors of the Caverns.

Seeing him for the first time, one who did not see the depths of his eyes might have guessed his age at, perhaps, twenty-five.

The shipyard was at the far north end of the Caverns; Cain's quarters, and those of his subjects, were, for reasons of safety, at the far south. The walk from Cain's quarters to the shipyard was a lengthy one, mostly uphill. The living quarters were deep in the Earth; the shipyards were only one level beneath the surface. It never crossed Cain's mind to bring bodyguards with him, walking alone at night through his own domain. He was the most feared, and likely the most hated, human then alive on the face of the Earth.

Cain was, in his own person, quite certainly the deadliest. The Worker or Workers who made the mistake of an attempt on his life would die, quickly and surely.

Possibly the Ruler Loden was more dangerous than Cain; it was likely he was feared by a greater number of sentient beings. But Loden, Cain believed, was not a human being.

Cain walked down the corridors. Doors opened at his approach, closed again as he passed. Once he crossed the path of two pair of his barbarian ken Selvren guards, changing the guard at the East Gate. One was a half-breed, with darker skin than his fellows, but the same silver eyes. Cain did not speak to them, but merely continued on his way. The guards, after a brief pause, went about their business. In the dim lighting that was the norm for the night hours, one might have thought that the guards had not noticed his passage.

THE RING

They were ken Selvren.
One would have been wrong.

Despite the hour, the shipyard was acrawl with activity, the center of which was a slim needle of black metal, utterly unlike any of the other fighter craft arrayed across the yard. The ship bore no visible weapons; no mountings for lasers, no heatseeker grips. The smooth black hull was one surface, without seam or weld anywhere upon it. It seemed to absorb light; its surface gave no reflection.

It was the result of over ten years' labor by the finest human engineers in existence. It was, so far as Cain's engineers could make it, an exact duplicate of a Falcon-class slipship, the smallest faster-than-light starship ever built. The hull, the instrumentation, the reaction engines, all were modeled upon the starships that the Ruler Donner Almandar had built in the third century A.T.F. to serve as scouts for the great fleet of starships which he had led from Earth in that century. The subwave motor was more than "modeled" upon one of Donner's ships; it had actually been taken from the shell of a thousand-year-old Falcon found at the edge of the Glowing Desert, far to the south. They had reconditioned the subwave motor; repaired the casing which held it, replaced with new materials all the parts which they were capable of understanding. But the core of the engine, the blocks of molar probability circuitry, they could not touch; had they, however accidentally, harmed that circuitry, decades would have passed while they strove to re-create it.

Half a dozen junior Commanders stood behind them at rigid attention.

Cain and Mersai stood together in the Command Center, before the huge star chart, with a full sixteenth of the galaxy spread across its surface. A bright blue dot—the solar system, and Earth, though at that resolution they were the same—glowed at its far left side, and near its far right side was a single green dot. The chart was twice the height of a man; a Giant would, just barely, have reached its top.

The image was ludicrous, of course. Standing there in his grimly efficient combat fatigues, Commander General Orrin Mersai's age-ruined visage moved in a faint smile. The Giant who made his way into the Caverns, for whatever reason, was a dead Giant.

"We don't have decades," Cain was saying without heat. "There's something happening at Parliament, and there's something happening in orbit. The Rulers are getting ready for another campaign, I think. In any event," he said, with cold amusement glinting in the hard dark eyes, "even if they are not preparing to break the Treaty, we *are.*" Cain turned away from the old General, looked again at the star chart. He touched the green dot, and the map flickered; the next instant it held the image of a planetary system with eight planets and a pair of asteroid rings. The fourth planet out was a super-Jovian; in orbit about the gas giant was a single satellite of approximately Earth's size: the planet Cassandra. Cain's comment was utterly unrelated to the image on the screen. "The Rulers still hold nearly half this Valley, my friend, from Singer to Parliament itself, the entire length of Almandar; and Maston holds nearly one fifth of what is left. That is not acceptable."

General Mersai nodded. "I am not arguing, my lord. I merely wish we might send someone other than yourself."

Cain was silent for a moment. They were on a level with the shipyard; through the observation bay windows they could see the final work being done on the starship: the fusion cells being loaded and the lifeplant being lowered into position near the rear of the cockpit. The soundproofing was not perfect; the clang and rumble of heavy equipment in operation was, in the silence, just audible. Cain's reply, when it came, surprised Mersai somewhat. He was used to the bravado of the Warriors and did not doubt for an instant Cain's courage; he had followed Cain into battle too many times, had on one occasion seen Cain defeat five skilled Warriors at once in unarmed combat. "I wish that also, my friend. The day following the day of my death, the Rulers will bring Eastmarch to its knees. And I am frightened, in some measure, for myself. When the Rulers were at the height of their power, when Donner Almandar led his fleet of ships from Earth, he was warned away by the Sisterhood of the Ring from their home and did obey the warning. This is a desperate measure, for a desperate time." Cain's gaze came back from a great distance, and he smiled at the expression on his senior Commander's face. "Death does not frighten me, my friend. But I dare not fail."

Over the intercom came the call, the voice of the engineer

Dailen. "My lord Cain." There was a pause so brief it was nearly imperceptible. "Your ship is ready."

Cain took a deep, slow breath. "Well."

Mersai stood stock-still for a second and then stretched forth his arm to Cain. Without hesitation Cain reached over and grasped his forearm.

It was in Mersai's mind to wish Cain good fortune.

The dark eyes touched his for just a second, and Cain said simply, "I will take your wishes with me." He released his grasp, turned, and without looking back strode to the gates leading out onto the floor of the shipyard. The gates slid slowly aside at his approach and closed just as ponderously behind him.

The words fell, soft. "Cain . . . only Cain would try something so foolish. Yet if he succeeds, he could rule as the Rulers have, forever. . . ." Commander General Orrin Mersai was not even aware that he had spoken aloud until he heard a sharply indrawn breath behind him. He turned to look at the junior Commanders; one of them, newly promoted to his rank, held a visibly shocked look upon his features. *Getting old*, he thought wryly, *talking to myself.* "Is something wrong, Commander Third?"

"Sir? No, sir!"

Mersai cocked his head to one side. "Was it the description of our Lord as foolish that shocked you . . . or the idea that he might rule this world forever?"

It was a horrible question to pose a junior Commander—a Third, just as low as one could be in rank above Warrior—who was still unsure of himself. "Sir, no sir. I mean, *neither*, General Mersai . . ." His voice trailed off.

The aging General's voice was as gentle as he was able to make it. "Young man, Cain often does foolish things, to my way of thinking. He has the advantage of having been right on every occasion thus far. If it was the second half of that comment that upset you—how old are you?"

The abrupt question startled the man. "Sir? I've just turned twenty, sir."

"In other words, you were not even born when Cain returned from the Exile. I grew up as a slave of the Rulers; so did every other

Warrior in this service past the age of forty or so. You might," he said softly, "want to ply one of the old bastards with drink some evening and learn what it was like."

The Third was so pale he might have been one of the barbarian guards Cain employed. "Sir," he half whispered, "I shall. Thank you, sir."

Through the observation windows Mersai saw the canopy of the starship closing upon Cain. Absently, he said, "You are quite welcome."

It had been fifteen years since Cain had flown a fighter craft of any description. Nonetheless, he had followed the construction of the starship with minute attention to detail; the cockpit of the starship was as familiar to him as that of the simulator he had practiced in.

The canopy closed above him, a near-invisible shield of monomolecular crystal with a refractivity index near zero. Immediately behind him, the lifeplant was already flooding the cockpit with oxygen; more oxygen than Cain needed, but the lifeplant was another piece of genetic engineering from the far past, and Cain's engineers did not know how to alter the level of its oxygen output.

It was not a major inconvenience. Had it been, Cain could have locked the helmet ring at his neck and breathed the bottled air supply from his flight suit. Instead Cain merely slowed his breathing and regulated his heartbeat to adjust.

"Ten minutes, my lord. We'll be dropping the Shield."

Cain did not tender a reply; none was necessary. He brought the fusion cells on-line and watched calmly as the temperature of the reaction engines climbed upward. Tow cables pulled the starship into launch position at the center of a huge painted circle. Running lights blinked around the exhaust safety perimeter, inside which the technicians were not permitted.

"No activity upstairs, my lord. We're opening the silo doors."

Above Cain the massive panels that covered the shipyard cycled slowly open. Through the widening aperture, bright starlight glinted down on Cain. Nearly a millennium had passed since the Earth had held an industrial civilization to speak of; the night sky over the Valley was achingly clear, filled with stars.

General Mersai's voice. "My lord Cain; is the Command given?"

The ritual was necessary; in some ways the Caverns and its Warriors were as ruled by the customs of the Valley as any Worker in the fields. The High Lord could not enter danger without giving over the Command he left behind to some one of his Commanders; it did not have to be the highest-ranking Commander, though usually it was. "Commander General Orrin Mersai, the Command is given."

Another voice, one Cain did not recognize.

"My lord . . . Shield down."

Cain touched a stud on the control panel.

The ship lifted. The Earth fell away beneath him.

He flew south and east, still in atmosphere. The Rulers of Earth, as they styled themselves even now, had ships in geosynchronous orbit. If fortune smiled upon Cain, the Rulers would have missed the brief moment when the Shield over the Caverns went down; and if they missed that, they would miss everything.

South he went, across the Glowing Desert, hugging the ground. Near the equator he began to climb at last on a slow arc. He was over the Antarctic when he finally reached low Earth orbit. He took a brief moment to adjust his inclination and then, for the first time, ignited the fusion engines.

Three gravities of acceleration slammed him back into the cocoon of his seat. The starship dropped below the ecliptic plane of the solar system, accelerating away from the sun and its gravity well. Cain bore the acceleration stoically, almost without thought. His attention was far away from the mechanics of the journey.

Calm, the words whispered deep within him, in the voice of a man who had been dead since before Cain's twenty-first birthday. *Center yourself; the enemy lies only in the lack of balance.*

He submerged his identity in the depths of control, and the world grew very distant, a series of events happening to someone else entirely.

On the monitor on the instrument panel, the number representing the gravity well of the solar system dropped beneath a glowing horizontal line. The fusion engines cut off quite suddenly, and Cain's weight vanished; he hung loosely in the restraints of his cocoon. In the engines behind Cain power flowed through the subwavicle engines for the first time in at least a thousand years.

Cain moved one finger, and touched a stud set in the armrest of his cocoon.

The ship hung motionless for an unmeasurable instant.

Dropspace yawned before Cain. The ship submerged itself beneath reality.

An infinite time passed in the blink of an eye.

He hung above the plane of Cassandra's planetary system. The ship was tumbling slightly on its axis. Cain had no idea where the momentum had come from and did not care. He touched the attitude jets lightly until the tumble ceased, brought the ship around to face Cassandra, and punched for the fusion engines.

There was no triumph, anywhere within him.

From space, Earth was the blue of the One Ocean, the white of clouds, and the brown of baked desert.

The world beneath Cain was *green*, with less white cloud cover than was normal for Earth. There were no oceans, no mountains to speak of, no deserts. Cain hung in high orbit over Cassandra for nearly an hour, examining the information that his passive instruments brought him. The reports were curious, conflicting. Spectroscopic examination of the atmosphere showed a percentage of light gases far higher than Cain had expected: seventy-three percent nitrogen, twenty-two percent oxygen, and nearly a full four percent split evenly between the noble gases argon and helium. Possibly, he thought, that was the result of the gas giant primary's nearness.

Presumably the air was breathable; the Sisterhood had not left Earth for an unlivable world.

The planet's magnetic field was incredibly powerful.

. . . *the dim radiance built, and built, a flickering curtain of white fire at the edges of Cain's awareness.*

Tectonic instability, of course. There was a strong tide from the gas giant primary. Cassandra must have horrible quakes, as the planet was literally stretched in the waxing and waning of the tide. It explained the magnetic field as well; the magma flows in the planet's core must be impressive.

The place seethed with life. Carbon dioxide on Earth was never more than a trace element in the atmosphere; on Cassandra it comprised nearly a full percent of the air's composition. The ambient temperature differentials were drastically different from those on Earth; the poles were only some thirty degrees Centigrade cooler than the equator. Life there was, yes; but not, apparently, civilization. Nowhere on the planet did Cain find the characteristic neutrino emissions of working fusion generators. At their greatest resolution his ship's telescopes could not find anything that resembled a building, anywhere on the surface of the world.

One of his instruments was a device that measured, to the best of Cain's understanding, fluctuations in quantum uncertainty. Just before and just after the Drop it had flickered erratically.

The needle went off the scale.

Cain jerked back in the cocoon as some power arced across him like a physical blow, danced like fire across the surface of his skin. An incredible pain touched him. . . .

It ended almost the very instant it began.

"Okay," he said aloud, slightly breathless by the suddenness of the pain, "so there is civilization. I was wrong, I admit it."

There was no response, nothing overt.

Cain's attention was drawn to a spot near Cassandra's equator, one of the few cloud-covered areas, by appearance no different from any other stretch of cloud cover across the surface of the planet. Without stopping to consider the action, his fingers danced across the controls. The fusion engines lit briefly, accelerating down into geosynchronous orbit. He hung over the spot and slowed his breathing further, and further. His heartbeat stilled, until both his breathing and heartbeat moved synchronously, ten times per minute.

His eyes dropped shut.

A vast emptiness opened before him, filled with nothing but a hissing silence. A presence hinted at its existence, and then the words came, random phrases without meaning.

. . . *and so . . . but who . . . T'Pau's treaty with them . . . and their lack of the power . . .*

Cain roused himself from the near-death trance, plotted the path of his descent without hesitation, and brought the ship down into the atmosphere.

Into insanity.

The ride down was rough. High winds struck the ship, once Cain descended beneath three kilometers, and fought with him for control of his vessel. Unchained from the forces of gravity, vast, forested islands appeared just below three kilometers, floating stony-bottomed above the hard surface of the planet, drifting like piloted vessels through the deep banks of the clouds. Though he suppressed the emotion savagely, something inside him took a vast, prodigious offense at the very sight. Though the Sisterhood of the Ring might have fooled his instruments, they could hardly have done so to his eyes; those great, floating islands of stone were really there.

At eight hundred meters he broke through the cloud layer, into clear, quiet sky, running still at twice the speed of sound. A vast tropical rainforest stretched out beneath him as far as the eye could see.

He made a pass over an empty clearing covered with some green sward—grass, perhaps, brought by the Sisterhood from Earth, or some similar native plant. A likely place, amidst the overwhelming stretches of the huge trees. Cain banked, brought the ship around, and made a vertical, belly-first landing.

Despite himself, his breath quickened when the ship finally touched ground. He sat without moving in the cockpit, waiting for the moment to pass. When it had, he touched the stud that released the cocoon's hold upon him, opened the ship's canopy, and in a single smooth movement made the drop to the ground. Standing next to his ship, he touched his right wrist with his left index finger, touched his left wrist with his right index finger, pulled the gloves from his hands, and tossed them into the open cockpit. There was no need to remove the flight suit itself; it was skintight, both light and comfortable.

With his bare hands he removed his helmet. He did not have to unlock it; it had not been necessary, so he had not bothered to seal it entirely at any time.

The air was unreal.

Once, as a child, Cain had made the journey from his home

village of Eastmarch to nearby Telindel. Along the way he and the minstrel Loukas had camped one night at the edge of a field of flowers, and all that night Cain had kept coming up out of sleep under the prodding of the floral scent on the cold night air.

The air here reminded him of that, as, confronted by a great work of art, a man might think of the first reproduction of that art he had ever seen. Cain could have grown drunk on it had he let himself; his breathing threatened to grow erratic for the second time in as many minutes.

With rigid self-control he forced himself to a still inner quiet, reached out for the invitation of the glow . . .

He stood motionless for an instant and then began walking.

Despite the cloud cover, enough light reached the ground to illuminate everything with an indistinct glow. The grass was not the grass of Earth, but so similar it needs must be related. The trees, similarly, bore some resemblance to the trees Cain had known all his life. He passed through one meadow perhaps half the size of the one he'd landed in. There was a small spring, and he came there upon a group of animals, like and unlike deer, grazing around the spring. The animals froze for an instant at his appearance and then went back to grazing. If there were predators on this planet, they did not look like Cain. He passed through the meadow without disturbing them; that which he was searching for grew closer and closer. He could feel the presence of the power, like a storm of needles striking his exposed skin.

The pulsing power grew stronger, and stronger, and abruptly a barrier of overgrown shrubs and brush raised itself up before him. The light knife was in his boot; he pulled it free, set the control on the variable laser to a blade of one meter, and pressed on, slashing his way through the forbidding overgrowth.

Suddenly there was nothing in his way.

He stood at the edge of a vast clearing, so huge he knew there was no conceivable way he could have missed it in his search for a landing spot.

By inescapable logic, if Cain were to trust his eyes, his instruments, and his memory, then ten minutes ago this clearing had not been here.

Perhaps ten meters of the emerald grass separated Cain from the beginning of the water. A lake stretched away from that spot, almost perfectly circular, nearly one hundred fifty meters from one end to the other. A waterfall fed the lake at its far end, the water falling from so high above that Cain, looking up, could not see the spot where the waterfall originated; it was lost in its own mists.

As he stood at the far end of the clearing, the spray from the waterfall touched Cain's face with coolness. The lake was rough and turbulent at the far end, the water boiling where the waterfall crashed into it; the water near Cain was still, almost tranquil.

From that quiet water the woman erupted upward, into the air. A fountain of water sprayed up with her, and beautiful mocking green eyes touched Cain's for just a moment, before her lithe nude form twisted inside the spray of water and returned to the depths of the lake.

Cain had no warning there was anyone behind him; no human, nor Ruler, nor Giant could possibly have come so close to him without his knowing.

A hand came over his shoulder, spread wide to clasp itself over his face, and pulled him down with astonishing strength.

A woman's hand.

He lay flat on the ground, looking up into the overarching trees. He could not move. Three indistinct female shapes hovered above him, looking down upon his helpless form. A light shone down into Cain's eyes, made it impossible for him to see them clearly. Their probes ran through his thoughts, examined in minute detail the carefully crafted layers of his upper mind. One mind reached further yet, down into the quiet where Himself crouched, waiting; but in the secret darkness He was very still, still as death itself, and escaped notice.

When, at last, it seemed they had decided he meant them no harm, the voice came to him in a long, ethereal, soundless whisper. *Who are you?*

The portion of Cain's mind that was submerged tried to move his body, and could not, not a centimeter in any direction. The surface of his mind merely answered their question.

My name is Cain. I'm a leader from Earth.

The low chuckle of their amusement ran through his mind. *Of course you are. Why are you here, Cain? How did you find us?*

I've come to seek your aid. The light fell away from Cain's eyes, and though still he could not move, he could see the women clearly for the first time. They were lovely, in an exotic fashion very unlike the beauty of the women of the Rulers, or of his own people. *I found you with Donner Almandar's star charts. When he took his fleet from Earth, his charts marked this star as the place to which the Sisterhood had gone after the Fire, and this planet as Cassandra, the home of the Ring.*

The woman in the center was looking at him with a gentle understanding, and yet her thought held an undertone of concern. It came to Cain that she was the one who had probed him so deeply. *Your people —Workers, they call you. Servants . . . .*

Slaves.

. . . slaves of the Rulers, whom we called T'Pau's People. You fight them?

We have been at peace for a decade. Before that there were twenty years of war. But the Rulers have been building this last decade, planning something, we do not know what, with the aid of the Giants. War will, I think, come again soon.

The thought came to him again, more insistent this time. *Why have you come to our world? Earth is not our concern, and the Rulers are not our enemies. The Creator T'Pau was our enemy, but the Rulers— they are her children's children and her children's children's children. They know more of the Light now than they knew when we left Earth. Shall we give them our enmity now when we did not then?*

I am here, said Cain, *because before you left Earth, you created a weapon of Light they could not stand against. When they conquered Earth, they did not dare attack you because you held the power of the Ring. Will you not help us?*

No. The thought was somber. *The Light is not a weapon, Cain. It cannot be used as such.*

Knowledge, a very wise man once told me, is the only weapon. What do you know of the Light?

This time their laughter tore across the surface of his mind, and the three voices were one: *He wants to know about the Light!*

Golden brilliance glared around them, a raging light that illuminated the entire clearing around the lake, blazed up from the surface of the lake itself, and set the water roiling. In a sudden swift motion, the three women vanished, and in the next instant Cain found himself suddenly freed of restraint and dragged, flight suit and all, into the waters of the lake. Something like a small sun, dozens of meters in diameter, flared beneath the surface of the water, pulsed with a beat like that of a human heart. He'd had no time to even draw a breath, and kicked to the surface, treading water. The three women were already far across the surface of the lake and widening the distance between them. Cain was pulled along with them, into the stunning, numbing presence of the Light. Shrieks of laughter came from the three as they played in the rough water. Cain reached the far edge of the lake, close enough to the waterfall that its thundering fall would have made normal speech all but impossible, made his way up onto the shore, and sat, watching the inhuman play.

One of the women came back to him, moving easily through the rough water Cain had made such hard work of. She held her place ten meters from Cain, shining green eyes fixed upon him. They all looked much alike, but the voice; Cain recognized the voice as that of the woman who had probed his thoughts so deeply. She gestured behind herself with something like challenge. *The Light, Cain.*

Cain made no response, and her lips curled in a smile. She turned away, dove back into the depths. Her thought reached out to him. *The resting place of power, Cain! With this power we made all you see; the Light, made real. Join us in the Light!*

Such a quiet, trustworthy man I am, Cain agreed. *Perhaps I should.* The comment obviously meant nothing to the women; their only response was a distracted puzzlement. Cain took a long, slow breath. "Okay." There was, perhaps, the very faintest trace of alarm in their thoughts. "Here I come." Deep within, the locks broke, the chains snapped apart, and Himself came up from the darkness.

For the first time since the landing, Cain smiled.

He strode forward, into the lake, and plunged beneath the surface of the water. The Ring pulsed hotly in the water, its power touching Cain's nerves like a fierce wind across the strings of a harp. He kicked and moved down into the warm water, to where the monstrous arc of the Ring waited for him. The water was uncomfortably hot by the time he had reached the huge crystalline structure, almost painful.

He was vaguely aware, as though from a great distance, of the three women who were the Sisterhood of the Ring, and their beginning realization that something was horribly wrong.

With the full cold power of his will, Cain of Eastmarch reached out and laid hand to the Ring of Light.

There came a scream the likes of which Cain had only heard once before in his life. The last time it had been his; this time it was the Ring's.

Awareness vanished in a silent white explosion.

Only an instant could have passed.

Cain came back to himself, floating senselessly in the depths of the dark, boiling-hot water. The Ring was gone, and the world was an aching empty place. His face and hands, the only exposed parts of his body, were near burning from exposure to the searing water, and he could not remember the last time he had taken air into his lungs. There was a great roaring sound in his ears.

There was something clutched in his left hand.

He kicked with all his strength, and an eternal instant later his head broke water. He sucked in the precious air in a huge gasp and was moving again even as the oxygen came flooding down into his lungs. Cain dragged himself up out of the water, onto the grass, and pulled the variable laser from his boot, lit the blade and extended it to the full three meters of which it was capable.

He ran.

A shriek composed of equal parts pain and terror broke around him. The illumination that had lit this world ever since his landing was failing, the sky darkening toward a murky black. Cain did not slow, did not even look back to see if he was pursued. The wind came blasting out of nowhere, directly into his path, and sent him staggering. A pair of the deerlike creatures blocked his path and Cain sliced one of them in half with his light knife and broke the other's neck with a blow from the hand that held the chunk of glowing crystal.

They chased him, of course; the world itself rose up against him, wind sending the branches of the trees slashing against his face as he ran, and scores of the peaceful grazing animals blocked his path. He cleared a path with long swings of the variable laser, and still they followed; something dark and wetly cold settled about his shoulders, and Cain rolled across the ground until it was gone, came back to his feet and kept moving; they chased Cain in their fury all the way back to his ship, shadows and terrors and screaming horrors that would have driven many men mad.

If they did not drive Cain mad, the possibility must be considered that it was only because he was mad already.

In the end, like so many before, they were powerless to stop him.

The starship fled at the full five gravities' acceleration of which it was capable.

Cain, wrapped in the acceleration cocoon, was almost relaxed. The chunk of crystal glowed in his clutch, a tiny, exact duplicate of the huge Ring of Light in the lake. He thought perhaps it had been larger when he first left the planet. Now it was almost small enough to slip onto one of his fingers, like a true ring.

Cain.

"Yes?" Despite the acceleration, the word was not slurred at all. Nonetheless, his throat hurt.

Cain. Bring back the Ring. The thought was urgent, desperate.

"No." On the monitor Cain was watching the solid bar that showed the degree of curvature of space. The bar was dropping steadily toward the bright white line at which the Drop would occur.

Cain, we will not be angry, we will not harm you. Please bring back the Ring! It is not yours!

"True, it's not." He rested, eyes fixed on the dropping bar. *I recall asking for your help nicely, but it didn't work.*

There was silence then, and Cain was content to let the silence lay. He was not thinking, not planning, not exulting at his success.

He was waiting.

He watched the dropping bar.

Far away, as distance was measured in traveling, but very nearby in the universe of mind, Cain felt a slow raising of power. He paid it no attention; without the Ring the Sisterhood was no more powerful, and perhaps less so, than an equivalent number of the Rulers.

Perhaps he was correct to pay the raising no heed; when their power struck him, he barely flinched. The words that came with the sending echoed after the sending itself was gone: *You have stolen the Ring. Whoso steals the Ring will die. You will die.*

In the silence of his ship Cain said through a raw throat, "That's a hell of a curse you've got there." His voice sounded odd in his ears. He was very tired.

They screamed after him. *You will die!*

"Everybody dies," said Cain.

Reality twisted away into dropspace.

The Sister

The Year 1253 After the Fire

Thirty-one years before the theft of the Ring, Barra Lusende went hurrying out into the courtyard to greet the rider. He came in the last hour before dusk, only minutes before her son Davyd would have closed the gate for the night.

The letter the messenger gave her was written on a substance the likes of which Barra Lusende had never seen before. One of the librarians at Parliament could have told her what it was—memory-writing plastic—but even in the Library at Parliament it was scarce. Once, before the Fire Wars, it had been common, but the orbital factories where it had been created had not functioned in nearly half a millennium by the date of Barra of Eastmarch's birth.

The messenger who delivered the letter was no one whom Barra knew: a hard-faced young man about the age of her eldest grandson, with skin so pale it was visible even beneath the dirt of the road, in dusty brown riding clothes without a hat, on a big bay horse that was trembling visibly with exhaustion. That in itself was cause for comment in Eastmarch, for Eastmarch was a small village at the very edge of the Valley of the Rulers, and received visitors but rarely. It had been nearly a year since Barra had last seen a stranger, and that one was a Ruler, a teacher from the Academy. One such came every four years to test the children of Eastmarch and perhaps find some likely candidate for the Academy at Parliament.

Barra turned the envelope over in her hands, frowning. The messenger, without asking her permission, filled the bucket in the garden from the garden spigot—Barra and her husband Anton had piped water, not like some steadings in poverty-stricken Eastmarch—drank from the bucket and splashed his face liberally, and then gave the rest of the bucket to his horse. The horse drank with quivering eagerness.

Finally Barra looked up from the envelope. For some reason she could not explain, her palms had grown damp. "What is this?"

The rider looked at her in surprise. "Surely you can read?"

"Of course I can read." She continued to look at the envelope. "But the envelope doesn't open." Anton Lusende had appeared in the doorway, hovering uncertainly behind her.

"Oh." The messenger seemed sourly amused by that. "Here, you run your thumb over the pressure border. Like this, and it opens." He demonstrated for her and then remounted his horse to leave. "Thanks for the water." As he brought the horse about, the setting rays of the sun struck him in profile, and for just a moment, a dim orange line glowed there, so faint that one who did not know what it meant might have missed it.

Barra drew her breath in sharply.

The rider turned back slowly to look at her. "Is something wrong, madam?"

She blurted the words. "You're wearing a Shield."

The man cocked his head to one side. "So?"

She swallowed. "The . . . Rulers, the Rulers wear Shields."

"Oh?" The grim young man brought the big bay forward a step and leaned forward in the saddle. "And do you think I am a Ruler?"

"I . . . I don't know, sir," Barra whispered. Behind her she heard a sound as though her husband Anton were stirring.

The man nodded slowly. "Fascinating. Well, rest your mind, my lady. I'm not a Ruler. I've never even seen one of your infamous Rulers, although—this person 'Loga,' he's one, is he not? I've a letter for him as well. And I've one for your sister Siva, except I'm told she's dead."

"Loga? Yes . . . yes, he is a Ruler." Barra stood staring at the youngster in increasing bewilderment. "You've never seen a Ruler?"

He nodded. "I assure you, it's the truth. They're not common where I come from."

Barra stood gripping the memory plastic in both hands, vaguely aware that she was crinkling it. "What . . . where *are* you from?"

It was too dark for her to make out the color of the man's eyes; they glittered oddly. "I think you know."

The trembling that seized her came from the depths of her memory, from a time so very long past that she had not really thought about it—about *him*—in at least a decade. "Oh, my."

"Yes," the man said gently. "Your brother sent me."

Standing in the middle of the courtyard, in front of the affluent Merchant's house and the wealthy Merchant who had allowed her to dig her way out of the poverty of Eastmarch, Madam Barra Lusende fainted dead away.

Without further word, the messenger brought the big bay wheeling about and rode him out into the gathering night.

The date on the letter was nearly a year old.

Summer 18, 1252 A.T.F.

My very dearest Barra,

You will be surprised to hear from me, given the circumstances I was in when last you heard of me, and the time that has passed since then. If my messenger survives his journey—and I think he will, for the journey is no more dangerous than the one I undertook after my Exile, and Kavad, besides being ken Selvren, with experience in desert ways, has the advantage of maps and other resources that I did not—and, if you are still alive, you will receive this letter sometime in early Spring.

I have missed you. I think you will believe that, for it is true. I cannot tell you where I have been nor what I have done. I've no time to write a letter so lengthy, nor would you believe all of it. Nearly fifty years—it seems unreal to me that so much time could pass. I still remember you, Barra; I have never forgotten that promise. I hope that life has been good to you while I have been gone.

There is much that I would discuss with you, and will, soon, for I am coming home again, and the Rulers themselves cannot stop me.

I was right, you know; I was.

Don't worry about recognizing me; you'll know me; I have not aged a day in all these years.

I am coming back. Tell them that, in Eastmarch. Spread the news.

THE RING

I'm coming back.
With an army.

It was signed in a big scrawl, with just the word:
Cain.

Elena

The Year 1193 After the Fire

• 1 •

It was the year 1193 After the Fire, ninety-one years before the theft of the Ring.

Cain was six years old when his father died.

Their family lived on the slopes of the hills at the far eastern end of the Valley of the Rulers, just outside and above the village of Eastmarch. Cain's father, Marric, took his living from the sea, fed his family with the fish and crab and white silkies, and sold his surplus, when there was any, in the market at Eastmarch. Often enough, there was surplus; the Valley was located far enough to the north that the waters of the One Ocean were reasonably cold. Cold water holds more oxygen in its mix than warmer waters do, and with oxygen goes life; Marric's fishing was generally good.

Each morning before the sun rose Marric would leave home with his nets and ride up the hill until he came to the place, near as high as the highest hill in the east end of the Valley, where the hill melted into the stonesteel of the great barrier that kept the sea from pouring down into the Valley of the Rulers. The waterlock was unmarked, only a dark recess in the sheer wall of the stonesteel. Entering the recess, lights came up, a dim blue-white radiance that emanated from the smooth ceiling of the corridor. Perhaps five meters in, there hung a doorfield that was all but invisible except at night, when it glowed with an eerie phosphorescence that made Marric more nervous than he ever admitted even to himself. Through that doorfield, slightly obscured, one could see the vague outlines of an opening that let out upon the bright blue of ocean. That first doorfield Marric had never even managed to touch entering the waterlock from the Valley side; it always vanished at his approach. Two meters past the faint line that marked where the doorfield had been there hung yet another doorfield. The first doorfield would re-form behind Marric, and the second vanish.

The doorfields were not very smart. Try as he would, Marric had never managed to make them both stay open at the same time. In fact it was impossible for both doorfields to be turned off at once; but like the rest of the inhabitants of Eastmarch, Marric knew nothing of spacecraft, and even had he known it, the fact that the waterlocks mimed spacecraft airlock design would have meant nothing to him.

Had he ever attempted to speak to the doors—in, for example, the same peremptory tone that he sometimes took with his wife Elena, and his children—and *tell* the doorfields what he wanted of them, Marric would have been vastly surprised at the results. But he was a practical man, imaginative and curious only to the extent that the world and the things in it affected his work and his family, and he would no more have spoken to a door than to the fork he ate his dinner with.

Past the second doorfield there was a great ledge, overlooking the One Ocean. It was five meters wide and ran away to the west as far as the eye could see. To the east the ledge narrowed, and at last vanished into the wall of the Great Dam. The Great Dam itself ran on another six or seven kilometers, and then came down to merge with the Gray Mountains, beyond the far eastern end of the Valley of the Rulers. As one left the waterlock, there was, immediately to the north, a series of steps cut into the stonesteel, which led down directly into the sparkling blue sea. Once, Marric swam down as far as his lungs would bear, following the flight of stairs down into the Ocean. The stairs extended down as far as Marric had ever been able to swim, and as far beneath that as he was able to see in the water-greened sunlight of midday.

Marric's boat was kept on the far side of the waterlock. The waterlock doorfields would allow only a single man, and as much as he could carry, to pass through at any one time. Marric had fooled them by carrying his boat through a piece at a time, and rebuilding it on the other side as he sat on the ledge four meters above the surface of the ocean.

Once he figured out how to get his boat through the waterlock, he dismissed the subject of the doorfields from his mind and never thought about it again.

For over fifteen years Marric fished every day that weather would allow. When the weather turned foul and the Ocean threw itself against the barrier of the Great Dam, the waterlocks stayed resolutely shut. Marric could not even get past the first doorfield on those days. The first time that had happened, Marric had lost his boat. The weather had seemed fine the day before, and he had neglected to weight down his boat. By the time he knew the weather was turning foul, late that evening, the waterlocks had already decided that it was unsafe for him to go through, and so when the storm came and then left, it took his boat with it.

After that Marric never neglected to weight his boat down with stones and to drag it up the ledge until it was inside the stone overhanging where the inner waterlock doorfield glowed. The boats were not very large; the early boats would carry only Marric himself, and the later boats, after his eldest son Misha began aiding him, carried only two. Still it was not cheap when one of the boats was lost. It happened on occasion—every two or three years, on average, some storm more terrible than the norm would steal his boat away from him. There was nothing he could do about it. The ledge on the north side of the Great Dam was utterly smooth, the stonesteel so silky that the Great Dam's builders had been forced to cut grooves in the surface of the ledge so that there would be a secure surface to walk upon. Perforce, there was no way for Marric to tie the boat down securely; weighting it with stones was the best solution he'd come up with. Marric accepted the situation stoically; it was merely one of the costs of doing business, and he always had the cured timber ready to build a new boat when the current one was lost.

Marric was not a wealthy man, but neither was he poor, not by the standards of Eastmarch. Their house, high on the hill overlooking the village, had three rooms, and the floors were made of wood rather than packed dirt. The walls were painted white, both inside and out. It was a great contrast to the manner in which he started out. His first two years of fishing, Marric had lived in a canvas tent. Two years passed before Marric, then still a young man, succeeded in convincing Elena's father Garret that fishing done through the waterlocks could be commercially successful. He'd a monopoly, of sorts. There were other fishermen, of course, at the villages of Telindel and Saerlock, who were, like the fishermen in all fishing villages, serviced by one of the thirty Great Locks, which could usher a dozen large boats at a time through the twenty-meter thickness of the Great Dam. But while crab traveled well, fish from Telindel tended to smell strongly by the time it had reached Eastmarch. Saerlock, sixty kilometers further west than Telindel, did not bother to send even their crabs to Eastmarch. And neither village ever sent silkies, though they were accounted a great delicacy and priced accordingly; the flesh of a silkie turned black within a day of its death, when it did not turn the gorgeous shimmering red of one of the incredibly toxic species of silkie genegineered during one of the desperate later stages of the Fire Wars.

Marric had built his house upon receiving word from Elena that her father would allow him to marry her. Despite a formal education that had ceased when he was only eleven, he knew that it was inappropriate to expect a woman to come live with him in a canvas tent. He was, in his fashion, a considerate man. He took his bride-to-be up into the hills one day shortly after they were betrothed, up to the place where the hills ceased and the stonesteel of the Great Dam began, so that she might pick the spot where he would build her house. The ride up took them most of a day, up winding paths that cut back and forth across the hill many times. The day was bright and warm, and they rode in shadows beneath the cover of the pine and redwood trees until they neared the top of the highest of the hills. There Marric led Elena off the path. They tethered their horses at the edge of the trees, not far from the entrance to the waterlock where Marric had fished for the last two years, and walked hand in hand across barren rock. Without any abrupt transition the rock became stonesteel, and they walked out over a wide expanse of the gray substance. Marric halted a few paces away from the edge of the stonesteel and let Elena look out.

From where they stood they could see, faint with the distance to the southwest, the ring of the mountains that marked the far border of the Valley. The Great Dam curved around them, rising away to the west as though it would touch the sky itself. Only slightly further to the east it turned contrary to the main curve of the Great Dam and ran slightly north before vanishing into the Gray Mountains. Immediately before them the hills fell away to the floor of the Valley. The river Almandar was a far blue-silver gleam, at the limits of their vision. The Black Mountains, where the Rulers at Parliament governed the entirety of the Valley, were almost lost beyond the edge of the horizon; only their very peaks were available to sight.

Elena stood back from the edge. Never in her life had she been so high above the village, and she hoped never to be again. She was a young girl then, only fourteen, with a simple beauty: light brown eyes, skin very pale, and clean black hair bound in an ivory clasp. Though she spoke in an educated fashion and could indeed read and write, her family was as poor as any in Eastmarch, and her dress reflected it: plain brown linen and sandals that were clean but old. Finally, under Marric's gentle prodding, she laid down on her stomach at the edge of the great drop and, chin propped up on the backs of her hands, peered cautiously over the edge.

Her voice floated back to Marric, sitting cross-legged next to her, running one hand across the long black hair. "My father will want to know how my dress got dirty."

"And what'll you tell him?"

"That you ravished me against my will, threw me down in the dirt and had your way with me."

Marric frowned. "And got the *front* of the dress dirty?"

"I shall tell him that you secretly prefer other men, and treated me so."

Marric nodded. "That won't do my reputation any good. What'll Garret think, do you suppose?"

His tone was very grave. Elena turned her head to the side slightly, to see his expression. He was smiling, so she smiled in return and turned back to look down again at the tumbling hillsides. "Oh, he shall, I suppose, be enraged and want to kill you."

"Well, that won't do," said Marric decisively. "You must take the dress off, and we'll beat the dust out of it before I take you back to your father."

There was a brief silence as the wind whispered around them and the warm sun beat down upon them. Elena said thoughtfully, "I suppose we could tell him that I fell down."

"And what will he think about that?"

"Oh, he won't believe it," said Elena seriously, "but he won't care either, since we are betrothed."

Marric grinned broadly. "He won't care?"

"Put your tongue back in your mouth," said Elena without looking at him. "*I* care. You shall wait until we are married. It's not that long now."

"No," he agreed after a moment, stroking her hair again, "it's not. And you're worth the wait."

". . . there." Elena raised herself up on one elbow and pointed down the hillside. "Right there, in the clearing."

Marric did not even look where she was pointing. He'd had a bet with himself that she would pick that spot. It was near the brook, and they had in fact passed it only half an hour or so since, on their way up to the waterlock and its lookout. "Very well," he said. "We'll build there."

On the day Marric died, Cain awoke in cold darkness, to the sounds of stirring out in the main room. He could hear his mother's gentle voice and now and again the rough sound of his father grunting some word of reply. His sisters Siva and Barra were cuddled in the bed with him, helping to protect him against the fierce cold, and he climbed out of bed carefully, so as not to wake them. Cain was six years old; Siva was almost five, and Barra was only two, and they were girls besides; Cain knew they needed their sleep.

His older brother Misha's pallet was empty.

Misha was the only one of the children who slept alone. He'd been five when Cain was born and had never gotten used to having to sleep with the other children. Misha was eleven that winter, and already near as tall as their mother Elena. He'd been helping Marric with the fishing for over three years now, since he was eight. Cain did not see Misha when he came out into the kitchen; he was probably out saddling the horses for the ride up the hill.

His mother saw him first; Elena said only, "Good morning, Cain."

Marric was sitting by their small brick firepit, warming his boots in front of the fire his breakfast was cooking over. His mother's grill was set up over the pit, and four eggs were frying on the grilltop along with a half dozen slices of brown bread and three thick strips of silkie.

Marric turned in his chair to look at the boy. In the flickering red flames from the firepit the child looked eldritch enough to bring a touch of uneasiness to Marric, which the man banished with guilty firmness. The nose and chin were Marric's own, and the black hair was Elena's; but the black eyes came from Elena's father Garret, and the firm set of the child's mouth had no place in a boy of six. He was the only one of their children to take the dark coloring in both his hair and eyes. Misha and the girls had brown hair, and besides Cain only Barra had Garret's dark eyes.

Marric patted his right thigh, and Cain came obediently enough and climbed up into his father's lap. Marric addressed Elena: "Do we have any milk?"

Elena did not even look at the jug sitting on the other side of the kitchen window, to be cooled by the night mists. The window was real glass, lightly glazed to keep the warmth in. "Little enough, and Barra will need most of it."

"Give him a half cup." Marric turned back to his son. "What're you doing up so early?"

Cain said simply, "I want to go with you, Da."

Marric said just as directly, "Can't, son. You're not big enough yet."

A draft of cool wind struck them, and a moment later Elena came around the firepit and put a half-full cup of milk into Cain's hands, bent over and quickly kissed him on the cheek. She went back to cooking breakfast and lunch for Misha and her husband without a word.

Cain drank a sip from the milk. He did not really want it. "That's what you said last time, Da."

"Last time" had been two mornings ago. Marric kept a smile back by force of will. "Not much longer, Cain. You're growing fast."

"But . . ."

Marric shook his head and said flatly, "No more. Ask as many times as you like, but don't argue with the answer or I'll tan your hide. You have to stay home and take care of your sisters." He gestured at the cup. "Finish your milk." The child drank the rest of the cup all at once and put it down on the bricks next to the firepit, by his father's boots. Marric picked him up off his lap and set him down on his feet. "Back to bed, now."

The front door opened quickly, and Misha, already dressed in his overshirt and boots, slipped inside, a small patch of mist coming with him. He did not even look at Cain, but stood there in front of the door. "Horses are ready, Da."

Cain faded back into the darkness of the passageway leading to the children's bedroom, and stood watching; he had been forgotten already. He watched as his father pulled on his boots and his overshirt. Misha was saying, "You ought to let him go, Da, at least once. He'd be a nuisance, but being kept here all the time, it's eating him inside."

Marric said calmly, "He'll get over it." He was lacing up the front of his shirt, slowly; his hands, after over fifteen years spent handling the nets nearly every day, were no longer supple. He came around the firepit to where Elena was standing and kissed her thoroughly. "Be back early tonight if the weather doesn't change." Unnoticed by either of them, Misha was pulling the silkie steaks and the bread from the grill and putting them into the lunch sack he carried. "The way it looks, the doors might not even let us through, and we can spend a day together."

Elena smiled. It took the years from her face, and Marric kissed her again. "That would be very nice," she said softly. Marric let her go, and then she kissed Misha as well, with that same smile still on her face. "The both of you be careful."

Misha said with a perfectly straight face, "I'll see Da doesn't fall out 'a the boat again."

Marric sighed—the incident Misha referred to had happened only once, two years ago, and it was the *only* time in fifteen years that he'd fallen from his boat—but said nothing about it, and opened the door. "Come on," he growled, and the two of them went out together into the mist.

The happy expression was still on Elena's face when Cain silently retraced his way back to the bedroom and climbed back into bed with Barra and Siva. He lay in bed with his eyes closed, lay perfectly still, and tried not to think about the expression on his mother's face when she kissed Misha.

Tried not to think about it, because she never looked like that for him.

He was still lying there, wide awake, when his mother came to wake them at dawn.

That morning Cain went through his chores quietly, without any particular thoughts uppermost in his mind. Their one cow was sickly, and Cain knew his father was thinking of slaughtering it and buying another. Cain checked the cow's fodder in the pen out back of the house and found only a little of it gone from the day before; nonetheless he conscientiously cleaned out the old fodder and replaced it with fresh-cut long grass and then did the same for the young mare Marric had purchased the prior quarter.

They had no well, because the ground that high up was too stony; Cain spent a fair chunk of the morning carrying a pair of empty buckets down to the stream, a little further down the hill, and back up again with the buckets sloshingly full.

The year was well into Winter season. There was no snow on the ground, but the day was bitingly cold, and Cain's hands, where the water splashed on them, were so cold he could barely move them. The air itself felt strange, with a sort of tense stillness. Once he thought he heard a crack of thunder, very far away, but it did not come again, and the gray dome of the sky was clear of lightning flashes.

One instant the air was perfectly calm, without the faintest trace of a breeze. It seemed to Cain that he was the only thing in all the world that moved within the mist. He was on his way back with his third and last load of water, and despite the cold he was sweating in the still air.

The wind struck him like a sledgehammer.

Cain was not even aware of any transition; one moment he was trudging uphill, and the next he had been slammed into the ground and the water he'd been carrying was all over him. His first conscious thought was nothing worse than annoyance: now he'd have to go back and refill the buckets.

It was not until he tried to stand up that he realized how bad the wind was. He could not get to his feet; the wind knocked him down again. While he was lying there, trying to think of what to do, the hail began slashing down into the grass around him. One large stone struck him in the back of his neck, and then another struck him on his shoulder, and for the first time Cain was afraid. He could not walk; the wind would not let him attain his feet.

He began crawling up the hill.

The hail fell down upon him, and Cain knew very shortly that he would not make it back to the house. There was a ringing sound in his ears from the hailstones, striking him in the back of his head. He could not see in the swirling wind-blown mist and the hail. The hail was coming down on a slant from the north; Cain tried to remember where exactly he'd been on the trail back to the house when the wind had struck. There was a fallen redwood, an ancient gnarled tree that had toppled the prior Winter, somewhere on the way back to the house.

If he could reach the shelter of the fallen redwood, he would be safe.

The glazed window in the kitchen had blown out in the first instant of the wind.

Now Elena sat in the middle of the kitchen, with Barra and Siva in her arms, clutching them tightly. The house shook around them, and Elena knew there was a very real possibility that the house might come down upon them.

Siva was silent; Elena thought the child was too frightened to cry. Barra wasn't old enough to understand what was happening, and her screams were nearly as loud as the wind. Elena sat quietly, holding her children and praying to the Lords of Light with everything that was in her, praying that her husband and son would be returned safely from the storm.

After an hour the house stopped shaking, and a half hour after that the wind had lessened to the point where Elena could make the girls hear her. The hail turned to rain while Elena was telling the children to stay in their bedroom and wait for her to come back. She did it quickly, before Barra's screams could make her change her mind, and went outside into the still-fierce wind and around to the back where the mare was penned.

She knew a moment's despair when she saw what had happened to their garden and the pens where the livestock had been kept: the fences of the pens were flat on the ground, and the mare and all of the chickens were gone. The cow, which Elena expected to die soon anyhow, was still there.

For a moment it was almost too much for her; it had not occurred to her that the mare would be gone. She could still hear Barra's wailing, near buried in the sound of the wind. Elena looked up, up the hill to where the Great Dam rose above them, barely visible in the whistling gray sleet.

It was not that far. Fighting against the wind, Elena began trudging uphill.

Nobody came for Cain.

After a while, he was never sure how long, the hail had turned to rain, and the wind quieted. He was vaguely aware, lying on the south side of the fallen redwood, of the fact that blood was trickling down his face from the places where the hailstones had cut him.

Eventually he realized that nobody was *going* to come for him.

For a long time he simply lay there. As the wind died, the angle of the rain lessened, and the tree ceased to be a shelter. He was very tired, but the water was quite cold, and there was the faintest trace of stinging salt in it, ocean spray taken right over the top of the Great Dam. Cain's cuts began to bother him, and he came to his feet and without even looking around went back up the path to his father's house.

In the driving rain he could not see how bad the damage was. At first the door would not open, and he thought his mother must have blocked it with something for some reason. His muscles were trembling; he tried again, not expecting success, and the door swung wide. There was the sound of crying from within, which ceased briefly at the sound of the door opening.

He heard his sister Siva's voice from their bedroom. "Mama?"

"No, it's me." Cain went through the kitchen. The table had gotten knocked over, and the firepit was wet and the window broken, but otherwise it looked all right. In their bedroom, Siva was sitting in the center of the bed the three of them shared, holding Barra on her lap. The covers were half wrapped around her. There were still tears on Siva's face, and Barra was crying almost soundlessly. Cain climbed into the bed with them and took Barra from Siva's lap. "Where's Mama?"

Siva sniffled. "She went to get Da."

Holding Barra on his lap with one hand, Cain used the other to pull the blankets up around them, and then put his arm around Siva and held her close. Tears were still tracking down Siva's face. "Don't cry," he said quietly. "I'll take care of you until Da comes back."

THE RING

In later years Elena could not remember that day clearly, only images, moments. It took her nearly an hour to reach the waterlock, and it was still raining solidly when she did. Her thighs ached from the fight against the wind, and the water that streamed steadily down her face was mixed with tears. She had never been through the waterlock and did not know how to operate it, or if indeed it required operation. When she reached the clearing where, thirteen years ago, she had first learned that she loved the man she was going to marry, she realized that she did not know what to do next.

Their horses were tethered at the edge of the clearing. One of the horses had broken a leg, and its screams made Elena wince. The horse would have to be destroyed; she did not have the stomach to do it, not now. Their other horse, although it was skittish and shied away at her approach, seemed fine. Over the sound of the rain and the thunder and the horse's screams there came a low rumbling noise which Elena could not place. Had she known it for what it was, the sound of the One Ocean throwing itself against the stonesteel of the Great Dam with such violence that the Great Dam itself shook under its force, she could not have been more frightened.

She could not cause the doorfield to open.

Through the doorfield she saw a still shape, lying on the floor of the passageway. Immediately past the form was another of the invisible doors. The Ocean threw itself against that entrance in vast, slow surges, but did not reach the still form in the dimly lit passage. Elena pushed on the door; it was like touching a surface of smooth steel. She searched the walls of the passageway for a control. There was nothing. She struck the door with her hand, but still the door would not open. Sobbing with frustration, she kicked the door again and again and finally sank down with her back to the door, while the tears coursed down her cheeks. "Damn you," she whispered over her hopeless tears, "why don't you open?"

A cool voice, utterly lacking in emotion, almost buried in the wind, said, "Because I have not been so instructed."

Elena could not remember coming to her feet. The first thing she knew, she was backing away from the doorfield, looking wildly about her. *"Who said that?"*

"I did," said the voice. "I am the door. Would you like me to open?"

"I . . ." Her voice broke. When she finally made her throat work, the only word it could produce came out as a croak. "Please."

The doorfield vanished.

Elena stood utterly still. Suddenly she could hear the low rumbling sound much better, a dull booming as the One Ocean raged against its barrier. Something snapped within her, and the next thing she knew she was outside in the clearing in front of the waterlock, with her son Misha's head cradled in her lap and the rain pouring down into his open eyes. She must have entered the waterlock to bring him out, but she could not remember having done so. "Misha," she whispered raggedly. "Misha?"

Her son did not answer her. He did not blink as the rain came straight down into his eyes.

The expression in his eyes was quite mad.

Elena of Eastmarch sat back on her heels and cried as she had never cried before in her life, cried for the loss of her husband and her eldest son, cried for the loss of the only two men whom she had ever loved in her life.

· 2 ·

The next morning they went down the hill, the four of them together, and Misha. Before the sun rose, they packed all of their belongings such as could be carried with them and, with their one surviving horse, spent most of the day in the journey down to the outskirts of Eastmarch, where Elena's father Garret kept a small house of brick at the edge of Lord Malachor's estates. Siva and Barra rode the horse, with Elena holding the reins to guide them. Misha walked beside Cain. Cain had been told to hold his older brother's hand, and indeed, as long as Cain grasped Misha's hand Misha walked beside him willingly; but if Cain let go, for whatever reason, Misha would just stand there, until something or someone made him move again. He did not answer when addressed, and had not spoken since the previous day, when Elena had taken him from the waterlock.

The day was gray with clouds, and cold; and it rained once, though not badly, during the journey. The road they took down out of the hills hardly deserved the name. It was just a track where the grass had been beaten down somewhat by Marric and Misha on their way back and forth from the market in Eastmarch. Twice they had to make detours from the road, where trees had fallen across it. They made poor time, but Elena was in no hurry. She was very pale all that day, and never spoke at all except to call halts for resting. Once she had to pull a bush from the road before them and caught her forearm against one of the broken branches, cutting herself deeply. They continued on their way, and it was not until Elena felt her hand grow slippery, as the blood flowed down her forearm, that she realized she had cut herself.

She had not felt it.

They reached the foothills in midafternoon and came down onto the Traveler's Road, which hugged the curve of the Great Dam. East and west it ran, linking the villages and towns of the north Valley: Eastmarch and Telindel and Saerlock, and then Moorstin and Allietown and Singer, which was built on the shores of the great lake T'Pau. From Singer one could journey south, by boat down the river Almandar, through the rich heartlands of the Valley of the Rulers, where the skipper-wheat and corn were grown which fed Rulers, Workers and Giants alike, throughout the world. Follow the river Almandar far enough, past towns too numerous to list, past the burned shell in the territory of Semalia that once was the city of Erebion, and one came in time to Goldriver, at the base of the Black Mountains. There Almandar was diverted, and flowed both east and west in numerous small streams, until finally the streams became brooks and creeks, and vanished.

Ride west . . . .

The Traveler's Road continued, dirt in places, in others plain flagstones laid end to end, brick and stonesteel near the city of Singer on the lake T'Pau, which, it was said, had been built by Giants; continued, past Singer, through Trenton and Isoldè and Camberville, looping south then, away from the Great Dam, where the city of Eagles was nestled up high in the southwest hills that became the Black Mountains. It was the second highest town in the Valley, bar only Parliament itself, and the highest town accessible by a road of any sort. Past Eagles lay Volta and Domè and Flynnton, and, at the far west end of the Traveler's Road, the great city of Westmarch, as unlike the village of Eastmarch as the day was different from the night.

At the age of six, Cain knew nothing of these things, not even the name of the road they took into Eastmarch. It was not an impressive road, whatever its name might be; wide enough for two carts to pass each other at once, of dirt which was, for the moment, turned to ten centimeters' thickness of mud. Elena did not even glance to the west as they reached the road; they turned onto it and trudged slowly east through the mud. They were the only persons on the road; with the weather as it was, only those with excellent reason for traveling bestirred themselves.

They did not see the sun all that day. As evening fell, they entered the outskirts of Eastmarch. It was immediately obvious that the worst of the previous day's storm had missed Eastmarch; the shanties at the west end of the village were still standing. It was a small village, with only eight thousand residents, and Lord Malachor's estate was appropriately sized. The estate was on the east side of the village, and it was while passing through the fine houses at the east end of Eastmarch, over streets of cobblestone, that for the first time that day Cain saw others, men and women in good dress of leather and wool and cotton, and one lady in a coach wearing a gown of what Cain knew was sunsilk. They all of them looked directly at Cain and his family, with a variety of expressions that Cain did not entirely understand, but knew already that he did not like. One woman called out a word at them that Cain did not know; but his mother Elena went rigid and pale, kept her family moving and did not reply. Cain kept hold of Misha's hand and followed his mother's poker-straight back through the wet streets until they reached his grandfather's house.

The house that Lord Malachor had given to his chief gardener Garret was a small one-room affair of brick, on a tiny plot of land at the edge of Malachor's grounds. A small copse of trees hid Garret's house from the sight of the big house; otherwise it would have been in plain sight. The bricks were scrubbed clean, though obviously used at least once before they found their way into what was now Garret's home, and the garden in front of the house, though small, was as finely kept as the gardens surrounding Malachor's estates. The outhouse was back off from the road perhaps twenty meters.

Elena stood in front of the door for a moment before knocking. It was a stout door, oak with iron bindings across it, and her first knock she herself could hardly hear. She struck it more firmly, and an irritable voice from inside called out, "By the Light, I'm not deaf! Let me get my pants on and I'll be there." Moments later the door opened a crack, and an old man whom Cain had never seen before peered out through

the crack. He was backlit by the fire, and his features were indistinct to
Cain. Presumably the old man saw them more clearly, for after an
instant he opened the door more widely, and said slowly, "Elena?"

Elena's voice sounded shockingly harsh, even in her own ears.
"Marric's dead, Father."

"Ah." The man looked out past her. "These are the children, are
they?"

Cain's mother nodded jerkily.

The old man stood in the doorway for some time, and Cain began
to wonder if he was going to let them in. At last he sighed as though he
were very tired, and said simply enough, "Tie up the horse, then, scrape
the mud off yourselves, and come in where it's warm."

That night, lying on the floor in front of the fireplace, letting the
embers of the fire bake the stiffness from his bones, Cain had the first
dream of his entire life that he was able to remember.

Despite the aching tiredness that permeated his body, he had
difficulty getting to sleep at first and lay awake in front of the fire
listening to the pop and crackling of the dying logs. Once, he thought
he heard his mother crying and propped himself up on one elbow to
look over at where she lay, further away from the fire than any of her
children. Her eyes were closed, her breathing still and regular. Disturbed, by what he was not sure, Cain lay down again on his back and
closed his eyes.

He did not see the tear that trickled down through her closed
eyelid, or the one that followed it.

Cain's last thought was that he did not think he was going to be
able to sleep.

This was the dream:

He was standing on a smooth hard surface, so smooth he had
never felt anything like it before, stone like silk. There were straight
lines cut in it, and water running down inside the lines. He was standing on a ledge, with the Great Dam rising above him, and the One
Ocean, which he had never seen in his life, stretching out before him to

touch the horizon. The water shimmered blue in the bright sunlight, the blue of sapphire, and the same hot bright sunlight touched him, dazzled his eyes with reflections from the peaks of the dancing waves.

Suddenly the water turned dark, and the sun hid itself behind swirling gray clouds, stole away the warmth and the light. Tears tracked down his cheeks, though Cain did not know what it was he wept for. The sea was falling away from him, falling five meters, and then ten, and there were women's voices, three voices sweet and pure, and they spoke to him:

It is not for you. The power will be for your son; it is not for you.

From the north came the great tidal wave, a thundering wall of dark water that would smash the Great Dam beneath it, and Cain. The sky grew blacker and blacker, until the mountain of water reached up to blot out the sky itself.

It is not for you, the women said again.

Cain's last instants before the wave crushed him were filled with a terrible, desolate grief.

He knew that he would never have a son.

· 3 ·

Elena dreaded the audience with Lord Malachor.

She was all too aware that her best dress was none too good, and that she would have to present her plea to him in open court, with the other Eastmarchers—the men and women who'd known her as a child —there to see the state her husband's death had left her in, and to learn of the madness of her eldest son.

The evening of their first day in Eastmarch, Garret came home from the big house after work and ate in silence the dinner that Elena had prepared for them all. The food was good: carrots with honey, baked in a pot that had hung most of the day in the fireplace; roast chicken; and apples for desert. They ate sitting on the polished wooden floor, except for Garret himself, who sat on his bed. He'd brought home a jar of ale, and drank that himself; there was water for the others.

Cain sat watching his grandfather as dinner progressed, quiet but for the sounds of the crackling fire and the moaning of the wind outside. He was not sure what to make of the man. His mother had rarely spoken of him, or of her dead mother, or indeed of anything from the days before she'd married Marric. They'd slept the sleep of exhaustion the night before, all of them, even Misha, and when Cain had arisen that morning, before anybody except his mother, his grandfather had already left for the day. Now, eating his dinner, he studied the man surreptitiously; Garret was a tall man, though he walked with a stoop. His eyes were black, as dark as Cain's own, or Barra's. His hair was pure white, and he was beginning to bald; he wore a beard, near as white as his hair. His hands were quick and nimble, moving from one item to the other on his plate with an almost hypnotic grace, moving and flashing in the flickering firelight. The plain band of steel on his hand caught the red firelight, sent it slashing back into Cain's eyes, and behind the rubygold light a pair of dark eyes caught his own, behind the brilliant light, the color of blood and copper . . .

Very deliberately, Cain turned away from the old man and looked directly into the fireplace, into the leaping flames.

Nobody seemed to have noticed anything. Garret said without any emotion in his voice at all, "It's not polite to stare, boy."

It was the first thing he'd said since coming back from the big house. Elena was almost startled at the sound of his voice and glanced back swiftly at Cain. Cain was looking fixedly into the fire. She turned back to her father. "Was he staring at you?"

Garret finished his plate and drained away the last of the jar's ale. He did not thank Elena for the dinner. "Why not? He's never seen his grandfather before. I've been looking at them." He looked directly at his daughter. "Are you ready to talk about what needs to be done?"

Elena met his glance squarely. Her chin lifted. "Yes."

"Good," he said brusquely. "How much money've you got?"

"Sixteen stars, twenty-eight golds. There were twenty-nine, but I broke one for the apples and the chicken. I'm afraid I took the carrots from your garden."

The old man stared at her. "That much? Business must have been good."

"Marric . . ." She stopped, bit her lip, and tried again. "My husband was a good businessman."

"I know." Her father said the words as though conceding a point in a contest. "And now he's dead."

Cain was vaguely surprised by the comment; he was never certain how adults were supposed to behave, but he had the immediate impression that this was not how. Beside him, Siva was sniffling as though she were looking for an excuse to start crying again.

"Thank you for reminding us," said Elena, very evenly. Cain was not sure whether the firelight had put the color into her face, or anger. "The next time any of us come near forgetting, I'll seek you out to freshen our memory of the real world."

Garret continued as though Elena had not even spoken. "And so you'll need to plan. You're fortunate, having so much platty and gold. You might find a decent marriage again." He paused as though waiting for a response, and then actually smiled. "You've matured a bit, child. You surprise me."

Cain saw his mother choke back a reply. The muscles along her jaw clenched. "I had thought to move to the village. I'm a good seamstress, and I can cook a bit. It might be enough, with the money Marric's left us. And we've the title to the house in the hills, if some enterprising young man wants to take over Marric's trade." Garret was nodding, and Cain's mother added quietly, "It's a good spot."

"It is that," said Garret agreeably. From the shelf over his bed he had taken a small bone comb and was running it through his beard with great care. "At any rate, there might be some luck for you. Hogan the dressmaker, his wife died not two weeks ago. He's let it be known he's looking for someone to help him keep the store. Interested?"

"Yes."

"Good. Here's another thought for you as well. Do you remember Kenzie?"

". . . no, I don't—wait." Elena's eyes half shut. "He was the bootblack, who used to hang out down with Sam Kephard—oh, what was that place called, it was something long?"

"Was called Bulling's Place of Lodging, Fine Wines and Eating," said Garret. He replaced the bone comb on the ledge above his bed. "Now it's called Kephard's Inn, since Bulling's died and Sam Kephard's the new owner. They serve whiskey now, and vodka when they can get it. Bulling would have crapped red silkie over something like that, but Kephard likes hard drink. Anyhow, Kenzie died this past summer— transform fever, and a bad case too—and there's no bootblack yet picked up the business to replace him. I was thinking about Cain here."

For the first time Elena seemed startled. "Cain?"

"Aye. He's too young to be apprenticed, and I don't figure you're planning on school for him; even with the head start you've got with those sixteen stars, you won't be able to afford Schoolmistress Sandahl's rates long enough to get him past the barest tricks of reading and writing." The old man looked at Cain again, and this time Cain met his eyes. "How about it, lad? Do you think you could do that, black boots for pay?"

There was a moment's silence as Cain considered the question. Cain could see that his mother had not paid attention to Garret's question; she was thinking about something else.

Cain said, "Yes." That was all.

Garret nodded again, rather thoughtfully. *Of course.* "Well, that's got Cain, and you also, I'm thinking. The girls I think we can leave for now. They're young, too young for schooling with Sandahl—if that's the way your thoughts go, and I'd bet it is—or anything else." Elena nodded, almost reluctantly, and Garret spoke with the closest thing to gentleness Cain had yet seen in him. "So, what do we do about Misha?"

Almost involuntarily Elena glanced over at where her eldest son sat with his back to the wall. His face was utterly blank of expression, and still he did not blink. He'd eaten when food was put in front of him, but merely sat holding the wooden plate when he was done. Mention of his name did not change the placid quiet in his eyes.

Elena's voice was low, so low that Cain could hardly hear her. "Petition the Lord to send for one of the Rulers," she whispered. "When Mahgred's son Keri cracked his skull open, when we were children, the Ruler Athel came and took him away, and when he came back, he was whole again." She was looking down at the floor, not at her father. "I'll go see Lord Malachor and ask him to send for one of the Rulers."

"Daughter? Look at me." Elena brought her eyes up to meet his, and Cain saw that the color that had been there was anger, not firelight, for now she was very pale. "Will you do that? Go to the Lord Malachor as a supplicant?"

"Yes."

"It'll be hard for you, pleading helplessness in front of the crowd like that." The old man spoke without any sarcasm at all; he was studying his daughter's features.

Elena said simply, "He's my son."

Her father nodded, sighed again. "So he is." He still had not taken off his boots from the day's work. Now he did so, and dropped them next to his bed. Still in his work clothes, he swung his legs up onto the bed and lay back, closing his eyes. "The Lord Malachor will be coming by in the morning."

"*What?*"

"Well, midmorning, likely. They don't rise too very early over at the big house."

"But . . . Father, how?" she whispered in bewilderment.

"I've served the man forty-three years," he said quietly. "It counts for something, and the Lord Malachor, I guess he figured it wasn't so great a favor. He's a good man, like his father was." He was silent a moment. "Besides, I pleaded with him."

Elena rose slowly, and began gathering up the wooden plates to wash in the tub outside. She had her back to the old man when she said, "Thank you."

"Parents do such things for their children."

"I know."

"I know you do. Good night, Elena."

"Good night, Father."

Eric Malachor, Lord of Eastmarch, was a tall bluff man, with soft brown hair and a flushed look to his skin, dressed in clothes so fine that Cain had never seen their like before. His boots were of softest black leather and came to midcalf, and his cloak was blue sunsilk. His breeches and shirt were a lighter shade of blue wool. The bracelet on his wrist was pure gold, and he wore a diamond on a collar-guard at his throat. At his waist there hung what looked like the haft of a knife, molded to fit a man's hand, except that there was no blade in it. Though Cain knew he was as old as Garret, or nearly, he had aged better; there was no gray in his hair, and he moved like a man with half his years.

He came alone with Garret, without bodyguards. Cain did not know enough of the ways of the royalty to be as surprised by that as he might have been.

The door to the house was open; there was no window, and if they'd left the door closed there'd have been no light. It was warm enough; the sun was out for the first time in a week, and though there were clouds, they were high and white.

There was no warning of the Lord's approach. Elena was still brushing Misha's hair when Eric Malachor appeared in the doorway, and came hesitantly through. He had to duck slightly to get his head in under the lintel.

Elena was on her knees instantly, dragging Misha and Siva down with her with one hand on each of their shoulders. Barra was asleep on Garret's bed. It left Cain standing alone, in the midst of the silence. Lord Malachor did not seem to notice the boy. His first words were, "Get up, please. You're not in court." When they had obeyed, he stood silently for a moment, looking at them, and then at Elena alone. "I do remember you," he said after a moment. "Garret said I might. You argued with my second wife once, I've forgotten about what, and got whipped for it." He smiled briefly at the memory. "A serving girl with the guts to argue with that witch—it impressed me with your courage, if not your sense. It might please you to know she's passed away." The smile faded. "I am sorry to hear about the loss of your husband, madam. I'll miss the silkie steaks he brought to market."

Elena kept her eyes downcast as custom required, rather than meeting the man's gaze directly, but her voice was firm. "Thank you, my lord."

Lord Malachor seemed to look around at the inside of the room for the first time. "Damn, this place is cramped. Come outside with me, madam, and let's talk out where there's room to breathe." He turned and strode out, without looking to see that Elena was following. Once they were gone, Garret, who had stayed outside the entire time, came inside where the children were waiting. He stood staring at Cain. There was something that Cain could not identify glittering in the black eyes.

Finally he said, "Was your father a damn democrat, then? Or did he sing the diamond to you, maybe?"

Cain shook his head. He answered carefully. "Sir? I don't know what you mean."

"How old are you, boy?"

Cain looked at his grandfather warily. The old man was clearly angry about something, and Cain could not guess what. "I'm six, sir."

"And you've never been taught to bend the knee in the presence of royalty?" Cain glanced down in obvious confusion at his knees, and suddenly his grandfather laughed, albeit a trifle sourly. "Well, I guess you haven't. Could be Marric was a democrat, or could be he figured you'd never likely run into royalty, up there in the hills. 'Bend the knee,' Cain, it's a figure of speech. It means to kneel. Do you know how to kneel?"

Cain never had a chance to reply; Lord Malachor came back then. He could not have spent much time speaking to Elena. The instant Malachor came back in, Cain knelt promptly. Malachor roared with laughter, laughed until he was wheezing. He clapped Garret on the shoulder. "Well, he's learned a new trick since I met him."

"Yes, my lord," said Garret stonily.

Malachor crossed the length of the house in two long steps. "Stand up, boy. Let me look at you." Cain did so, and the Lord Malachor studied him for a long moment. He glanced away once, to look at Misha, and then back again to Cain. "He's very like you," said the man almost absently, and Cain knew he was not speaking to Cain's mother; and then he shrugged, as though dismissing the entire subject from his consideration. "Well, doubtless we'll see." Malachor turned away from Cain and said to Elena, "You'll be taking up residence in town?"

"Yes, my lord."

Malachor nodded as though he did not really care. "Make sure my secretary knows where you are. I've a rider going to Saerlock in two days. They've a mail transmitter in Saerlock, and the message will go from there to Parliament the same day. When the Ruler comes—if one comes—he'll not want to be kept waiting while we track you down."

"Yes, my lord," Elena said quietly. "Thank you."

"You're quite welcome." Lord Malachor stopped in the doorway, nearly blocking the entrance with his bulk, and looked at Cain's mother. "May the Light protect you, madam."

He left without waiting for a reply, as though he did not expect one.

The rooms they moved into were on Merchant's Way, just south of the intersection of Merchant's Way and Center Street. The rooms were located on the second floor of the building, which faced onto

Merchant's Way; the building itself was a plain affair of third-grade wood with only enough of a coating on it to help keep the water off.

It was very ugly.

The interior was no better than the building's outside had led Cain to expect. They had two rooms, and one of those, intended to be the kitchen, was very small. The bedroom was larger, fully large enough to sleep all five of them without crowding. The door from the hallway opened onto the kitchen; there was no door between the kitchen and the bedroom. There was no fireplace, and the cooking firepit, in the kitchen, was small and poorly ventilated. The walls were warped slightly in places, so that the draft crept through them. The one window was tiny and heavily glazed; it looked down on the alleyway to the building's back.

It was Hogan the dressmaker who found them the place. He was a cheerful fat man somewhere past his fortieth year who sweated constantly and dressed somewhat better than his station in life warranted. "Why, consider the possibilities!" he boomed. "Rugs over the floors, hang cloth—thick yellow linen, maybe, that I've got so much of on the shelves right now—hang that down the walls to cover the cracks. And a water drain right there in the kitchen! Never have to carry a bucket of dirty water out of here, just dump it down the drain!" Cain noticed that the drain Hogan spoke so proudly of stank badly, and that Hogan did not stay near it very long.

There was pumped water in Eastmarch, and in their building, but it had not been run into the rooms they were renting. To get water they had to go down the hallway to where a single dripping spigot was shared by everybody on the second floor.

After they'd spent most of half an hour unpacking their goods, Cain asked Hogan where the outhouse was. Hogan laughed as though Cain had said something very funny indeed. "Outhouse? Why, this is a modern building, Cain; it has a flush toilet!"

Cain stared at the man with dark suspicion and found, rather to his pleasure, that it made Hogan look distinctly uncomfortable. "How many people use it?"

"Well, everybody on this floor, I'd guess," said Hogan after a quick glance at Elena. "But you can get a butt-rest at the leatherworker's so's you don't have to sit on the same stool all the rest of them use. As long as you keep your butt-rest clean, why, flush toilets are a great convenience!"

Cain looked over to where his mother was standing, unpacking one of the traveling bags that had her dishes wrapped in it. Her shoulders were shaking, and he had no idea at all whether she was laughing or crying.

"Thank you," he said to Hogan with cold politeness. Then he went outside, down the stairs and around the building, and pissed in the alleyway.

They had spent just better than a week in their new home before the Ruler came.

Misha had improved not at all in that week; he still stared vacantly ahead, from whatever spot he had been left in. If he ever slept, he did not close his eyes to do so. If taken to the toilet, he relieved himself. The one time they forgot to do so, he soiled his pants, and after that they were careful about making sure that somebody took him to the toilet first thing in the morning and again before he went to bed.

The rooms changed slowly over the course of that week. On their first day there, Elena brought in bucket after bucket of water and scrubbed the entire place, floors and walls and firepit. Siva spent an entire hour washing the window, until it could nearly be seen out of. Elena bought acid from Eastmarch's only physician, poured the acid down the stinking drain in the kitchen, and then bought a clay stopper to cover the drain when it was not in use. That evening she lit a roaring fire in the firepit and kept it burning most of the night as hot as was safe, to dry out the wood before mildew could set in.

The next day Elena, Cain, and Siva patched over the worst of the gaps in the walls with caulking, and again that night the fire burned high, to help the caulking dry. Hogan came through on the offer he'd made their first day there, and brought over nearly two full rolls of yellow linen, which he and Elena together hung from the walls in both rooms. They sold their horse that week, for a fair enough price, and with the money from the horse bought a large rug to cover the floor in the bedroom and a smaller rug for the kitchen. Elena dug into their precious store of stars and bought a fine long black oak table, about seventy centimeters high, and cushions to go around it. It was something they had not had even at their home in the hills, and both Cain and Siva were mightily pleased with it.

On the day the Ruler Elyssa came to them, Siva went to the store to buy bread and had come back with both the bread, and daisies for Elena. Elena stood motionless for several moments, and then in a very quiet voice thanked the girl, and was putting the daisies into a jar when a pounding came on the door.

"Hogan?" called Elena. It was a natural enough assumption; Hogan had been by every day after closing his store for the evening, and it was near that time.

Cain said, "It's not Hogan," and then a voice bawled out through the door, "We are the Lord Malachor's messenger, with the Ruler Elyssa. Let us enter!" Cain did not even look at his mother; he was the closest one to the door, and he opened it without hesitating. A man in the gold and brown livery of the messenger service stood just beside the door, at rigid attention. In the doorway itself was a woman whom Cain caught only a glance of before dropping to his knees.

In the dimness of the hallway, the woman was glowing.

The woman who entered from the hallway was both like and unlike any other person whom Cain had ever met. If he had never heard the name Ruler, he might still have ascribed such a title to the Lady Elyssa. She carried herself with a complete and almost innocent arrogance, moving slowly into the room, examining everything in it with a sort of curiosity. Cain watched her out of the corner of his eye; she seemed as intrigued by the linen hung on the walls as by any of the people in the room. Her hair was a pale, almost white shade of blonde. He did not get a clear enough glimpse of the Ruler to even guess at the color of her eyes. Her clothing was as strange as the rest of her. In a woman of Eastmarch it would have been considered immodest: a blouse of pale green that hung loosely almost all the way down to her knees, with big silver buttons that were buttoned only over her breasts. She wore breeches like a man, though tighter than the breeches men of Eastmarch wore, and of a black material that Cain had never seen before; it reflected the light of the firepit so brilliantly that sunsilk, had there been any in the room with her, would have seemed a cheap material by comparison. She wore black flat-heeled boots, in shape not very different from the boots Marric and Misha had worn to go fishing in; but the Ruler Elyssa's boots had lights that appeared like starbursts deep within the surface of the boot. And over it all, the pale golden shimmer that clothed her like a second skin.

Had Lord Malachor been within the room with her, her presence would have rendered his nearly invisible.

Time stretched while the Ruler looked through the two small rooms. She must have known instantly that Misha was the one whom she'd come to see; he sat stupidly in the corner of the bedroom and did not appear to notice her when she stood for a moment immediately in front of him. Finally she turned away from him and returned to the kitchen.

The word "Arise" seemed to drift from her direction; had the silence been any less profound Cain would not have heard it. She spoke almost indifferently to Elena. She neither introduced herself nor asked their names, but said only, "Tell me how it happened."

Elena met the Ruler's eyes once and looked quickly away. "Madam . . . Rul . . . I don't know how to call you," she said suddenly.

For the very briefest moment Cain thought that something like anger might have touched the Ruler's features, but then it was gone, and he was sure he was wrong. She smiled graciously enough, and her teeth were amazingly white, even against her pale skin. "I am the Lady Elyssa; you may call me so."

"Lady Elyssa, my husband Marric fished in the One Ocean, and brought his catch back through the waterlock in the hills over Eastmarch. Misha helped him. Ten days ago there was a terrible storm, and Marric . . . died. Misha was trapped between the invisible doors until I came to get him. Once I had brought him out, he was as he is now."

The Ruler nodded. Her accent was strange, unlike anything Cain had ever heard before; different from the accent of Eastmarch, different again from that of Saerlock. "That is what I was told. There are two possibilities, Worker. The likeliest is that your son's brain was starved of oxygen—of air," she said gently to Elena's look of incomprehension, "while he was between the doorfields of the waterlock. The other is that he is mad, driven from his mind by the loss of his father and the violence of the storm." The Ruler examined Elena before continuing.

"If it is simple madness, we can likely cure it. If his brain cells have died, there will not be much we can do for him. Some retraining, perhaps."

"If . . . if Misha's brain . . . *cells* . . . have died, then you cannot help him?" Cain's mother was staring at the Lord of Light with disbelief.

"Madam," the Ruler Elyssa said flatly, with something very near anger, "we are the Lords of Light, and we are more powerful than you can ever know." She held Elena's eyes a moment as a snake might hold a bird's. "But even we cannot turn back the day."

Standing by the door, watching the two of them, for the first time in his life Cain thought that his mother was not beautiful. Elena looked instantly at the floor at the tone of the whip in the Ruler's voice. "Lady Elyssa," said Elena, "I would count it as a blessing if you would do whatever you can for Misha." She bit her lip, and added, "Please."

The Ruler nodded. "I must take him to Parliament. You know this?"

"Yes."

"Misha!" For the first time the Ruler raised her voice, and to Elena's surprise Misha appeared in the doorway to the bedroom. He walked docilely to where the Ruler stood in the center of the kitchen, and the Ruler Elyssa placed a hand on his shoulder. "Turn your eyes away," she said softly. "The Light can dazzle those who are not prepared for it." The Ruler Elyssa gave them no time to think about her command; the blazing Light that took her, and took Misha, turned the kitchen to brightest noon. Elena turned entirely away from the radiance and covered her face until it was gone.

When it was finally dim enough to see again, she found the Ruler Elyssa gone; Misha gone; Siva, staring at her mother with big eyes; and Barra, screaming from the other room.

Cain said, "My head hurts."

Then he collapsed.

The messenger's name was Boran. On his way back to the Lord Malachor's estate, he turned over the evening's events in his mind. Boran was hardly ignorant of the ways of the Rulers; as a very young man, before entering Lord Malachor's service, he had once traveled to

Goldriver, where Rulers were near as often seen in the streets as human royalty.

He still did not understand why the Ruler Elyssa hadn't had the woman Elena and her mad son brought to her. It was not like a Ruler— or at least unlike the small number of Rulers whom Boran had known— to care overmuch about the convenience of the simple folk.

He'd overheard part of a conversation between the Ruler Elyssa and the Lord Malachor when he was summoned, and he half thought that a statement the Ruler Elyssa had made might have explained her obvious desire to be done with the night's work.

"No, no," she'd been saying when Boran entered the reception hall where Lord Malachor had met her, "I can't. I'm late already for a party in Singer. We take at times," she said flatly, with plain displeasure, "entirely too much effort over you Workers."

The very next day Elena began work in Hogan's shop, and Cain took up his position in front of Kephard's Inn as the village of Eastmarch's only bootblack.

And the village bootblack he remained, for over four years.

The Minstrel

The Years 1193–1195 After the Fire

Cain found that he enjoyed shining boots. His kit consisted of nothing more than the box he kept his brush and polishing cloth in, clear wax and bootblack, and his own spit. Eastmarch was not a large village, nor a wealthy one; on an average day he might shine seven or eight pairs of boots, at a half-estar apiece. He soon found that there'd been a reason why the previous bootblack had been such a permanent fixture in front of Kephard's Inn, on the Traveler's Road at the west end of town: business was better there, and Sam Kephard kept a wooden sidewalk with an overhang that kept the rain and snow off in winter and the sun off during the rest of the year. It was, all considered, a pleasant place to work. He came to an understanding with Kephard: one tenth of whatever Cain made in the course of a day went to Kephard, for the privilege of sitting on Kephard's sidewalk.

The hours Cain spent in front of the Inn, listening to the conversations of his customers, might not have been as useful as a true education, but in some ways it taught him more. His clients were generally vain members of the upper class—Merchants and Land'ners—as only such could and would spend half an estar just to have his boots cleaned. They were barely aware of him as a person; things a man would not have said in front of his wife, and might not have admitted in front of most other men, Cain heard often. His personality, already that of a skeptic, was profoundly affected by the conversations he overheard. Before he had reached the age of seven they had left him with a deep, ingrained cynicism about men and their motives which stayed with him through the rest of his life.

Cynicism was not the only thing Cain learned, of course. The work brought Cain his first exposure to money; until Marric's death, only his father, and sometimes his mother, had ever been allowed to handle money. When he began working the trade of bootblack, Cain did not even know the names of all the common coins. That was changed quickly; before his first day on the job, Hogan's brother Thomas, who kept books for most of the Merchants in the village, taught him the coinage of the realm, and the basics of addition and subtraction. He learned to count all the way to a hundred by rote, and how to make change. He learned that five aluminum pent made an iron half-estar, and ten pent made a full estar; that ten estar made one of the silver lunès. That was as high as he learned to go for some time. There were larger coins, suns of gold and stars of platinum, but he had been shining boots for nearly half a year before he saw his first gold sun, and that only because a drunken Trader dropped it while sorting through his coin for a half-estar. He never did see a star; one star would have been more money than Cain could have made in a full year shining boots.

He had no real friends. Most of the children his age were free to do as they pleased, from Malachor's children down to those as poor as himself. His place was on the porch of Kephard's Inn, except on Sun-Days, when Elena went, with all of her children, and later with Hogan and his daughter Katya, to worship at the Church of the Light, in Eastmarch's center square. Some of the boys became casual acquaintances; he enjoyed talking with them, but he was too distant a person, and also too confined in terms of where he could go with them, for any of them to grow close. Some of the others tormented him, almost casually, until Sam Kephard put a stop to it with a club.

Once, on his way home, he was waylaid for the money he had made that day, and robbed of it.

There were four of them, waiting for him in the alleyway he walked home through, running parallel to Merchant's Way. Two of them appeared in front of him, and without even having to think he knew what was happening. He did not consider fighting; the other two were each larger than he was. Instead he turned to run and found the other two immediately behind him.

Then he fought with a savagery that surprised them, struck one boy a blow in the stomach that put him down on the ground writhing in pain, and landed nearly half a dozen other punches before the sheer weight of the three remaining boys pulled him down to the ground. While two of them held him down, the third boy struck him in the face repeatedly, vicious blows that kept coming even after Cain's struggles had ceased in the haze of the pain. At one point Cain remembered crying out, *Help me! Please help me!*—but nobody came, and finally the boys stopped hitting him, took his money and scattered his boot-black's kit across the alleyway.

One of them kicked him in the ribs, hard, before they ran off.

Cain lay in the alley, distantly aware of the sound of the village around him, voices far away, the occasional passage of one of the rich folk in a carriage on nearby Merchant's Way. At no time was he actually unconscious; he simply could not move.

It was night when a tall figure appeared over him, and his grandfather's voice was saying something his ears could not interpret except as sound. Later other voices came, and somebody picked him up and carried him back to the rooms he shared with Elena and his sisters.

Fall came and went, and the year 1193 After the Fire gave way to the year 1194. They heard nothing of what had happened to Misha, and as the quarters slid by and became years the subject ceased to be discussed. Finally Cain ceased thinking about Misha much at all.

With the income from both Cain and herself, Elena reckoned they could afford schooling for Siva. Siva was enrolled in Mistress Sandahl's School early in 1194. Her first day of school was Winter 8, the day Cain turned seven. She learned her lessons well enough that Mistress Sandahl did not raise her rates after the end of Siva's first year. It was only one of the ways in which Mistress Sandahl encouraged the correct attitude toward learning in her students. A student who learned poorly or not at all she charged more for than a student who learned quickly and retained what Sandahl taught of reading and writing and history. She was a fierce old lady whom Cain never saw smile. With the exception of his own mother she was perhaps the only woman he had ever met of whom he was at all afraid.

Not counting the Ruler Elyssa, whom he did not even think of in such terms.

As a woman, that is.

Sometime during Siva's second year at school, Cain was never sure exactly when or how, he grew into the habit of walking Siva to school in the morning and walking her home again after school. They got along well enough, and the things she told him about from school were interesting enough to hold his attention. What math she knew held no interest for him, except as it related to the handling of money; but reading, after he found out that there were books with stories in them, was a thing he desperately desired to learn. During Winter Quarter 1195 he learned secondhand about the Fire Wars which ended the evil first world, and how the Rulers had taken over and fought wars with the Giants and the barbarians and such to keep the evil from happening again. That in itself did not interest him much—with the cynicism that his work was engendering in him, he supposed that the Rulers *would* say that things were terrible before the Rulers had taken over, whether that was true or not.

But—once Siva had been exposed to the Rulers' official explanation of why the first world had been such a terrible place and why things were so much better now—after that the students were given books to read, some of which had been written before the Fire. Cain listened in rapt wonder as Siva read to him, slowly and fumblingly, from works such as *Macbeth*, by Master William Shakespeare, and *Huckleberry Finn*, by Master Mark Twain. Once Siva tried to teach Cain to read, but it grew dark while she was trying, and their mother would not allow them to light a candle to continue the lesson.

The school Siva attended was only a large room that Mistress Sandahl lived over, at the far eastern end of the Traveler's Road, where the Traveler's Road, the longest continuous road in the Valley, quietly and without fuss petered out into nothingness. The next day, when Cain came to pick up Siva from school, Mistress Sandahl was waiting outside the room with Siva. She stood there with one hand gripping Siva's shoulder while the other students filed out of the schoolroom and went running down the cobblestone street. The old woman glared at Cain with an expression that was only a hairbreadth away from hostility.

Cain stood there, wondering what he could possibly have done to get the old woman so angry. When all the children had gone, except for Cain and Siva, Mistress Sandahl let Siva go. What she said then was not remotely what Cain had been expecting. "Your sister tells me you're very bright."

Cain glanced at his sister. Siva looked embarrassed. "Yeah," he said after a moment. "I s'pose."

Sandahl looked at him. She spoke as though the words hurt her teeth. "If I send work home with your sister, will you do the work with her?"

Cain was startled. He said the first thing that came to mind. "Maybe."

"As you please," she said shortly. "I'll send work home with her and correct it if you've a mind to do it." She did not wait for a reply from him, but turned about and went back inside the warm schoolroom, and began swinging the door closed.

Cain said suddenly, "Thank you. I will."

Sandahl looked over at him fiercely. "You miss even one lesson," she said sharply, "and I stop." She slammed the door shut.

Cain's mother, when he told her later that night, was clearly displeased, but said nothing; and so Cain and Siva did their lessons together.

On the day of Summer 16, 1195, as evening encroached upon afternoon, a man rode out of the west. Sitting on the porch in front of Kephard's Inn, Cain watched him coming, riding for most of half an hour down the pale white ribbon of the Traveler's Road from Telindel. It had been a dry summer, and the rider rose a cloud of dust as he passed. Cain saw the dust before he saw the rider, and sat in the shade watching the rider approach for the entire time. He'd had no customers that day, not one. He was not alone in his misfortune: Sam Kephard had let Jenny, the barmaid he'd just recently hired, go home for the day a little while after lunch, with instructions to come by again at dinnertime and see whether or not Sam needed help. It was a sleepy summer day in the middle of the workweek; neither Kephard nor Cain had expected much in the way of customers, and by the luck of the day they got even less than they expected.

Watching the man, Cain had the odd illusion that the rider was heading straight for him. It was nonsense, of course. The man was riding east, and Cain was in the path the man had chosen to take. Still, the impression was very strong. In the next half hour the horseman entered the outskirts of Eastmarch and rode without pausing right up to the hitching post in front of Kephard's Inn. Cain stared at him, quite openly, while the man tied up his horse. Cain could not quite make out his features, even though he was only a few meters away; the sun was lowering itself to the horizon immediately behind him.

The man came and stood before Cain. He was not looking at Cain, but rather at his surroundings, the village of Eastmarch.

Cain waited patiently.

The man finished examining the village at length and turned to look at Cain. Cain let him look, and looked back. He was elegant enough, for someone just in off the Traveler's Road; tall, perhaps a full two meters, some thirty years of age. He wore a beard and full mustache, and his hair was quite long, past his shoulders. The hair was an odd mixture of black and silver, though the black was not the same shade of jet black as Cain's, and the silver was not the color of age. His skin was darker than that of any Eastmarcher Cain had ever seen, either naturally or else from the sun in his travels, and his eyes were an odd shade of brown. He wore good traveling clothes which had seen better times: a leather jerkin and breeches, and the jerkin had been dyed a deep shade of scarlet. His belt was plain leather, but with a gorgeous silver buckle in an intricate style. He wore more jewelry than Cain had ever seen before on anyone, even a woman: three rings hung from his left ear, and there were silver and copper bracelets on both wrists. His necklace appeared to be of true gold, with some green stone hung from it. There was a haft that hung at his waist, and it raised a memory in Cain that he could not place for a moment; then it came to him. Such a thing, like a knife with the blade removed, the Lord Malachor wore.

His boots were of good quality, though travel-worn.

"Well, lad," said the man after a moment, in a voice fluent and musical as any instrument, "will you shine a poor traveler's boots for him?"

"Half-estar."

"Indeed?" The man managed to put a world of surprise into the word. "Why, lad, that's robbery!"

"It's what I charge. Do you want me to shine your boots?"

"Lad, in Telindel the going rate's three pent for a shine." The man looked at Cain in a fair approximation of honest amazement. "Three pent, lad, and in Saerlock some would do it for two!"

"This isn't Telindel," said Cain evenly, "and it's not Saerlock either. It's Eastmarch, and I'm the only bootblack in Eastmarch . . . and it's five pent."

"Oh." The man absorbed that news for a moment. "Well, seeing's you've locked the business down so smartly, five pent it'll be." He did not sound upset at all. He placed one boot on Cain's raise. "If you would." Cain got out his brush and began scrubbing the dust from the leather. The dirt was caked into the crevices; the man must have been on the road some time. "I suppose I must compliment you on your fine business sense, setting up in front of a saloon as you have. Get the young ones going in, to look their best for their ladies, and the old ones coming out, to clean themselves up before going home to their wives. Why, there's many a grown man's gone bankrupt for lack of such simple business sense. How old are you, lad?"

"Eight."

"Really?" The man looked startled, and Cain finished up with his first boot and started on the second. "You look older." Cain was aware of the man looking down at him. "No, I take it back," he said more slowly, "you act older."

"I know. 'Scuse me, sir, let me get at the heel here. There's a nasty gouge in it." Cain rubbed bootblack into the gouge, and then more until the gouge was filled out to the surface of the leather and appeared to have vanished. It wasn't the job a leatherworker would've made of it, but the man wasn't paying for anything better. Cain dabbed polish wax on and smoothed it over the boot, finished up with a soft cloth buff of the boot tops, and closed his box. "That'll be a half-estar, sir."

The man paid him absently, studying the sign that said Kephard's

Inn with a doubtful eye. "Tell me, could you, if there's another saloon in this town?"

"There was one once," Cain informed him, "but it burned down and the man who ran it went to Telindel."

The man snorted, and said with a twist to his lips that might have been a smile, "I see this Master Kephard has the same fine business sense as yourself."

"He tells people," said Cain, "when they ask, that there's not room in a village the size of Eastmarch for more than one inn. I think he means it," he added in a totally factual tone of voice.

The man looked down at Cain again, as though in reappraisal. "I don't doubt. What's your name, lad?"

"Cain. What's yours?"

"Loukas, Loukas of Semalia. Is your name really Cain? That's the name of a demon in the kriss religion, you know."

Cain looked up at him. "Is it?"

"Aye," said the man who called himself Loukas. "One of the first two mentioned in their holy writings, in fact, and Lucifern is the other. Your parents wouldn't be kriss, would they?"

"And name me for a demon? Hardly. They named me for the kainan bird."

"The kainan? Is that an Eastmarcher word?"

Cain shrugged. "It's a kind of a shrike."

Loukas laughed. "So instead of naming you for a demon, they name you for the bloodiest carnivore in the air?" He seemed amused by the thought. "That's not much of an improvement, is it?" Cain simply shrugged again, and Loukas looked at Cain with a brief frown. "Lad, do you ever smile?"

"Sometimes."

Loukas cocked his head to one side and grinned suddenly, very widely. His teeth were startlingly white against the brown skin. "I rather think we'll improve on that." He ruffled Cain's hair and went inside the inn to get drunk.

. . . *The golden Light poured through him, held him weightless as a leaf in its grasp. There was pain in the Light, and beauty, and the cold aching whisper. . . .*

His mother had to shake him twice before he came up, out of the golden dream, and into the dim darkness of reality. The expression on his face must have been odd, even in the poor light from the firepit in the kitchen; Elena said, almost gently, "Cain? Are you feeling well?" She touched a hand to his forehead.

Cain shook his head irritably. "Yes. I had a dream."

Her hand snapped away as though scalded. "Up with you, then," she said, suddenly harsh. "It's time to take your sister to school."

As Cain was walking Siva to school, later that same morning, they passed a huge tent that had sprung up overnight, pitched on an empty stretch of grass and brush at the very side of the Traveler's Road, near the far east end of town; past the residences, but somewhat west and considerably south of Lord Malachor's estates. The tent was of some brilliant green material which caught the early-morning sun like an emerald mirror. Tethered to a small apple tree was the horse that Loukas of Semalia had ridden into Eastmarch on the prior day. It was a good spot; there was nothing behind him except the hills, rising toward the Gray Mountains.

Loukas was sitting out in front of the tent, wearing only his breeches, writing on a tablet of some sort. He was much cleaner than the last time Cain had seen him; his hair and his beard looked to have been brushed, and the dust washed out. Loukas nodded to Cain and called, "Good morning," to them; the words echoed after Cain.

They passed by the tent without speaking. They were halfway to school when Siva said, "Do you know who that was, back there by the tent?"

"Why would I know?"

She shrugged. "You sit in front of Kephard's every day. I thought maybe the man in the tent went there."

"His name is Loukas. I think he's a Trader."

She did not seem surprised that he knew the man's name. "If he was a Trader, he would stay at the Inn."

Cain said nothing for a moment. Then he conceded, "Maybe."

"I wonder why he's here?"

The grin that flashed across Cain's face might have surprised most of those who knew him. "Why don't you ask him, you're so interested?"

"I'm not interested," Siva protested. "I'm just curious."

"Oh," said Cain. "That's different."

Siva was carrying a pair of writing tablets in her right hand, hers and the one Cain had done his work on; she shifted that to her left hand and punched him suddenly in the shoulder.

Cain looked at her in surprise. "Why did you do that?"

"You're mean."

"I am not!"

"Don't you care why he's here?"

Cain was rubbing his shoulder. "No."

"Do you think he's going to stay?"

"How would I know? Maybe. He sure didn't come to Eastmarch on his way to somewhere else."

Siva was silent for a while then. They were nearly to the school when she said, "Could you *ask?*"

Cain asked Siva, as though he did not care what the answer was, "Do you still like me?"

Siva sighed in exasperation. "Yes."

"Okay. I'll ask him."

Siva smiled at him. Most of the time Cain was only vaguely aware of the fact that his sister was very pretty. "Did I hurt your shoulder?"

"No. Of course not."

Cain did not tell her what was in his mind, that there was nothing that could have stopped him from going back to see Loukas.

Nothing in the world.

Loukas was still there at the side of the road, taking a breakfast of apples and beer when Cain returned. Two apples were roasting over a small fire of branches and twigs. It was still relatively early in the morning. There were folk on the roads, but only a few. He must have purchased the beer from Kephard's; the containers were beer bulbs, and only Kephard's Inn in all of Eastmarch had the machine to fill them properly. He had put on a shirt, a fine thing of yellow sunsilk, and looked good in it.

Cain stopped on the other side of his fire. "Good morning to you, too."

Swallowing the last of one beer bulb, Loukas gestured to the damp ground near himself. "Have a seat, Cain. I was thinking you'd come by. Want a beer?"

"Sure." Cain took the beer bulb curiously—it was surprisingly cold, as though there were ice in it—picked a spot for his bootblack's kit, and sat on it to keep from getting wet. "How do you open this?"

"Easier to show you." Loukas took the bulb from Cain and ran one finger along the shiny ring at its neck until the ring went *click*. He handed it back. "Never drunk from a bulb before? I'd guess Master Kephard doesn't sell to you?"

"Says I'm too young." Cain sucked at the bulb experimentally and was rewarded by an icy draft. "Jenny gives me beer sometimes, when he's not there, but just in cups. He counts the bulbs."

"Jenny'd be the serving girl? She wasn't there yesterday."

"He sent her home early, things were so slow. She's nice," Cain added.

"I take it business is better, usually? Kephard said it was." Cain nodded, and Loukas seemed to relax just a bit. "That's good. It had better be, if I'm to stay here."

"Why are you here?"

The question came out abruptly, and there was a hanging moment of silence before Loukas replied. He seemed a bit amused. "I'm a minstrel, Cain. I sell my songs for entertainment. There are eight minstrels in Saerlock, and three in Telindel. There's none here, I'm told."

With a perfectly straight face, Cain said, "Just good business sense, then?"

Loukas shot a quick grin at Cain. "You could say that." He reached into the fire without apparent thought for burns, bracelets jangling slightly, pulled the spit with the two baking apples on it from the fire and set them aside in the damp grass to cool. "Want a baked apple, Cain? I put on a second, just in case."

There was almost nothing in the world that Cain liked better than baked apples; some days, when he'd made good money, his mother, or sometimes Siva, baked them for him.

Cain was aware of the minstrel's eyes on him, awaiting a reply.

Cain said, "Why are you here?"

The saddlebags from Loukas' horse were immediately behind him; he propped himself up against them, leaning back slightly, and took a long draft from his beer bulb. "Let me put it this way—why are *you* here?"

Cain answered warily. "You called me."

Loukas shook his head. "No," he said softly. "I called, and I was expecting *someone.*" He nodded at Cain. "*You* came. I was hoping it would be you."

Cain drank some of his beer, looking down at the bulb thoughtfully. "I think my sister heard you too."

Loukas shook his head again. "If she'd heard the call, she'd be here now, with you. Oh, I'm sure she heard *something.*" Loukas was looking at Cain as a man might look at a horse he was considering buying, and the look did not please Cain. "But she did not hear what you heard." He made a long arm to where the apples were sitting in the grass and brought back the spit and the baked apples. He slid one off for himself, and bit into it. "Do you want one, or no?"

The smell struck Cain like a blow. With his mother angry this morning, he'd had nothing to eat yet. "Please." Loukas tossed the apple to him, and he ate it swiftly, pausing only long enough to pick the seeds out and toss them over his shoulder for luck. Loukas watched him with some amazement.

"Damn, Cain, were you not fed this morning?"

Cain looked up at him, still working on the core. "No. I got my mother mad at me." He looked straight into the minstrel's brown eyes. "I told her I had a dream."

"Ah."

Loukas seemed to accept that as sufficient answer, and Cain finished his apple in silence. He wiped apple juice from his chin with his forearm and said with what might, in another boy, have been shyness, "Thanks. That was good."

"I could tell," said Loukas dryly.

"Loukas?" Cain said it hesitantly.

"Yes?"

"Why are you here?"

"That's an important question to you, is it?" Loukas looked directly at him. "Cain, you're here because I called you last night. I'm here because you called for me."

"I don't understand."

" 'Bout a year ago, pretty near. I was passing by Singer and set up my tent at the edge of the Road. Been a long day's traveling, started before dawn, and I was tired. Come evening I was ready to sleep, and I'd got set to. Had my tent pitched and laid down inside with my knife in my hand and my head on my pillow." Loukas paused. "The bitch hit me square between the eyes. I thought I'd been struck, went rolling out of my tent with the blade lit on my knife. If some poor bastard had been riding by on the Road just then I'd've had his head off. Scared my horse half out of her wits." It was hard to bear up under the gaze of the calm brown eyes. The gaze was heavy, like a weight. Like his grandfather's black eyes. As other folk, Cain supposed, must feel his own. "Then it came to me what it was, a cry for help from a child. It ended so sudden, I thought sure whoever made that cry had been killed. I knew the cry came from the east, so I headed that way, stopping off at every town and making the sending, and failing at every town. Eastmarch was the last place you could be." He drained the remains of his beer bulb and opened another with a slight *click*. "And the whole time to get here, Cain, the whole time I was afraid you were dead already."

Cain said slowly, "All the while I was watching you ride down the Traveler's Road, I was thinking how you were riding to me. It seemed silly."

Loukas said simply, "I came for you, Cain. I didn't come for anything else."

A thought was hovering in the back of Cain's mind, and at last he brought it forth to the light. "I think . . . I think my grandfather probably heard the sending last night."

Loukas glanced at him swiftly. "Oh?"

"Yes," said Cain more certainly, "I think he must have. He's like me. Like *you*."

"What's his name?"

"Garret. He's the Lord Malachor's gardener."

Loukas chewed his lower lip. "Hmm. I don't know the name— was your grandfather ever a student at the Academy?"

Cain looked at him blankly. "The what?"

"Well, the . . ." Loukas broke off, stared at him. "You don't know of the Academy? Where did you spend your life, child? The

Rulers sweep through these parts every four years to select likely children for training, and more often than that in populous areas. The last time they tested in Eastmarch would've been in Summer Quarter 1192."

"We lived in the hills until my father died. That was two and a half years ago, not long after newyear. Winter 22, 1193. We didn't come down to Eastmarch until after that."

Loukas sighed, and rearranged his bulk against the saddlebags so that he was more comfortable. "I'd forgotten how far I was from civilization. By the Light, children in Goldriver know who Loden *slept* with on any given night!" The comment obviously meant nothing to Cain; Loukas brushed by it and continued. "I'll teach you about the Academy, then. Indeed, I'll teach you many things. But back to your grandfather for now. He probably didn't go to Academy; my memory's good, and I don't recall anyone name of Garret. Is he loyal to the Lord Malachor?"

That Cain knew the answer to. "Yes. They're friends, I think."

"And is he a churchgoer? Church of the Light, I mean, not foolishness like the kriss or elrons."

"Yes, every SunDay. So's my mother."

"And the Lord Malachor? Ever heard any rumor that he was less than proper in his regard for the Rulers?"

Cain merely shook his head. "No."

"Well." There was a world of summation in the word, and Cain had the impression Loukas had just reached a decision. Suddenly Loukas laughed and leapt to his feet. He vanished into his tent, came out with an instrument like a lute, though with a longer neck and a longer, wider hollow. "I'm keeping you from your work, and myself from mine. You need to be off, to shine your boots, and I need to be at work, writing new songs and practicing old. I'll be at Kephard's toward evening, to play for the dinner crowd. Will you stay for that?"

"Not tonight. I'll have to ask my mother when she comes home from work. And I have to wait until Hogan's not there. She doesn't like me to talk when he's there."

Loukas had slung the instrument around his neck and was running his fingers across the strings. At Cain's words he stopped, and seemed about to say something; Cain thought he changed his mind. "Mornings," he said instead, "they're a slow time for you, business-wise?"

Cain nodded. "Yes. I could come here for a while. It's on the way from the school to Kephard's."

Loukas cocked an eyebrow. "And what might your mother say to that?"

Cain said simply, "I won't ask her."

Loukas grinned at him. "That's the spirit. Never *ask* for anything you can *take*. You should go now."

Cain stood and picked up his bootblack kit. He turned to leave, powerfully aware, even now, of Loukas' eyes upon him.

He turned back. "Loukas?"

"Yes?"

"You really came for me? Just for me?" Asking the question, it was the first time Cain had ever felt vulnerable in his entire life.

Loukas' hands ceased moving on the instrument. He said directly, "Just for you, Cain."

Cain could not meet his eyes. He nodded, accepting it. "Okay." He wanted to say something else, anything else, but he was afraid that if he did he would cry like a girl. Loukas stood looking at him, waiting patiently for whatever Cain chose to do.

Cain ran all the way to Kephard's.

That night Cain's grandfather Garret passed away in his sleep. It was Lord Malachor himself who found the body, when he and several of his men went out to see why it was that Garret had not come to supervise the planting of the white roses that had just arrived, all the way from Singer.

At the time Cain thought nothing of it; his grandfather was old. It was not until several years later that he learned that Loukas had killed his grandfather.

By that time he could not find it within himself to blame Loukas.

Loukas had only done what Cain's grandfather would have done to him.

The Diamond
of the Day

The Years 1195–1201 After the Fire

· 1 ·

Cain spent six years with Loukas. He was a child when they met, nearly a man when the Rulers took Cain away to the Academy at Parliament.

Looking back on that period, long years later, Cain's memory brought back, for the most part, only flashes; moments and colors, fragments of incidents that he could not place in any context that made sense to him. Jenny was there, the pretty blonde serving woman at Kephard's, and Kephard himself, cracking skulls with the club he kept behind the counter. Siva he remembered sharply, arguments and reconciliations alike; Barra, attentive and wide-eyed, came to him with less clarity, but more warmth, of SunDays and evenings spent telling her, secondhand, the stories Loukas had told him. Other folks he recalled only dimly. His mother and Mistress Sandahl were mixed up together, fierce, forbidding women who were, in memory, very similar to each other. He could not remember even the name of the fat man who had shared his mother's bed, though the sense of distaste was still there. Thomas, the man's brother, he remembered rather more clearly, the occasional kindnesses that were so rare for an adult of Eastmarch to direct at the child who was, after all, only the village bootblack.

He remembered the excitement that had filled him the first time Thomas, while teaching Cain the trade of bookkeeping, had made him understand the structure and reason for the higher maths, the beauty in the way the numbers tumbled together, the clear elegance of geometry and the calculus.

They stayed with him also, the long mornings and afternoons spent sitting quietly on the porch in front of Kephard's; those came back to him sharply, the feel of the cold in winter, cutting through the thin clothing that was all Elena could afford; or the blessed warmth of summer. They were the bright memories of his childhood, and until the day he died he did not lose them.

But before all else, his memories of those years were his memories of Loukas, the youthful minstrel who had seemed so old to Cain when first they met. Fully a century later Cain could recall entire conversations, nearly word for word, played out as the two of them were seated in front of the fire by Loukas' tent at the edge of town. Far more so than the village of Eastmarch, Loukas of Semalia became his world; Loukas' thoughts became Cain's; and long years after Loukas was finally dead, his dreams and plans lived on in Cain.

And after Cain, in Orion of Eastmarch.

· 2 ·

The week following Loukas' arrival was a jumbled one. They buried Cain's grandfather two days after his death, and so for two days Cain was unable to see Loukas again. Elena took her father's death harder than Cain would have expected; she aged visibly in the course of that week.

Garret's death was almost incidental to Cain; if he thought about it at all, it was only with a distant sort of relief that he would not have to explain Loukas to his grandfather. To Cain's surprise, his mother did not object when he told her he wished to take his dinners with Loukas. She was, he guessed, still distraught over her father's death. He did not worry about the why of it, but simply accepted her permission as a blessing.

They did not own a mirror; Cain could not have seen his own face when he asked her. Elena had seen that look in her father's eyes. Seeing it that morning before Cain took Siva to school, seeing it for the first time in Cain's eyes, she knew that she had lost the argument before it had ever begun.

She went through the rest of that day visibly more cheered than at any time in the last week; Hogan remarked upon it.

Elena said quietly, "It seems that there are things in the world that you can count on." She smiled wanly. "Perhaps not the things one would desire; I doubt I shall ever see the likes of Marric again."

Hogan nodded. He was not even offended.

"But Cain . . . ." Elena shrugged, and her lips twisted. "He reminded me of my father this morning."

Hogan patted her clumsily on the shoulder, and they went back to work.

Cain and Loukas ate their dinner that evening at the inn, as they had grown accustomed to. There were beef pies, special on the menu that day besides Kephard's customary fare, and Cain ate two of them, cleaning the meat from the insides of the pie and then using the crusts and his skipper-wheat honeyroll to get the last of the dark brown gravy. Kephard had finally unbent to the point where he would serve Cain beer, though only enough to go with his meal; two glasses, or on a hot day, when the beer warmed quickly, perhaps three, diluted with ice.

The ice was a luxury. Cain had never realized that Kephard liked him until the day that Jenny pointed out that he had never been charged for it. Kephard had the only beer machine in Eastmarch, unless there was one in the Lord Malachor's home. The beer machine fascinated Cain. Kephard kept his beer in kegs in the basement, same as the shopkeepers on Merchant's Way who sold beer in jars; but where the shopkeepers had ice for the beer only during winter, when nobody cared, Kephard's beer machine made fine round balls of ice during the hottest days of summer, and chilled the beer besides. There were two input bins, where beer and water were poured into the machine, and a spigot where beer came out, frosty cold. The ice dropped down, in a steady stream, into a holding bin at the side of the machine. When Cain asked Kephard how the machine worked, Kephard told him, with a straight face, "There's a piece of the sun inside it," and so after that Cain did not ask again.

He never attempted to touch the machine; Kephard would have busted his arms.

The inn was a small place, with eleven tables large enough for two or three people apiece, chairs scattered through its length, and a row of private booths along one wall. The bar itself was like any bar, a long barrier behind which Kephard kept his hard alcohol and foodstuffs and the beer machine. On the evening Lord Malachor came to the inn, it was, being entirely too hot a day, rather more crowded than usual for a TwosDay. Loukas had been playing the same song, uninterrupted, for nearly a quarter of an hour when the Lord Malachor, with half a dozen of his men, appeared in the entrance. The song, which Cain had already heard part of, concerned the troubles of a young farmer in Saerlock who'd gone with a friend to eat at Alice's Inn and, contrary to the garbage-dumping regulations, dumped some garbage off at a cliff along the way. Except for the choruses it was more of a story than a song, backed by the repetitive, almost hypnotic melody from the instrument Loukas called a guitar. Loukas was leading the crowd cheerfully through the choruses, and fully half the inn was singing when they came around.

The ignorant farmer had been inducted by the legate Kierin into the service of the Lord Deremor, the Lord of Saerlock, along with a group of criminals. ". . . *there was mother rapers, and father killers, and father rapers, and one particular big father raper came and sat down aside me on the bench there . . .*"

Loukas probably saw the Lord Malachor before anyone else in the inn; his customary stool, to the back of the inn, faced the door directly. The Lord Malachor took over the three tables nearest the door as silence descended around the inn. Loukas never missed a word, but simply looked a question at the Lord Malachor. Malachor waved a hand at him, to continue, and Loukas did, another full five minutes of song in the midst of utter silence. When he was done, he laid his fingers over the strings at the neck of the guitar and said to Lord Malachor, "My lord, did you enjoy the song?"

There was an empty stool directly in front of Malachor. He gestured to it. "Very much. A bit disrespectful of authority, it seemed."

Loukas was up from his stool in an instant, nudging the box with his coins in it over so that it rested by Cain's feet as he did so, and crossing the room to where Malachor sat. He slung his guitar around so that it hung on its strap over his shoulder and seated himself before Malachor. "Aye, my lord, it was that. Such songs are popular." He shrugged. "Being only a poor singer, I cannot say why."

Malachor grinned at Loukas. His men sat with their eyes on Loukas, the way dogs might watch a stag about to be brought down. The legate Stenno sat quietly just to his lord's right, with an unpleasant smile on his ugly face. "You're as impudent as they told me, Loukas the Semalian. Whereabouts in Semalia are you from?"

"I'm the son of a farmer from Tubadin, my lord."

"Ah." That seemed to impart something to Malachor. " 'The son of a farmer'—this farmer, what was his name?"

They might have been alone in the inn. Aside from their conversation there was no sound at all; nobody ate, nobody drank.

"Jerald, my lord. And, having been asked these questions before, I'll answer your next; to the best of my knowledge, sir, none of our folk fought with Erebion when it rose against the Rulers." Loukas met the Lord Malachor's eyes directly. "You look to be of an age to have fought in that war, my lord."

"I did." Malachor shifted the subject abruptly. "Where did you get the variable laser?"

The first stupid expression Cain had ever seen on him crept across Loukas' face. "My lord? The varbal what?"

"The light knife, minstrel. I wear one, gifted me by the Ruler Alber during the war with Erebion. I'm the only one in Eastmarch who does. They're not easy to obtain." Malachor's eyes were intent upon Loukas.

"I bought it, my lord, in Singer, eight years ago. Paid five stars for it, and the horse I'd ridden into town on as well. Took me two years' singing before I'd recouped the investment in it." Loukas shrugged. "It's saved my life more than once, my lord. A man traveling alone is hardly safe these days."

Malachor said suddenly, "Do I know you?"

A soft humming sound seemed to touch Cain. Loukas cocked his head to one side and said gently, "My lord, how could you?"

The humming grew louder, and Cain was amazed that nobody in the inn seemed to hear it. Eric Malachor seemed confused and shook his head slightly as though to clear it of something. Suddenly he relaxed and grinned, and the humming sound ceased as though a harp had been silenced by a hand laid across its strings. "Well, doubtless it'll come to me. Perhaps I saw you play once, elsewhere. At any rate, it's good to have a minstrel here again; it's been ten years since our last died, and unless my memory fails me you're far better than he ever was. You must come play for me sometime." He stood and gestured at the quiet inn. "Clearly," he said with humor, "I cannot come here to listen to you, and ruin these good folks' dinner."

Loukas came to his feet and bowed quite low. "My lord, I would be honored."

Malachor gathered his men to him with a wave of his hand— Stenno was visibly disappointed—said, "Welcome to Eastmarch, minstrel," and they left.

Time passed, quietly, without incident. Loukas became as much a fixture at Kephard's Inn as Cain, or Jenny, or Sam Kephard himself. There were those in Eastmarch who thought the minstrel an odd man; for Cain, there was no basis for comparison, and it never occurred to him to make the attempt.

Loukas was Loukas.

On Winter 8, 1196, Barra started school with Mistress Sandahl; by that time Cain was probably better educated than his sister Siva, though not, perhaps, in subjects Mistress Sandahl would have found appropriate.

One night he and Loukas were walking back to Loukas' tent. Cain was leading Loukas' horse, which Loukas had named Sunflower for the color of its coat. Everything that Loukas possessed in the world was kept in Sunflower's saddlebags, except for the tent itself, which he refused to pitch every night. Sunflower went everywhere with Loukas, and as for the tent, Loukas said, "The tent's made of *monomolecular electropolymers*, stiffened by a weak electric current. The man who tried to take it down and fold it so's he could steal it would have a hell of a time of it without my thumbprint for the smartlock. It *could* be stolen, if he'd a mind to drag a three-meter-long bright green tent to wherever it was he wished to take it. But it's hard to hide, hard to move, and well known as being *my* tent, which makes it hard to sell."

Cain tried sorting through the two words that Loukas had spoken in the Old Tongue. *Monomolecular* became "single-piece," but *electropolymer* he could make neither head nor tail of, and said so.

"*Electricity*, Cain, is the root of the first half of the word. *Polymer* is just the Anglish word for plastic. Electricity is the force that makes the beer machine work, like lightning, only tamed so that men can get work out of—"

Cain interrupted him. "I *knew* Sam Kephard was having me on! He told me the beer machine worked off a piece of the sun."

Loukas shook his head. "He wasn't lying to you, though I'm sure he thought he was. The beer machine leaches energy from what's called a fusion power supply. It takes a gas called hydrogen—you read on my video tablet about the periodic table?"

"Yes, but I didn't understand it all."

"I'd have been a bit surprised if you had," said Loukas dryly. "I don't entirely understand it myself, and I've studied it a good while. At any rate, the hydrogen atoms join together—*fuse*—into helium atoms, and give off light and heat in the process; the fusion motor turns the heat into electricity in a way I confess I don't understand. The sun, Cain, is powered by the same thing: hydrogen burning by fusion to produce helium. So Sam Kephard wasn't entirely lying to you when he told you there was a piece of the sun in the beer machine. Even if the sun does come by way of hydrogen cells bought in Saerlock." They walked along in silence for a bit, except for the sound of Sunflower's hooves on the cobblestones. "I needn't remind you, I'm sure, that you don't talk about things like this, even to your sisters."

Cain nodded his head. "Because of the Rulers?"

"Aye. They suppress technology, the Rulers do."

"And *technology* is . . ."

Loukas laughed. "Damn. So many words to teach you. *Technology* is many things, Cain. It means 'techniques of knowledge,' near enough. Knowing ways of doing things. It's an Anglish word from before the Fire, and at that, the Anglish word was based on a pair of words from an even more ancient language called Latin." He paused, and scratched his beard. "Or was it Spanish? I've forgotten. At any rate, so say the Rulers, it was technology gave men the weapons that caused the Fire Wars. It was weapons—bombs, they were called—based on the knowledge of fusion, that caused the Glowing Desert, off to the south, and nearly destroyed all the world." His voice took on the rhythms of story-telling. *"The survivors were divided, and the warring continued. Only the Rulers learned the power of the Light, and with it defeated in battle the Giants, defeated the barbarians and the mutants, and so brought the first true peace the world has ever known."* He paused. "I may have mislaid a word or two, but that's near a direct quote, from the lips of a Ruler named Loga, who taught me while I was at Academy—and who is a dead man, believe me, does he ever make the mistake of coming within striking distance of my knife. At any rate, see you, the Rulers believe technology caused the downfall of the first world; and, could be, they're right. They're right about a lot of things."

The thought came to Cain very slowly. "But not . . . everything?"

Loukas answered near as slowly. "I do hope not."

" . . . the sun, here in the center. I don't care what your mother thinks, it's the Earth travels about the sun, not the other way 'round. Here, in orbit around Earth, are the few ships left to the Rulers. That orbit's what's called *geosynchronous*. It means the ships stay put directly above one spot on the Earth's surface, though only in the equatorial plane. That orbit's also where they put the automated orbital factories. My variable laser was built in such a factory, as were the fusion cells that drive both the light knife and the beer machine. The factories are breaking down now; the Rulers no longer know how to repair them, and they're afraid to take the Giants up to look at them. The Giants might learn too much. The Rulers beat the Giants in battle once, but that was while Loden's son, the Ruler Donner, was still on Earth. To hear tell, he was near as tall as a Giant himself, and a Warrior the likes of which the Rulers couldn't field today. Those factories are the best of what's left of the technology from before the Fire, but they go dark, Cain, and they are not replaced. . . ."

The bombs fell.

In a nuclear rain that lasted for days, through a peremptory first strike and a retaliatory second strike, through retaliatory second and third strikes, until only a few lonely submarines cruised through the ocean to fire their weapons upon an enemy who no longer existed, through all of this the bombs fell, and fell. Billions died, of the planet's seven and a half billion persons, in fire and blasting shock waves and radiation. Billions more died in famine, and the firestorms caused when the bombs went down. But that was not the worst.

Vast clouds of dust and earth were blasted into the sky. Whole continents disappeared beneath them; the skies grew dark, and temperatures began to drop.

And the glaciers came south.

"What *are* you reading?" asked Loukas. His eyes were closed; he was lying flat on his back inside the tent, almost asleep. That happened sometimes, that Loukas fell asleep before Cain was ready to go home; when it did Cain simply remembered to bank the fire and give a drink to Sunflower before he left.

It was a history of the first Fire War; Cain told Loukas so. "I'm only on the first chapter, though. Why do you ask?"

"No reason." Loukas' voice floated out from the tent; he sounded sleepy. "Well, actually, there is a reason; you got very quiet, boy, and there's some of the books in the video tablet you're not old enough to be reading."

Cain looked down at the video tablet, at the words, shining silver-blue on a dark gray background. "Which ones?" he asked immediately.

Loukas laughed. "Damn, Cain, if I mean for you not to read them, why would I tell you which ones they are?"

"I guess you wouldn't, except to save me from going crazy with wanting to know." The one he'd been reading had been depressing him, but he was hardly going to tell Loukas that.

It was almost as though Loukas had heard the thought. "If you really want to know, just go to the index and try opening files at random. The ones you can't get into I don't want you in. The one you're reading I'd not have let you read just a year ago."

"Why not?"

Silence from the tent. Then: "It was written by a machine that killed men."

Cain laughed.

"You think I'm lying to you?"

"No, Loukas," said Cain quickly.

"Well, I'm not. It was a war machine in orbit, before the Fire, and it was very smart. It controlled X-ray lasers to shoot down fusion missiles—and other things. It used them, the day of the Fire, and kept the damage to the world from being as bad as it might have been, by preventing many of the fusion missiles from reaching their targets. After the Fire, it wrote down what it had learned about humans—

about its creators—and then, because it had killed many humans while protecting others, shut itself down. By the time T'Pau's People had got back to orbit again, the parts of it that it had kept its memories in had decayed to where they couldn't bring it back."

"A killing machine?" asked Cain incredulously. "Why would they want to?"

"Finish the book, Cain."

"Loukas!"

"The machine had killed, Cain. It had been built to kill. But it felt regret. It was *sorry.*

"This is a guess. But—if a machine could learn that, perhaps T'Pau's People thought its example might help all the humans who couldn't."

"The machine felt sorry," Cain repeated, "for killing men."

"The word you are looking for," said Loukas very, very softly, "is *guilt.*"

" . . . And 'twas only then that they realized the sea was rising. In those days there were *many* oceans, Cain, not just the one. You wouldn't recognize a map of that time. Immediately after the first and largest of the Fire Wars, there came a small ice age, when the dust and smoke from the Fires blocked out the light from the sun. In the Old Tongue it was called *nuclear winter.* This was right after the war with the White Flame Tribe, after the Sisterhood of the Ring told everybody they were tired of all the fighting and were leaving Earth to those who were willing to fight for it. So the Rulers—they were called T'Pau's People then, after T'Pau Almandar, the genegineer who designed them and gave them their psychic abilities—the Rulers came north, where the radiation was not so bad, and brought normal humans with them and settled in this Valley. They did not know, then, that the Giants even existed; rumors they'd heard, no more. Many mutants were created during the Fire Wars; most of them died out. The Giants did not. They survived, up in the far north, by virtue of their skills at engineering. The Rulers became aware of the Giants when they heard that the Giants planned to do no less than warm the entire world again. So say the histories, then, that Loden and Donner and Loga went north, to the home of the Giants, and waged war upon them until the Giants submitted. The warming process was already under way by then, and the Giants could not stop it. The process, if you're interested, is called a *greenhouse effect*, and I'll explain it some other time. The oceans began to rise, and the Giants, under threat of destruction by the Rulers, built the Great Dam to protect the Valley from the rising waters. And see, it has done so, these thousand years. Aye, it's a long time. T'Pau's People became the Rulers, normal men and women became Workers, and for a thousand years there has been no war more serious than that rebellion in Erebion . . ."

• 3 •

They were seated before Loukas' fire, on a SunDay evening late in Winter of 1196. Rain was threatening, and Loukas seemed moodier than usual. He'd been tuning his guitar with half a mind and plucking out odd tunes with it that Cain had never heard before. Cain paid only slight attention; he was reading, on Loukas' video tablet, a text about the Sisterhood of the Ring, the quasi-religious order that had at one time contested—not warred, but competed—with the Rulers for mastery of the Earth. The text was one written by a Ruler named Gabriel, and Cain was taking what he read with Loukas' recommended grain of salt. T'Pau Almandar had inflicted a terrible defeat upon the White Flame Tribe and sent her son, John Almandar, to negotiate with the Sisterhood, the only significant power left upon Earth that might oppose them.

The video tablet was an astonishing device, had Cain ever thought about it. It held, listed in its index, five times as many books as Mistress Sandahl had in her entire school.

He never thought about it.

What finally brought him up from the history of the Rulers' dealings with the Sisterhood was the playing of the guitar, and the feel of eyes upon him. The melody was haunting, unlike anything else Cain had ever heard by Loukas, or anyone else.

> *The greenest hills are fading*
> *Than I've ever seen*

THE RING

The singer's voice is silenced
In dreams of could-have-been

The amber light is waning
The darkness takes the day
The singer's voice is silenced
Still the harpist plays

Loukas' voice softened and then stopped. "That's from a song called 'The Diamond.' I wrote it for . . . well, I guess it doesn't matter why it was written, such a long time ago it was." He sat quietly with the guitar in his hands, running his fingers along the strings, but not playing; simply sitting, looking at Cain. "The first thing is to build your knowledge of the world and how it came to be, for knowledge is a weapon deadlier than a sword, with a longer reach than an arrow. *Learn,*" he said intensely, "learn your enemy not just until you know your enemy better than your enemy knows you, but until you know your enemy better than your enemy knows himself."

They had skirted the subject before, covered it in glances and fleeting touches. Cain put it into words for the first time, with an odd disquiet in his stomach that he could not control. "Are the Rulers my enemies?"

"They are killing you as you sit there, Cain. If they are not your enemies," said Loukas, "then the word has no meaning, and we must make us a new one."

Cain nodded without argument, accepting, taking the answer on faith. "Tell me about them."

Loukas was silent for a long moment.

"Academy," he began, "is a group of buildings, Cain, buildings in the city of Parliament, and also the name of the school that occupies those buildings. See, the Rulers have a dilemma, Cain. They believe in peace, justice, honor—and the power of the Light. And they are not hypocrites, they behave as they believe.

"To each other.

"They live forever, I'm sure you know—or at least, do not die of old age. Loden and Loga are older than the Great Dam itself, and there are probably a dozen other Rulers of similar age. I heard once Loden was actually born before the Fire, though I don't know if that's true. I

don't know as much as I might about the Rulers on a number of fronts
—rumors fly around Academy same as anywhere else. But what I know
about the length of their lives I did not learn from rumor, but cold
experience. Cain, these long lives, they're not a part of the Rulers'
genetic makeup. It's a thing that comes with control of the Light. A
Ruler who's injured, for instance, can heal himself almost instantly by
joining himself to the Light. Age, so they say, is only an injury of a sort
itself, and the touch of the Light aids them in preventing it." Loukas'
words rolled across Cain, a rhythmic steady cadence. "But—even lacking their control of the Light—we can lead lives as long, as productive
as theirs. Not through control of the Light, but with a drug, Cain, a
drug that was developed in the last days before the Fire."

Cain squirmed under Loukas' unfocused gaze; or, not unfocused,
only fixed on something behind Cain, and far, far distant.

"A drug called youthbooster."

Cain literally whispered the words. "Tell me."

Thunder rumbled in the distance.

"What would you know of it, Cain?"

"Why do they not let us have it?"

Loukas grinned suddenly. "The crux of the question, to be sure.
You've a knack for coming to the point, lad." Loukas unlooped the
guitar from his shoulders, made a long arm inside his tent, and hung it
just inside the flap on a peg. "The moisture's not good for the wood,"
he said absently. "I'll have to teach you to play it sometime soon; I
think you'd have aptitude." He sat very still, forehead creased in
thought. He was, Cain saw, having great difficulty putting his thoughts
into words. "I wish you to understand without hating. The hating will
not help, only blind. Cain—there is much to admire in the Rulers.
They are in large measure a good people. And yet they are your enemy
and mine, because they will not let us share their lengthy lives, because
they hide the secret of youthbooster so well I misdoubt there is anyone
in all this village even knows the word. The Rulers live so long, Cain,
they have learned to take a long view of events, to plan not for the
morrow nor the next season, but in *lifetimes*, as Workers measure them.

"They breed slowly, do T'Pau's People; they are not a fertile race.
Homo sapiens—the species you and I are members of—we breed like
treebunnies by comparison. It is only death that keeps our numbers low
enough that the Rulers are not threatened by us. Did we not die, we

would, within two to three generations, have filled this Valley from the Great Dam to Parliament itself with such numbers that the Rulers *could not* control us. We might then threaten them. And so, they must deny us youthbooster.

"There is this, also. They love luxury, a life of ease, as much as any Worker. In the days before the Fire, machines did much of the labor Workers do now. All men lived in the style that today only the Rulers can maintain. So, unless they choose to raise up the old science—and remember, they believe it was that science caused the Fire—they must, to maintain their fashion of living, be served, and served well, with each Ruler commanding the instant obedience of many Workers."

The words came slowly. "Justice, Loukas? All of the things you have told me of the Rulers—their belief that war and killing are wrong, their concerns over what behavior is ethical, what is not, all of it—it does not mix."

Loukas nodded, stirring the fire moodily with a stick that was itself burning at one end. "No, it does not. They're aware of it, too." Sparks flew from the depths of the fire. Loukas' eyes were lost somewhere in that heated light. His next words seemed at first irrelevant. "You should study kriss theology sometime. I did once, when I was younger. It's full of such nonsense, a god who's infinitely powerful, infinitely merciful, infinitely good, all-knowing—but he keeps a private torture pit and has a demon adversary named Lucifern whom he can't or else won't destroy. It always struck me, if he couldn't destroy Lucifern, he couldn't very well be infinitely powerful, and if he wouldn't, he couldn't be infinitely good." Loukas grinned somewhat wryly. "Understanding the kind of arguments the kriss use, Cain, will be good practice for the sort of arguments whereby the Rulers justify denying youthbooster to the Workers. The truth, Cain, the plain truth, is they're afraid of us, and they're afraid of technology. We breed too fast, and the technology that could make our lives something other than a simple struggle for survival is the same technology that caused the Fire Wars, the same technology that let Donner Almandar tell the Ruling Tribunal to go to hell during the Great Schism.

"That's the truth." Thunder rumbled above them once again, and a flash of brilliant white lightning lit up the Valley all around them. "But the Rulers tell each other—for they do not talk about youthbooster to Workers at all—that because we cannot control the

Light as they do, we are in some way less due the ethical consideration they extend to one another. On that point, the vast majority of them, it seems, have come to agree. And yet there is dissent on another point, and one of great concern to you. The question that divides them is just this: can a Worker learn to control the Light? To answer that question they created Academy, to teach the best among the children of Workers in the same fashion in which the children of Rulers are taught. Those Workers who learn to control the Light, to assimilate the Light within themselves and become Light, will become Rulers and thereby live forever." He shrugged. "Lies on top of lies on top of lies; that is not what the students at Academy are told, of course. To tell them that they might, by learning to control the Light, become Rulers themselves, is much the same thing as telling them that there is such a thing as youthbooster. The Rulers tell *one another* that if one of us is proved worthy—by controlling the Light—then they will raise that Worker up to become a Ruler."

It happened rarely, but was becoming more common as Cain learned: Loukas answered Cain's question before Cain had even asked it. "Make no mistake, Cain, for all we look alike, we and the Rulers are a different race of beings. When we lie with one another, we do not create children. And they are born with the power to harness the Light to their will. Whether a Worker can learn to control the Light . . ." He was silent for a moment, as though remembering. "I do not know. But in answer to your question, Cain, all the answer I have for you, there was one. *One*, Cain. Once in history has someone who was not one of T'Pau's People become a Ruler. And he, damn him, was not a Worker at all, but a barbarian from beyond the Glowing Desert." Loukas thrust his stick savagely into the fire. "A barbarian."

"A mutant?"

"How not? It's said, as a child, the Ruler Loga had silver eyes and skin the color of chalk. It was the genegineer T'Pau who injected him with a transform virus that gave him the darker skin and blue eyes that most of T'Pau's People have." Loukas saw the look on Cain's face and interpreted it correctly. "Darker by comparison, lad. Most Workers are darker than the Rulers, though not many are as dark as I. But there are barbarians beyond the Glowing Desert with skin like cloudy ice, and eyes of silver."

"You talk like you know." It was as close to asking as Cain had ever come. Cain was intensely aware that Loukas had never questioned him about subjects Cain did not wish to discuss. "You were not always a singer."

Loukas said only, "No, I was not always a singer."

The vision struck Cain suddenly, sharply, of what he somehow knew was the Glowing Desert, with the wavering ghost aurora flickering above its surface. In a Shield that protected him from the radiation, he staggered across its surface, dying of thirst, and there was beauty, great beauty . . .

He came back to himself and saw Loukas staring at him in concern. "Yes, lad, once I journeyed through the Glowing Desert—but I do not recall having been so thirsty. Or tired . . ."

Cain shook himself slightly, and the image faded. His ears were ringing. "Loukas . . . when were you a Warrior?"

"It is becoming harder and harder," said Loukas conversationally, "to tell you things at a pace of my own choosing. I was a Warrior, Cain, a long time ago. The city of Erebion rose in rebellion against the Rulers. I think you know which side I fought on. The Rulers wouldn't dirty their hands fighting against mere men. They hired other men t'do it and sent them against us. Damn near all Erebion, and much of Semalia Province, rose in that war. Erebion's gone, and Semalia's still recov—"

"Loukas?"

"—ering from the loss of that war. Not . . ."

"*Loukas!*"

Loukas seemed to rouse himself from the depths of memory. "Cain? What's wrong, lad?"

Cain was not sure why the question was important to him; he knew only that it was indeed important. "Loukas, how old are you?"

Loukas sat, staring into the fire. One hand reached up, toyed with the curls of his beard. "Cain . . ." He stopped after speaking Cain's name. After a while Cain thought Loukas was not going to answer him, and was beginning to regret the question. At a level so deep he was not even aware it existed, the thought that Loukas might be displeased with him was perhaps the most terrifying possibility in Cain's world. Finally Loukas stood, slowly, and undid his belt.

He caught Cain's startled look and laughed. "Relax, I haven't developed a taste for boys since the last time I bedded Jenny." He withdrew the belt from its loops and handed it to Cain. "Look at the buckle. It comes off easily enough; if somebody's of a mind to rob me, they'll take that." Cain pulled the silver buckle off, admiring the workmanship, and put it aside. "Turn it over, though. See the dark spot midway to the back? Give me the belt." Loukas took the belt back from Cain and touched the spot with his thumb. "There's a smartlock sewn to the surface of the belt, same as the one on my tent and Sunflower's saddlebags. If anyone but me touches this spot, nothing happens. And you can't cut the belt open; for all it looks like uncured leather, it's not." Loukas turned the belt over again in his fine, strong musician's hands, and did something to the belt Cain could not quite see. The belt folded open along one edge, and from the exposed interior Loukas withdrew a small, transparent packet.

He handed the packet to Cain with the dry comment, "Don't drop it in the fire."

Glancing from Loukas to the package, Cain examined the packet and its contents. Six spheres were within the packet, six spheres filled with some blue liquid that shone brilliantly in the flickering firelight, a pure deep blue like that of the ocean. His throat was suddenly very dry. He looked back up at Loukas. "It's youthbooster, isn't it?"

"Aye. Supposed to take one every seven or eight years." Loukas offered no more explanation.

"Loukas, how?"

"Not from the Rulers, to be sure." Loukas picked his words with care, like a man picking his way through a field set with bear traps. "Cain, my name is not Loukas. Or was not, at any rate. It was Artemis; I am sixty-seven years old; and I led Erebion in its rebellion against the Rulers."

Cain stared into the fire. Silence, stretching silence. The rumble of thunder came again, and the twigs in the fire crackled as though in response, glowing in orange heat death. He looked away from the fire and found the minstrel's brown eyes, looking at him across the glare of the fire. Cain simply waited, trusting, and Loukas smiled softly, as though Cain had said something in which he found meaning; and told him.

"I was a student at Academy for eight and a half years, Cain, but by the time I was failed as being unworthy and sent home—knowing nothing, still, about youthbooster—I had met with certain Giants, who, for reasons of their own, after I was well away from the grasp of the Rulers, educated me. You haven't learned much about the Giants, Cain. Not yet, at any rate, but you must; they're important. Having been beaten so easily the last time they challenged the Rulers, they believe they cannot defeat the Rulers in battle. I think, today, they might challenge the Rulers and win. But they will not, as a group, because as a group they follow the instructions of the Skaald, their leader; and the children who might become Skaald are taught never to dream of fighting the Rulers, for in the last such battle the Giants were almost exterminated.

"But sometimes Giants split off from their people, to act alone. Two such Giants," said Loukas quietly, "aided Erebion when it rose. If they had not aided us, we'd likely not have fought against the Rulers, nor lasted as long as we did. One of those Giants was a genegineer named Riabel. Among Giants, the word *genie* is a curse; indeed, the very name T'Pau is another of their swear words. The Giants are genies themselves, though reminding one of the fact can cost you your life. They were created by genegineers before the first Fire War and, in some ways, badly created. Though they are strong, they are too tall for Earth's gravity; too tall and too massive. They lead painful lives and tend to die of degenerative bone disease, which is not an easy death. The science of genetic engineering is banned among them; and one such as Riabel, who studied it and was caught, is either killed or exiled. Riabel's crime must have been mild, or his judges bribed; he was not killed, which is unusual for a Giant caught playing at the genegineer's art.

"Oh, Riabel was not a genegineer such as T'Pau Almandar, no creator of races—but he knew how to make a variant of youthbooster that worked for both men and Giants alike. Youthbooster is what is called a transform virus, Cain. It's not a proper chemical-based drug, but actually a disease that happens to do something benign. The opposite of transform fever, so to speak. Riabel and his aide Kenoir, for reasons of Giant ideology I will *not* get into tonight, gave us youthbooster and weapons such as rifles and mortars."

The words, *rifle* and *mortar*, meant nothing to Cain. "But why did you fight the Rulers, Loukas?"

"We didn't exactly declare war upon them," said Loukas with some humor. "They did so upon us. But when the battle came to us, we fought. Boy, of course we fought." His eyes met Cain's, with the glitter of the fire still in them. "We wanted to live forever."

• 4 •

Time flowed. It seemed to Cain, caught without perspective in the events as they happened, so young that each day was an eternity, that his life was as it had always been. Loukas was simply *there;* Cain had sat in front of Kephard's Inn forever. He rarely thought of his father, and never of the house in the hills. He did not examine his own life; despite his ingrained cynicism, it never occurred to him to ask why Loukas spent such effort on him. With the innocence of youth he took the world as it came to him, and did not question. He did not know he was happy, and would have denied it without an instant's thought if accused.

Loukas taught him. He taught him history, and something of science, and as much of the small amount of math as Loukas owned. He taught Cain to sing, taught him to play the guitar with such skill as he found within Cain. Cain enjoyed the guitar, but the gift for the instrument was not within him.

If Cain failed his teacher in some ways, he surpassed him in others. He learned in stillness to hear the thoughts Loukas sent him; passed beyond that, and learned to hear any thoughts Loukas did not intentionally keep from him. With concentration the power grew within him until he could, almost without effort, catch the surface thoughts of nearly any person whom he met. Some people held their minds tight, so tight that Cain could not, without considerable effort, even feel that there was anything there behind their eyes. To his surprise—and relief —his mother was one of those, though neither of his sisters were.

He learned other skills as well: how to breathe properly, to control the speed at which his body took in oxygen and the speed at which it burned it; how to slow his body and his heartbeat for meditation; and how to speed himself, bring oxygen and adrenaline surging up together in unison for bursts of strength and a flickering unreal speed that amazed him. He learned things that in an earlier age men had called witchcraft: how to make dice fall as he willed them; to see the other side of a card without turning it; to bring, from the darkness, a light that was bright enough to read by. By Loukas' instruction, he did not use the skills except when Loukas was present, and under Loukas' direction. That he did not was a promise Loukas had extracted from him; and Cain could not break the promise.

Cain's grasp of ethics—a subject that Loukas found of primary importance—was perhaps the least well learned of the subjects that Loukas tried to instruct him in, and certainly the least cared about. Nonetheless he found he could not break his promise to Loukas, though he had given it without any intention at all of keeping it.

It disturbed him.

He learned, and learned, and time flowed past him, the river around the stone that was Cain.

Two significant things happened when he was ten: Hogan's brother, Thomas, the only bookkeeper in Eastmarch, had a stroke; and Cain was taken west, out of Eastmarch territory for the first time in his life, to see the town of Telindel.

Thomas had his stroke early in Spring, one of the coldest Spring quarters in memory; Spring 21 was SunDay, and he'd gone to church with Elena and Hogan and their children, same as always, though shivering badly from the cold. After the service was over, Thomas tottered off to his home, not far away. Though he did not have a surname, as the village's only bookkeeper he was, if not wealthy, surely the closest thing to a rich man the village had who did not also have a surname. His house showed that—it was not far from the village's center.

Cain waited until Hogan was out of earshot to speak to his mother on their way home. "Mama?"

Elena looked down at him. "Yes?" Her breath plumed in the icy air.

"Thomas is going to have a stroke tonight."

She did not stop walking; she did not even break her stride. Cain was not surprised to see that she believed him instantly. "When?"

"I don't know, Mama. Sometime before morning. Somebody should go see him in the morning. He's going to need help."

"Okay." They walked on in silence a bit longer. "Thank you for telling me."

"You're welcome." There were times—rare, to be sure—when

Cain almost liked his mother. If nothing else, she was not nearly as stupid as the other adults he knew.

It was nearly six weeks later that Cain came home from his dinner with Loukas and found Hogan and Thomas sitting at the table in the front room. Elena had served them wine, and they all seemed in good enough spirits. Thomas looked well, though the left side of his face still sagged. Cain nodded to them, dropped his coins on the table for his mother, and went into the bedroom to do Mistress Sandahl's lessons with his sisters. He rather enjoyed the lessons, and was careful not to do too well at them. He did still, on occasion, learn things of value from them.

Besides, the look of contempt Mistress Sandahl would give him if he dared quit was something he could picture too well, and tried not to think about.

That night his mother called him away from his lessons to come sit with the adults. They did not offer him any of the wine. *Jenny,* he thought, *would ask me if I wanted a drink.*

"Cain," she said, "I've been talking with Thomas. He hasn't been getting around very well since the stroke, and he needs a boy to help him out at his offices: bring him his books, carry them from place to place when he sees his clients, clean the office, help him to dress when he has to dress fancy, and the like. He's offered five estars a day for it, which is a bit more than you usually make, and going up to six estars if he's pleased with you; and no tenth-cut for Sam Kephard." She looked as cheerful about it all as Cain had seen her in a solid quarter. "I don't see any reason why you can't start tomorrow."

"Reason," said Cain slowly. He looked up abruptly and smiled at them all. "No."

His mother looked as though she refused to believe the evidence of her ears. "What?"

"The reason," said Cain politely. "I don't want to do it."

His mother sat and struggled quietly with her anger. Hogan was flushed red, but with embarrassment, and Thomas was simply looking at him. "You will," said Elena at last, "do as you're told."

Cain sat quietly, biting his lip, thinking. Finally he looked up into his mother's blazing anger. "Or what?" His voice did not even raise.

His sisters were staring at him from the bedroom. "Will you strike me? Will you throw me out? I can rent a pallet at Kephard's as good as the one I've got now for an estar a day. I could buy both of my meals for an estar apiece, and even after Sam Kephard's cut I'd have something left over which I don't have now."

Elena came to her feet screaming. "Get out, then! *Get out, you little black-eyed bastard!*" Hogan stood up between her and Cain, preventing her from coming around the table to where Cain sat, watching his mother struggle with the fat man.

"Mama?" Cain waited, and said again, after she had calmed some, still flushed with her anger but calm enough to listen, "Mama?"

"Don't call me that." Her breath came very short. "Don't you ever call me that again."

Cain sat very still for a moment. When he spoke again, it was with the vast, simple coldness of a child who truly does not care, who has schooled himself not to care. "Very well, madam. Elena, what will pay for the schooling? It costs you two and a half estars a day to send Siva and Barra to school, three when one of them's out sick. You don't have it. Where will it come from? Will Hogan give it to you?"

The words penetrated. Elena knew without having to look at Hogan that the very suggestion had made him uneasy. Cain continued. "So it's not going to be Hogan. Mistress Sandahl has let me do my lessons with them, even though you can't afford to send me to school with them. If you can't afford to send either of them, do you think she'll let them go to school for free?" Still there was no answer. Cain nodded again. "So it won't be Mistress Sandahl's generosity that'll see the girls schooled either." He lowered his voice slightly, so that his sisters could not hear him. "Before Da died he told me to take care of the girls. If he hadn't said that I'd have left a year ago." He stared at his mother, and when he spoke again his voice was filled with a purity of disdain that no adult could possibly have matched. "You don't really think I *like* it here?"

Before Cain's mother could answer, Thomas said, speech slurred slightly, "Everybody wait." His manner was grim and even somewhat surprised. "Cain, I want you to come for a walk with me. Will you?"

Cain glanced at his mother and then at Thomas. "Sure."

Thomas nodded and reached for his walking stick. "And Elena, I want you to calm down while I'm gone. Sit and think a bit and ask yourself if the boy's said anything you didn't know already, eh?" He turned to Cain, getting to his feet painfully. "Let's go."

It was Spring 60, the third day of the work week. Eastmarch was quiet that late in the evening, just the occasional carriage and even more occasional passerby. Thomas leaned heavily on his stick as they walked down Merchant's Street. Cain did not offer to help him; Thomas was a big man, and Cain was not sure that his help would have been of use. Thomas was troubled; Cain could feel it, and might with some effort have learned the source of the disquiet. He did not bother, but walked down the street with the old man. There was ice on the street, but no snow, and though it was cold, there was no wind to speak of. In all, not a bad night, by comparison with the weather they'd been having the last few weeks.

Thomas said finally, "What got your back up, Cain? Is it working for me you don't want to do? Perhaps I'm wrong, but I've always thought we got along well enough."

Cain's lips moved in an empty smile. "I'll apprentice to you if you like. And I'll do it for, oh, four estars a day—whether you like my work or not."

Thomas sighed. "Cain, you know I can't do that. My clients are mostly Merchant and Land'ner class, Cain. They're proud folk, very conscious of their class. If I apprenticed a boy who'd been shining their boots the week before, they'd stop using me. There's other people in this town can do the math necessary to keep a store's books; I don't dare anger my clients."

Cain said without heat, "Okay."

Thomas waited a beat, until it became apparent no further reply would be forthcoming. "Okay, but I should lick the ice somewhere else, eh?" Cain did not reply, and Thomas sighed. "Cain, *why* will you not work for me?"

Cain did not look at him. "It would mean another estar or two a day for my mother, which she doesn't need. It won't send the girls to a better school, because there isn't one. It would probably mean a new dress three times a year instead of twice for the girls." He shrugged. "I don't care about that. They have nice dresses now. So it won't help my sisters to come work for you, it won't help me to come work for you, it won't help anybody except my mother. She doesn't like Sam Kephard very much, and she doesn't like Loukas hardly at all. She won't admit it, but part of the reason she likes the idea of my going to work for you is because it'll hurt them if I'm not there: Kephard because he'll lose some money, Loukas because he likes me." He did look at Thomas then. "Besides," he said evenly, "I don't like your brother, and if he thinks it's a good idea, it probably isn't."

To Cain's surprise, Thomas laughed at the comment. It was a strange-sounding laugh, perhaps because of his stroke. Thomas said, "No, my brother's not the most charming of men, and I know you don't like him." He walked silently a moment. "Still, he's not so bad, boy, and the job he gave Elena is one she had little training for, at least when he gave it to her. Your mother's a woman in her thirties, Cain, looks older yet, has two young girl children and a son who's not yet fit to do a man's work. She'll not marry again, Cain, and my brother, poor manners, fat and insecure, all surface and no depth, still he's decent enough. I mean to say, as good as poor Elena's likely to do, and better than she might have got." He sighed as though he were in some pain, but did not miss a pace. "You should have known your mother when she was a girl. She was a sight—ambitious, that's the word, coming of the poor family she did. And doing well until your father died, and Misha . . ." Thomas broke off, and then continued a moment later, more slowly. "I think she knows now her own lot won't be much better than what her mother's was, but she's determined for the girls to have a better chance."

Cain nodded silently.

"And as for yourself . . . Cain, I can't apprentice you. I'd go bankrupt if I did. But I can teach you what I know, same as if you were my apprentice. Someday you could make your living doing it, keeping books."

Thomas saw the skepticism on Cain's face and grinned at the boy. "Oh, not here, I won't yank your cork. There's too many won't forget the boy who sat in the gutter and shined their shoes for a half-estar. But in—well, not Telindel, it's too close—but Saerlock, it's further and bigger, or better yet Moorstin or Allietown, where there'd be nobody who knew you as a child—there, Cain, you'd have a shot. And not a bad one. You ride into town one day on a fine horse, with a purseful of

stars, rent an office and hang out a sign. At first you won't get much
business, but you hang with it and charge less than the other bookkeep-
ers, and do better work to boot, and flatter your clients shamelessly with
how impressed you are by their fine business sense—"

Cain laughed at that.

Thomas broke off. "Have I said something funny?"

"Do you know Loukas?"

"Your friend the minstrel? Well, I've stood him a drink a time or
two—oh. 'Fine business sense.' " Thomas nodded. "Perhaps I did pick
the phrase up from him. The Light shine on my words, I've heard him
use it. You might take that as your model, if you would—aside from
being irresponsible, the minstrel's a sharp man. But I was saying, Cain,
do those things, build up a clientele, and the day'll come when there'll
be nobody in the town who'll ever remember you weren't born to the
Merchant class. By the time you're old, there'll be enough money there,
if you've saved wisely, you can start talking longingly of the old hometown of Eastmarch; sell the business, pack up the wife and kids, and
head *west*. Travel a good long ways down the Traveler's Road, pick
some likely-looking town—I can't even mention 'em, I've never been
further than Moorstin, and I don't know what's out there—but pick
some such town, ride into town with your family in your finest clothes
and with the best horse and carriage you could buy, tell 'em all with a
straight face that you're Land'ners from Eastmarch. You had to leave
Eastmarch on account of difficulties with the local Lord—people are
always willing to believe the worst about you, and while they're busying
their dirty little minds with wondering about what got you exiled, they
won't be wondering if you are what you say you are. Drop your money
down on the table in front of the town's Lord and with unctuous
politeness demand somebody sell you a plot of land." Thomas smiled at
him, a somewhat tremulous smile. "They'll do it, too, and there you
are, from bootblack to Land'ner in one man's lifetime. It's been done.
If I'd ever married and had children, I'd do it myself. But before you
can do it, Cain, first you need a skill. Will you come work for me,
Cain?"

Cain did not miss a beat. "Sure."

The simple answer seemed to startle Thomas; he peered at Cain
with a moment's surprise. "Well," he said after a moment, "seems I
can still persuade people a'times."

"You didn't persuade me."

"Eh? What's that?"

"You finally," said Cain quietly, "*asked* me."

One evening near the beginning of summer, Cain showed up at Loukas' tent, bleeding and beaten, but still walking under his own power. Loukas took his appearance in stride, washed his face of the blood and bound up his arm in a sling; he had a dislocated shoulder. He did not ask Cain what had happened, and Cain did not volunteer the information.

Loukas walked him home, light knife in his hand, blade lit and glowing at a meter's length. Those who were on the streets when Cain and Loukas came by got out of their way.

They stopped in front of the stairwell entrance. "Cain?"

"I won't tell you who did it, Loukas. You'd hurt them."

"So?"

"I want to be the one."

In the radiance from the variable laser, the gleam of the teeth appeared in Loukas' dark face, sudden and quick. "I understand *that*. Tell your mother you'll be taking a trip to Telindel with me. We'll be gone three, perhaps four weeks. I'll tell Master Thomas. I don't think he'll be too angry. When you come back you'll know more about dirty fighting than anyone else in this silly damn village."

"Okay." Cain stood there a moment. "Thanks, Loukas."

"You're welcome." Loukas turned off his light knife and hung it from his belt. "Good night, then."

For the first time since Loukas had known Cain, Cain hugged him, hard and swiftly. Cain had the impression he'd surprised the man. "Thanks for being my friend." He ran up the stairs without waiting for a reply.

Standing alone in the dark street, Loukas smiled again, rather more gently than was usual for him. "You're welcome, boy. The Light knows, you're welcome."

Cain supposed, years later, that Telindel must have made *some* impression on him. It was the first town he'd ever seen in his life, a place with four times as many people just in the town as in all of Eastmarch territory. Nonetheless, while he remembered the trip clearly, both there and back, Telindel was only a confused blur in his mind, a remembered impression of confusing size and numbers. Superimposed on whatever might have remained of Telindel were the images of the town during the War. It was his first headquarters, before he built the Command Center in the Caverns, and his memories of the city from those years were memories of a town—and a small one, at that—being torn down and rebuilt, almost overnight.

He remembered with great clarity his first sight of the Caverns: Loukas making, with just a thought, the ghost light that followed them and going right down beneath the surface of the Earth, into the great echoing empty spaces beneath the ground. The Caverns amazed him far more than anything in Telindel, so much so that even while he was in Telindel, with the town's wonders there before his eyes, he had difficulty keeping the remembered feel and smell and sight of the Caverns from rising up before his eyes to overwhelm reality.

One night they camped at the side of the Traveler's Road, next to a field of flowers. The floral scent on the crisp night air was simply astonishing, and Cain lay awake most of the night, strange images running through his mind whenever he dropped off: three women, and a pale golden light, and the light became a circle . . .

A ring.

The next morning they entered Telindel, and Cain forgot the dreams that had plagued him all that night. Two days in Telindel, wandering through the town as Loukas made his purchases, watching as Telindel readied itself for the Summer Games, and they started back for Eastmarch. Dreams did not bother Cain all the way home. They spent an hour in the morning and an hour every evening, practicing several different kinds of fighting. There was not a night they were on the road together but that Cain went to bed exhausted.

He learned to handle a knife properly, as well as the variable laser Loukas carried. Loukas had bought a pair of swords and a composite bow in Telindel, and they practiced with those weapons as well, for all the world as if Cain were one of the privileged Malachor children and not a Steader's brat from the hills of Eastmarch.

Cain knew already, while meditating, the techniques for bringing speed and strength up in one coordinated surge. Now Loukas taught him to do so under any circumstances: rushed without warning, raised from sleep by an attack, or while he was deeply engaged in some other task.

They were gone not quite five weeks. When they came back to Eastmarch, Cain learned that a Ruler had been there in their absence, testing children for the Academy. With the exception of Cain's mother, there was certainly nobody in all of Eastmarch who found anything at all suspicious in that; and even Elena was only suspicious, not certain.

Cain was not suspicious. He lived in Loukas' world, and in Loukas' world there was no such thing as coincidence.

It did not even occur to him to ask Loukas *if* Loukas had known the Ruler was coming. He did wonder *how* Loukas had known, but did not ask even that. If Loukas wanted him to know, Loukas would tell him.

Instead he tracked down three boys, each of them several years older than himself, and beat them to within a centimeter of their lives.

For the first time in his life, Cain knew victory.

The taste was very sweet.

Time flowed . . .

Somewhat to his surprise, Cain found that he enjoyed keeping books with Thomas, and enjoyed even more their forays into the higher maths, trigonometry and the calculus—what Thomas called "numbers for fun," because it was utterly useless for keeping books. He never even made a mark in one of the books while one of Thomas' clients was there, but when they were gone, he did as much of the work as Thomas would let him. In time that came to be most of the work that Thomas did. Sometimes his clients caught sight of Cain's big, somewhat sloppy writing next to Thomas' neater marks and questioned Thomas about it. Thomas let out that he was developing arthritis in his hands and that Cain wrote the numbers for him at times; the Land'ners and Merchants who did not have the math to do their own books found it more than believable that the former bootblack did not either.

Cain had been a bootblack for a bit more than four years; he was Thomas' helper for four years likewise, and they were, once he got used to what Thomas wanted of him, and how he wanted it, the four best years of Cain's life. Thomas needed Cain at the office less and less as he recovered from his stroke, and as long as Cain performed the tasks that Thomas set for him in the mornings, and was there when the clients came to visit Thomas after lunch, Thomas largely did not care how Cain spent his afternoons and evenings. As a result, though Cain actually spent less time at Kephard's, the time he did spend there was better spent; more time to learn the songs Loukas sang and more time to simply relax, drink beer, and listen to the other patrons in the Inn. Sam Kephard was not entirely civil to Cain at first; Cain was costing Sam Kephard perhaps as much as three estars a day by not sitting on the front steps waiting for Land'ners and Merchants to come by to have their boots blacked. Aside from the money Kephard made when that happened, from his cut of one tenth, those same folk had often wandered on into Kephard's afterward, even if they had not planned to originally, and usually spent there considerably more than the half-estar that Cain'd gotten out of them.

As the seasons flowed by and became years, Kephard appeared to forget his pique and once again stopped charging Cain for ice.

Cain fell in love with Jenny, the serving girl, at least a bit. He knew Loukas was seeing her much of the time, and he half hoped that they'd settle together and maybe get married. She was a pretty blonde girl, though not the prettiest woman Cain had ever seen, and she didn't care for her looks the same way some of the women in town did. Cain hardly ever saw her with makeup on. He did not care; privately he thought she was beautiful. Aside from Loukas, who did not count, she was the only adult he had ever met who had never treated him like a child.

Cain sat in the corner with Loukas, drinking his beer. He was in a strange mood tonight, as was Loukas. They were so close, Cain to Loukas and Loukas to Cain, that sometimes Cain did not know whether it was himself who threw Loukas into one of the dark moods or Loukas who did so to him. Cain wasn't sure what might be eating at Loukas; he knew what his own problem was and knew well enough there was nothing to be done for it.

Cain came to the Inn late that afternoon, stayed for just a moment, and then went to walk his sisters home from school. When he came back for his dinner, Loukas was sitting on the porch outside the Inn with a black scowl on his features.

Cain did not say anything to Loukas, just stood waiting until Loukas came to his feet and they went back inside for their dinner. Jenny served them with rather particular quiet. Cain had the distinct feeling that, like both himself and Loukas, Jenny was upset about something. The brief thought flashed through his mind that the way things were going, he probably ought not to go home this evening; his mother was sure to be angry about something. The day had just been going that way; even Thomas, normally the kindest of men, had been unusually cranky all that morning and afternoon.

Near nightfall he went outside, just in time to watch as the Merchant Jaime Lusende closed up his shop for the night and escorted his daughter Risa home. Like Cain's sisters, Risa was schooled at Mistress Sandahl's; it was where Cain had first seen her. The first hour after school let out, she worked in her father's glassworks shop. Only a moment after Cain had come out into the night air, Loukas followed him, wearing his guitar slung over his shoulder.

Loukas saw where Cain's gaze lingered, but he said nothing, not even to advise Cain that he stood no chance with the girl.

Cain thought, years later, that it was not any sudden attack of manners on Loukas' part that prevented the comment; it was only that Loukas was not the sort of man to waste his breath telling Cain something Loukas was already sure he knew.

"Come on, lad," said Loukas, more gently than was his wont. He ruffled Cain's hair a bit awkwardly. "Come on inside, and I'll teach you how I cheated you at dice the other night."

Cain shook his head. "I don't think so, Loukas." He watched the man and the girl walk away down the darkening street. Master Lusende's hand was gripping the knife that hung at his waist. He was aware of Cain's attention, and not pleased by it.

"How about I'll play you a song, then?"

Cain looked around at him, aware suddenly that his friend was, despite his own poor mood, trying to cheer him up. "Yes," he said after a moment, somewhat awkwardly. "I'd like that." He followed Loukas back inside and took their table again. Jenny came by and collected their empty glasses, bringing refills without a word. Loukas did not even look at her, and behind his back Jenny made a pair of horns over his head. Cain kept his face straight with an effort.

Strumming a light tune that Cain did not recognize, Loukas set in on a bawdy song about the exploits of a Trader from Saerlock, beginning with the Trader's unlikely birth and becoming more unlikely as he continued. Not one of the verses could have been sung in polite company. Cain actually saw Jenny blush after one and suspected he was blushing himself. Loukas grinned and concluded the song two stanzas later, and then whispered to Cain during the applause, "And I didn't even sing the dirty parts, where Jocko falls in love with the mule."

Jenny came by again and replaced Loukas' empty glass. She glanced at Cain's near-empty cup, and Cain shook his head.

"Loukas?"

Loukas looked over the edge of his mug at Cain and put it down. He wiped foam from his mustache. "Ah . . . singing's thirsty work. What?"

Cain looked down at the tabletop, at the old scarred wood. "Will you sing 'The Diamond' for me?"

Loukas' expression did not change. "Lad, I'd rather not."

Cain looked up at him. "Please?"

Loukas stared at Cain with an odd expression that Cain could not read. Finally he said, in a monotone, "As you wish." He looked down at his guitar as though he were only now realizing that it was still slung around his neck and spent a moment tuning the instrument although it did not need it. Finally he looked up and growled loudly, "Can I have a bit of quiet to work in?" He did not wait for the requested quiet, but began:

> The greenest hills are fading
> Than I've ever seen
> The singer's voice is silenced
> In dreams of could-have-been

The sound from the other patrons in the Inn faded like water into parched ground and became utter silence as Loukas sang.

> The amber light is waning
> The darkness takes the day

THE RING

The singer's voice is silenced
And still the harpist plays

Oh, will you dance? Oh, will you sing?
You cannot know
What morning brings

The harpist plays, the sound so true
You cannot know
What the dancer will do

The candles flare and the singer's blind
And so the lovers glance
And though you see it can you find
The dancer in the dance?

Morning comes and takes you
And though you're gone I play
Pale gold it rises
Oh, will you know
The diamond of the day?

I played for you
But it's been so long
Shall I keep playing
For the sake of the song?

Loukas tore his hands from the strings with shocking abruptness, as though the touch of the guitar pained him.

Someone over at the far end of the inn clapped, uncertainly, and then stopped. The silence was palpable. Loukas staggered to his feet and slung his guitar over his shoulder. "I've had too much to drink," he said roughly. "See you in the morning, lad. You should be getting home to your mother, she'll want my hide."

He walked straight as an arrow to the exit, and out into the night.

Old Sam Kephard himself came over to Cain a few minutes later, and picked up the empty glass Loukas had left. "Loukas had a bit much, did he?" asked the old man quietly.

Cain said simply, "I don't think so."

He finished his beer, dropped his last coins on the table to pay for it, and left.

He walked aimlessly in his moodiness, through the empty dark streets. The moon was only a sliver, hidden at times by the scudding gray clouds. The village seemed unreal, leached of color in the white glow of new moon and the stars. The air tingled with ozone, and Cain knew that it would rain soon. The mist came after he'd been walking for a while, and with a sudden sharp ache he was reminded, briefly, of the day his father died. Lost in his own thoughts, he paid no attention to where he went. It was with something like surprise, then, that when he finally heard a voice calling his name and looked up, he found himself back on the west side of the village, not far from Kephard's Inn. He was disoriented for just a moment, and then placed himself.

The woman across the way called his name again, and Cain saw that it was Jenny, wrapped tightly in her shawl against the cold, making her way home from the Inn. "Cain! Come to walk me home, have you?"

"Jenny?" Cain did not miss a beat. "Of course. What else?" The sudden appearance of another human in the pale mist and the simple friendly sound of his name being called warmed Cain as nothing else could have. He ran lightly across the damp stones of the street to where Jenny stood waiting for him. The woman offered him her arm as though he were one of her many callers, come indeed to walk her home, and Cain laced his arm through hers without smiling. She grasped his wrist companionably.

"You're going home kind of early, aren't you?"

Jenny turned slightly to peer at his profile. Her left breast brushed against his arm as she moved. "Cain, it's past midnight."

"Oh?" Cain considered that. "I didn't realize that. I . . . was walking."

"I don't doubt," said Jenny dryly. "Walking must be a powerful interesting activity to twelve-year-old boys."

"I'm thirteen," said Cain flatly.

Jenny sighed, her breath pluming out into the air. "Foot in my mouth again. This seems to be the night for it. I got Loukas upset with me earlier tonight with another such comment. By the Light, Cain, I meant no harm."

"It's okay, you didn't hurt my feelings. It's just that I'm thirteen." He looked up at her; she was nearly a head taller than him. "Not twelve."

"Very well," she said in feigned exasperation. "I *understand*. All right?"

"All right."

"So what were you thinking about, then, all alone out here?" Jenny cocked her head to one side. "Risa Lusende, might be?"

With sudden fierceness, Cain pulled his arm from hers. "By the Light, does it matter? I've heard as much as I care to about my place in life. I know thinking about her is stupid, all right? I know it."

Softly, Jenny took his arm back, linked it once more through her own. She said, so gently that he could not take offense, "Ah, she's too old anyhow. You should get yourself a girl your own age, break her in proper."

The thought struck Cain and he asked the question without stopping to think. "How old are you, Jenny?"

A faint smile graced her lips. "Older than the Lusende girl, to be sure."

"Oh. Oh," he said again with sudden embarrassment, "that's not what I meant."

"Of course it wasn't," Jenny said gravely. The woman was silent for a moment, and then laughed. "Well, my age isn't such a great secret, I guess. I'm twenty-six, Cain." Her voice was not wholly without bitterness. "Young enough that the men still call on me, old enough I'll not get a husband worth having. It's not so bad, really. I get ten percent of the profits from Kephard's place, and by the time I'm old enough the men don't come to see me—well, that'll be another ten years, the Light willing. I should have enough saved to buy a part interest in the Inn." Her voice dropped slightly. "And sometimes the men who I see, they leave gifts—coin—when they're done. I take it."

Cain assimilated what she was saying, and then said curiously, "Are you a *whore*?"

Jenny stopped dead in her tracks and stared at him in amazement. Then she laughed, loudly and with considerable humor. She calmed slightly and, still laughing, said, "Where did you learn that word, Cain?"

Cain was startled by the laughter. "I . . . it was . . ."

Jenny shook her head, not waiting on his answer. "Never mind," she said with good humor, "it was Loukas, must've been. That's a Saerlock word; I've never even heard it from the lips of an Eastmarcher. Come on," she said, turning to resume the walk home, "let's not stand here all night." She felt silent then, as a thought struck her. Not looking at Cain, she said, "Did Loukas tell you I was a whore?"

"No," said Cain honestly. "He's never talked about you to me, except . . ." The word was out of his mouth before he realized it, and, aware of her eyes on him, he finished the sentence awkwardly. "Well, he said you were the best time he'd had since a week he spent once in Goldriver, and he couldn't remember the week in Goldriver; he was only told about it."

Jenny was silent then, and Cain was afraid he'd offended her. His tone was defensive. "Well, that's what he *said.*"

She snorted. "Oh, I believe it, it sounds like him. And men talk that way, I know. I guess I'll take it as a compliment." Jenny was silent again for a bit, and then said, "But that word, *whore,* you shouldn't use it, Cain. Most Eastmarchers won't know what it means, but some will, and in Saerlock it's an insult and a word you don't use in polite company."

Cain nodded easily; he did not really care.

"Besides," Jenny continued, "it's not what I am. A whore takes money from a man so that he might lay with her. I never do that, and if a man wants to leave money, well, that's his affair; I never ask. What was Loukas brooding over tonight?"

The question came so smoothly, with no break between it and what had come before, that Cain was caught off guard and answered honestly. "I think there was someone he loved once, and he wrote that song for her. He started to play it for me once, and stopped."

"Oh?" Jenny seemed to consider that. They crossed the street, heading into the south side, where the buildings lost their sheen of polished stone and became rough, rickety affairs of brick and unpainted wood. "That's not how I took it."

"How else?"

Jenny hesitated, fingers stroking slowly across Cain's wrist. "He was singing to you, Cain."

Cain shook his head. "I asked him to. So?"

"I think he loves you."

It took Cain a long moment to sort through what she was saying. Then he used a phrase that would have shocked his mother and added, "Don't be stupid."

In the near dark he could not see her expression. "You've never guessed anything like that?"

"No. We're friends—he teaches me things. That's all."

"Then I'll say no more about it. I understand about being friends. You should treasure them, Cain. You won't ever have that many to speak of." She felt him go tense and said swiftly, "No, no, I don't mean *you* personally. Don't take on so. It's just that good friends, they're rare no matter who you are." They walked in silence another few blocks until they neared Jenny's room, a walk-up in a squat brick building at the very edge of the village.

She released his arm when they reached the stairs that led to her room. "Thanks for walking me home, Cain. It's a boring walk, most nights." She leaned forward and kissed him swiftly on the forehead. "You should be heading home now. Your mother'll be worried."

Cain shook his head. "She'll be bedded down with Hogan. She probably won't even notice I haven't come home, and if she does, she won't care."

"Oh." His words seemed to disconcert her. Jenny regarded him, standing there in the darkness.

"Jenny?"

She shivered suddenly and hugged herself. "Yes, Cain?"

"What you said, about Loukas . . . did you mean that?"

The question was not what she had expected. "Yes."

"Oh."

"I don't mean anything bad, Cain. Look at me, please." He raised his head to meet her eyes. "Have you never stopped to wonder what a man of his years sees in the company of a boy your age? I don't mean he covets your arse—not that it would surprise me, it's nice enough— just that, well, do you really think it's your sparkling wit brings him to share your company? Or—well, it doesn't matter. If he loves you, it doesn't surprise me, you're almost as pretty as a girl. That's what got him angry with me tonight. I pointed that out to him. *I* thought I was making a joke." She shrugged. "Maybe it was only the memory of a lost love caused him to behave as he did tonight. And maybe it was something else."

Cain stood motionless in the cold, thoughts swirling through his mind like fireflies. He said nothing, but simply stood looking at her.

She finally spoke with what might have been reluctance. "Would you like to come on upstairs with me, then?"

Cain spoke slowly. "What?"

"Oh, come on," she said, teasing suddenly, "your hearing hasn't gone bad so quickly. You must have been thinking about it, walking home with me so far. Would you like to come up with me?"

Cain stared at her. The thought had not even been in his mind. "I . . . why?"

Jenny put her hands on her hips. "Why, the very question!" Then she saw he meant it, and sighed. "Cain, I like you. It's reason enough, and by the Light, it's *cold* out here. We can lie in bed all night and gossip about the people we're in love with if you're too scared to do anything else, but I'm freezing my tits off standing here. Yes or no?"

"I spent all my money at the inn," Cain blurted.

"Lords of Light," she swore, "bring me flowers in the morning! It'll be enough." She turned without waiting for an answer, and Cain went quickly up the stairs after her.

The next day, when Cain took his dinner with Loukas, Loukas was in good spirits. Neither of them mentioned the previous night, and if their dinner together was quieter than usual, why, the one the night following was more normal, and within a week it was as though that evening had never happened.

Loukas only mentioned it to Cain once, when he gave Cain a sheet of paper, the writing in Loukas' spidery hand, with the words to "The Diamond" on it; and even then all he said was, "I'd like you to have this. So's you don't mess up the words while you butcher the tune."

Cain took the sheet without a word and was searching for something to say when Loukas turned and stalked away.

· 5 ·

On the third day of Summer in Cain's fourteenth year, the Ruler Selene came to Eastmarch to test children for the Academy at Parliament.

Cain had no warning; he came that afternoon to walk his sisters home from school, arriving several minutes after class should have been let out, so that Risa Lusende's brother Anton would have had time to get Risa and take her home. It would not do for him to arrive while Risa was still there. While Cain did not think Anton would dare use the knife he carried—Anton had limped for three weeks after their last fight—it was better not to make him decide.

Cain found, rather to his surprise, that they had not even been let out of class yet. Anton was standing impatiently at the front gate; Cain took up a position a few meters away and waited with as much patience as he might. Unless Anton's glare at Cain's approach were counted as being communication of a sort, the two did not speak. The door to the schoolroom remained stubbornly closed. It never crossed Cain's mind to knock on the door, or even, the Light forbid, go inside and see what was keeping them; Mistress Sandahl would have his head.

Standing at the gate, waiting, Cain tried to remember the last time Mistress Sandahl had been late letting her students out. Due to the memory-retrieval techniques Loukas had taught him, Cain's memory was better than that of anyone in Eastmarch except, perhaps, that of Loukas himself; after searching his memory, Cain could not recall a single instance when those doors had not opened *precisely* at the seventh bell.

Finally, better than a quarter of an hour late, the door did open, and the students came out. Cain was struck immediately by the strangeness of their behavior. Rather than the sudden loud babble of children's voices which was usually the sign the children were being let out of the prison of school, the students were quiet, almost grave. They filed out of the schoolroom with great decorum and did not run, but walked, out into the street where Cain and Anton were waiting.

Cain's voice sounded strange in his ears. "Something's wrong."

Anton Lusende snorted at the sound of Cain's voice, but did not quite dare a comment in return.

In an odd, time-shattered moment Cain *saw* the Ruler, standing in the doorway, and then shook his head again irritably, and she was gone, and the children were again there before him, walking with that unnatural quiet.

Cain barely saw Risa Lusende walk by him, with a smile for him that turned cold as he ignored it. The forty or so students who made up Mistress Sandahl's current class had almost entirely filed out of the classroom before Cain knew where the sinking feeling in his stomach came from. His sisters remained inside, and an indistinct form was standing motionless just back of the classroom's one window, looking straight out at him.

Options flew through his mind with the speed of storm winds. The Ruler had kept his sisters, but *why?*

The answer came to him almost immediately: because of Barra, of course, for where Siva had no more than a trace of Cain's ability, Barra had it in much greater degree, and the Ruler might reason that an ability that showed in degree in two sisters might show itself also in the brother; and Mistress Sandahl, good woman and churchgoer that she was, would have talked freely.

No matter how Cain weighed his options, the least suspicious thing he could think of doing was to go inside, with all apparent innocence, and see what was keeping his sisters.

Like a man going to battle, Cain walked through the gate.

Cain had only been inside the schoolroom twice, in all those years, to deliver schoolwork to Mistress Sandahl when his sisters had been sick. The workbenches were arranged inside in four double rows; they were long things of crude wood, at which five students would sit to work. There were over a hundred books on the shelf behind Sandahl's desk—probably two thirds of the books in Eastmarch. The thought flickered through Cain's mind that he, who had never been allowed to touch the books in that room, had probably read most of them on Loukas' video tablet.

Loukas had told him that most Rulers were not particularly sensitive telepaths; nonetheless Cain suppressed the damning thought savagely.

Barra and Siva were sitting at their desk—they sat right next to each other, near the back, with the other children of low class—and Mistress Sandahl was standing nervously in the spot from which she usually lectured her students. The Ruler was standing next to the window, having turned to watch Cain enter. It was a woman, though not, Cain knew at a glance, the Ruler Elyssa, whom he had seen for only a few moments, eight years past. The woman did not glow visibly, which he filed away to ask Loukas about, and her dress, though it was a fine thing of pale gray, was not as immediately, obviously abnormal as the clothing of the Ruler Elyssa had been.

Like the only other Ruler Cain had ever seen, the woman seemed very young, perhaps only twenty, and pretty enough, though not with the same sort of unworldly beauty the Ruler Elyssa had shown. Pale blue eyes and sandy blonde hair, straight and so long it reached the small of her back and cascaded forward over her shoulders, in fine contrast to the dove gray of her dress.

Then her eyes caught and held him, and Cain had a moment to wonder that he had ever found Loukas' warm brown gaze intimidating. "You would be Cain?"

Though Cain could not know it, he did perhaps the worst thing possible at that moment. Likely any other Worker in Eastmarch, from the lowliest Steader to Eric Malachor himself, would have been down on his knees in that instant—not counting Loukas, of course, who would have killed her already.

Cain met the gaze of the icy blue eyes.

"I am, my lady." He did not turn to Mistress Sandahl. "Why are you keeping my sisters? Have they misbehaved?" Mistress Sandahl did not answer him, and Cain glanced at her quickly; no help there, Mistress Sandahl was almost paralyzed with fear.

"No," said the Ruler softly, "they've not misbehaved. Do you know who I am?"

"No, my lady."

"I am the Ruler Selene." The woman waited a moment and said with a dangerous edge to her voice, "Do they not teach Workers how to kneel in Eastmarch?"

"Oh. I'm sorry, my lady," said Cain, and knelt, quickly and without hesitation, and did not so much as raise his head again until she told him to get up.

"How old are you, boy?"

"Fourteen, Lady Selene."

"Your sister Ba—why do you call me that?"

Cain slowed his racing pulse with an effort. "My lady, call you what?"

"Lady Selene." Selene took a step toward him, cold blue eyes probing. "That's a Goldriver usage, boy. I've never heard it from an Eastmarcher before."

"I . . . the Ruler Elyssa, my lady, when I was a child, she took my brother Misha to Parliament because he was mad. To help him. My mother asked her how she would be addressed, and she said as the Lady Elyssa. I guess I remembered that."

"How old were you when this happened?"

"Six." After a moment, Cain remembered to add, "My lady."

"Eight years ago. And you remembered that title all this time, until you might have the opportunity to use it again?"

"My lady, I have a good memory."

"It seems. Cain, your sister Barra did quite well on the tests for Academy. Not well enough for admittance, but well enough that I asked Mistress Sandahl if the child had any brothers or sisters not in the school; she mentioned you." She was silent for just a moment. "How did we manage to miss you in the tests—twice now, is it not?"

"We lived in the hills, ma'am. My father fished through the waterlocks until he was killed in a storm. The testing in 1192, we didn't hear about it until after the Ruler who gave the tests was gone. The hill people don't always. Last time, I'd gone to Telindel on a visit."

"What an interesting coincidence."

The statement did not seem to require an answer; Cain offered none. The Ruler Selene turned very slightly to address Mistress Sandahl. "Teacher, the girls can go home. I'm going to test the boy." The assessing, measuring gaze came back to Cain. "He's going to do very well."

"I'm supposed to go with her tomorrow."

Elena's reaction was nothing like Cain had feared or hoped for. Neither anger nor pleasure showed on her features. More than anything else, she seemed tired. After a moment she said, "What about your sisters?"

"I told the Ruler Selene I couldn't go to Academy unless their education was arranged for with Mistress Sandahl. She didn't—"

His mother stared at him. "You said what?"

"She said she would arrange for the girls to go to school until they got married." Cain shrugged. "I don't think she was angry. I think it pleased her I was worried about them."

"Cain?"

"Yes, Elena?"

His mother bit her lip. "When you get to Parliament, will you go to see Misha?"

Cain said simply, "Yes." His mother said nothing more, and Cain kissed his sisters swiftly and picked his overshirt off of its peg, just inside the door.

"Where are you going?"

"To see Loukas." Cain pulled the overshirt on. "Where else?"

Loukas took the news calmly. He and Cain talked while walking from Kephard's back to Loukas' tent. "It sounds like you did well enough. I could wish you'd kneeled to her a bit quicker, but . . ." Loukas let the sentence trail off. "It's done."

"Loukas, I don't understand. The tests—they were like the ways you test me, guessing the cards, rolling the dice—I did as badly as you can do on the tests. When they were done, the Ruler Selene was more pleased than when we started."

Loukas chuckled. "Figure it out, Cain. Missing all the cards, for example, tells her just as much as if you'd got them all. What're the odds against your not guessing *any* of the cards?"

"Oh." Cain thought about it. "Pretty high. Then she knows I was trying to hide things from her."

Loukas nodded. "Yes, but you handled that already. Your protests about your sisters—if she was worried about why you didn't want to go to Academy, your obvious concerns about Siva and Barra probably put her worries to rest. No, given she caught me by surprise coming so early, this hasn't turned out badly. I was going to see you sent to

Academy this year anyway. It's time." They walked slowly, Sunflower's hooves clopping on the cobbles. The night air was cool, the smell of the flowers from Lord Malachor's gardens reaching out to them. "Eastmarch, it's not your place, Cain. It's time you saw Academy and learned the things I can't teach you."

"Time I learned about the enemy," said Cain quietly, "firsthand."

Loukas only nodded.

Cain could not sleep that night. He lay on his pallet, without moving, practicing his breathing exercises. After a time he lost his body and floated in a quiet gentle darkness. If he reached, he could feel, somehow close and far all at once, the minds of his sisters. His mother he could not feel at all without more effort than he was willing to put into it. Loukas was even further, but clearer and sharper, his sleeping mind like a structure scrubbed clean of all but function.

The Ruler, who was spending the night at Lord Malachor's estate, was a bright hard spike of light in whom control reigned so strong that Cain could find nothing human behind the glare—no warmth, no uncertainty.

Only power, and discipline.

Though it seemed to take forever, morning came.

Cain rose with his sisters and sponged himself clean with the hot water that his mother had boiling in the kitchen. His mother had washed his best tunic and pants for him, the pair he wore to church on SunDays. His only shoes were of simple canvas that was laced to cover his feet from the worst of the cold.

He walked his sisters to school.

The streets were unusually busy for so early in the morning. It did not occur to Cain that they were up to see *him* before the Ruler took him away to Academy. He noted the abnormally large number of folk on the streets, but did not make the correlation.

Thirty-two years had passed since the last time an Eastmarcher had been taken to Academy, and that student had been sent home before the end of her first year.

Cain half expected to see the Ruler at the gates to the school; she was not. The students gathering there before the start of class stared at

him with expressions ranging from envy to admiration to simple disbelief. None of them talked to him.

His sister Siva had walked all the way to school with a stony
expression. Neither she nor Cain had responded to Barra's occasional
attempts to start conversations. Now she put their writing tablets down
on the ground and without any particular ceremony hugged Cain
tightly. She did not say the word aloud. *Good-bye.* When she released
him her eyes were bright, but she did not shed so much as a single tear.
She stooped in what was almost a curtsy, exactly as Mistress Sandahl
taught girls to retrieve an object from the ground, with near-perfect
grace.

Barra was crying and made no attempt to hide it. She flew into
Cain's arms and spoke through her tears. Nobody but Cain could have
heard her. "You won't forget me? Promise me you won't forget me?"

"I won't forget you." Cain made no move to remove her arms,
but simply held her until Mistress Sandahl rang the bell for classes.
"Sunshine, you're getting my good shirt wet. You have to go. Siva, take
her inside."

"Okay." Siva took their little sister's hand and did not look back
as she led Barra inside.

I won't forget you, said Cain. He was not certain either of them
heard him. Barra froze for a step, and even Siva seemed to hesitate.

Just for an instant. The door closed on them without either of
Cain's sisters looking back.

Cain had not planned to see Loukas again; saying good-bye once,
last night, had been difficult enough.

He was heading to Lord Malachor's house before he realized he
had not said good-bye to Jenny. A desire to avoid seeing Loukas again
warred briefly with the necessity of bidding Jenny good-bye, and lost.

If Loukas had taught him nothing else in those six years, he had
taught Cain to make decisions quickly and abide by them without
regret. Cain turned in midstride and headed back to Kephard's.

It was still early in the day. The breakfast crowd at the inn had
cleared away, and only a few serious drinkers were there, secluded in
the booths. Loukas was at his customary spot, and he lifted an eyebrow
at Cain's appearance. Cain nodded to Loukas cordially.

Jenny was behind the bar, wiping glasses clean. Her face lit up when she saw Cain. "Cain," she said softly, lips turning up in a smile she could not restrain. "I didn't think to see you."

Cain smiled back, somewhat embarrassed despite himself. "How not? You didn't think I was going to leave without saying good-bye to you?"

"Oh, I thought you might." Jenny put down the glass she'd been wiping without thought since Cain had walked in, took off her apron and came around the bar. "You and emotions don't get on so well, sometimes. Come here."

Without looking at anything else in the world, Cain went forward and kissed Jenny good-bye swiftly.

A man in one of the booths whistled. "Try it again, lad!"

Jenny still had an arm on his shoulder after he'd kissed her; she smiled again and said, voice low, "You can do better than that, and I know it."

Cain glanced around. Everyone there was watching, frankly unabashed, even Loukas. He thought to himself, *The hell with them all*, stepped in, and kissed her properly.

The world went away for a while. When it came back again, he heard applause and whistles from far away. Jenny whispered, lips just next to his ear, "All right, now you can go on to Academy. You take care of yourself." Cain disengaged himself and saw, to his utter astonishment, Sam Kephard actually smile at him.

"Best of luck, lad."

Cain had to pass by Loukas on his way out the door. He stopped and stood looking at the man. He could not think of anything to say that he had not said the night previous. Finally he said, "Good-bye, then, Loukas."

Loukas nodded, but did not move. Cain found himself still standing, rooted to the spot. He meant to move, to leave, but nothing happened. The gentle brown eyes held him.

Loukas stood slowly, whispered, "Cain."

Cain could not move.

I'd hoped that Fate would send me a tool. Someone to share the dream with, and then you came, and I thought that tool had been sent me. From kilometers away Cain was vaguely aware that people were staring at them. *In all the years I looked, never once did it come to me that the tool would be a person, would someday stand before me, made flesh and blood, a boy whom I have found that I love.*

Cain stood frozen in place, shivering, trying to hold on to some shred of dignity. To the others in the inn it must have seemed that the two men simply stood silently, looking at one another. When Loukas saw that Cain could not move, or would not, he grinned, a wry, crooked thing, and took Cain into his embrace. He was not surprised that Cain held onto him then, held him hard and tight. *Cain,* he said quietly, *be careful.* And aloud, he said softly, "Go. She'll be waiting. You mustn't make her wait."

Cain ran until, turning back, he could no longer see Sam Kephard's Inn.

The sun was very hot as Cain walked through the village to Lord Malachor's estate.

The Ruler Selene was waiting for him at the front entrance to Lord Malachor's house. She was not doing anything, just sitting with her eyes closed on the polished stone bench in front of the house, waiting for him beside the white roses with a stillness so profound Cain found it almost frightening. He had the sudden impression that had he spent an entire week taking his leave of his family, the Ruler would have waited there without even noticing the passage of the time.

She opened her eyes at his approach and came to her feet with a grace that stirred a painful ache of desire within Cain. "Are you ready?"

Standing irresolute on the raked lawn before the estate, Cain nodded jerkily. "Yes." He bit his lip, and then said it anyway. "You're making a mistake, you know."

The comment seemed to amuse the Ruler. "Am I?" The too-old eyes caught his and held him with a knowledge so personal that Cain flushed hotly. Simply being looked at by her in that way made Cain vastly uncomfortable. "I don't think so."

In the face of her gentle mockery Cain was almost unable to order his thoughts. But he did, raised his head and said defiantly, "I know myself better than you do. If it turns out I can't learn what you want to teach me, I want to go home again."

Her laugh held no malice. "We do not bargain, child. And yet—if

I am mistaken and you are not suitable for our needs, rest assured we shall not keep you at the Academy."

He shook his head stubbornly. "Not staying at Academy isn't the same thing as going home."

A flash of anger crossed the Ruler's features, and passed. "Cain, we're not monsters. Truly, we're not. And I'm not wrong about you. There is power within you." Still Cain let the doubt sit plain upon his features, and the Ruler Selene smiled, and her voice was very soft. "As you wish."

The whiplash of the Light came from nowhere, tore itself from the air around them, and Cain heard himself screaming in the instant before he was taken.

They came back into existence on a high ledge of stonesteel, far above the rest of the world.

Cain's scream cut off instantly. He stared wildly about himself and then caught Selene's eyes upon him. He forced himself to calmness and said, his voice only slightly ragged, "I'm all right."

The Ruler nodded. "I know." She held her hand out to him, and, tentatively, he took it. Together they walked to the very rim of the ledge and looked down. Eastmarch lay spread beneath them, and beyond that the entire Valley, as far as the eye could see before the distance turned detail to haze.

Selene stood just behind Cain. She released his hand and ran her fingers up his arms, left her hands resting on his shoulders. Cain trembled almost uncontrollably. The Ruler began speaking, just behind Cain, her voice a low, soothing flow of words that made no sense to him, the pitch of the words rising and falling hypnotically.

Far inside him, Loukas' voice, almost drowned out by the power building around them, whispered, *Silence, boy, and calm.*

A golden light grew about Cain, and a warmth that reached through him and into him. A beat began in his skull, and his breath came short. Something was about to happen. There was a roaring sound in Cain's ears, and a voice that was not Selene's, insistent and probing.

What do you see, Cain? Tell me, what do you see?

Cain tried to slow his breathing, to breathe in the slow deep way Loukas had taught him. But the pounding in his skull would not stop, and his voice moved of its own accord. "The water . . . the water comes, and the people, they're screaming . . . the doors have closed, and they cannot swim . . ." The words ripped up out of his throat, and Cain heard the voice from far away, harsh and strident, before the whiteness took him entirely.

Somebody was speaking, had been for some time. It was a quiet voice, the voice of an adult, a voice of power and age.

". . . and against that darkness I have raised him up, and against that darkness I have set him. For I have seen a coldness, and in the coldness a man, and in the man decision; and though I die I shall not die, and though I fail I shall not fail, for in him have I been made complete."

It was his own voice, and it ended. He was standing on the ledge of stonesteel, only a step away from the edge and the long drop. His legs were shaking, and his whole body trembled.

The woman was standing behind him, holding him, arms wrapped around him, hands linked tightly together over his chest.

His voice was little better than a whisper; his throat was raw. "Let go of me. Please." She did, and he stepped backward from the edge, turning slowly to face her.

The Ruler Selene's features were still and composed. "How do you feel? You look terrible."

"I feel fine." He swallowed, tried to wet the back of his throat. "What did I say?"

"You told me you had power." Cain felt her drawing the Light about them, and this time he did not cry out.

He did not see Eastmarch again for almost fifty years.

The Academy

The Years 1206–1207 After the Fire

· 1 ·

Cain crawled up from sleep, bleary-eyed and disoriented. His head ached as though a dozen Goldriver smiths had been at work inside and hadn't bothered to clean up after themselves once they'd finished.

The voice that addressed him was the last voice in the world that he wanted to hear at that exact instant. "Well, you've made a mess of yourself again."

Cain opened one eye. He was lying in bed in his cottage, one cottage among the hundreds that were set aside for Academy's students at the lower north end of the city of Parliament. Sitting cross-legged at the foot of his bed, wearing nothing but a clean white robe, his fellow student Ellian Temera was looking at him with disapproval plain in her features. Cain groaned, and let the eyelid crash back down again. "Am I dead?"

"No, but I'm not sure I wouldn't rather you were. At least I wouldn't keep finding you like this."

Cain sat up in bed, slowly, and swung his legs over the edge. Somebody had moved the floor far enough that his feet took forever to reach it. He opened his eyes, both of them this time, and the cottage spun around him briefly, then stabilized. "Elli," he said softly, "you said I was to amuse myself last night, and so I did." His voice echoed oddly in his ears.

The girl sitting at the foot of his bed looked at Cain, disturbed. She was a dark-skinned girl from the town of Soret, in Turrin province south of Semalia, who'd grown up along the banks of the river Almandar. Aside from the shade of her skin and the cast of her eyes she did not resemble Loukas at all; but at times, Cain heard him in her voice, in the accent with which she spoke the common tongue. She was two years older than Cain, and due for the Test that summer. Even with the displeasure plain to see in the quiet brown eyes, she looked desirable enough that Cain had a momentary impulse to grab her and pull her back into the bed with him.

Unfortunately, the mood Elli was in, that was probably the worst thing he could do. He *reached* slightly, extending one hand, and the water jug on the cottage's table lifted itself and came to him. He drank deeply from it, paused to let the cold water settle in his stomach, and drank again.

"Cain, I had to study. I'm testing on three subjects on OneDay. Alber's testing me, worse luck. You *know* that."

The Ruler Alber was a member of the ruling Tribunal; he, Loga and the Ruler Gabriel were the only members of the Tribunal who took any particular interest in Academy. Alber's interest seemed to be mostly negative; if he had ever said anything good about Academy or any of its students, the comment had not reached Cain's ears.

Cain nodded, and regretted it instantly. "Sure. And I didn't have to study, so I went to a party. What's wrong with that?" Elli did not answer him. "What time is it?"

Elli's eyelids drooped slightly. She reached out, for the telepathic cast that let the students know what the time of day was. The idea of breaking the day up into divisions—hours, as the Rulers called them, ten to a day—was familiar to Cain, though not by the word the Rulers used. Their obsession with time was one of the large number of things Cain found particularly alien about the Rulers. Bad enough they needed hours, but the hours themselves were chopped up into *minutes*, a hundred per hour, and the minutes were chopped up into a hundred ridiculous small things called *seconds*. "By the cast . . . 4:84:74. Not quite noon. Are you too hung over to even listen for the timecast yourself?"

"Damn." Cain ignored the question, took a long, slow deep breath to flood oxygen through his bloodstream. "I promised Loga I'd make sure he made his class on time. But I forgot to ask for a wake-up call."

Her voice was very quiet. "You were out with him again last night?"

"*Yes.* So?" Cain made it to his feet and considered the horrible length he needed to walk to reach his shower. After five years in Parliament, the shower, with both hot and cold running water, did not even feel like a luxury anymore; it was just a part of his life, one that, at this particular moment, was rather too distant for convenience.

"That Ruler," she said quietly, "is a disgrace."

Cain nodded. His head did not quite threaten to come completely off. "Indeed. Great company, though."

"What do you see in him?"

"A Ruler with a sense of humor? You have to ask?"

"What, for that matter, does he see in you? Why the sudden interest?"

"I don't know," said Cain, which was true enough, as far as it went. He had a guess, though, one that worried him as much as he ever allowed himself to worry about anything.

Elli sighed. She came of a family of Land'ners in Turrin; more so than Cain, she was aware of, and cared for, distinctions of class. Cain had never told her about his childhood, and she had never really asked. He suspected she knew his social status was—or had been—considerably beneath her own, though now, as students at Academy, they were both as high in class as any Worker might ever hope to become. Students at Academy, once they had failed the Test—and they did always fail it—usually entered one of the administrative posts: magister, legate, tax collector, something where the Rulers preferred, when possible, to employ one of their highly trained Academy students rather than the ignorant and often illiterate Workers who were the Valley's norm. "Cain, you have a chance to pass the Test."

"So does everyone else."

"That's not true, and you know it. Almost nobody ever passes it— I've never heard of it happening, and the students who were here when I came hadn't heard of it happening either. But you're different. You might make it, Cain. Don't screw up your chances by antagonizing people."

"You mean the Ruler Alber." Cain made a rude gesture. "*That* for Alber. He doesn't like to see Workers associate with Rulers, he should stay out of the bars in Goldriver. Want to wash my back?"

"No."

Cain shrugged, walked a careful straight line through the two-room cottage, stood under the shower, and turned the cold water on.

Elli was gone when Cain came out of the shower, feeling as though he might live and half hoping he wouldn't. He dressed with reasonable speed, pulled on a pair of boots given him as a gift by the Ruler Selene, left his cottage and started walking uphill, through the city of Parliament, to the estate of the Ruler Loga.

Parliament, in the early 1200s, was a city at the height of its glory. It would never be larger, or more peaceful, or more productive. Better than two hundred thousand persons—some forty thousand Rulers, the balance of them Workers—lived within its boundaries. Singer, at the edge of the Lake T'Pau, was the only other place on Earth where Rulers lived in any number; some five thousand had made that city their home.

Parliament was a city planned by the Rulers, for their own benefit; there was nothing in all the city that did not serve their needs in some fashion. Except for, in small measure, the city of Singer, there was nothing in all the Valley to match its glories, its structures of white marble delineated by black, of shining silver and platinum facings, streets all of ferrocrete, and walkways of tended grass. There were buildings in Parliament of twenty stories, rearing like Giants above the others. There were hospitals renowned for their healing skills; Workers of sufficiently high status came from the length and breadth of the Valley to be treated there.

Academy, the school founded for the purpose of finding and encouraging psychic talents among the Worker population of the Valley, grew more successful with each passing decade. The students, the best of the current Worker population, came, and learned, and were sent back out among the Worker population with newly high status; wealthy enough to bear numerous children without strain, and so, over the course of centuries, to raise up the general genetic level of the Valley. It was, in essence, a breeding program for the Workers, though it is possible that most of the Rulers did not think of it so, and certain that those who did, did not explain it as such to their students. With the death by suicide of the genegineer T'Pau, the Rulers lost most of whatever skill in genetic engineering they had ever had; and so they could not raise the Workers up to their level in that fashion. Because they had an extra pair of chromosomes, they could not breed with the Workers and so bring the Workers up to their level by sharing their genetic heritage.

And so, through the subtle mechanism of Academy, they bred the Workers instead, exactly as though they were racehorses.

The program was based on sound eugenic principles; and, without much surprise, the Rulers found, as the centuries rolled by, that it *was* working. In some areas the Workers studying at Academy came near to surpassing the Rulers already; there were Worker telepaths and seers, for example, to better anything of which the Lords of Light themselves were capable.

And then, in the very dawn of the thirteenth century After the Fire, the likeliest student Academy had ever seen was brought to them by the Ruler Selene. To many of the Rulers, it seemed that the culmination of the dream was near; here was a Worker so powerful, so near attaining the Light, that he might very well pass the Test.

And if he did not, surely his children would.

They could not know, of course, that Cain of Eastmarch would never have children.

The doorfield shattered.

"Good morning, Thea."

Loga's servant corrected Cain gently. "Good afternoon, Master Cain. Have you come for Lord Loga?"

"Yes, Thea. He asked me to make sure he made it to his 5:50 class."

She nodded. "Well, you just come right in, then, Master Cain." She led him in through the entryway and down a short staircase into Loga's cavernous home. It was the first Ruler's home he'd ever been in and was still one of only a few. The first several times he'd been through Loga's estate Cain had found himself by turns astonished by the opulence and enraged at the waste—all of this for just one person— but after the first few visits the sensation had faded, and today he hardly noticed it.

The Ruler Loga was sprawled facedown, naked and senseless on his bed. There were no blankets or sheets on the bed, only the stretched fur coverlet upon which he lay. A fireplace not far from the bed, grated so that the fur coverlet was safe from sparks, kept the room warm. Weapons of every description, from the most primitive to weapons which had actually been used in the later Fire Wars, hung from his walls in barbaric splendor; variable lasers, blasters and tangler bags mixed in among lances and swords and knives, spears and shurikens and nunchaku. Cain had seen other Rulers grow physically ill after a short visit in that room.

Loga turned his head slightly, opened one horribly bloodshot eye at the sound of Cain's boots echoing on the polished marble tiles. "By the Light, what time is it?"

Cain barely had to listen to hear the counting in the back of his mind, the telepathic cast that made sure the students reached their classes on time. "5:22, Loga. You're supposed to be teaching a class at half past."

"Oh. I can't, I'm dead."

Cain nodded. "I thought so too, when I first woke up. Sadly, it turned out I was alive. I'm afraid you are too."

The redhead looked distinctly displeased by the thought. "Yeah, that's what you think." He worked his mouth as though there were something in it. "Maybe I am alive, but then something's dead in my mouth. What did we drink last night?"

"I don't remember. Some kind of whiskey with bubbles in it." Cain shivered. "It was sweet."

"What are you doing here?"

"You have a class," Cain repeated. "Half past five."

"I remember. I asked you to come get me." With great effort, Loga rolled over onto his back and stared up at the ceiling. "And another one at 6:50, damn it. Well." His eyes were amazingly motionless, like those of a blind man. "You'll have to teach the 5:50 class. I'm too ill. I'll do the 6:50 class myself—they're not even Academy students, just Warriors from Singer, coming to study up on hand-to-hand combat."

"Hand-to-hand combat," said Cain politely.

"Yes." The ceiling must have been fascinating. "You, of course, don't know anything about unarmed combat."

"Not a thing," said Cain mildly. "Where would I have learned such a thing, in a village such as Eastmarch?"

"Of course." Loga closed his eyes again. "The Light shine on my words, Cain, you're the first person in five hundred years has drunk me under the table."

"Uh . . ." Cain cocked his head to one side, trying to remember a conversation he'd had with another student, several years ago. Something about . . . "I don't think I can teach your class, Loga."

"Why the hell not?"

"Loga, I'm a student, a Worker, not a Ruler. Academy's seven hundred years old; in all that time, has a student ever taught a class, in any subject?"

"Hmm." Loga had not, Cain thought, blinked once since opening his eyes. "That's a good question. Boy named Lewin or something like that taught one a hundred eighty, ninety years ago. On self-hypnosis. He got washed out of Academy for it."

"My point."

"Oh, not because he was a Worker, Cain, because he was really bad at it." Loga shook his head at the memory. "It was just amazing. Special case."

"What's the class, Loga?"

"Telekinesis." Loga rolled over onto his side and propped himself up on his elbow. "Teach the little bastards how to cheat at dice."

Cain had a sinking feeling in the pit of his stomach. " 'Little bastards'? How old are they, Loga?"

"Seven, eight. I can't face that today, Cain. All those innocent wide eyes . . ." Loga's voice trailed off, and when he spoke again his voice was firm. "No. I can't do it. I just can't. I hate children."

Cain sighed. "Loga, you handle the children better than almost any other Ruler I've ever seen."

"Yeah? Well, only because they know I hate them, and I know they hate me. It puts the relationship on a proper basis, so we get along."

"Loga, I really—"

"Cain." The word was flat. Without expression, Cain looked into the bloodshot blue eyes. "Cain, I'm not asking. Go teach my class."

"You're really looking to provoke Alber, aren't you?" Loga sank back, spread-eagled on his bed, and did not answer Cain. "Very well," said Cain quietly, "but, for my own sake, I really hope you have some vague, general idea of how you're going to handle this. Okay?"

"You're a horrid, self-centered person, Cain. Go."

"We are much alike," Cain agreed. He had the pleasure of seeing a brief change of expression flicker across Loga's face, and then went.

They lay in bed together in Ellian's cottage, not coupling, only holding one another against the cold. Cain had blocked his mind, so that it seemed he perceived the world through layers of thick glass. He'd been forced to do it, merely to get to sleep; Elli was worrying over his problem with Alber as though the worrying might accomplish something. The chatter of her thoughts, running an endless treadmill, was actually unpleasant; and her compulsive talking was not much better.

Finally Cain said gently, "Elli, would you *please* shut up? I'm not sure what Loga thinks he's doing, either, but I am sure neither of us are going to figure it out tonight."

"Cain, you didn't see Alber this evening when he heard about you taking Loga's class. I've been here since I was nine years old, Cain, and I've never seen one of *them* lose his temper before. They just don't do that where we can see them."

"Yes, I know."

"*Cain.*"

"Elli," he said quietly, "listen. Nobody's going to execute me for doing what I was told. They may send me home, and that wouldn't be the end of the world; I'd like to see my sisters again, and it hardly matters whether I'm officially graduated or not. With what I've learned here I could ride into any village or town in the Valley—including your hometown, Elli—and be running the place within a decade. So, what's the worst that can happen? Expulsion, I think, and that's almost certain to happen regardless once I've failed the Test. And the best? Loga may force Alber out of day-to-day operations at the Academy; I hope that's his idea. In any event there's nothing we can do about it right now. So let's go to sleep."

Elli was silent for just a second and then burst out, "Cain, I *told* you to stay away from Loga! It's not good to get involved with the Rulers when they argue. They're so gentle all the damn time some Workers don't understand how ruthless they really are. And they treat us so well, some of us—especially those of us who—" she stumbled slightly over the words "—didn't come of very high class, they lose track of the fact that we're here for them, not the other way around."

Cain chuckled, alone in the darkness. "Elli, are you implying that I'm naive?"

"Cain, you can't trust them, *you can't trust Loga.*"

Cain rolled onto his side and ran one hand lightly over her nude form. "Do tell. Someday, Elli, I'll tell you about my teacher Loukas."

"Loukas . . . you've mentioned him. He was the minstrel in Eastmarch?"

"Yes. I think he'd like you, and you him, did you meet. When we've both left here, will you come with me to Eastmarch, to meet him? You're the two most important people to me in the world."

"Perhaps." She lay very still. "Cain, do you love me?"

Cain sighed. "I don't really know. I'm not sure I know what that is. You're very important to me."

"I know."

Cain dropped his lips to hers, ran his tongue over her lips. "Will you come with me to Eastmarch?"

Ellian was silent a long moment. "Let's wait until we reach that point, Cain. Many things can happen."

"Will you," he whispered, "come with me where I go?"

The woman did not hesitate at all. "Ask me again, Cain, after you've passed the Test."

Alone in the bed with her, Cain turned on his side, facing away. After a moment he felt the warmth of her pressing up against his back and her hot breath on the back of his neck.

He slept, and did not remember his dreams.

Cain had to check in at the hospital's front desk before they would let him go through into the gardens behind the fences that surrounded the hospital.

"Good morning, Cain," said the Worker who watched the door. She was a pretty brown-haired girl whose accent Cain could not place; she'd only recently taken over from an older woman named Patra, and Cain still did not know the girl's name. She finished typing his name in on the keyboard that was a part of her desk, glanced up and smiled at him. "You can go in. He's been excited all day, waiting for you."

Cain smiled. "I'm sure." He held up the small bag he'd brought. "Sweets. Is it okay, or is he on medication?"

The girl glanced back down at her computer terminal. "No problem. He doesn't go on medication for two more days."

Cain thanked her and went back.

There were eight hospitals in Parliament; during the years Cain was at Parliament, he never learned all of their names. Each one was named after some Ruler hero who had died in one of the various wars in which the Rulers had consolidated their power over Earth.

The first hospital whose name he learned, and the only one whose name he could remember, many decades later, was the McKenna Memorial Hospital for NeuroPsychic Research. It was one of the oldest buildings in Parliament; Cain could tell, because the sign at the entranceway, which held the name of the hospital, gave the name in two usages, both the common tongue and Old Tongue, and the Anglish version was *above* the common-tongue inscription.

Cain went there, every OneDay during the entire time he was at Parliament, to see Misha.

Misha worked in the gardens at the hospital. He was, Cain was not surprised to find, an excellent gardener; their grandfather Garret would not have been displeased with him.

He was also quite simple.

Misha was on his knees with his back to Cain when Cain came to see him that OneDay, weeding among the even, laser-straight rows of the flowers. He was humming the tune to a song that Cain had taught him, and which Loukas had taught Cain. Cain stood on the lawn that flanked the garden, watching Misha weed. There were times when he envied his elder brother. He did not remember Misha very clearly from before his brother's accident, and so had little to compare Misha against; but the person whom Misha had become was as happy as anyone Cain had ever met. His body had aged, but not his mind.

He was always happy to see Cain.

Misha finished with the weeding of that section and gathered up the weeds to place them in the small canvas bag at his side. Doing so, he looked up and saw Cain standing there. His face split with a wide grin. "Cain!"

Cain smiled back at Misha, went forward and hugged him. He'd

had to school himself to do that at first; the Workers at the hospital
were firm in their belief that the patients should be hugged and
touched as much as possible. For perhaps the first year after his arrival
in Parliament, Cain had been unable to bring himself to hug his mad
older brother as they requested, and his inability to do so had made
Misha scared and depressed; Misha always thought Cain was displeased
with him for some reason.

To Cain's considerable surprise, Misha had recognized him instantly the first time Cain had gone to see him; the passage of eight
years between Marric's death and Cain's arrival at Academy did not
seem to exist for him at all.

Cain disengaged himself gently from Misha's embrace. "Hi,
Misha. How are you feeling today?"

Misha did not stop smiling. "I'm very fine today, Cain. Today the
Ruler Calandra came and took some flowers I grew for her. Did Da
come with you today?"

Once, and only once, Cain had tried to explain to Misha about
Marric's death. "No, Misha. Da said you were to take care of your
garden today; he had to go fishing. Probably next week he can come."

Misha looked momentarily disappointed and then smiled again.
"Okay." *Next week* was sufficiently distant that Cain knew he would
have forgotten about Cain's answer by the time it came around. "Did
you come to have dinner with me?"

"Afraid not," said Cain with a straight face. "I think the Ruler
Loga's going to want to see me."

Misha's face sagged. "Oh." Cain grinned at his brother's woebe-
gone expression and handed Misha the bag he'd carried in. Misha
seemed to notice the bag for the first time. "Candy?" He looked at
Cain with an expression that was almost suspicious, opened the bag and
looked inside it. "*Chocolate?* Oh, Cain, thank you!" He flung his arms
around Cain and hugged him again.

"Hey, that's enough." Cain disentangled himself, grinning. "You
were going to show me the new roses you planted, remember? You
promised."

Misha nodded eagerly. "Yes, I remember." He took Cain's hand
like a child and together they walked down the path through the park
behind the hospital.

THE RING

"A wise man," Cain had once heard a Trader say at Kephard's Inn, "does not gamble in Goldriver." At the time the comment had meant nothing to him; shortly after his arrival in Parliament, it had come clear. Cain himself could make dice fall however he wished, could read cards from either side. The same was true of many of the other students at Academy, and of most of the Rulers. A Ruler, in addition, once he got drunk enough, was more than capable of destroying an inn with a thought. Barely a season passed when some inn was not destroyed in such fashion. A plea from the owner of the inn to the Tribunal usually saw the place rebuilt; but there was no reimbursement for the income the innkeeper lost while his inn was ruined.

Goldriver was only a twenty-minute monorail trip down through the foothills of the Black Mountains. It held forty-five thousand Workers, and those forty-five thousand Workers were often counted with the Workers of Parliament as being one group of Workers dedicated to the service of the Rulers; nonetheless, Goldriver was its own city.

The two cities were as different as night and day; Goldriver was a city of Workers alone—there were no Rulers who lived within its boundaries—and though it was cleaner and wealthier than most Worker cities, it did not compare with the sparkling cleanliness and tended gardens of the city up the mountain.

Goldriver would have been nearly an hour's ride from Parliament, downhill all the way, had it been possible to reach Goldriver by horse at all. From Parliament, it was not; one of the few functioning pieces of machine technology Cain had ever seen, a maglev monorail powered by Parliament's fusion generator, linked the two cities together. The trip from Parliament to Goldriver, aided by gravity, was only twenty minutes. Going uphill nearly doubled that travel time, and not only because of gravity. The monorail coaches, going downhill, were generally empty of all but passengers. For the uphill journey, some fifteen times a day, the coaches were loaded down with foodstuffs from farm towns throughout the south end of the Valley; Parliament did not grow its own food.

After better than five years in Parliament, Cain rarely even noticed the hundreds of ways in which that city was significantly different from any other city on the face of the Earth—except briefly, upon arriving in Goldriver. The first thing he noticed, disembarking from the monorail, was, as always, the *smell;* food being cooked, the simple tang of dust in the air, and other, less pleasant odors—surely nobody had ever urinated in an alleyway in Parliament. Five years in Parliament had not made him feel at home; in Goldriver he was instantly at his ease. The place was like Eastmarch grown large—eight inns, and two inns called restaurants, meaning they did *nothing* but serve food to those too lazy to prepare their own.

Among which number one might count Cain.

He walked down Prospers Avenue, a wandering avenue most unlike the arrow-straight streets of Parliament, which went north and south or else east and west, but never both. Prospers Avenue began near the edge of town, where the monorail line from Parliament ended, and looped around most of the outskirts of Goldriver before petering out along the banks of the small creek that was, that far south, all that was left of the mighty river of Almandar. Cain was not far from either Samuelson's Inn or Anna's Restaurant, and was trying to decide between them when he felt the faint disturbance in the fabric of reality; an instant later a gentle wind buffeted him, and the Ruler Loga appeared on the street beside him. Most, though by no means all, of the Workers on the street knelt briefly at Loga's appearance and went on about their business.

Cain merely said, "Hello, Loga. Dinner?"

"Sure." The redhead glanced around; his long hair was bound up in a long braid that reached down to his shoulders, and it moved with him. "Anna's? It's been a few years since I've eaten there."

A few years, to a Ruler, might mean anything from just that to some time before Cain's parents had been born. Indeed, there was a custom in Goldriver that did not, quite, have the force of law, that businesses were generally not renamed when ownership changed hands; it upset the Rulers when they went searching for a place they had not been to in a hundred years and were unable to find it because its name had changed.

They went inside and were taken to the table near the back where Cain usually found himself seated. The lighting was dim, which Cain preferred, and the clientele was disreputable enough that folk tended not to bother one another.

"You know," said Loga thoughtfully on the way to their table, "I think I burned this place down once."

"You don't remember?"

Loga shrugged. "Afraid not. It's been a while. It was an accident, if it's the same place."

Once they were seated and had ordered and had their ale brought them, Loga said cheerfully, "You probably want to avoid Alber for a while."

"Great."

"Fortunately," Loga continued, "that won't be so hard. He's been reassigned, out of Academy entirely. I got him sent off to the Library."

"Oh?" Cain considered that. The Library held the massed knowledge of the Rulers, everything they had ever learned or known. There were students who chose to labor there, after failing the Test, rather than be forced to leave Parliament entirely. It was the only way a student could stay in Parliament after failing the Test. It was an irrevocable choice; once a Worker was exposed to the documents in the Library, he or she could not go home again. The Rulers would not allow it. "How did you manage that?"

"I argued that Alber was not serving the Academy's best interests —emotionally caught up in his work, so to speak. Between his supporters and mine, we had a great old time in the Chamber last night."

"Congratulations."

The smile faded. "Cain, what the hell's wrong with you? I had the rather distinct impression you didn't care for Alber. I know he doesn't like you."

"The man hates me," said Cain quietly.

"He hates me too," Loga protested. "Doesn't that count for anything?"

Despite himself, Cain grinned. "Not really." The grin faded quickly enough, and he burst out, "Damn it, Loga, it's great you got rid of Alber. But did you have to use me to do it? More ale," he said to a passing serving girl.

"Yes." Loga looked at Cain, with an attempt at wide-eyed innocence that he almost carried off. "Cain, you're the only student in Academy who I could have teach a class, and then defend the choice and be clearly right because you're talented as any Ruler. There's no law against Workers teaching, only custom because they're presumed not to have the skills. I wanted to break that custom and establish a precedent—that teaching is a position one is awarded not because one is a Ruler but because one has the skill—and yesterday we did so."

Cain drained the last of one mug as the serving girl placed another at his elbow. "Try to keep in mind, please, I'm only just a Worker. By the Light, Loga, I don't need the likes of Alber as my enemy. *You*—you're his equal, or better. I'm just the Worker who cost him his job."

Loga shrugged. "What's he going to do to you?" He grinned at Cain. "Come on, *think*. He's not at Academy any longer, and he's hardly going to hunt you down and attack you as though he were a Worker himself."

"And once I've left Academy? You'll tell me next any assignment I get, magistrate or legate, won't be reviewed by the Tribunal before it's approved?"

Loga did not answer him for a long time. Their meals came, sizzling steaks on wooden platters, with hot bread and baked beans. Cain sat across the table from Loga, staring at the Ruler. Their server left, and finally Loga said, "True. *If* you are assigned to the post of magistrate or legate, you will need to be approved by the full Tribunal, and, of course, Alber will not approve the posting."

Cain raised an eyebrow. "If?"

"Sometimes," said Loga conversationally, "when you attempt sarcasm, you remind me of a Worker I knew once, a student of mine here at Academy. He'd be an old man, today."

"Really?" Cain appeared to consider the comment. "Is that a compliment?"

"In some ways." The bright blue eyes invited Cain to share a joke. "You know who else reminded me of that student?"

Cain did not think he paused. "Who?"

Loga grinned widely at him. "Why, Loukas, of course."

"Loukas? I don't think I know a Loukas."

"I've been to Eastmarch, Cain. It's a depressing place."

"Eastmarch? I don't—oh, you mean the minstrel. Is that who you mean?"

"Yes, Cain, your minstrel friend." Loga chuckled. "He was gone, of course, when I got there. Left Eastmarch, I'm told, about a year after you went to Academy. Long enough almost nobody there except your mother connected the two events. Cain, I described my old student to these folk, my old student Artemis, and do you know, to a Worker they agreed it was the description of the minstrel Loukas?"

"You've lost me, I'm afraid. You say this Artemis"—Cain mispronounced the name exactly as Loga had, with the accent on the *e*— "would be an old man now. Loga, Loukas was a young man. Thirty or so, the last time I saw him."

Loga nodded, cut a piece of his steak, and ate it. "Couldn't, of course, be the same man. Still, an amazing resemblance, eh?"

Cain sipped at his ale. "Perhaps. Still—you and I look a bit alike. If I were to dye my hair red and let it grow some, get out in the sun and darken my skin just a bit, how many folks out there might take a description of you and say, 'Yes, that's Cain, that's the very one.' Hmm? Loukas was a handsome man with a black beard and black hair, dark skin and brown eyes. How many men are there, Loga, in Semalia and Turrin, who meet that description? Twenty thousand? Fifty?"

"I went to Eastmarch," said Loga, "and saw your mother. Why don't you ask about her, rather than arguing with me about this minstrel? I'd think most men would ask how their families were doing."

"I don't like my mother." Cain smiled at Loga. "How are my sisters?"

Loga laughed as though Cain had said something clever. "Fine, they were just fine. Would you like to go dancing tonight?"

Cain made a dismissing gesture with one hand. "Sure. Why not?"

"Fine. There's a party in Singer. You're to come with me and pretend to be a Ruler."

"As you wish."

"Cain," said Loga, suddenly dead serious, "your only worry about Alber comes if you find yourself up for a position in the administrative services. And that will only happen if you fail the Test. The answer to your problems, then, is clear."

Cain had seen it coming. "Don't," he said, "fail the Test."

Loga chuckled and raised his mug in something like a toast. "You're a smart boy, Cain."

Sometime in the course of that night, Cain found himself on a tree-lined pathway that wandered along the edges of the lake T'Pau, singing drunkenly at the top of his lungs. Sailboats cruised the lake's surface, bright and gaudy in the cool night air. An entire evening being treated with the same sort of deference that a Ruler received as a matter of course had left him feeling very strange. Loga had passed him off to the Rulers at Singer as the son of some Ruler Cain had never heard of. "She's dark-eyed enough—closer to brown than black, but still, I doubt anyone'll look at you askance." And indeed, the Rulers had accepted Cain as one of their own without any apparent suspicion at all.

Five years at Parliament had worn away the edges of Cain's Eastmarch accent; still he kept his mouth shut and did not seek out the company of the Rulers at the party. The estate the party was held at was a huge one, larger than any Cain had ever seen at Parliament; it sat on a rise overlooking the lake T'Pau. From its huge windows Cain could see, rising up under the moonlight, the vast bulk of the Great Dam.

It was the first time he'd seen the Dam since leaving Eastmarch, and the mere sight of it made him feel very strange, distant and disoriented. He stood watching it with a sweet, powerful drink in one hand; the drink had been served him in a crystal goblet that was worth as much as everything his family had ever owned put together. Finally one of the woman at the party had taken his hand, without even a word, and led him off into one of the empty rooms. She was a small, delicate woman with hair nearly as red as Loga's, and she coupled with an energy and a degree of imagination that left Cain drunkenly amazed.

Another voice joined Cain's, horribly off-key, and he turned about carefully to look behind himself. Loga was there, still shining ever so faintly with the afterglow of his jump. The lights and glowfloats of the estate twinkled behind him. Loga broke off in midstanza and came to walk beside Cain. "Cain, what the hell did you leave the party for?"

Without surprise, Cain saw that Loga was at least as drunk as he was himself. He spoke carefully, to keep his words clear. "I'd gotten laid, damn it. Why else should I stay? They were all talking about things I know nothing about."

"You got laid?" Loga looked at him indignantly. "I haven't, yet. Who with?"

Water was lapping at Cain's ankles; he looked down in surprise and realized he was walking into the lake. "I didn't get her name. Redhead, sort of short, nice breasts, gorgeous bottom. She looked a little bit like you." Cain paused. Thoughts were coming slowly. "I tried not to think about that."

"What's *wrong* with the way I look?"

"Well," said Cain carefully, "nothing . . . in particular." His feet were wet again, cold and wet. Oh, yes, the water. *Stay out of the water*, he thought to himself clearly. "Was that woman one of your descendants?"

"No, just . . . chance resemblance." Loga nodded. "Yes, that's it, chance resemblance. I don't have any children, among the Rulers anyhow."

Cain studied Loga drunkenly; they were on dangerous territory, a subject about which Cain was not supposed to know anything. "That makes it sound like you have Worker children."

"I don't, at the moment. I have had, in the past."

Cain let a puzzled look cross his features. "You can't."

Loga stared at Cain. "Why the hell not?"

"Rulers and Workers can't breed together. Everybody knows that."

Loga looked at Cain with a disturbed expression. "Not . . . *exactly*. T'Pau's People and Workers can't breed with one another. I'm not one of T'Pau's People; I can sire children on Worker women, but not on a Ruler woman."

Cain shook his head slowly. "I don't understand."

"Cain, what makes a Ruler?"

"What makes a Ruler?" Cain laughed, and the laughter came forth with grim cynicism. "Hell if I know. The fact that you live forever? Or is it just the fact that we don't live forever, that we die without youthbooster?"

Some incredible force took him, slammed him back against one of the trees at the side of the path. "*Where did you hear that word?*" It was like being pinned by a mountain; Cain could not have moved if saving his life had required it. Loga screamed the word. "*Where?*"

Cain stared at Loga, abruptly perfectly sober, stared at the wild expression in his friend's eyes. Cautiously he brought forth a partial truth: "The word was there in your thoughts, Loga."

Loga's breath came fast, and he stared at Cain as though he would find the truth on Cain's features. He was standing, legs apart, with his hands gripping Cain's shoulders. The grip was painful and growing more so; Cain was considering kicking Loga in the groin when he was suddenly released. "Okay."

"Loga?"

The Light gathered about them. "Come on. I want to show you the Test." The glow was very fierce. "It's time."

They appeared in a place of stark emptiness. A small square room, with yellow sunpaint on the ceiling, black walls and a black rug.

The room was bisected by a huge panel of some transparent material, flush against the surfaces of floor, walls, and ceiling. Cain turned around slowly. A doorfield glowed behind him; on the other side of the panel there was a doorway, but no door or doorfield. That was all there was in the room. "Where are we, Loga?"

"Parliament." Loga ran one hand over the barrier. "This is the Test. It's a panel of transparent monocrystal. It's the strongest material known to the Giants."

"I thought diamond was the strongest material."

"Hardest, yes, but hardness is not the same thing as tensile strength," said Loga, enunciating carefully. "It wouldn't be that difficult to break a thin sheet of diamond."

Cain touched the barrier tentatively. It was smooth, almost slippery. "I don't understand the purpose of this."

Light flared. Wind touched Cain as air rushed in to fill empty space.

Loga stood on the other side of the barrier, looking at Cain with an unfathomable expression. His voice was distorted by the barrier. "Join me. Come to me." He laid the palms of his hands flat against the barrier, pressed himself against the transparent wall. "You know about youthbooster."

Cain took a step forward. "Yes."

Loga's voice shook. "I've been alone for a long time. You can do it. Make the jump, Cain."

"Loga, I'm drunk."

THE RING

"You want to know what makes a Ruler, Cain? Here. Being here. I am here, and I am a Ruler." The bright blue eyes bored into Cain's with terrible urgency. "You can do it, Cain, I know you can. *Make the jump.*" The words touched him directly. *Make the jump, Cain, and live forever.*

"Loga . . ." Cain did not finish whatever it was he had planned to say; the whiplash of the Light curled through the room, and Loga was gone.

He stood in the empty room for a long time, staring at the ghostly, almost invisible barrier. Finally he backed out of the room, found himself in a building of the Academy he had not had occasion to enter before, and walked through the echoing empty streets of sleeping Parliament until he came to his cottage.

There he sat, wide awake, and thought, and wished desperately to be able to talk again to Loukas, or to anyone who would just answer him honestly.

That summer Elli took the Test and failed it as she and her instructors had expected.

She did not tell Cain she was going to try; he found out only after she had gone home.

There was a note on the pillow of the bed in his cottage.

Today I am taking the Test, and then I am going home to Soret. There's a school there, and I'm going to teach; it's what I came to Academy for, after all, so that I would know something worth teaching. Once you have taken the Test, join me there if you will. I'll wait for you for three years before I marry somebody else.

I'm sorry I can't say good-bye to you, but I don't want my last memory of you to be saying good-bye. Besides, you always have such a hard time with that sort of thing.

I love you.

Ellian Temera

Cain read the note and knew she did not expect to see him ever again.

He sat nude in the darkness, in full lotus. His breathing was calm, very slow, very deep. One hand rested upon each knee. The sweat trickled scalding down his body, and his skin felt raw.

A voice tickled at the edges of his mind. Memory . . . but so real. The voice whispered to him, the voice of a dream and a vision, *Make the jump, Cain. Make the jump, and live forever.*

His breathing stilled, slowed even further. He drew the cool air down into his lungs, in incredibly long slow draughts, brought the air deep within himself. His heartbeat slowed, gentled into a rhythm that matched the serene intake and exhale. The voice faded from the edges of his awareness as he centered his being into a profound peace unlike anything he had ever known before in his life.

His body fell away from him.

Cain reached out for the Light.

And screamed.

The sound was high-pitched and wavering, a terrible scream that sounded as though it held the pain and failure of the entire world.

It did not stop for a long time.

Cain came back to awareness slowly, as though rising from a great depth of water.

He could not move.

Voices murmured around him.

"By the Light, do you see what happened to the barrier?"

Another voice—Loga's? "Am I blind? Of course I see it. Watch your feet; the shards will be very sharp." There was a pause; somebody touched Cain. He felt the touch from far away.

"Is he alive?"

There was some pain, very distant.

"Barely. Hard to tell through all the blood. He must have caught pieces of the barrier everywhere."

A third voice. "The Light shine on my words, he looks like something from the last battle at Erebion."

"By the Light, Loga, what could have done that to the barrier? The damn thing's *shattered.*"

The voice was very short; of course it was Loga's. "Don't be a fool. Him."

There was a brief silence. In the devastating awareness of his aloneness Cain found the silence welcome.

Loga said grimly, "What else?"

And then there were no more words or sounds or Light, only endless hurt and emptiness and the tight hungry pain in his belly; hands lifted him and Cain screamed once and descended into the dark wave-covered depths of endless night.

· 2 ·

It's a fallacy, Cain, Loukas was saying, *to say the Rulers live forever. They don't; they merely live longer than we do. They do not die of old age or disease, but that does not mean they do not die. Accident can kill them, and murder; most of them do not pass four or five centuries before some mishap catches them.*

They were walking together along the shores of the great dark ocean. There was no sun, no moon, no stars, only the shore and a dim pearl-gray illumination. The water lapped silently at his feet.

So then, if there is no true escape from death—and there is not— then death is merely life's conclusion, no better and no worse. That is all there is to life, Cain; that we live it as well as we might, and die bravely when our deaths are brought us. Fate is cruel at times; for all you are young, perhaps this is your moment.

They continued on, toward the greater darkness that lay further down the beach. Cain said finally, *What is this place?*

Loukas said, *I do not know. I have never been here before.*

Oh.

Shall we go back?

Cain's steps slowed, and then stopped. He turned to look back the way he had come; far, far distant there was a faint lifting of the grayness.

Yes, he said at last.

Good choice, said Loukas simply. *It's damn cold out here.*

Some time later Cain opened his eyes. He was incredibly weak; just opening his eyes drained him utterly of such energy as he had. He was lying in a bed in one of the rooms at the hospital where Misha lived. A window facing him opened out onto the gardens that Misha tended. He could see by the length of the shadows that it was late afternoon.

There were two people in the room with him; Misha, sitting quietly without expression, and the Ruler Loga, who was yawning as Cain opened his eyes. Misha caught Cain's awakening instantly; he was up out of his chair and on his knees at Cain's bedside. "Cain, we were worried!"

Loga rubbed his eyes and leaned forward. He did not get out of his seat. "I'd say we were. You were nearly dead for a while there." Cain rolled his head slightly to one side to look at Loga. His head felt like a boulder. "It was amazing," Loga said. "I was dozing last night, just after midnight, when I woke up briefly. You know, your brother doesn't look anything like my student Artemis, but when I awoke, it seemed to me for a moment that it was not your brother sitting there, but Artemis himself. Just after that, your breathing deepened and your heartbeat steadied, and I knew you were going to live."

Cain's throat was sore, so sore that for a moment he was not sure he could shape the words. When they came, they were so hoarse he was not sure Loga would understand them. "Go away."

The Ruler shook his head. *Why do you think I am his enemy, Cain? I'm not. I'm not yours. I've tried to be your friend. I tried to be his.*

Misha looked back and forth between Cain and the Ruler. "Cain? What's wrong?"

Cain could not raise the strength for speech. *Go away, Loga.*

Cain, you will answer me.

You betrayed him.

Cain, I stopped a war. I saved thousands of lives, scores of thousands.

All those whose lives you saved, Loga, are they not dead now of old age?

Loga whispered the answer. "Yes."

Cain let his eyes close. *Go away, Loga. Go be friends with somebody who won't die on you.*

"Yes." Loga's voice held a plain regret that was audible even through the muffled layers of Cain's pain. "I suppose you're right. Who ever said choices were easy?"

Cain did not answer him. Shortly he was aware that Loga was gone.

Misha leaned close to Cain as soon as Loga had left. "Loukas," he said very quietly, "says you're to go to the Library."

"Okay."

Misha sat back, clearly satisfied with having delivered his message.

Cain said quietly, "Misha?"

"Yes?"

"Hold my hand, please. It's cold."

Misha looked at him in surprise and then grinned in simple delight. "Okay." He took Cain's hand between both of his own.

He sat there with Cain through the long night.

The next morning Cain tendered his application to enter the Library.

He spent nearly two full weeks hospitalized, unable to move from his bed for the first week of that time. Misha tended to him conscientiously, feeding and bathing him.

A Ruler whom he had never met before, Loden Almandar, the Tribunal Elder, came to see him before he was released. Though Cain had not seen him, he had seen Loden's pictures in enough of his history books that the Ruler's face was instantly recognizable; Cain made a valiant attempt to rise so that he might kneel, before the Ruler's hand on his shoulder stopped him. "That is not necessary, young man. I know you are ill." He spoke the common tongue in an archaic style, like some of the other very old Rulers whom Cain had met; he used the long forms of words, without contractions.

Loden dragged up one of the visitor's chairs and seated himself by Cain's bedside. "I am informed you wish to enter the Library."

Cain's voice was stronger now; he did not worry about it breaking. "My lord, yes. I would like that."

"Why?"

"I would like to stay in Parliament, my lord. I have failed the Test."

The ancient Ruler nodded. "True enough, you did." He did not smile. "A spectacular enough failure, to be sure, but failure nonetheless. Worker Cain, you are—" the Ruler hesitated only slightly "—not loved by the Ruler Alber. If you are permitted entrance to the Library, it is likely he will not treat you equitably."

"My lord, I know. But my brother Misha is here in Parliament. He's mad and cannot be sent to Eastmarch with me; he needs someone to watch him constantly. He was lonely before I came; if I leave him now, I think he will die."

"I was told about this," said Loden. His broad features were empty of any readable expression. "Cain, I would prefer to keep you here in Parliament. You, and, if I am honest with you, your children. But I am as constrained by custom as any other Ruler; the only proper way for me to do this is to see you inducted into the Library. You know you cannot go home again once you have worked with the Library's private documents?"

Cain said, "Yes."

Loden Almandar's eyes flickered shut for just a moment. "Ah." He smiled very briefly, nodded and stood. "Then I shall see your application is approved. Alber will not argue with my decision. Once you have entered the service of the Library, if Alber abuses you, let me know. It may be that I can do something about it."

"Thank you, my lord."

Loden stopped in the door. "Cain?"

"Yes, my lord?"

"Loga tells me that you attempted the Test after a student whom you cared for had left you—that your mind was not settled. Is this true?"

The wave of pain that struck Cain was amazing, like nothing he had ever felt. He could not speak.

Loden, standing in the doorway, winced. "I see it is. Cain, if you wish to attempt the Test again, inform me. I will see that it is arranged." His voice was as gentle as Loden Almandar was capable of making it. "Good day, Cain."

His application was accepted, and Cain, at the age of nineteen, entered the Library.

The Ruler Alber was a short man and slightly overweight, and a poor telepath to boot; Cain skimmed the surface of the Ruler's thoughts as easily as he might have done to any Worker.

It was not of much help; all that it told Cain was that Alber hated him because he was tall and handsome and skilled, and that much he knew already.

Alber stared at him without blinking. They were in one of the Library's reading rooms, with the door closed. Alber had not bothered to get up when Cain entered. Cain stood, waiting for Alber to speak.

"You should not have come here," said Alber finally.

"My lord, I had to. Because of my brother."

Alber nodded. He did not seem particularly angry, though the clean, unwavering hate never varied. "I've been told about him. I do not, Worker Cain, consider your desire to please your mad brother sufficient reason for you to have disturbed me, again, here at the Library." He shook his head again, and said again softly, "You should not have come here."

There was something dead inside Cain; he stood and waited for Alber to continue.

"How old are you, Cain?"

"Nineteen, my lord."

Alber leaned forward, clasping his hands together on the reading table's top. "And Workers live, what, sixty, seventy years when they receive medical care?"

"Something like that, my lord."

"So I have perhaps half a century to make you regret your intrusion into my life?" Alber smiled. "That should be enough."

Cain smiled back at him. "No doubt, my lord."

Alber's knuckles went suddenly white, and the Ruler himself went utterly rigid in his chair. "Do you find something amusing in this, Worker?"

Cain let the smile die slowly. "I? My lord, no."

"You are dismissed, Cain." Cain inclined his head slightly and turned to leave. Behind him, Alber said, "I will teach you your place in the world, Worker."

The words stopped Cain in midstep; he turned in the doorway. "I have," he said evenly, "had better teachers than you. Good day, my lord."

He closed the door behind himself and walked away, half expecting that Alber would come after him.

Alber did not.

Cain spent nearly a year in the Library at Parliament. At first the other Workers in the Library treated him with a sort of wary deference; and even Alber, though he made his distaste for Cain plain enough, did not bother him greatly once Cain had learned his duties. Cain's duty schedule was always, the entire time he was at the Library, heavier than that of his fellows; he took it as a blessing, for when he was not on duty there was little enough to do but sleep.

And in his sleep he could not stop dreaming about Elli. *Why* had she left in the fashion she had? Had she never understood that he cared for her?

Perhaps, Cain thought in the still, empty moments late at night, he had simply not been clear enough.

It took most of half a year before Cain managed to make himself comfortable in the Library. It was a different world from anything he'd ever experienced before. Academy, once he'd gotten used to the luxury, was not so different from the evenings he'd spent with Loukas; teachers who presumably knew more than Cain did had taught him, and he had learned, either acceptably or well, but never poorly.

In the Library nobody cared what he knew or how well he knew it; all that was cared about was how well he tended the hundreds of thousands of books the Library held, or the computer systems which held as much information again; and how quickly he could get the information into readable form when one of the instructors at Academy, or one of the Rulers researching some project of his own, requested it.

He was not surprised that he found himself to be skilled at the use of the computer systems; once he'd learned the rules of syntax with which the computer demanded it be addressed, it generally obeyed him without the misunderstandings that were common when other Workers attempted to search through the infobase. With the passage of Fall Quarter of 1206, and of Winter Quarter 1207, Cain's life settled down into a certain numb predictability; and he was not displeased with that.

There were things that Cain disliked about the Library. Foremost among them was the way the Workers were kept track of, like property; he was not allowed to so much as leave the Library without checking out with the Worker on duty at the door, giving his destination and business and the time he would be back. If he was to be gone for more than a single hour it had to be cleared with one of the Rulers. He could not leave Parliament at all; if there was something he required from Goldriver, he had to write it down on a sheet of paper and submit it to the Worker whose duty it was that week to facilitate such things. A day or two or sometimes a full week later, one of the students from Academy would make the trip and get it for him.

Cain's quarters in the Library were plainer than the cottage he had lived in as a student at Academy; he hardly noticed, and did not care. There was only one room, with a private shower and toilet, and the bed was large enough for only one person; apparently Workers at the Library were not intended to sleep with one another.

At least not comfortably.

It was another of the things Cain paid no attention to. The other Workers at the Library he found of little interest; they were, with few exceptions, Academy's most egregious failures, men and women who could not bear the thought of returning to the company of their fellow Workers after having been exposed to the glories of Parliament. There were about a hundred and twenty of them, and Cain found only about fifteen of them worthy of any interest at all. Though most of the Workers at the Library were there because of nothing more interesting than a lack of willingness to leave Parliament, some few had chosen to enter the Library service because, like the Rulers, they were engaged in some research they could not bear to leave uncompleted.

Cain followed their example. He was in the midst of knowledge no Worker outside of the Library had ever been given access to; as he was certain Loukas intended, Cain studied.

There were three categories of books in the Library; Open, Proscribed, and Censored. The books marked Open were available to anyone, Worker or Ruler. The Proscribed books were not available to the average Worker; in theory, they were not available to the Workers at the Library either. But Cain found that nobody really cared if he read books on the Proscribed list; the computer would grant him access to those files if he requested it, and the Proscribed books that were actually on shelves, in bound editions, were not segregated from the Open books by any barriers.

Books that were marked Censored in the Library index Cain

could not find in bound editions, and the computer would not grant him access to the files.

Some of the other Workers at the Library told him that there was, according to legend, a room somewhere in the Library that held all of the bound copies of Censored books. According to the ancient rumor, the room had no doors, so that there was no way for anyone but a Ruler to enter it.

Careful snooping in the minds of the Rulers who came to the Library confirmed that the rumor was correct. Cain got occasional glimpses of the room in the minds of some Rulers, just before they made the jump there. Cain abandoned any hope of getting to those hardcopies; even were he to attempt the Test again, he did not intend for his first target to be a room whose existence the Rulers of Earth did not even acknowledge.

The computer was his obvious target; the only way it knew who was accessing it was from the passwords it requested. One who had the correct passwords was able to read literally anything in the infobase. Without any exceptions of which Cain knew, only Rulers were allowed access to the Censored books. If there was a Worker anywhere in the world with the necessary passwords, Cain never learned of it.

And so he stole the passwords from the mind of a Ruler.

Alber.

It happened on the afternoon of Winter 81, in the year 1207. Unlike Loukas, Cain did not believe in fate, or destiny; but it seemed to him that there must be something besides chance to explain the fact that it was the very day that Cain discovered the location of Donnertown that the Ruler Alber made it impossible for him to continue his research.

Cain was sitting at an empty terminal in one of the reading rooms, scanning through a text about the Great Schism. There were four broad categories of subjects to be found on the Censored list. Science was at its head; better than two thirds of the Censored books dealt with the advanced hard sciences in one way or another. Youthbooster was the second subject, and the third and fourth subjects were historical events: the self-imposed exile of the Sisterhood of the Ring from Earth and the Great Schism between Donner Almandar and his father Loden, when most of the technical knowledge of the Rulers of Earth left Earth aboard the fleet Donner Almandar had built at Donnertown.

Cain browsed through the pages. The text was moderately interesting; it contained information that Cain had not seen in any other texts on the Schism, concerning the progress of the debate that had begun in 221, when T'Pau's People learned to heal themselves through the power of the Light, and had blossomed in the following decade, when a Ruler who was now dead discovered that the same technique could effectively prevent aging. Almost immediately—only ten years after that climactic discovery—the Great Schism took place; the Tribunal formally decided to destroy the youthbooster factories because T'Pau's People no longer needed them. The response was predictable, of course. Reading the man's writings, Cain felt clearly the horror that had struck Donner Almandar upon the implementation of that decision. Donner took some sixty percent of T'Pau's People and some eighty percent of the rest of the population of the Valley and went south with them to Donnertown. The testimonials shed considerable light on *how* the decisions that had led to the Schism had been reached; under other circumstances Cain would have found it fascinating.

Now there was no time.

Cain touched the button marked "Page," and the screen reformed with the image of a map. The map was of the Earth, dated 244 A.T.F., and did not differ very greatly from the maps of the modern Earth. The Great Dam had already been built—it was shown on the map—and the One Ocean had risen far enough that the outlines of the land approached the outlines Cain was familiar with.

The map contained one thing that no map Cain had ever seen before did. A small star, at the edge of the Glowing Desert, was inscribed with the words *Donner's Town.*

Cain stared at the map. This was the twenty-second text about the Great Schism that he had searched; he'd started to wonder if the books on the Censored list were themselves censored. He did not dare print out a page from a Censored book; instead he fixed the map in his mind so that he could not forget it, and continued with the text.

Perhaps half an hour before Cain was due to go on duty, the Ruler Alber shimmered into existence in the reading room.

Cain had enough warning that Alber was coming. He closed the file he'd been reading and had opened one more innocuous by the time Alber ceased glowing. "Lord Alber," he said politely, not looking up from the terminal. "What may I do for you?"

Alber grinned at Cain. It struck Cain as an even more unpleasant expression than the Ruler's normal look of aggressive self-pity. "You can answer some questions for me, Cain."

Cain did not blink. "Surely." He struck the "Page" key as though he were still reading.

"Did you know, Cain, that every Ruler has a different password for gaining access to the Library computer?"

"Oh?" Cain lifted an eyebrow. "Actually, my lord, no, I did not know that."

Alber chuckled. "I didn't think so. And I'll bet you didn't know that when you're signed on to the computer—with my password—I can't get on."

"Oh." Cain stood slowly. "I'm afraid I didn't know that, either. So, what happens now?"

"Well, that's a good question." Alber could not seem to stop smiling. "I suspect even your good friend Loga will be upset with you when he learns about what you've been doing, eh? I've only been monitoring you for the last hour or so; once we've polled the computer for its records of every book that's been accessed under my password in the last quarter or so, I think there might be sufficient reason to have you executed."

Cain thought swiftly. In that instant he had already decided to kill Alber. When he spoke it was with the most perfect seriousness of which he was capable. "So . . . even you think I've got more to fear from Loga than yourself?"

"What?" The smile left Alber. "Explain yourself!"

Cain shrugged, taking a step toward Alber. "I mean only that it does not surprise me that you've decided to leave the handling of this matter up to Lord Loga." Cain thought about it for several seconds before he said it. "It's a shame you haven't the guts to do it yourself."

The glow covered Alber, and in that instant, for the first time, he actually resembled what Cain thought a Ruler should be. Cain was reminded strongly of the first time he had ever seen a Ruler, when the Lady Elyssa had come to take Misha away. Alber slapped Cain, twice, as hard as he was able. Cain tasted blood inside his mouth. He stood motionless, staring straight forward. Alber was screaming at him, a swift tumble of words that Cain did not even listen to. Alber struck him again, and the blow jolted Cain down to his shoes.

Enough. He did not even think about the action; he simply *did* it, as Loukas had taught him. Time slowed around him, and in the next instant Alber struck at him again. He leaned out of the way of the blow, brushed Alber's arm aside, and kicked Alber in the kneecap. He heard the sound of the bone cracking clearly.

Alber shrieked, a sound composed of equal parts fear and rage, and vanished before he could strike ground.

Cain took a quick step forward. He felt *something;* Alber was not far away. He made for the door, and Alber appeared before him, a knife in his hand, the leg Cain had kicked healed in the instantaneous way only Rulers could heal themselves. He leaned in and touched Cain with the knife, a long slash on Cain's forearm. The glow never left him; he vanished instantly, and a cut stroked along Cain's shoulder. Cain whirled, and the Ruler was gone again, and the cut took him high on the cheek.

Cain stood without moving. The knife flickered against his skin, touched him again and again. He waited, waited for the moment to come, and then when he felt the hot touch of the knife at the side of his neck he *moved* backward with blinding speed, right hand extended and fingers stiffened. He felt his fingertips touch Alber's windpipe and continued, pushing backward until suddenly the flesh was gone and he was lunging back against empty air.

Alber appeared again, standing just before Cain, the bloody knife still in his hand. His eyes were wide with shock. He dropped the knife and reached for his throat with both hands. Cain sank back against the wall, and sat. Alber staggered forward two steps and collapsed to his knees; Cain sat, watching him, as the Ruler Alber pitched forward onto his face. He was still grasping his neck as though he were attempting to strangle himself, and succeeding.

His body twitched for perhaps half a minute before it finally spasmed once, wildly, and went limp.

Cain was not certain how long he had sat there with the body before it finally occurred to him that he should do something about it. He thought briefly about trying to leave the Library, walk undetected through Parliament, take the monorail down to Goldriver, and flee to—where? After several seconds of thought he shook his head and decided to surrender himself instead. He got up, carefully cleared away the book he had been reading, and turned the terminal off.

His cuts were starting to hurt.

The first Workers he approached did not believe him; after he showed them Alber's body, they went into hysterics. Finally Cain found a Ruler in one of the Library's reading rooms. He knocked on the open door, and when the Ruler looked up, he entered and knelt. "My lady?"

The Ruler was nobody whom Cain knew; she examined him curiously. "Yes? Why are you bothering me?"

"My lady, I've killed the Ruler Alber."

The Ruler stared at him.

"My lady?" Cain looked up at her. "Forgive me, but I'm not certain what to do now. In Eastmarch I would surrender to the legate, but I don't think there is one in Parliament. Is there?"

The Ruler continued to stare at him in shock.

Oh, hell, thought Cain, and reached out. *Loga!*

Cain? What is it?

I've killed a Ruler, Loga.

Cain sensed a moment's amused disbelief and then, suddenly, a pair of words in a language he did not know: *Te rashia, you're serious!*

Cain glanced at the Ruler, sitting there with a book opened, pages fluttering in the faint breeze from the ventilator. She had not moved since being told he'd killed Alber. *Maybe two.*

• 3 •

Cain had not even known that there were prison cells in Parliament.

The cell was small; wide enough to lie down and sleep in, but no more. There was a toilet in the opposite corner. The cell was bisected by a monocrystal barrier, very like the one in the room of the Test.

A pair of ventilators kept the air moving through the cell. There was no entrance into the cell itself; there was no opening in the barrier at all. A pair of Rulers, trained in hand-to-hand combat by Loga himself, each one holding him by one arm, had jumped through with him and left him there. A female Ruler whom Cain did not know came twice a day and transferred through a meal for him, taking at the same time the tray from the previous meal.

The days stretched on. Knowing the Rulers as he did, Cain assumed that they found no reason to hurry in determining what to do with him, and because he could do nothing about it, he refrained from worrying.

Sunlight did not reach the cell; Cain knew only by the telepathic timecast when the days changed. Six days had passed when the Ruler Gabriel came for him, manacled Cain's hands behind him, and without further word of explanation took him away.

They appeared at one end of a long, mirrored hall. Immediately behind them there was a doorway by which a Worker might have entered; before them stretched what seemed an infinity of reflecting panes.

"Walk with me," said the Ruler Gabriel quietly. He took a step down the way, without waiting for Cain, and after a moment Cain followed him. Gabriel's melodious baritone flowed smoothly, the words seeming to come at Cain from all sides. "As you walk this path, remember. There was a time, Cain, when our survival was uncertain, when the Light flowed in us but weakly. We fought, Cain, merely to live. But, see, we have remained while all else has passed by, and see, we have grown powerful. The Earth is ours; there is nothing that walks on its surface or flies through its airs or swims in its Ocean that may harm us.

"And yet the reverse is not true. Where there is power, there is responsibility. My actions, Cain, they are mine; they are not imposed upon me from outside, for there is no power in the world so great that it could so impose its will upon me. You are a Worker, Cain, and yet unlike other Workers, your actions, Cain, they are *yours;* they are not imposed upon you from outside, for there is no power in all the world so great that it can impose its will upon you.

"Shortly you will stand in the Chamber at Parliament, before the Tribunal of the Rulers of Earth. You are the first Worker to do so, Cain. Workers did not build the Chamber; we raised it up ourselves, with our own hands we laid its foundations, shaped the stone that became its walls, and brought the Light within it."

They came to the end of the corridor, and Cain stood motionless, hands bound, waiting for what would come next.

"The Chamber is only a place, Cain, nonetheless. A place that any Ruler may appear in without ceremony, for it belongs to us all. T'Pau Almandar understood this." Gabriel turned to Cain. "Yet the Creator T'Pau said to us, Cain, 'Build you the hall I have described, and line it with mirrors as I have shown you; and time to time you shall walk that way, and see yourself in the mirrors, and reflect upon yourselves.' The Creator, Cain, had a sense of humor." Gabriel's lips quirked upward in a brief smile. "And then she said, Cain, 'Do not forget.' And she killed herself because she had."

Cain said dryly, "Thank you. I will treasure your words."

"She made a mistake, Cain. She gave us an extra gene and made it impossible for us to merge back with the rest of humanity. In all the tumbling years that have passed since her death, Cain, uncounted have been the numbers of the Workers who have died for that mistake. I hope that you do not add to that number."

The Light bound itself to them.

They appeared on the debating floor in the Chamber at Parliament.

Cain looked about, curiously. He had seen holos of the Chamber before, but they had not served to convey the sheer magnificence of the place; in his young life Cain had not seen anything remotely like it.

There were more Rulers gathered there than he had ever seen before in one place—thousands at least. There was not an empty seat anywhere in the upper Chamber. Eleven seats ringed the edge of the debating floor; seated in those places were eight Rulers, whom Cain knew either personally or by reputation: the Rulers Elyssa, Selene, Michael, Athel, Maria, Calandra, Julian, and Loga. Three of the eleven Tribunal seats were empty. One had belonged to Alber, who was dead; Gabriel stood beside Cain, in the middle of the debating floor, and Loden Almandar stood behind the black spar of the podium.

No word was exchanged; Loden raised his arms, and the Light showered down upon the Chamber, the golden radiance flooding through the thronged building. Alone in the midst of the communion, Cain watched the ceremony transpire with an empty expression; he felt its presence, but in the midst of the outpouring, the Light did not touch him.

After a moment of silence had passed, Loden Almandar fixed his gaze on Cain. Behind Loden, Cain could see the entire Valley, spread out like a map. The view was astonishing.

Loden's voice struck out like a weapon. "Cain, you stand accused of the murder of the Ruler and Tribunal member Alber I'chai'andra. What say you?"

Cain was uncomfortably aware of being the focus of thousands of pairs of eyes, most of them clearly hostile. Their attention disturbed his concentration, made it hard to focus upon what was transpiring. Nonetheless, he cleared his mind as best he could and made his reply. "My lord, except that I dispute the word *murder*, I do not argue the fact of the event. As I admitted when I summoned Lord Loga, I did kill the Ruler Alber."

It was a blunt, single word.

"Why?"

"My lord, in self-defense. The Ruler Alber and I were arguing, and he struck me several times. After the third blow I struck him back. He brought the Light to him and vanished; he returned with a knife and cut me as you have seen. I bear the marks still. I could not even flee, else I would have. His last cut touched me on the neck, Lord Loden, not a centimeter from the jugular vein. When next he appeared, I delivered him a blow to the throat that crushed his windpipe, and of that blow he died. My lord, so it happened."

Loden nodded. "Cain, you are not the first Worker in history to receive a blow—even an unearned one—from an angry Ruler. Most Workers have the sense to endure the blows. You are not a fool, Cain, and I do not think you are a hothead. Why did you strike back?"

"Because, my lord," said Cain evenly, "of overwhelming pride. I am not a *thing* to be used in whatever fashion a Ruler may choose. The Ruler Alber made the mistake of thinking otherwise, and for that mistake he died. I am a Worker, my lord. The Workers are my people, and I do not disown them. But I am first a man, no less so than any person in this Chamber. I stand by my deeds. If you strike me, my lord, I shall strike you back. It is the first law of living creatures, Loden Almandar, that they will defend themselves when threatened. You can kill me, and perhaps you will, but you cannot take from me the will to defend myself where I may."

"What do you think we should do with you, Cain?"

"Return me to my post in the Library." Cain turned slightly, hands manacled behind him, and looked around the Chamber at the Rulers who were watching him. "I have done nothing wrong."

"Gabriel," said Loden, "we have heard enough. Take Cain back to his cell. We will wait for your return before attempting a consensus."

The Ruler Gabriel bowed his head slightly. One hand touched Cain's shoulder. "I shall return shortly."

They vanished together.

Cain sat in his cell. In the afternoon, the Ruler Gabriel came to Cain and informed him that he would be brought before the Tribunal again in the morning.

With nothing else to do, Cain waited.

The day passed, and became night.

They flickered into existence in a cellar warehouse near the south end of the city of Parliament.

Selene said irritably, "What is it you have to show us, Loga, which could not wait until morning?"

Her father stood behind her, expressionless.

Loga glanced quickly between the two of them. "This." They had materialized in front of a huge brace. In the poor light, it looked as though there were nothing at all in between the brace's grips; Loga rapped against the empty space, and his knuckles struck a barrier. "It's the replacement for the wall Cain shattered Testing."

Loden sighed. "So? My daughter is right, Loga. It's late."

Loga said carefully, "I believe it is generally agreed that I am among the more powerful Rulers in my ability to control the Light— am I not?"

They were intelligent enough; Loga saw them both get his point.

"Guys, I can't break this. I've tried for a couple of hours, and I can't do it. It shivers, and once when I made myself incredibly dizzy concentrating, I made it ring like a bell."

"So," said Selene, "Cain shattered one. Are you afraid he'll break the barrier in his cell? If that's your worry, I wouldn't concern myself, Loga. He was unconscious for three days last time."

"That's not my point. My point is," said Loga intensely, "that he did it—and I can't." He gestured to them. "You try, if you like. Or yourself, Loden. Break it." He walked around to the other side of the barrier. "What is it makes us Rulers? The ability to control the Light? Or is it just the ability to deny *them* youthbooster?"

They simply stared at him.

"Break the barrier, Loden. Break the barrier," he whispered, "and live forever."

Loga vanished, and left them alone with the unbroken barrier.

It was Winter 88, 1207 A.T.F.

They brought him to stand in the center of the Chamber, in the center of the circle of Rulers, once again. Again the Chamber was packed, and again there were three empty seats among the eleven reserved for the Tribunal.

Cain stood silently, with the Ruler Gabriel a pace behind him. There was no raising of the Light; Cain guessed that the ceremony had been performed before he was brought to them. That boded nothing good.

Loden wasted no time in ceremony. From behind the podium he spoke as soon as Cain had oriented himself. "Worker Cain, you have been found to be guilty of the murder of the Ruler Alber. It is the judgment of this Tribunal that two days hence, on the first day of Spring, you be exiled from the town square at Goldriver, into the Glowing Desert, so that by your removal from the company of Rulers and Workers alike you may be rendered unable to cause further harm."

Cain absorbed the words slowly.

They were going to kill him.

He was a young man; the thought of his own death was something he could not quite credit. It was not even the thought of death that shook him the most; it was simply the very idea that the most powerful beings in his world had decided to take his life from him.

For, though the Rulers might speak of "exile," and thus preserve for themselves the fiction of mercy, an unprotected man would die within a day from the radiation in the Glowing Desert, still lethal better than twelve centuries after the Fire.

Oddly, it was the thought of Loukas that brought Cain the strength to raise his head and meet the hostile glares of the crowd without flinching. Loukas would not have wanted Cain to show weakness before the Rulers; and therefore Cain would not.

He became aware that the assembled Rulers were waiting. For what? Cain stood silently, looking around the immediate circle of Rulers. Truly, they were not, for the most part, even acceptable telepaths; most of them Cain could read like a book. Where he did not find hostility he found, at best, resignation. Loga alone Cain could not read at all; the bright blue eyes, the lines around the man's mouth, held nothing at all for Cain.

Cain came back, at last, to Loden. The silence had stretched through a minute, unbroken. Cain said mildly, "Are you waiting for me to say something?"

"Twice since the coming of our people to this Valley," said Loden, "a Ruler has slain another Ruler. In both instances we granted them the right to speak after they had been judged. It seems fitting to us that we extend the same courtesy to you."

"May I ask a question of you, my lord Loden?"

The ancient Ruler nodded. "You may."

"Is there anything I can say that will persuade this Tribunal to reverse its judgment?"

Loden Almandar actually smiled. "I am afraid there is no likelihood of that."

Cain nodded. "Thank you. I appreciate your frankness." He took a deep breath. "I do, in fact, appreciate your concern for ethics, even while judging my life forfeit. But then, that is something at which you have had considerable practice—ethics become an art to justify the killing of folk who do not have the power to harm you." With a small part of his attention Cain saw a startled expression touch Loga, and vanish; his voice grew stronger. "You speak of ethics. The teaching of ethics is one of the primary reasons, so I have been told, for the existence of Academy. For nine hundred and thirty-six years, ever since the Great Schism, the Rulers of Earth have kept as slaves a people as noble, as wise, and in their own way as talented as any of T'Pau's People. Because they cannot do a simple thing; because they cannot control the Light as do T'Pau's People; because of this, the Rulers of Earth have denied them youthbooster."

Cain paused at that point. He had been almost certain of his response; he got it. A babble of sound and thought exploded around him, a rising wave of reaction more hostile and no less severe than that Loga had exhibited on the shores of the lake T'Pau. He stood in the center of the Chamber and rode out the pandemonium.

When it was quiet enough, Cain addressed the Tribunal Elder. "May I continue?"

"Where did you learn that word?"

Cain turned slightly and grinned directly at Loga. Surely nobody in all that vast crowd missed it. "Does it matter, my lord Loden?"

"Perhaps not. You may continue, Worker."

"Thank you. There is, Rulers, a contradiction here. I know you are aware of it. I know what fraction of your writings on ethics has gone to explaining away the contradiction. Erebion exists as a tribute to your willingness to honestly face the grim realities of your decision to deny youthbooster to the Workers. There is only one way for you to justify this to yourself, is there not? For you to allow Workers to die so, you must believe, deeply believe, that we are not your equals, that in some way our right to *live* is less real than the rights of the Rulers to their power and their security." Cain said quietly, so that those in the higher tiers of the seats must strain to listen, "The power of the Light is an astonishing thing. Its control must be a source of wondrous pride to you, and rightly so. And yet—it is only power. Your own philosophers tend to reject the notion that there is any inherent morality to be found in the exercise of that power.

"It is," said Cain again, "only power. And therefore your rule is based not in moral right, but only on the fact that you *can* rule, that there is no force on this Earth sufficient to prevent you. There is in the Light a great power, for healing, for building. Yet there is also in it a great power for destruction; and it is that power that has subjugated a people as deserving of freedom as your own for nearly a millennium.

"In all that time," said Cain of Eastmarch, "the Workers have persisted. Despite you they have survived as a people, they have retained a dignity; as Erebion shows, they have retained their courage, and, with knowledge, their will to act. Therefore there is some greater force than the force that you are capable of wielding; and if force is the only basis of law that you acknowledge then there is some higher law than the law of the Rulers of Earth.

"To that law I adhere.

"I reject you. I reject your authority.

"I have no more to say."

They took him back to his cell.

Loga came to see him late that afternoon. He did not use the door, of course; he shimmered into existence on the other side of the cell barrier.

Cain was half asleep on the cell's cot; he sat up at the edge of the cot, yawning slightly. His greeting was not particularly civil. "What do you want?"

There was a single chair on the other side of the barrier. Loga sank into it, and sat slumped in the chair. His depression was honest, and evident. "I'm sorry, Cain."

"*I'm* going to die, and *you're* sorry?" Cain shook his head. "Go to hell."

"In Goldriver, last night," said Loga, "somebody tacked up hundreds of posters about you, about the fact of Alber's murder. We were trying to keep it quiet. There was a very good chance, Cain, that you'd have been allowed to return to your post at the Library, that eventually you'd have been allowed to take the Test again. But the posters changed that. They didn't mention youthbooster, but they hardly needed to. The Rulers can't allow it to be known that a Worker killed a Ruler and was not punished for it. You're right, yes, the Rulers govern through force. But things aren't as black and white as you'd like it, either. We simply aren't the villains you'd like us to be. We've kept a peace the likes of which this sorry old world has never seen; we've prevented another Fire War from destroying us and all our works utterly. You've studied Rational Ethics; the first precept is that intelligence must exist to contemplate ethics, for without the existence of intelligence there can be no vantage from which to contemplate questions of ethics. Therefore the survival of intelligence is the first good. Our rule has prevented another Fire War like the one that nearly wiped out self-aware intelligence on this planet. That has been, bluntly put, a *good* thing."

Cain cocked his head slightly to one side. "Eloquently said. You argue well, though I'm not sure why you bother."

"Cain, were the posters necessary? Were you looking to blow this into something that could not be settled quietly?"

Cain shrugged. "I didn't place the posters, Loga. I was in a cell. And before you say it, I don't know who did place them either. That's the truth. Until you told me, I didn't know it had been done." He thought about it a moment and then looked up again. "But I'm not sorry for it. I only wish the damned posters had mentioned youthbooster. I doubt you'd have razed Goldriver the way you razed Erebion, to prevent spread of the news." He paused. "Of the truth. There is this about the truth, Loga. I misdoubt it is any more powerful, in and of itself, than a lie; lies are believed so easily by so many. But because it is the truth, it can be rediscovered when the lie is long forgotten. Long-lived as you are, you will appreciate the power of time in this regard."

"Cain," Loga whispered, "you could have lived forever."

"Live forever? With the likes of you?" Cain stared at Loga. "Damn you for the hypocrite you are. I'd rather die."

Loga's voice held obvious pain. "You're getting your wish."

Cain laughed bitterly. "Sometimes things work out."

The days slid past. Winter 89 passed, and Winter 90; Winter 91 was of course a SunDay, and the hush that had fallen over all of Parliament, and all of Goldriver as well, seemed to reach Cain in his cell. He spent the day lying quietly on his cot, remembering the people whom he had known, saying good-bye to the memories. He expected to die the day following; and while the thought did not frighten him, he did not feel prepared to die.

There was so much left to do.

Not entirely to his surprise, he found that he could not sleep; the idea of passing what few hours remained to him in an oblivion that would soon enough be permanent was revolting.

The night crept away.

Just before midnight the door to Cain's cell opened, very slightly. A single figure in a traveler's cloak, hood pulled far forward, slipped in through the door, and the door shut quickly behind him.

Cain sat up on his pallet, somewhat wearily. "By the Light, is it too much to ask to be allowed to get some sleep before you all kill me?"

The voice sent a chill through him like nothing he had heard in six years. "I'm afraid it is." The man pulled the hood back from his face, and Loukas said simply, "Well, this is a damn foolish thing you've done."

· 4 ·

Cain stood, staring at him in wild amazement. "Loukas? By the Light . . ." His voice was rising.

"Calm yourself!" said Loukas sharply. "If you were not taught the proper breathing exercises at Academy, you surely learned them from *me.*"

The tone penetrated. Cain stood silently, until he could control his pulse again. His voice was almost steady. There were too many hundreds of things he wanted to say or ask, all at once. Finally he said only, "Hello, Loukas."

The man moved forward, until he was right before the monocrystal barrier. "Hello, Cain. Let me look at you."

Cain searched the face in return. The same warm eyes, the same well-tended beard and mustache; he felt the years slide away, and for one very strange moment felt *young* again for the first time since the Ruler Selene had taken him to Academy. "Loukas, you haven't changed." Cain took a step forward, until the barrier blocked him, and realized with slight but real shock that he was taller than Loukas.

Loukas seemed to be realizing the same thing. "You have, Cain. You're not a child anymore."

Cain hardly heard him. "By the Light, Loukas, it's good to see you. I've missed having you to talk to."

"Oh?" Loukas lifted an eyebrow. His voice was dry. "Have you, now?"

"Yeah." Cain heard the thought that Loukas did not say aloud, and smiled. "I've missed *you*."

Loukas nodded thoughtfully, and then grinned. "Fair enough. I've missed you, too. I wished to come to you, you must know that, but it wasn't safe. Loga fastened on you too quick; by the time I'd arrived in Goldriver he was watching you almost constantly." The grin did not fade. "After a while, I came to wonder whether you would even really want to see me."

Cain flinched as though he'd been struck. "How could you think that?"

"Six years had passed, Cain. You were a boy the last time I saw you; you're a man now, and such a man as the world does not often see. I'd been your teacher, and your friend, but there is not much left for me to teach you, and I was not certain the friendship would survive exposure to the Rulers. Power is seductive, Cain, and it's a drug that I think would please you."

The words troubled Cain for a moment, before he shrugged them off. "Well, you were wrong. I'm glad to see you. I could never change so much I would not be, Loukas."

"Okay." Loukas said nothing more, but stood there, smiling at Cain, eyes roving over the young man's form. "By the Light, I can't get over how you've grown."

Cain let him look, and said after a moment, "There's a problem. Unfortunately . . ."

"Yes?"

"Our reunion is liable to be short."

"Oh, yes."

"You see, they're going to kill me tomorrow."

Loukas nodded. "Perhaps we can do something about that."

Cain let out a breath he was not even aware he had been holding. "I was hoping you were going to say that. Loukas?"

"Yes?"

"I found Donnertown. I know where it is."

Loukas' grin grew even wider. "Sit down, then." He appropriated the lone chair, on the other side of the barrier. "Let's talk."

They spoke for only two hours before Loukas said he must go. Most of that two hours did not concern the immediate problem of arranging for Cain to survive the exile of the Glowing Desert; that problem Loukas solved simply enough at the beginning of their conversation. "The Glowing Desert," he said, "is not so hostile as men believe. I rode through it once, with a personal Shield set to wide dispersion; it kept both me and my horse alive long enough to get through the desert before we died of thirst. You won't have a horse, so you won't be able to get through the desert as quickly; but by the same token, your Shield will need to protect only you, rather than the greater bulk of your horse. It'll last longer, I'm saying." Loukas withdrew a personal Shield from within his cloak.

Cain had seen them before; a Ruler who intended to spend any significant time outside the Valley wore one as a matter of course. Even a small amount of radiation damage to neural tissue was irreversible, and over the course of centuries those small amounts added up. The personal Shields protected Rulers from that danger. "How will you get it to me? There's no opening in this damn barrier, Loukas. They even have a Ruler jump my meals across it."

Loukas glanced at Cain. "As you say. Bide a moment." His eyes dropped shut, and his breathing evened into a gentle rhythm. The Shield held between his hands began to glow, not with the orange radiance that meant it was working, but with the warm yellow-white incandescence of the Light. Cain watched in disbelief, almost unable to credit his eyes. The Light built slowly, creepingly, pooling between Loukas' hands.

There came a thunderclap as the Shield disappeared, and air rushed in to replace the space it had filled, and a smaller clap as it appeared in the air in front of Cain, a meter above the ground.

Purely by reflex, Cain caught the Shield before it could fall to the floor of the cell.

Sitting on the other side of the barrier, Loukas was nearly drenched with sweat. "I must be getting old. I swear that didn't used to be so hard."

"Loukas?"

"Yes?"

Cain turned the Shield over in his hands. "Loukas, when you were

—when the Rulers said you had failed the Test and sent you home to Erebion—could you do this then?"

Loukas produced a cloth from inside his cloak and wiped his face dry. "Yes."

"I see."

Loukas shrugged. "But it's hard for me, Cain, very hard. I can't move myself; I mass too much. They weren't impressed; any Ruler child can do better." He put the cloth away. "I suspect you could do that, Cain, and perhaps better. I heard what you did to the barrier in the room of the Test."

Cain turned his attention to the Shield. "So . . . I turn this thing on just before I'm to be transported into exile? You're sure they can't stop the sending at that point?"

"No. But it's a reasonable gamble. That's an awful damn lot of power to be raised up without sending it somewhere."

"My hands are liable to be bound."

Loukas repeated, "I've heard what you did to the barrier in the room of the Test." He chuckled. "If you can't snap the chain of a pair of iron manacles, you can bloody well fry in the Glowing Desert."

Cain nodded. "As you say." He tucked the small Shield within the waistband of his breeches and covered it with his shirt. It was completely hidden; unless they searched him, they would not discover the Shield, and Cain doubted they would search him—after all, they would think nobody but a Ruler could have gotten anything to him, and no Ruler would.

They talked, after that, of the things Cain had seen and learned in his time in the city of Parliament. They talked, as much as Cain could allow himself, of Ellian; and about her, Loukas simply listened, and did not waste his time trying to tell Cain what his mistakes had been. Cain knew what they were, and told Loukas about them, not so much in what he said as in what he did not say about the woman.

He did not say he had loved her.

They discussed Loga briefly; they had both of them, during their years at Academy, enjoyed the same sort of relationship with the wild Ruler, and things Cain had not understood about the mutant came clear in the course of their talks. Loga was, as Loukas pointed out, alone as no human had ever been in all the history of the world; not one of

T'Pau's People, not a Worker, nor yet a barbarian such as the silver-eyes from whom Donner Almandar had rescued him.

Loukas told him, briefly, about the events in Eastmarch in the year before Loukas had left. Not much had changed; Eric Malachor had died, and his eldest son taken over his duties. Siva received a proposal of marriage from the youngest son of a rather poor Merchant family, which was still being negotiated when Loukas had left. All else was essentially unchanged; and that, five years old, was the most recent news Loukas had for Cain. Their conversation ended abruptly; Loukas looked up suddenly. "The second hour's nearly done. They'll be changing the guard outside your cell shortly. I have to leave before that happens; the Warrior replacing the night guard is not one of ours." He stood, closing his cloak about himself. He did not look at Cain. "I wish we had more time together, Cain. Still, if wishes were horses, we'd be belly-deep in horseshit, eh?" He finished lacing his cloak shut and turned back to Cain. "Live well, Cain."

Cain whispered, "Loukas."

Loukas looked away from him briefly. "I must go, lad. I'd hate to have to kill one of the Rulers come to see you before your execution." He turned back, almost unwillingly it seemed to Cain, and met Cain's eyes. "If I'm found here inside the buildings of Parliament itself . . . I've spent a long while placing people inside here. I can't endanger that."

"I'll do what you've said, Loukas."

"Good-bye, Cain."

Cain found it very hard to say the words. "Good-bye, Loukas."

Loukas did not leave. He stood looking through the barrier at Cain. It was as though he were waiting for something.

"Loukas?"

"Yes, Cain?"

"I . . ." Cain swallowed. ". . . Loukas, you are the only friend I have ever had."

Loukas' eyes closed, and he stood still a moment longer. Then he smiled, and there was no pain in the smile. He opened his eyes and said, "I understand." He brought the hood back up to cover his features, knocked quietly on the door behind him, and spoke the last words Cain ever heard from him.

"A martyr and a returning hero; I think that'll do it. Come back, Cain. Just come back, and it will all have been worth it."

He left swiftly, through the crack in the opening door.

After he had gone, Cain told the empty cell, "I love you."

· 5 ·

The day on which Cain was supposed to die dawned bright and beautifully clear.

Cain knew, because his sadistic morning guard made a point of telling him.

The day wore on slowly. The ceremony of banishment was not to take place until midday. Cain simply sat, and waited.

And waited.

Eventually they came for him.

The crowd came from all over the south end of the Valley, to see the spectacle of the murderer Cain's exile. Such a thing had not happened within living memory; the curious and the foolish flooded into Goldriver, filling the inns to bursting, sleeping in the streets and in the horse-drawn carts they had arrived in. They were still arriving that morning, on the first day of Spring, jostling for positions at the edge of the town square. The whipping post at the center of the square, where commoner sorts of criminals were punished for their crimes, was set up to receive Cain. Goldriver's entire contingent of Warriors was there, keeping the center of the square clear of Workers, so that the Rulers, when they came, might perform the sending without interruption from the gaping Workers.

The day was a glorious one, the skies an achingly clear blue, without clouds. The sun was bright and warm, and gentle breezes wandered through Goldriver with as much ease as the pickpockets moved through the crowds of Workers.

Goldriver was a Worker city; at noon the bells rang, five times. Before the final bell had ceased echoing through the town square, a group of some thirty persons simply appeared in the center of the square. The thunderclap of their appearance was huge; wind blasted away from them like a hurricane, buffeting the crowds at the edge of the square.

At first the watching Workers could not make out the murderer among the massed rank of the Rulers. Excited Workers called out the names of the Rulers they recognized, with as much familiarity as though the Rulers had been members of their own family. Loden, some called, and Loga, Elyssa and Selene and Gabriel—all were easily recognizable. It took the massed crowds of Workers some time before someone realized that the tall man walking beside Loden Almandar, for all his bearing suggested that he, and not the Rulers, controlled the situation, was in fact walking with his hands behind his back because they were chained so.

Many of them had brought rotten fruit and eggs for just that moment; unfortunately, the condemned man was surrounded by Rulers, who likely would not take kindly to being showered by the Worker's missed throws. Then the Rulers led Cain up to the platform atop which sat the whipping post and wrapped the links of the chains that bound his hands behind his back to the post. Then they descended from the platform, and many in the crowd let fly.

Perhaps a half dozen of the missiles reached their target; then the Tribunal Elder, Loden Almandar, flickered, vanished, and appeared on the platform with Cain. The Ruler looked around at them. It did not seem that he raised his voice, but somehow his voice was amplified so that it boomed like the voice of a Giant. *"You will stop that now."*

Cain endured it stoically; one egg had been truly foul, and the odor nearly made him sick right there on the platform.

In that same booming, artificially amplified voice, Loden said, *"We have come here today to punish the Worker Cain. He is convicted by his own words of the murder of the Ruler Alber, whom he came upon unawares and strangled in a fit of madness. Bear this day in mind as long as you live, for this is the fate of those who disobey the Rulers of Earth. We shall send him forth into the Glowing Desert, and there his skin shall peel from his muscles, and his muscles in time decay from his bones, until there is nothing left but the skeleton of the murderer. Bear this man's fate,"* said Loden Almandar, *"in mind."*

Standing immediately behind him, Cain said loudly enough for Loden to hear him, "Good advice, that." Something was moving, at the very edge of the crowd.

Loden Almandar touched a slight discoloration on the collar of his tunic, and when he turned to face Cain, his voice was normal again. "You had potential. I regret this, Cain."

Cain met the Ruler's eyes and gave him a hard grin. "Not as much as you're going to."

Loden nodded thoughtfully and backed away from him, out into the empty square where the other Rulers were waiting.

Cain endured, waiting, standing in the village square, while the Rulers, ignoring the yells and cheers from the crowd, began the summoning of the Light. Only Loden did not join in the raising, but stood watching Cain. Cain felt the hot tingle of their power, assembling itself in the square before him. A sending such as they were performing, where the object must be sent without a Ruler to guide its passage through the otherworld, was vastly more difficult than a traditional jump. Fifteen Rulers, working together, took as long to prepare for it as Loukas had taken to send the Shield through the cell barrier.

A silent voice reached out to Cain. *Now.*

While the power of the Light grew in front of Cain, Cain summoned what power was his own and concentrated on the chains restraining him. The manacles on his wrists snapped cleanly. Without trying to hide it, Cain brought his hands around, to show the masses the broken chains. The roar of the crowd took a quantum leap upward.

The Rulers raised the Light and brought it down upon him, and as the Light grew around him, pulsing and sharp, Cain spoke to Loden as though they were the only two in the square.

He met the old Ruler's gaze head-on. He shaped the words silently, concentrating upon the sending with all his might; Loden would never have heard Cain's voice over the roar of the crowd. *I'll be back.*

Perhaps Loden read his lips; perhaps the sending reached him. The Ruler simply shook his head *no.* His thoughts touched Cain clearly. *I don't think so, Cain.*

Cain waited until what he judged was nearly the last possible moment and then, without pause, withdrew the smooth oval of the Shield from beneath his tunic and turned it on. The Shield caught the glow of the gathering Light, reflected it in a fierce glare back at the crowd of Rulers and Workers.

Loden understood instantly what was happening. Cain could almost see the swift thoughts as they passed like clouds across the surface of Loden's face. His first impulse would be to stop the sending, but it was already far too late for that. The other Rulers could not have ceased the gathering of the Light had their lives depended on it. Cain watched Loden as a slow, almost glacial anger descended upon him; and Cain smiled grimly. In almost the same instant Cain saw Loga shake himself free of the rest of the Rulers and come forward to join Loden, with a terrible knowledge come to him in that moment.

The glare was very fierce now. Cain could barely see his tormentors. From the edges of the crowd a tall man in dark clothing was making his way through the press, forging steadily to where the Rulers Loden and Loga stood watching Cain.

The crowd had grown momentarily silent at the sudden unexpected glare, and Cain's last words to Loden rang clearly across the square.

"I'll be back, you son of a bitch."

Cain's last sight was of the man whom the world knew as Artemis of Erebion. Several Rulers who had attempted to stop him lay dead in the square; light blade in hand, he was crossing the square to where Loga and Loden stood.

And then it was over, and Cain of Eastmarch was gone before he could see how it was that Artemis of Erebion met his death.

The youngest children in that crowd were old when he finally returned.

· 6 ·

. . . *and so he wandered, children, wandered through the ruins of the world. On that first night, after killing Artemis, the Lords of Light hunted him, and on several nights thereafter, their forms flickering into existence over the Glowing Desert and blowing away again like candles in the wind. But they did not find him, for it was not Cain's destiny to die at the hands of the Rulers; and in time the Lords of Light fooled themselves into believing that Cain had died in the Glowing Desert, and ceased to search for him. Even I, who did not believe he had died, did no more than save a belt buckle and a silver bracelet; Artemis' dying request of me was that I give them to Cain, and in time I did so.*

How he survived the Great Desert I do not know, but survive it he did, and began his own hunt, for what was, by then, the nearly mythical

THE RING

Donnertown, where Donner Almandar lifted himself, and those who would follow him, away from the Earth in a fleet of starships the likes of which this tired world had never seen before and never will again. For in Donnertown, as nowhere else on the planet, could be found the tools Cain desired: machines, and knowledge, and what was, for him, the key to everything—the blood-burning youthbooster. . . .

. . . what? Oh, child, of course he found it.

He did not believe, pitted as he was one man against the entire might of the Lords of Light, that he could not succeed, though any sensible man would have told him so.

Yes, child, you are correct. He was quite mad.

He was also, sadly, right.

PART TWO

The Ring of Light

Senta and Solan

The Year 1284 After the Fire

• 1 •

The antigrav crane lifted the huge slab of white and gold marble into position and lowered it gently into the alloy guides. The crane left the slab there and was going back for the ferrocrete panel to which the marble would be bonded, when the marble slab cracked and fell, slowly and with as much majesty as a Giant, and with much the same effect; it shattered when it struck the ground. None of them had any construction experience; Allain, the Worker with the misfortune to be in charge of that group, stood looking at the mess, and then went in search of the supervisor.

He listened for the sound of swearing.

". . . air too bloody thin . . ."

The work area stretched out across nearly fifteen square kilometers, a patchwork of dirt and building materials, of ferrocrete and filler cement, hardening beneath the bright false suns. Stacks of marble and lumber reached ten and fifteen meters into the sky. Near three thousand Workers, men and women both, labored there.

". . . suns too damn hot, and too bloody *many* of them . . ."

Artificial suns glittered in low orbit, warming the planet. On Earth the Rulers had divided one full day into ten hours; this new planet turned on its axis in just over nine of those hours. The orbits of the artificial suns were designed so that they made a complete circuit of the equator once every four and a half hours, so that they matched the period in which the planet's sun was in the sky. The planet was set much too far back from its sun for comfort. The sun was a mild G-2 star not quite forty light years from Earth, and similar to Sol. The planet itself, though very like Earth in size and gravity, had been, only ten years ago, a cold world utterly without animal life, with an atmosphere similar to that of Earth over a billion years in its past. What plants had existed were simple things resembling mosses and ferns.

". . . too *heavy* . . ."

That much, at least, was undeniable. The planet's gravity was 1.15 times that of Earth; not uncomfortable, really, unless one was engaged in heavy labor.

As the Workers were.

Allain came upon a group of some fifteen of his fellows, standing around a flooded basin where plumbing was being laid. Every person there cast a total of five shadows, one from each of the four false suns, one from the real one. Water sprayed into the air, came down in a blessedly cool rain.

Perhaps that was why nobody was in any hurry to do anything about the disaster; and even the supervisor—a man of middle years and florid complexion who went by the name of Pauli, who had been a house builder back on Earth before the work crews had taken him away from Earth, along with most of the rest of the province of Turrin—even he, standing there with a video tablet in his hand that showed a section of the blueprints, merely continued with his litany of complaints:

". . . and to top it all, as the Light shines on my words, this marble is *shit!* Maybe it's beautiful and maybe it ain't, but it doesn't work the way they want to use it! Maybe the wood we build with is ugly —but at least wood don't shatter," Pauli finished in disgust.

"Sir?"

The supervisor turned on Allain and screamed, red-faced. "*What?*"

Allain eyed the supervisor. "I've got a problem, sir. You want to listen to it?"

Standing in the drizzle, water dripping down his cheeks, Pauli visibly bit off his immediate reply. "What is it?"

"We're trying to mount a marble facing so we can bond the ferrocrete, but the marble keeps cracking before we can get the ferrocrete slabs in place."

Pauli closed his eyes and stood stock-still. He counted to ten once, and then again, and when he opened his eyes to look at the mess his voice was almost controlled. "Try mounting the ferrocrete slabs first."

"Oh." After a second, Allain nodded. "That would work, wouldn't it?"

The supervisor said gently, dangerously, "Yes." After Allain had left, Pauli shook his head. "They give me Giant-sized equipment to work with, and idiots with midget-sized brains to run the equipment." He screamed at the Workers standing around him. "Is it any *wonder* things are behind schedule?"

"So poorly you're treated, Pauli." His assistant, with a slight motion of his head, gestured up the hill behind them to where the watchers came to observe when they had a mind. "Why don't you discuss it with them? You're lucky, they're together."

"Oh, hell." Pauli turned a full hundred and eighty degrees, and there, at the top of the hill looking down upon the work area, were a woman on a horse and a Giant dressed in pale, flowing green robes. "How long have they been there?"

"I just noticed them, myself." His assistant paused and said, "Pauli, we ought to do something about the water. I can *hear* Rome, in that booming damn voice of his—'You mean we built this whole mechanical heaven and you can't stop a leak in the garden?' "

"Rome's an ass," said Pauli irritably. "Even for a Giant."

"Pauli!" His assistant's eyes went wide with fear.

"What *now?*"

The Worker spoke in a panicked whisper. "The Ruler Senta is up there with him! They say the Rulers can read minds!"

"It wouldn't take a mind reader," Pauli said, "to guess how we feel about them. Somebody, please," he said wearily, "go down to the water main, and turn the bitch off."

After two solid days spent touring an entire planet turned into a playhouse, it was actually a pleasure to see something that was not *perfect.*

The Ruler Senta, daughter of the Elder Ruler Loden and the Ruler Elyssa, laughed until there were tears in her eyes. She sat easily astride her palomino near the edge of the drop, right leg draped casually over the saddle horn, enjoying the cool breeze from behind them. In the distance to their rear rose a city of gleaming silver and gold and ivory: New Parliament. When she found her voice, she said, "It's like watching one of the old movies, Rome! Charlie Chaplin, or the Three Stooges." Under the light from the suns, her pale blonde hair gleamed. A Ruler or a Worker would have found her desirable, attractive by virtue of a swift smile and quick laughter, easy enthusiasms, and a figure more appropriate to an athlete than to one of the indolent Rulers. Had she been told she resembled her mother, she would have disagreed— her feelings for her mother were, at best, mixed—but she would not have been displeased.

She was still, even by the standards of the short-lived Workers, quite young. "Have you recorded them at work?"

The Giant Rome, standing slightly behind her, shook his massive head. His voice, gentle and incredibly deep, drifted down to her. "No. I don't see the need." Fully four meters tall, twice the height of even a tall man, he stood well back from the drop overlooking the work camp, which would soon be a garden of surpassing loveliness. Simply tripping could be fatal to a Giant, as their vast weight came crashing down to impact the ground with bone-shattering force. "Whenever we do not supervise them personally, they behave so. They are an irresponsible, lazy people." Beneath the flowing green robes, Rome's legs were solid columns, tapering only slightly before becoming feet. His slightly mis-shapen skull sat atop shoulders so broad and muscle-corded they were more reminiscent of a wild animal than of a sentient being. His fore-arms were larger than a strong man's thighs.

Rome's people were one of the more gruesome leftovers of the Fire Wars; out of the union of genegineers designing for a superior race of warriors, and the inevitable mutations to the genome that had fol-lowed in the days after the first world's destruction, had the Giants been born. In military bunkers beneath the North Pole, they had sur-vived the Fire Wars, and survived also the small ice age that followed them, through a skill in engineering that only the Rulers had ever been able to match in all the history of the world. Since Donner Almandar had led his fleet off Earth, over a thousand years past, the Giants had not had competition as the premier machinists of Earth.

They were a grim people, the Giants. Nature had never intended a frame shaped like that of a man to grow so large in the gravity field of Earth. Here, on the planetary retreat that the Rulers had not yet named, with gravity even stronger than that of Earth, Rome ached all over, constantly, from the simple struggle to keep himself upright.

Senta turned back to him after another moment watching the Workers. "Can we go down?"

Rome winced at the very idea. "I would recommend against it. It's extremely hot down there."

"Oh?" She looked surprised. "It's cool here. The work camp's not that far from us."

"The atmosphere converters have not yet been installed in that work area. Oh, the air is breathable, but it's hot and very dry, not cooled and filtered as the air around New Parliament is. The converters aren't due to go in until the gardens are nearly complete; the ferrocrete dries faster that way."

Senta twisted in her saddle to look back the way they had come. "You installed the converters at New Parliament? I didn't see them."

"The converters are, of course, out of sight." It was quite an accomplishment, injecting that dry tone into a voice so soft and deep; nonetheless Rome managed it. "We wouldn't want to spoil the view of your beautiful garden world with crude mechanical devices."

"Your engineering is brilliant, Rome," Senta told him sincerely. "My father will be very pleased. They will all be pleased, I think." Suddenly she grinned at him. "Maybe even Loga will find this 'heaven' tolerable."

Rome simply shrugged; his mind was on something else. Coming from a Giant, even a shrug was an impressive gesture. His opinion of the Ruler Loga was well known.

Senta looked down upon the disorganized mass of Workers, laboring at tasks for which they were trained poorly or not at all—and achieving results despite those handicaps. "Have the Workers caused you much trouble?"

"Eh? Oh, them. Laar and I have overcome the problems. Oh, there's no love lost," he said with a short laugh. "They'd harm us if they could. My brother Laar especially, who's supervised them most days; he's not popular. We lost an entire colony of their fellows restructuring the atmosphere. That didn't help us at all, I'm afraid." With sardonic understatement, he said, "They don't want to work under us." Senta glanced up at him. He was behaving strangely, unlike the Giants whom she had, these past weeks, come to know and almost like. He caught the look, and the short, almost bitter laugh came again. *"You should understand that."*

Senta's open, almost innocent expression hardened into something far less attractive. "Save that discussion for Cain and Maston when you're in charge. When you're in power, you may better understand the difficulties of rule." The horse twitched restlessly beneath her, and with a thought she stilled it. "Do but finish the gardens, Rome, and *you'll* never have to work for us again."

"Ah, Cain and Maston," he rumbled quietly, and Senta knew they had reached the source of Rome's disquiet. "Laar shipped to Earth, two days ago; he returned this morning with, shall we say, interesting news."

Senta knew what the news must be. She had known of the theft nearly as soon as those of her fellows still on Earth, had known of it before Rome's brother Laar had made his journey. If she was surprised by anything, it was only that the Giants' spies had learned of it so quickly; their sources inside the Caverns must be nearly as good as the Rulers' own. "Yes, I know."

"I thought you might. Cain has stolen a weapon, a thing used in battle against your folk once before." If possible, Rome's voice became even deeper. "A weapon of the Light." Senta did not even look at him, and Rome almost whispered it: "A Ring."

In response Senta said only, "So?"

The Giant stirred with a sort of slow tension. His hands curled, closed into huge fists. Still the Ruler Senta was not looking at him. "So, things have changed. For this 'everlasting retreat' we built you we were promised your position of power, we were prom—"

Senta cut him short, almost angrily. "That's what you wanted, it's what we're giving you. By the Light, what else do you need?"

Rome's voice grew louder. Without conscious decision he found himself pacing slowly back and forth across the observatory point. "We want nothing more. Maston has not changed; him we can deal with. But now there's Cain, and Cain has changed." The volume of the deep voice lifted; Workers hundreds of meters away were looking up toward them. "When he was *only* the man who had caused the Lords of Light to flee Earth . . ."

"We are not fleeing!"

". . . we were not concerned." The surprisingly intelligent eyes glared at her out of the disfigured countenance. "There is no technology Cain's engineers possess that ours do not, and there is considerable ours have that his never will. We do not fear his artillery; we do not fear his fighter craft; we do not fear the fusion weapons from which the *Lords of Light* backed down!"

The Ruler Senta went pale.

Rome observed this, and his lips twisted. "We are only humble Giants," he said mockingly, "and the Light is not to be found within us; why, as simple a thing as hearing another's thoughts is denied us!" The smile died. "And so we have developed most excellent ears. I can quote to you word for word the conversation your father held with Cain a decade past, when Cain threatened to drop a piece of the sun on Parliament itself and gained himself a truce in the process. The point being, my lady, that our defense is more than a match for Cain's offensive weapons, and, for that matter, our attack capability easily outstrips Eastmarch's defenses."

Senta was staring up at him, without fright, gathering the Light visibly around herself. The tension seemed to leave the Giant in that instant, and he waved a tired hand at her. "I mean you no harm, child. Only tell me, what weapon of Giants has ever prevailed against the Light?"

The shimmering nimbus, only barely perceptible to begin with, faded into emptiness. Senta answered him directly. "I have been thinking on this subject for two days now. I cannot answer you from any personal knowledge of Cain; thankfully, I have never met the man. My father has told me of him, as has Loga. The description is that of a man out for himself, of a spirit set *against* the Light. Rome, I think he cannot use the power of that Ring. It is a focusing tool, perhaps a magnifier; we are not entirely sure," she said with a burst of something like humor: "The Sisterhood took us to task for our methods of dealing with the world, some eleven centuries ago. They were fairly upset with us, as I understand it, and did not find it appropriate that they teach us. But I do not believe Cain can focus or magnify something that is not there within him. If he thinks otherwise he is a fool."

"A detailed description, my lady, of a man whom you have never met."

"I trust my teachers, Giant."

"Perhaps. Yet—Cain has done what no Giant would have dared,

and accomplished what I think no Giant could have accomplished. Fine work, from a fool. My lady, that Ring may now be more important to us, to me and mine, than your gift of Parliament. You tell Loden that."

For all she was young, Senta possessed her full measure of the arrogance that was the birthright of any Ruler. "I shall tell my father what I please, Giant. I came to inspect your work; doubtless that shall be the major portion of my discussions with him after I have returned."

Rome studied the young woman for a moment. The adrenaline, raised in anger, did not leave quickly; but there was nothing more he would accomplish with this child. He nodded. "Are you satisfied, then, with what you have seen?"

With the speed of youth, she seemed already to have passed over their argument. Her smile was dazzling. "Yes, Rome. It's very beautiful."

The Giant looked around, at the sculpted blue mountains far to the west, at the glowing empty city of New Parliament, at the carefully force-grown forests and meadows. He had been raised, as had all Giants, in the far north, in a land of Arctic white, stark and elegant. Like all Giants, he found the pastoral leanings of the Lords of Light rather . . . cluttered. Curiously, he asked the Ruler, "More beautiful than Earth?"

He regretted the question instantly. Though he did not care for the Lords of Light at all, Rome did not enjoy inflicting pain.

She said flatly, "Nothing is more beautiful than Earth."

I shall miss my home.

· 2 ·

. . . some of you, children, know the history of that time, at least in small degree; how, during the Exile, the resistance against the Rulers continued, and upon Cain's return flared into the Twenty Years' War. Those in the Valley who rose against the Rulers were primarily in the east and the west; when the Treaty of Eastmarch ended the Twenty Years' War, the Rulers kept control of the Valley's center, of the lake T'Pau and the entire length of the river Almandar.

Cain claimed an area slightly larger than that of the Rulers, though it was split by their territory; a vast realm to the east that included the

Eastmarch of his birth and the cities of Telindel, Saerlock, Moorstin, and Allietown, and which included to the west the towns of Westmarch and Eagles.

The communities of the Valley were among the most rigid caste societies in all history, and the rebels were heirs to this tradition no less so than those who fought for the Rulers. It galled many among their number to take orders from one who was, after all, no more than the son of a fisherman.

One such was the Lord of the town of Eagles, a man named Maston Veramorn. In 1274, two days after the signing of the Treaty of Eastmarch, he declared independence and raised up the west territory in rebellion.

Against Cain.

Be it recorded that there were those, the Ruler Loga among them, who found this amusing. . . .

The slipship from Eagles came from the west, directly out of the crimson sun, in the last hour of the day. The ship circled the Caverns' landpad twice before the Shield went down, and the slipship dropped quietly straight down to a gentle vertical landing.

The Shield went up again instantly.

Cain was not sure how long the outspeaker had been addressing him with Kavad's voice.

"My lord . . . my lord Cain?"

Cain opened his eyes. He was seated in utter darkness, except for a dim spark upon which his entire being was focused; it seemed to float above the ground, two meters before him, the only source of illumination in the world. "Yes, Kavad?"

"My lord, Maston's emissary has arrived."

"Ah." Cain could not focus on the thought for a moment. With a great effort he drew his attention back from the blazing spark in front of his eyes, returned it to the problems of the real world. "Who is it?"

"A young man, my lord, Commander Captain Solan by name."

"So? Not Commander Captain Tristan, then. It seems I owe you a star, Kavad." He was silent a moment, motionless in the dark. "I could not credit that Maston would send this Solan. From what very little I've heard of him, he's supposed to be quite popular with Maston's Warriors. Not the sort Maston would send on a task guaranteed to make him even more popular."

"Unless, my lord, he is intended to fail."

"Yes. I know you don't trust Maston, sensible man you are." Cain came to his feet carefully, with nothing like his usual grace, stretched against the protest of aching muscles. "How very interesting. . . . Where is he now?"

"General Mersai, as you instructed, is leading him on a tour of the production floor."

"Good. Lights," he called, and the glowfloats in the room flickered into weak light. There was nothing in the room except walls of ferrocrete; rugs, for warmth; the glowfloats, for light; and a columnar enclosure of some flickering substance that resembled crystal.

For the Ring.

A moment's dizziness struck Cain, and he stood motionless until it passed. "Kavad," he said when the world had calmed itself again, "bring me whatever intelligence reports we have on this Commander Solan. Keep the man busy for at least another half hour. If he tires of the production floor, take him over to the Weapons Monger. He won't refuse that, he won't dare." Cain took a deep, steadying breath. "And send Keja in for my bath. Have her bring two tablets of *deoxymethamphetamine*. I must be in better shape when I see Maston's emissary."

"My lord? The word you used?"

"*Deoxymethamphetamine*." Cain repeated the Old Tongue word carefully; Kavad sometimes had trouble with words from the common tongue, never mind Anglish. "Keja will know what I mean. Two tablets," he said, as the world faded from his eyes for a moment. "And quickly."

The holo of Commander Captain Solan showed a clear-featured young man with straight sandy-blond hair and light blue eyes. Cain found him surprisingly young; twenty-two or -three at most, which would make him at least three years younger than Maston's "senior" Commander, a man whom Cain had met once named Tristan d'Volta.

This Solan was, if Cain's intelligence reports were to be believed, Tristan d'Volta's only serious rival as Maston Veramorn's heir apparent. Interesting, if true; and interesting also that Solan did not have, or did not use, a surname. Either his parents were disgraced—if he came from a family of high station—or, what was more likely, he was the child of a family of such low station that, like both of Cain's parents, they had never had a surname.

Not that Maston's other Captain was of such very high birth, either; d'Volta meant no more than that Tristan was born in the city of Volta, not far from Eagles.

Privately, though it was not a subject he cared about enough to spend much time on, Cain thought the Command setup at Eagles poorly planned. Maston Veramorn's insecurity was such that he dared not have officers of high birth around him, nor officers of any great experience either. Commander Colonel Gordal Stylion's "accidental" death, not two years past, had proved the last sufficiently well for Cain's mind. Maston's death would send his city, and those towns at the west end of the Valley that Eagles controlled, into a succession struggle that, by Cain's estimation, Maston's organization was not strong enough to withstand.

Cain cared little enough about it all, to be sure. When it happened, tomorrow or fifty years from tomorrow, he was more than willing to step in and pick up the pieces, and regain the territory that Maston's treachery had cost him.

The Caverns was an odd place.

Much of it was natural; more was not, had been excavated in the course of the last thirty years since Cain's return. Solan saw few Workers in his carefully guided tour, but the few whom he did see seemed in good spirits; there was none of the terror Solan had expected from Cain's reputation. The morale of the Warriors in the group that guided Solan was likewise high; one of them, the pockmark-faced pilot of the slipship named *Watchdog*, by whom Solan had nearly been shot down the summer prior, cheerfully offered Solan a rematch—weapons live or not, depending on how the truce talks went.

The tour of the production floor was fascinating. Solan saw production techniques such as vacuum welding that, though he was no engineer himself, he knew Maston's engineers would have paid dearly for. He came to suspect that there was some point to the tour beyond mere courtesy when they offered to show him the weapons monger's work areas. The shipyard alone was grim enough; Solan counted, as they clearly meant him to, better than three times the number of slipships that Eagles could have fielded on its best day. But the weapons-testing floor threw him even more badly. He was demonstrated new ship-to-ship missiles and ground-to-ship laser cannon that would have decimated an opposing fleet of slipships in mere minutes.

One thing that their spies had reported did indeed turn out to be the truth, as Solan's wife Rea had hoped: there *were* women among Cain's Warriors.

He was not sure whether he liked that or not.

Entirely to his surprise, Solan found that he very much liked Cain, High Lord of Eastmarch and its territories. He met Cain at dinner, a quiet affair attended only by himself, Cain, and General Mersai, Cain's senior Commander, and served by Cain's barbarian man-servant Kavad. The dinner was served in Cain's quarters, in a room large enough for five times their number, as they sat on cushions around a long low table of black oak. The table was old and rather plain, and Solan wondered briefly at its presence. Aside from that table the room was opulent indeed, with brightly lit glowfloats bobbing at the ceiling, rugs of finest deerskin, and tapestries of sunsilk hung from the walls. One tapestry depicted the Glowing Desert seen at night; it was almost as realistic as a hologram, blackness lit by the visible shining of radioactives with a half-life of tens of thousands of years. Another tapestry showed the ten-year-old signing of the Treaty of Eastmarch; in it, the Rulers looked rather uglier than Solan suspected was true of them, and Cain had been rendered somewhat older-seeming, and, if possible, even more handsome than he was.

Despite what Maston had told him, Solan found himself half doubting that the young man sitting across the table from him—he looked, at most, a few years older than Solan himself—could possibly be the legend whom men spoke of as Cain of Eastmarch. He was barefoot, dressed in nothing more elaborate than a plain black robe, fastened at the waist by a belt with a silver buckle of better-than-average workmanship. His only jewelry was not even of gold or platinum; just a single silver bracelet on his left wrist.

Cain seemed to be in fine health; he showed no signs of the illness that Maston's spies had reported.

They spoke but little during dinner, which was excellent, though not what Solan had expected: hot strips of silkie, lightly breaded with sweet skipper-wheat batter, with a variety of sauces in which to dip the strips; and roasted venison in a white cream sauce, which General Mersai told Solan was a silver-eyes dish. There were also hot rolls with butter and a dish of cold strawberries. Though good, the fare was simpler than Solan had been served at Lord Maston's table on far less important occasions.

Solan's only question during the dinner was directed at the servant, Kavad. "The silkie is excellent, barbarian. Where does it come from? Surely you're not using fighter craft to fly it in before it spoils?"

To his surprise, it was Cain who answered him. "No, of course not. There's a small waterlock in the hills to the northwest. We fish through it."

After dinner was cleared away, Kavad brought them hot wine and coffee. Coffee was a drink Solan was unfamiliar with and, after sipping at his cup, did not like. The barbarian brought him mulled wine, and he took it with thanks; the room was cooler than he cared for, and there was no fireplace.

It was Commander Mersai who first turned to the reason for Solan's presence. He did so with a single word.

"Peace?"

Solan glanced from Cain to Mersai, and back again. "The Games at Eagles are in three weeks; we won't have a better time. And it seems a good idea, all considered. Battling each other's done us damn little good."

Cain sipped wine from a goblet. "I don't argue the point. Indeed, twice since his break with me I've urged Maston that we join forces again. He's shown no interest before this. It makes me wonder, Captain Solan, why he makes the suggestion of truce now." For the first time, Solan realized why the man's black eyes were so prevalent in their spies' descriptions of Cain; it was the first time Cain had turned them directly upon him.

Solan did not think that his reply showed any hesitation. "The

Rulers have drastically stepped up the pace of their activities with the Giants. Our spies do not know why, but we must assume their plans are not friendly, to either of our parties. If war is due to come again, we *must* be united. The Rulers are still vastly powerful."

" 'Drastically,' " Cain quoted. His gaze did not leave Solan. "Orrin, tell him."

"Seven years ago," said Orrin Mersai, "twenty-four thousand residents of Semalia province were evacuated over the course of a single quarter, and sent elsewhere. Four and a half years ago, early in Winter of 1280, another eighteen thousand Workers were taken from Turrin province and sent elsewhere. Do you know where that elsewhere might be, Commander Captain?"

"Commander," said Solan stiffly, "I do not." The thought touched the back of his awareness, *And I'd no idea that the numbers were so large, either.*

Cain had laid down his goblet and was rubbing the silver bracelet at his left wrist with the fingers of his right hand. He looked up from the bracelet. "Solan, neither do we."

"Lord Cain, I don't . . ."

"Cain, please," the man said suddenly.

"Sir?"

"Call me Cain."

Solan glanced back and forth between the two of them. "Okay. Cain, I don't quite see what you're driving at."

"Maston has known," said Cain patiently, "for at least four and a half years, that the Rulers and Giants were engaged in some huge construction project, possibly in orbit, possibly not. Three quarters ago orbital traffic went crazy. The Giants launched an average of two freighter ships into orbit *every day*." Lifting his goblet from the table, he came to his feet, moving restlessly. "I've known for most of this decade that the Rulers have made some major decision as a direct result of the Treaty of Eastmarch, and so has Maston. I've gone half out of my mind trying to figure out what they're doing. Are they constructing orbital laser cannon? Are they thinking of boosting an asteroid out of orbit and dropping it on Eastmarch? They could, you know. Even I could do that, if I were insane enough and had started planning ten years ago—and a Shield that gives you some protection against a fusion bomb or laser cannon won't protect you from an asteroid's impact at all. Are they training those forty-two thousand Workers as Warriors and preparing to drop them on us directly out of orbit? It wouldn't be the first time they've done something like that. Before even *I* was born they sent Workers, trained briefly to handle the weapons of Warriors, against the rebelling city of Erebion, and razed that city to the ground. Are they planning none of those things? *All of them?* I don't know, and it's worried me sufficiently I was willing to work with even the likes of Maston Veramorn." Cain paused in his restless pacing and turned to Solan. He gestured at Solan with the hand holding the goblet.

"Then, one and a half quarters ago, every spy I had in Parliament went silent. Every one."

Solan bit his lip. "Ours also."

Cain nodded, returning to his barefooted pacing across the deer-skin rugs. "I know. So, assuming the loss of my spies meant the Rulers were about to move, I sent a messenger to your lord, urging strongly that he and I work together. Bad enough you fools raid the Worker steadings in Ruler territory, worse that you do the same to my own holdings . . ."

Solan protested hotly. "It was not our ships that first shot down *yours*, Lord Cain, but the other way around!"

Cain seemed startled by the outburst; but he smiled, and answered mildly enough, "True enough. Of course, your Warriors had just set afire a house belonging to one of my subjects . . ."

"It was disputed territory . . ."

Cain laughed aloud. "Boy, the man whose house was burning seemed to think he was my subject. By the Light, Solan, why were you sent to negotiate for Maston? You're very bad at it."

Solan opened his mouth to reply, and then closed it, slowly. Finally he said, "Am I?"

"Well, you've a tendency to speak before you finish thinking. If you were one of *my* officers, I would find it an enormously appealing trait; I've learned to trust men who say what they think as it occurs to them." Cain could not prevent the smile again. "But it's a bit disconcerting to have a man who's come to cajole me into a truce begin by leaping up to argue with me about irrelevant history."

Solan could not think of anything to say; he wisely remained silent.

Cain sank down cross-legged into the cushions, across the table again from Solan. "But I'm not looking to bring up those old arguments again; what's done is done."

Solan found his voice. "Not meaning to argue with you about anything irrelevant, Cain, but you are mistaken if you think I'm here to cajole you into anything at all. We will negotiate a truce acceptable to my lord Maston or we will not negotiate a truce."

"And now you're lying to me," said Cain softly. Solan flushed slightly with anger, and Cain continued, "Let me explain to you the way things stand, as I see them, and then you can either convince me I am wrong, if you wish, leave, if you wish, or work out the details of a truce—if you wish." Solan bit his lip again and kept his mouth shut. Cain leaned forward, across the table. "Good, you are smart. Now listen, damn it, and try to learn from someone who's smarter. One and a half quarters ago I sent Orrin Mersai to Eagles to personally deliver to Maston my urgent wishes that he and I work together. You might remember that visit."

Orrin Mersai grunted. "I reported having seen a new Commander, a Captain my lord Cain'd not heard of before. It was the first we really knew of your existence, aside from a report we'd never confirmed that Maston's daughter had been quietly married off to one of Maston's junior Warriors, four or five years ago."

"I'd only just made Captain before your visit, Commander General Mersai."

"I know," said Cain. "I know a fair amount about you already, and I'm learning more. Can you guess what that fool Maston told Commander Mersai?"

"I know."

"So," said Cain quietly, eyes locked to Solan's, "what's different today? What element of the situation exists today that did not exist then? We've better than three times the number of fighter craft Eagles has; but that was true in late Winter as well. We've more than twice the number of Warriors, but that also was true back in late Winter. So what's changed? You tell me."

Solan nodded. "It's hard for me to guess at what is in my lord Maston's mind, but—I know you know we've had reports that you've, uhm . . . obtained," he said carefully, "a weapon, a Ring, which even the Rulers fear."

To Solan's surprise, Cain did not deny it. He said merely, "So?"

"Well, you understand, this is merely a guess on my part, but I think, possibly, perhaps even *very likely* . . ."

"Yes?"

With a perfectly straight face, Solan looked right at Cain and said, ". . . in fact, I would say almost certainly, my lord Maston's change of heart on this subject is due entirely to the fact that basically he's a nice guy."

For a long, stretching moment, Solan was not sure it had been the correct answer. Then Commander General Mersai sputtered into his drink, and even Cain chuckled. Mersai put down his drink and stood. "I'm an old man, and I need my sleep. My lord, if I may?"

"Good night, Orrin." Cain did not even look at his senior Commander. "Sleep well. See me first thing in the morning, if you would. I expect we'll have the outlines of a truce for you to look at."

Solan came to his feet and took the outstretched forearm that Mersai offered to him, gripping it strongly. "Good night to you, Commander General."

"Good night, Commander Captain. I'll see you tomorrow."

Mersai turned, and lumbered out of the room.

They talked until very late, drinking the mulled wine the barbarian brought them. Though he knew better than to let it show, Solan was amazed by the contrast between the Cain of reputation—the man of scarlet rages and easy murders—and the man himself. He had, he knew within the first half hour of their conversation, never been in the presence of a better educated man. Before the night was through he was convinced he had never known a man more intelligent.

Solan could not recall having said so aloud—which was not surprising, as he was half drunk—but at one point, Cain said, "You're not exactly right, you know. Oh, I believe you've never met anyone smarter than I am, nor better educated; but only because you've never been to Parliament. There are any of a score of Rulers better educated than I, if only because they've had more decades to study. There are two Rulers in particular—Loga and the Tribunal Elder Loden, and I know you've heard of them both—and Loden's as smart as I am. Loga is smarter, which worries me, I tell you true." Cain looked troubled for just a moment; he'd had a fair amount to drink himself. "I do kill easily enough, I suppose, which is another thing the Rulers do not do. Weak stomachs, I think. They could have killed me once themselves, and been certain of my death, but they decided to exile me instead, thinking I'd die on my own and save their consciences." The troubled look vanished, and he grinned at Solan. "But then, they're fools, and that proves it, so it hardly matters."

And Solan laughed at the comment, and they moved on to other subjects.

At the suggestion of bed, Solan staggered to his feet. "Sounds a fine idea, that." He noticed with a twinge of envy that Cain, despite having kept up with him goblet for goblet, was perfectly steady on his feet. Kavad handed him his jacket, which he'd forgotten, and Solan thanked the barbarian politely.

Cain was standing by the door, waiting for Solan. When Solan reached him, he put a gentle hand on Solan's shoulder and half turned Solan to face one of the sunsilk hangings. "Give me your opinion, truly. What do you think of this hanging?"

It was the hanging showing the signing of the Treaty of Eastmarch. Cain took a step back from Solan as Solan examined the hanging in greater detail than his earlier glance had permitted. Neither the second look nor the wine he'd drunk since the first improved it much. "Truly? It's not very good, I'm afraid."

Standing behind Solan, Cain said silently, *I must have the artist executed sometime soon.*

Solan whirled about unsteadily. *"What?* You can't mean that!"

"No," said Cain after a pause, with an expression Solan could not have interpreted had his life been at stake, "no, it was just a joke. Would you like to see the Ring?"

Solan stared at him. Consternation and confusion warred in his expression. Finally he said with drunken clarity, "Cain, I don't understand you."

"I'd be amazed if you did. Would you like to see the Ring?"

"I . . . *yes,"* he said in sudden exasperation, "I suppose I would. Does what I would like have some importance to you I don't know about?"

"In the morning, then. I'll show it to you." Cain brushed by

Solan, through the door and into the corridor outside. "Come on. I've a spare room not far from my own. You can sleep there tonight."

With a glance back at the barbarian, who was cleaning up after them, Solan hurried after Cain's retreating back. The corridor was dark; it had, he thought fuzzily, been quite bright when he'd come down it for the dinner. Did they really turn the lights down in the Caverns at night?

"Yes, we do," said Cain absently. He opened a door into a wide stateroom with a bed in it large enough for three persons at once. "Will this do? There's a bathroom with a tub and civilized plumbing connected to it."

Solan did not even glance at it. "It'll be fine."

Cain nodded. "You'll breakfast with me, in the morning?"

"Of course, my lo . . . Cain."

"Shall I have a girl sent to share your bed?"

Solan only smiled. "Thank you, no."

Cain hesitated. "A boy?"

Solan did laugh at that, loudly. "No. All I meant is, I'm a married man, Cain, and happily so. I've a son, a boy just turned five." He dropped his jacket next to the bed, kicked his boots off and stretched out on the soft surface. When he spoke again, the love in his voice was plain, impossible to miss. "His name's Orion. He is the most beautiful thing I've ever seen in all the world."

Cain nodded again. "Good night, then."

Solan did not even think about the question; it simply came. "Cain, did you never love anyone enough to marry her?"

Solan regretted the question instantly. Cain stood stock-still in the doorway, as though he had been struck. After a moment he brought up a smile and said, "No, don't apologize. I spent forty years in Donnertown, at the edge of the Glowing Desert, Solan, building the army that gave us—you and me both—whatever freedom it is we enjoy. I'd been in Donnertown seven years before I learned to activate the Shield that protected Donnertown from the radiation of the Glowing Desert. If I sired a child it would be a monster. Good night, Solan."

Solan gave silent thanks for the dimness of the bedchamber, so that Cain could not see the bright redness flooding his cheeks. "Good night, Cain."

THE RING

It was only later, lying sleepless in the lonely bed he had been given, that Solan realized Cain had not answered his question.

· 3 ·

Solan had seen rooms with *nothing* in them that did not give the impression of barrenness so well.

He had difficulty taking his eyes from the enclosure that held the Ring. In the dim light from the glowfloats, there was a visible gleam around the Ring.

Dressed in his flight suit, helmet in his hand, he could not help but feel slightly ridiculous. Cain seemed to guess at his thoughts; standing behind the transparent column that held the Ring, not looking at Solan, Cain said, "Please, take off your gloves and put down the helmet." It was practically the first thing Cain had said to him that morning; breakfast had been particularly quiet, and Cain rather cool, as though the previous night had not occurred. Cain had appeared at breakfast dressed in the fashion in which most of their spies' holos showed him: the Warrior's uniform of the Caverns—a black uniform of conservative cut, with the starburst patch on the right breast, and within the patch, the glowing blue sphere that, Cain's propaganda said, represented the drug youthbooster—but without weapons, without any insignia of rank, and with no jewelry but the silver bracelet.

Solan tucked his gloves inside the helmet and dropped them to the rumpled deerskin rug at his feet. The Ring held his eye; an unprepossessing thing, to be sure. Surely this small piece of crystal was not the weapon that had turned his lord Maston into a quivering wreck?

"But it is," said Cain. Solan looked up at him and found himself caught in the depths of the dark gaze. "You're very young, Solan, but in nothing does your youth show more than in your lack of fear for the Light. We fought the Rulers twenty years; we had slipships and artillery and popular support among the Workers across the length and breadth of the Valley. The Rulers had only the Light, and they were damn near on the verge of winning the war before I threatened them with a weapon even Maston found horrifying." Cain grinned suddenly, a hard intense thing without any humor in it whatsoever. "Maston is a fool, and a treacherous one—but he fears the power of the Light."

Solan tore his eyes away from Cain's with an effort, took a step closer, and another, until he stood to one side of the Ring, with Cain across from him. "It's smaller than I'd have expected. Small enough to wear." He looked back up at Cain. "Why don't you wear it?"

"It was larger when I took it, so large it barely fit within the palm of my hand. When I first saw it on—well, the planet's name does not matter—then, it was thirty or forty meters across. There were three women who tended it, whom I saw, and perhaps, though I don't think so, others tending it whom I did not see." The object of their discussion was pulsing softly in the space between them. Solan saw for the first time that it was hanging there in the case, floating without support. "Since my return, it's shrunk. I think it desires contact, desires touch."

"Why don't you wear it?"

"Have your engineers," asked Cain seriously, "ever succeeded in modulating a Shield into its metastable form?"

The question seemed meaningless to Solan. "Yes. We don't do it often; it takes great energy." He looked down at the enclosure and suddenly understood. "You've enclosed the Ring in one? By the Light, why? I don't understand."

"Lights out," Cain said softly, and suddenly the room was plunged into blackness except for the glow of the Ring. "Shield off."

The blaze struck him like needles against his skin. Solan staggered back. Someone cried out, loud and high, and a voice that was not Solan's, which he did not think was Cain's, echoed deep within Solan's skull:

"Behold! Behold now the Face of Day; behold now the Light!"

A vast flaring light came straight at Solan, and a whispering hum that almost made sense filled his ears. He threw up his arms to cover his eyes. Half blinded, he heard Cain again, quiet and calm: "Lights on." The glowfloats came up, and Solan saw Cain, eyes closed, standing motionless behind the empty spot that had held the frozen column of the Shield, hand stretched out and open. A harsh, brilliant light nearly obscured his features from Solan's view, a light that came from the Ring, floating just before Solan, trembling in midair a meter off the ground.

Slowly, the Ring moved, back across the room, into Cain's outstretched hand. Cain's hand closed around the Ring, and Cain himself seemed to come back to life, eyes opening, and the tenseness leaving his form. "Excuse me," he said mildly, "just a moment." He glanced down at the floor, found the spot he wanted, and released the Ring at that spot. The Ring vibrated visibly, shaking in place. Cain stood watching it, a drop of sweat forming on his brow and running down his cheek.

One moment there was nothing there but the Ring; the next the nearly transparent Shield had appeared around it.

Cain said conversationally, "I bet you don't get to do things this interesting at home."

Solan was staring at him. "What . . . happened?"

"Hell if I know." With one hand, Cain wiped the trickle of sweat from his cheek. "But I think it's time for lunch."

"Lunch?" he said stupidly. "By the Light, what's going on here?"

Cain shook himself slightly and took a deep breath. "We've drafted a truce, we're coming to the Games, and we'll make peace. Aside from that we're going to have lunch now."

Solan said the only thing that came to him by way of reply. "We just had breakfast."

Cain looked at him curiously. "You're not hungry?"

"Uh . . ." For the first time, Solan realized that he was. "Actually, I'm starving."

"I thought you might be."

They ate in one of the few aboveground rooms that Solan had seen at the Caverns; up a lift into a building set in the side of a hill, looking out over the Caverns' landpads and the farmlands to the west. Barely visible to the northwest was a collection of ramshackle buildings; the remains of old abandoned Eastmarch, the village in which Solan knew Cain had grown up.

Cain sat silently at lunch, occupied with his thoughts. Solan ate ravenously, further confirming something of which Cain needed no more confirmation. Cain was hungry himself and ate well enough: two cups of coffee and one of the large beef sandwiches that Kavad brought.

Solan had three, and two glasses of wine.

It was Solan who broke the silence, after finishing off his third sandwich. "What did you do in there?"

"I'm not sure," Cain said. It was true enough, though misleading. Given that he did not entirely understand the Ring, any explanation he might give Solan would surely be, at best, only partially true. The idea of lying only because he did not know the truth galled Cain.

The answer obviously did not please Solan. Cain sat and waited for him to work his way through what troubled him. "I felt—at one point it seemed that your mind—that it was touching mine, that we were thinking the same thoughts."

"At one point, we were."

"Why?" With sudden anger: "Did you probe my thoughts because you doubt we'd keep our word? Do you trust us so little?"

"Trust? 'Us?'" Cain considered the word. "If Maston Veramorn is included in that word, I confess, I don't trust him any more than I'd trust a silkie gone red." He snorted. "Less. At least you can see the silkie's turned."

Solan sighed, rubbing at his temples. "This bespeaks poorly for our truce, my lord Cain. I mean, Cain. You trust Eagles—just not its Lord."

"I did not say that."

"Fine." The word was very short. "So now, ten seconds later, you do trust Maston?"

"I meant, Solan, that I do not trust Maston, and I do not, necessarily, trust Eagles either."

Cain gave the boy a point; he saw it coming. "Me."

"How not?"

Solan said bluntly, "Why?"

The answer Cain gave him was not the reason, and not an answer, and Cain saw that Solan knew it instantly. "You remind me of someone. I'm not sure who." Solan's face went curiously blank. "Who is your father?"

"I may not say, Lord Cain."

"Oh? You mean you don't know," said Cain mildly. "Well, there's no shame in that."

Solan spoke fiercely. "There's nothing in my parentage I need be ashamed of, sir."

"Did I say there was? *My* father was a fisherman." Cain studied him a moment. "You needn't wear your pride on your chin. It makes an easy target." Solan looked briefly startled at the image, and against his inclination a smile crossed his features. "It's just I've the strange feeling that I've met you before, and I know I haven't."

THE RING

With something like reluctance, Solan said, "Maston once said something that made me think he knows. I may be his bastard, or the child of one of the minor nobles from the early part of the Twenty Years' War." He shrugged. "If you'll remember, some twenty-two or -three years ago, when Maston was first consolidating his power in the west end of the Valley, there were, oh, half a dozen small nobles who opposed him. Some Maston destroyed, some he made treaty with"—his lips twisted into a wry grin—"and then destroyed. At a guess, Lord Cain, my father, if it was not Maston, was one of those nobles. Knowing my master as I do, I must presume that my noble father, if he is not merely the product of my imagination, is now dead. If your spies have told you anything about me, they've told you I was raised in an orphanage in Westmarch, so that might fit. All I know with any certainty is that the first time Maston ever saw me he looked as surprised as I've ever seen him since."

"You're very popular with Maston's commanders, and the Warriors as well, I'm told."

Solan frowned. "True."

"Knowing your master as you do," said Cain gently, "don't you think he might be worried by that?"

"No." The words were flat, intended to end the thrust of the conversation.

"So." Cain finished his coffee and gestured at Solan's wineglass. "More? Or must you be returning?"

The youth seized on the suggestion. "I'm afraid so. My wife will be worried about me."

Maston will think I'm turning your head, Cain translated silently. "Very good, then. May I walk you back to your ship?"

Kavad stood at his side and watched as Solan's slipship taxied briefly across the landpad and lifted into the clear blue sky. From where they stood, the Great Dam loomed behind the ship at first; as the ship gained altitude, it climbed gradually above the huge gray mass of stone-steel.

"He reminds you of someone, you said?"

Cain was watching the ship climb. "Did I say that?"

"Perhaps I was not meant to hear, my lord."

Eyes on Solan's slipship, Cain smiled. "Perhaps you were not."

Kavad said, "The boy impressed you."

Cain shot at glance at Kavad from beneath dark eyebrows. "You think so?"

"He impressed me." Kavad hesitated. "Maston's never married, has he?"

"No. You think Solan's his bastard?" Solan's ship vanished at last, cut off from their view by fleecy white cirrostratus clouds.

Kavad's silver eyes glittered thoughtfully. "They don't look very much alike, but fathers and sons don't always. It's been a few years since I've seen a holo of Maston's daughter Rea, but the boy does look something like her; and she *is* his bastard."

Cain said slowly, "He's not Maston's."

"Whose, then?"

Cain shook his head. "I don't know who that youth truly is, Kavad, where Maston got him or how—but that boy is the get of Rulers." The expression on his young face was nothing Kavad had ever seen before, old and somehow tired. And yet his voice was gentle, almost wistful. "There is Light within him."

The Lords of Light

The Year 1284 After the Fire

The Ruler Loden walked through the Hall of Mirrors, lost in the depth of his thoughts. He was in no hurry. If he could not escape his image in the mirrors, neither could he escape himself, nor the thoughts that plagued him, in their absence.

Cain, the thoughts whispered, *damn Cain.*

Loden Almandar was a classically handsome man; not surprisingly. He was only one generation removed from the direct work of the genegineer T'Pau, the greatest genetic engineer the world had ever known. Loden's father, John Almandar, had been T'Pau's finest creation. He was also her only son, as Loden had been John Almandar's. The Creator T'Pau had worked with only the finest genomes; it was the very best that there was in humanity that she took and altered into the mold that became known as T'Pau's People and later, after the last of the Fire Wars, as the Rulers of Earth.

Like quarreling children. Our last days here, and even now Cain gives us no peace.

Perhaps Loden was not, in the final analysis, human. It was a subject on which Loden himself held no opinion; he frankly did not care. There was an extra, twenty-fourth pair of chromosomes in his genetic makeup, and in that of all the others of the Rulers, which Workers did not have; and as a result Workers and Rulers were not interfertile.

There was one exception to that, actually. One Ruler there was who possessed only twenty-three pairs of chromosomes, the same as any

Worker, whose genetic makeup owed almost nothing to T'Pau Almandar.

Though it was hardly remembered these days, and mattered even less, the Ruler Loga was the only sentient being who had ever learned to control the Light who was not also one of T'Pau's People to begin with.

He was, in point of fact, a barbarian.

Near the end of the Hall of Mirrors, where the mirrors curved around and became a barrier themselves, Loden Almandar, the eldest of T'Pau's People, the Tribunal Elder at Parliament, came face to face with himself.

He gathered within himself the Light and with casual power stepped toward the barrier and vanished.

The raising of the power scarcely disturbed the path of his thoughts.

He was very, very old, and there was a sickness in his soul.

He appeared standing behind the black-and-gold marble spire of the podium, in the flooding daylight that illuminated the Chamber at Parliament. With one exception, no one who could not gather the power of the Light and make the leap Loden had just made had ever entered the open-aired Chamber through the Hall of Mirrors; from that Hall there was no other way to reach the Chamber.

One exception.

Cain had been brought by that path, had stood there, bound; and in that Chamber the Rulers had sentenced him to an Exile they had every reason to believe was his death. *Where was the error*, wondered Loden, seven decades later, *that we tried to kill him, or that we did not succeed?*

In a circle that closed itself at the podium, the other Rulers awaited him, standing in respect: nine of the ten Rulers who, with himself, comprised Parliament's Tribunal. Loden glanced around the room, drawing their eyes to him. His own wife Elyssa was there, and two of his daughters, Maria and his eldest daughter Selene. Michael and Athel were scholars; quiet men, and ineffectual, willing to be led. Gabriel was stronger-minded, but fortunately tended to agree with

Loden more often than not. The other married couple on the Tribunal,
Calandra and her husband Julian, were often a problem, and the fact
that the Tribunal's ninth member, a taciturn man named Eàmon, often
sided with them, did not help. Eàmon was the most recent Ruler on
the Tribunal; it was he who had replaced the Ruler Alber seven decades
ago. It did not seem that he would ever forget that Cain had murdered
his predecessor.

Loden raised his arms slowly, palms up, as though reaching out to
them. The other Rulers mirrored the gesture, and in silent communion
the glow began to build around each one of the Rulers, a hazy golden
illumination that crept across them like a liquid, pooling in their throats
and the hollows of their eyes, and reaching out . . .

The Light showered down upon them in a sudden fierce blaze,
blasted out of the Chamber in a brilliant beacon that outshone the sun
itself.

The Rulers stood in a world of incandescent coruscation, together
in the quiet joy and serenity of the Light, together and alone in that
which marked the inseparable difference between Ruler and all else.

The Light gentled, and vanished.

They stood silent for but a moment, lost each of them in private
reverie, and gradually came back to themselves. They took their seats
around the edge of the debating floor and waited for Loden. It took
him a long time, these days, to come back from those moments with
the Light. When he finally spoke, the words were anticlimactic. "Loga
returned today with the Giants." There was nodding from the various
members of the Tribunal; most of them knew that. Loden spoke carefully, placing his words. "The work on New Parliament is completed.
The Giants are on their way to ask this Tribunal for their payment. We
have what we want; and the Giants have, one would think, what they
want—to govern themselves. Senta has already told me the new world
is magnificent. The Giants, it seems, have been both diligent and honest in fulfilling our requirements."

Loden could almost see them thinking. It was Gabriel who finally
said, "So, why don't we dispense with the formalities, my friend? Make
the announcement that we're leaving, and then do so." He lifted an
eyebrow. "Pay them, in other words."

Calandra licked her lips, a nervous habit that she had not outgrown in six centuries, and said, "Yes. We are, many of us, wondering why you called this meeting, Loden. We are confident," and she met Loden's eyes with what might have been challenge, "that the Giants can rule henceforth and make their own peace with the Workers. When we leave, they have their reward." She gestured at their surroundings. "Our power and our place. Everything."

"If they can keep it." Standing at the podium, Loden grasped its edges tightly. The cusp had come. He said, quietly, emphatically, "They will not have the Ring."

The opposition he expected came from an unexpected quarter: his own wife, Elyssa, her voice low and husky. "We didn't promise them the Ring."

Loden stared at her. "Elyssa—Cain did not have the Ring when we made our agreement. If—"

She cut him short. "*We* have been honest in all our agreements. We made a pact to let them rule, nothing more!" Elyssa relaxed slightly and said quietly, "Quite aside from the fact that our ethical obligation to aid the Giants is, at best, questionable, our ability to do so is even more in question. Is someone to be sent into the danger of Eastmarch to *take* the Ring?" She spoke the words that all the other long-lived Rulers must surely be thinking. "Let time deal with Cain; it will. Assuming he raises any power out of that Ring—which I doubt—it will be short-lived for having defiled its source."

Loden looked slowly around the Chamber. They had guessed where he was going, and it was apparent already that there would be little support for him in the course of action he desired.

A movement drew his attention up, into the ribbon of open sky that was visible through the gap between the top of the walls and the bottom of the ceiling. "We can," he said, looking up, "think what we like—but the Giants fear the Light, and thereby the Ring, and thereby Cain."

A light was streaking across the sky. Although it would have taken one who had known Loden intimately for a very long time to see it— and even that person would have needed to be watching him closely at the moment—it is possible that the oldest living intelligent being on Earth smiled, at just that moment.

Or perhaps not.

THE RING

A brilliant pinpoint of light dropped out of nothingness, appeared in one end of the ribbon of blue sky, moving like a shooting star. The pinpoint became a ball of flame and struck the debating floor like the touch of a laser, crackling and hissing. The ball skittered aimlessly across the floor, spraying cool sparks in a brilliant fountain, and came to rest at the far end of the debating floor.

Loden's daughter Maria was smiling widely; Eàmon was visibly annoyed. Otherwise there was no reaction among the group of waiting Rulers.

The ball of light cracked open like an egg, and from the center of the egg there reared the shape of a huge king cobra, twenty times life-size, with blazing ruby scales and flashing adamantine eyes. The Cobra flared once, and when the image gentled into nothingness the Ruler Loga stood there, a red-haired man with bright blue eyes, grinning at them.

"Hi, guys." Loga glanced around at them. "How was that one? I've been working on it, you know." He took a deep breath and crashed into one of the many empty seats, not far from where the Ruler Athel was sitting, not far at all from where two Giant-sized seats of excellent workmanship and poor aesthetics stuck out from the rest of the Chamber like the glaring mistakes of amateur artisans. "*Hard* work."

"You're late," said Eàmon shortly.

Loga turned to Eàmon with an open, innocent expression. "Why . . . I hadn't realized I'd even been invited. I was hoping I was gate-crashing." The Ruler Selene chuckled aloud, and Loga winked at her before raising his hand to cover his face while turning to face her father; his features seemed to *run*, like water, and when he looked up again, a dead-somber expression sat upon his features. "Putting on my serious face," he said to nobody in particular. He glanced up, and met Loden's pale blue eyes. "I thought you might like to speak to me, before you speak to *them*," he said softly, pointing upward.

At that exact moment the first rumble of sound reached them.

Nine pair of eyes looked up instantly, to where the huge space-craft *Arskyld*, a ship sized for Giants, was approaching, still far distant at that moment. Loden did not even blink. In private comment Loga said quietly, *Too easy. Someday they're all going to be sitting around in a circle with their faces hanging out like they do, and I'm going to jump up and yell, "Look behind you!"*

The concluding thought was almost bored. *They will.*

A muscle in Loden's right cheek twitched. That was all.

Loga looked up himself; the Giants' ship was slowing, its engines all but deafening at this close range, dropping down to the landpad with which the Chamber of Parliament shared the clearing, high in the Black Mountains above the city of Parliament. Its approaching bulk grew and blocked the sun, threw the Chamber into shadow. "My fellow Rulers," he drawled, "our faithful engineers."

The Ruler Selene asked the question without expression. "Loga, have they completed the work to your satisfaction?"

Loga raised his voice over the growing thunder of the ship's atmosphere-only reaction engines. "Yeah." Loga did not even look at her. He watched *Arskyld* landing, dropping down to the landpad with a grace wholly inappropriate to anything of such size. The landpad, built by T'Pau's People in the days when Giants had been nothing more than a rumor to the north, was just barely large enough for a craft of *Arskyld*'s bulk to land upon. Loga was probably the most technologically sophisticated Ruler still alive; he was, by the same token, likely the only Ruler who appreciated what an awesome accomplishment *Arskyld* was. He'd have given much to see the schematics of the engines that enabled the ship to use a fusion reaction in atmosphere without radioactive pollution. The engines died down, and gentled into silence. Loga looked away from the craft and found, to his surprise, that he was the center of attention. "What?"

Elyssa said softly, "Perhaps some small details of your journey? If you would?"

"Look, what do you want? It's fine, really." He shrugged. "Gardens everywhere, if you like that sort of thing, you know, bushes, trees, flowers. New Parliament is nice, a little empty right now. It was all in the plans. Personally I think you could have just taken Senta's word for it all." Two large misshapen forms descended from *Arskyld* and, ignoring the too-small stairs carved into the mountainside, began the ascent up the steep slope to the Chamber.

"My daughter," said Elyssa, "is quite young."

"Then you shouldn't have sent her in the first place, but anyway," said Loga, not even glancing at the Ruler Elyssa, directing his words to Loden, "it's perfect. And see, now the Giants come for their payment. We did promise them complete satisfaction, didn't we? Loden?"

Elyssa said swiftly, "And what do you think, my husband? Have they not completed their bargain with us, to the letter?"

Loden did not even look at her, but only nodded, and his wife's jaw tightened visibly. Loden had no thought for her, with the crux of his problem ready to be dealt with. The two Giants had arrived—the Giant who held the most prestigious post a Giant might aspire to, Senior Engineer Rome, and his elder brother, who held the most powerful, the Skaald Laar. They were of the Giant clan of Janter, the clan that had, for a full four generations of Giants, near two full centuries, ruled the Giants in all things. Despite their long legs, they moved little faster than a Ruler, navigating their vast bulk with great care, coming in through the northern entrance to the Chamber. Loden stood there at the podium, facing them, with the other Rulers at his back.

"Greetings, Loden." The Giant Laar's voice was a deep, resonant sound—the way, Loga had once thought, that granite, speaking, might sound. The Giants' eyes were the most manlike features in their oddly deformed skulls, intelligent and sensitive. "I see you are all enjoying yourselves as usual. Dreaming." Laar's eyes did not look past Loden, but kept themselves locked to the old Ruler's. "Conferring. We don't wish to interfere with that pastime; let us conclude our business, and you may return to it. We have completed New Parliament, Loden. The atmosphere plants are in place. Most of one continent is fully terraformed, and the process, now begun, will not stop. The computer control network is the most sophisticated we have ever built; it is at your disposal. Within a century at most, that entire world will be indistinguishable from what you have created for yourselves here in this one city. It does," he said in tones that were half summation, half challenge, "meet your specifications in every way."

"Welcome," said Loden with subtle emphasis, "to *your* Parliament, Laar, Rome." He glanced up at the Giant Rome briefly and back to Rome's elder brother. "Please, seat yourselves. I know standing is difficult for you." The Giants did so, and Loden continued. "We have been discussing the situation in the Valley, as it will be once we Rulers have left it. We hope that our efforts to establish a lasting peace with Cain and Maston will not be lost in your hands. As you know, harmony between you and the Workers has always been our goal."

The two Giants laughed, boomingly, in high good spirits, as though Loden's comments were enormously amusing. When the laughter ceased, Rome looked around at the assemblage calmly. When he spoke, the words were laced with contempt. "Your efforts to establish a lasting peace . . . yes. Lords of Light, our spy satellites tell us that Cain and Maston's forces are fighting near Eagles right now . . . while you talk about some idealistic peace!"

Solan's tail was getting warm.

The baffles around his rear thrusters were of tantalum carbide; they would not melt and let the lasers through to his fusion engines at temperatures of less than three thousand eight hundred degrees Centigrade; and while the barbarian lasers reached temperatures that were sufficient to do it, the lasers had to stay on him long enough, or they were useless.

Commander Captain Solan was beginning to regret his impatience. A line of laser light slashed past his slipship. The ionization trail left a blazing afterimage in his retina. One of the barbarians was babbling at him in silverspeech, a language Solan did not understand.

Returning to Eagles, after the talks with Cain, he'd chosen to take a shortcut. "Barbarians . . ." The shortcut looked likely to cost him his life. *"Damn* barbarians."

The obvious way home was to simply follow the curve of the Great Dam. "Shortcuts," muttered Solan under his breath. As long as one stayed to the seaward side, it was safe enough, even when passing Singer, where the Rulers still held sway.

But it was slow. *"Damn* shortcuts."

Take your slipship up, over the Black Mountains, across the northernmost tip of the Glowing Desert, back up over the Black Mountains again, and there was Eagles; it would have cut his travel time by nearly a third. It was the route he'd taken on his way to Eastmarch; he had not even considered taking the long way going home again.

Unfortunately, the barbarian silver-eyes considered the Glowing Desert their territory. They were almost never this far north, though, and even two slipships they would not have bothered; but Solan was alone.

Beep. Beep. Solan slapped the antimissile switch, and did not even look at the rearview camera. His antimissiles missed the heatseeker. What was really galling . . . He took his slipship into a tight turn at eight gravities, to evade the heatseeker. He blacked out for a moment and came back to himself with a rapidly expanding fireball to his rear, momentarily blocking his view of his attackers, and their view of him. He took the moment to run through his tell-tales. What was *really* galling was that not one of those barbarian aircraft were any match for Solan's slipship.

But twelve of them were.

They were leaving the Black Mountains, flying north. Eagles was not far; Solan keyed open the comm. "Eagles, this is Captain Solan. I have barbarians on my tail, Eagles . . . *Eagles?*"

Laser light touched his slipship, ran across the stubby wings. Very bad; Solan took the slipship entirely over, three hundred sixty degrees around its axis, corkscrewing down toward the floor of the canyon they were in. Except for the very rear of the slipship, the light carballoys were not designed to take direct laser fire for any length of time.

"Commander Captain? This is Commander First Jonah. What is your loc—" The voice broke up in static as Solan lost altitude rapidly. The barbarian slipships followed him down, all but one which chose to keep its altitude, sitting up high and watching the excitement beneath; it was going to be a fatal choice. Not thirty meters above the ragged floor of the canyon Solan scooped air slightly until his speed had dropped to the point where the slipship wouldn't tumble when he took it up. Eleven ships on his tail, one above him. He took a steadying breath and tried not to remember the times he'd seen slipships come apart doing this.

Solan tipped the slipship's nose up. The wings caught the air, and the slipship slowed. It was like slamming into a wall of stonesteel. Then the thrusters cut in, and the slipship *climbed*, nearly straight up.

The barbarians were just beginning to realize that his ship was no longer there.

Solan came right up under the belly of the aircraft that was sitting up at the top of the mess, touched it with a laser nearly twice as hot as those the silver-eyes were using, and watched the aircraft disintegrate into a cloud of torn metal. He was nearing his original altitude when the voice came back.

". . . *you? Solan? You're not showing on our far radar, and . . . wait. There you are. Where are the silver-eyes?"*

The barbarians were regrouping, raggedly, and coming after Solan. *"Wait, we've got them on the radar. Nine craft . . . no, eleven."*

Another burst of gibberish came across on the hailing channel. Tuned to the higher frequency that Eagles used for craft-to-base communications, Solan knew the barbarians were speaking to him only by a flickering on his control panel. "Eagles, does anybody speak barbarian out there?"

"This is First Jonah, Captain. I speak it a little bit. Not perfectly, but well enough to—"

"Damn it, First, what are they *saying?*"

"Ah . . . Surrender, or get blown out of the air, basically. There's more, but it's all personal stuff about your mother."

"Oh. That's what I thought they were saying."

"Commander?"

"Never mind. Send somebody up to greet me and chase these mutants off. I'm coming home." The barbarian craft were no longer really close enough for laser fire; the heatwarp of the atmosphere was throwing the beams off to the extent that their chance of actually striking Solan was negligible. Not nearly as maneuverable as a slipship, but slightly faster, they were closing the gap. They must have been burning fuel at an incredible rate. There were some advantages to basing a craft designed for maneuvering in atmosphere upon chemical engines rather than thrusters powered off of fusion fuel cells. "It's going to be a race," said Solan quietly.

"Commander?"

"Never mind."

In the town of Eagles, high in the hills at the west end of the Great Dam, Maston Veramorn walked through the echoing empty corridors of what once had been his home, the Veramorn hearth for as long as there had been Veramorns: the huge stone and stonesteel structure of the Storm Keep.

He was a large, muscular man just entering his middle years, slowly going to fat, with iron-gray hair and wrinkles already settled around his eyes and mouth. As a youth he had not been handsome; others, even other members of Lord Veramorn's household, had called him the "small Giant," in reference to the renowned ugliness of Giants. As an adult he had acquired a certain rough charm, which served him well; not for nothing had the Lord Veramorn's youngest child become his heir apparent—even when Maston's brothers and one sister had still been alive.

The house was empty these days. Maston himself did not live there, had not since the outbreak of the Twenty Years' War. In air raids at that time the loyalist Warriors, fighting for the Rulers, had shown a nasty predisposition to shell the residences of the lords of the rebelling territories. Indeed, the Storm Keep had lost one wing in its entirety in one aerial attack.

After the war's end, he had stayed away for other reasons. His own domicile, built after the Treaty of Eastmarch, was far larger, as befit the keep of the man who ruled better than a tenth of the Valley. Further, the Giant Riabel was buried in the Storm Keep's courtyard, and Maston found that he was unable to separate his memories of the Storm Keep from his memories of Riabel and the Giant's insane, brooding presence.

Still . . . it was not a bad place at all. Maston was seriously considering giving it to Tristan. Commander Captain Tristan was still living in the Commanders' barracks, beneath the Command Post; an inappropriate place for Maston Veramorn's successor to be spending his nights. Maston thought he would enjoy that. Tristan had never had much beyond a certain dogged ability for hard work, and knew how to show appreciation. With but a little effort, the Storm Keep would be as bright and cheerful as the home of his childhood. . . .

The comm at his belt beeped. He picked it up.

"My lord?"

For a moment Maston could not place the voice; Eagles was a small town, had always been, and in his childhood he had never needed the skill leaders of populous cities such as Westmarch developed by necessity, of recognizing and remembering voices and appearances as easily as a falconer knew his falcons. Then it came to him. "Lieutenant Jonah. What?"

"My lord, Commander Captain Solan is on his way home. He's being chased, sir, by raiders—barbarians."

"ETA?"

"My lord, four and a half minutes before they enter the range of our guns."

The Storm Keep was not quite a kilometer away from the Command Post.

Maston Veramorn left at a dead run.

The Command Post was spread out across nearly a full square kilometer of what had once been a peak of solid granite. Before Cain's return from Exile, nobody in Eagles—nobody in the Valley, for that matter—had possessed the technology necessary to level that peak and build upon it. The Giants could have done it, surely; but Eagles was a small town of narrow streets and tall buildings, and if not poor, neither was it wealthy.

And the Giants did not work cheap.

Maston Veramorn ran downhill from the Storm Keep, along the Boulevard of the Falcons, past dozens of shops that still created handicrafts in the same fashion as their fathers and their fathers' fathers, past other shops that used manufacturing techniques developed by an industrial civilization that had been dead for nearly thirteen centuries by the date of Maston Veramorn's birth, straight through the crowds of his subjects without slowing. It was Summer 4, 1284, and the streets were crowded with people enjoying the fine weather.

Those who did not get out of his way were bowled aside. If the subjects of Eagles saw anything odd in the sight of their lord and master charging through the streets like a madman, they knew better than to do so much as smile about it.

He was not even breathing heavily when he reached Command.

The Command Post was modeled, in detail, along the lines of the Command Center at Eastmarch—a vast deck that overlooked the shipyard, flooded with bright yellow sunpaint. At the center of the Post were the holo clusters, in which the technicians monitored air traffic. Workstations radiated outward from the holo clusters in ragged groupings. Communications, defensive ground-to-air weapons, Shield control and slipship Command functions were separated in specific groups.

The Command Post's resemblance to the Command Center in Eastmarch was neither a coincidence nor surprising. Cain's engineers had built them both.

THE RING

The Command Post was fully manned when Maston arrived. Commanders and Warriors were at every post. His daughter, Rea Veramorn, and her five-year-old son by Captain Solan, Orion, were there already. The boy, a blond-haired blue-eyed mirror of his father, seemed unconcerned, watching the bustle of activity without comprehension, sitting quietly in the corner with his arms around his dog. Maston's lips curled in distaste at the sight of the animal—a perfectly useful dog being wasted as a *pet*, neither a sheep dog nor a hunting animal. Maston had been displeased at his daughter's decision to give it to the boy, when the child had no conceivable need of it.

Maston growled to his daughter on the way by her. "I told you to keep the child out of here."

Captain Tristan glanced up briefly at his lord's entrance and then back to the holo bubble. Rea was already seated at Weapons Station One, running white-faced through the setup routines. If she heard her father's words, she ignored them. The Warrior left in charge of that station stood beside her, at attention, his face a brilliant crimson. "My lord," said Tristan briefly, "you're just in time for the excitement. Solan's picked up an escort, it seems."

Maston grunted, taking in the computer-generated markers in the holo bubble with a glance. "You've got the top tier of lasers ready as soon as he's near enough? Good. Why don't you have Warriors up there?"

"There were no slipships ready," said Tristan steadily.

"Why the hell not?"

Tristan glanced at him quickly, with just the faintest perceptible trace of unease at the tone of Maston Veramorn's voice. "My lord, I've had no time to look into it yet."

"Do so at the earliest opportunity. Gunner Command!"

The Commander addressed did not even look away from his workstation. "My lord!"

"When he's below the first tier, give him protective fire." Maston looked back to the holo bubble. "Eleven craft? Who are they?"

Rea answered him. "Barbarians, silver-eyes."

Maston said sharply, "Cain's?"

The holo bubble showed the hills in which Eagles was nestled. From a spot deep in those hills a single sharp line of emerald laser light reached out, touched one of the pursuing ships. The aircraft vanished in a storm of disintegrating metal.

"Gotcha . . . No, can't be," his daughter said, the tension that was apparent in her face utterly absent from her voice. Her comment sounded almost casual. "Chemical engines, jets—look at the exhaust spectrum. Besides, If Cain had trained them, they wouldn't nearly be damn fools enough to come so deep into flight space we control."

"Eagles, this is Captain Solan." Orion looked up at the sound of his father's voice, trying to see where it was coming from. *"I'm going to drop under the tier . . . now."*

In the holo bubble the blue spark that was Solan's ship *dipped,* a drop perceptible even in the vastly reduced dimensions of the holo reproduction.

In Laser Tier One there were over one hundred eighty fixed lasers. It was Eagles' first line of defense, though by no means its last. A withering, nearly solid wall of laser fire cut through the air, with Solan beneath it and the barbarians above it. Maston watched the process in the holo bubble for just a second and then said, "Good. Gunner Command, bring the ceiling up on them."

Rea said quietly, "Yes, father." There was nobody in the Command Post who dared look at Maston except Tristan, and even Captain Tristan did so very briefly. Maston's face was nearly as scarlet red as that of the Warrior standing at attention near his daughter. In the holo bubble the wall of laser fire moved up incrementally, all one hundred eighty-three lasers in Tier One tracking upward at the same moment. The barbarian craft turned madly, scrambling to get out of the path of the decimating laser fire. Almost none of them survived; only two badly damaged ships made it through the curtain of laser fire and turned to flee south. Maston doubted that even those two would make it home. One of them was smoking badly enough that the holo bubble had included a cloud symbol trailing after it, and the other craft appeared to be having difficulty holding altitude.

"Eagles, well done. Open Landpad Five—quickly, please. I've got problems."

There was nothing more he could do here. Maston Veramorn turned away from them all and headed for the exit, down to the landpads. Orion was on his feet, staring wide-eyed at the strained sound of his father's voice.

He was not supposed to be there in the first place. With a very real pleasure, Maston backhanded the brat aside on his way out the door. The dog came to its feet, snarling, but did not leap. Fingering the light knife at his belt, Maston headed down to Landpad Five with something like regret.

It was not a bad landing. The crippled slipship made not even a single pass of the landpad, but came straight in, its tail shining so white hot that it was visible against the bright blue sky while the slipship was more than a kilometer distant.

Maston was continually amazed at how fast news traveled through Eagles. Probably every Warrior who was not at a duty post had assembled just outside the warning barrier at Landpad Five. As he stood on the observation deck, well back from the landpad himself, the thought flickered through Maston's mind that a sufficiently disastrous landing could cost him a significant fraction of his fighting forces. Still, he did not order them back. Captain Solan was extremely popular with the Warriors. Though the fact displeased Maston Veramorn enough that he planned to do something about it, he was hardly fool enough to antagonize his Warriors over something as trivial as a reasonably small danger to their own lives.

This fact was one that Maston had understood so long and so well that consciously he was not even aware of it; weapons are power, and men control weapons; and the men who control the weapons must follow their leader for some reason beyond blind fear, or they will not follow him long.

Solan dropped his slipship's landjacks, and the slipship slowed drastically as the belly thrusters cut in. He struck, moving far too fast. The landjacks snapped clean off at the first instant of contact with the landpad's high-friction plastisteel surface. The slipship canted to one side, and one of the stubby wings touched the ground and sent the slipship into a slow spin as it ground its way forward across the landpad. Before it had crossed forty meters, it had ceased moving.

Technicians in coldsuits rushed forward with their long hoses, spraying the glowing tail of the slipship with fire-retardant foam chilled to within forty degrees of absolute zero. The canopy glided open as though nothing were in the least bit amiss, and Commander Captain

Solan scrambled out of the slipship, out across the nose of the slipship to stay as far away from both the fusion thrusters at the rear and the foam spray, coldly lethal in and of itself. He touched the landpad's surface, stood still for just a moment; unbuckled his helmet, pulled it off and tossed it to a technician standing nearby, and with all the aplomb in the world walked away from the slipship he had nearly died in.

And the cheers and clapping began.

Though it had been many years since Maston had gone into battle, he remembered the feeling with great clarity: the high sharp blaze of adrenaline, the almost wild elation that came from having cheated death just one more time.

Maston watched from the balcony as Solan was reunited with his adopted daughter and their spoiled, undisciplined child. Near three score of Warriors crowded around him, those who could reach him pounding him on the back in jubilation.

While it was all happening, Solan looked around the floor and then up to see Maston Veramorn standing above the landpad, watching him. A grin split his face. "My lord!" he called, loudly enough that no man within a hundred meters could have missed the words, "I have brought you a truce!"

There was just a moment of near silence, and the landpad bay exploded with cheers.

Maston Veramorn nodded down to them, without expression, turned away, and went back inside.

No one watched him go.

The War Room was an anachronism. Spears and shields of the noble Land'ner families of Eagles and Westmarch hung upon its walls. The great composite bow with which Maston's great-grandfather had killed the shrike, in the famous hunt of 1212, occupied a position of honor above Maston's place at the head of the planning table. A workstation terminal, perpetually turned on, was immediately beneath it.

Maston sat there in the Commander General's chair, waiting. Though he was not, in theory, the Commander General—or at least, he had never bothered to assume the title—there was nobody in all the territory that Eagles ruled who would have been foolish enough to question his right to it.

A full quarter of an hour passed while he waited, brooding. Many of his Commanders filed in while he was waiting. He ignored them, letting them take their seats. Tristan would be hurrying Maston's daughter and second Commander Captain. Unlike both Rea and Solan, Tristan showed proper respect—and as a result, Maston knew, suffered somewhat in popularity with the Warriors.

And *that* Maston was well content with.

Rea was talking when she and her husband finally strolled in, arm in arm, with Commander Captain Tristan behind them. ". . . worried? *Me?* I wasn't worried. You wouldn't dare spoil your reputation." As had happened often enough before, Maston was struck by the resemblance between the woman the world thought his daughter and Commander Captain Solan; the same blonde hair, the same eyes, even something of the same mouth.

The brat, thank the Light, was nowhere to be seen. Apparently even his daughter was not arrogant enough to attempt to drag that spoiled, effeminate child into the War Room.

Solan did not continue their conversation, but gently unlinked her arm and, as custom demanded for a Commander returning home to his lord, went to one knee in front of Maston Veramorn. He touched his lips to the signet ring on the outstretched hand; in that instant, Solan realized for the first time that he had not, his entire stay at Eastmarch, seen a single person kneel to Cain. "My lord," he murmured, and rose again.

No one in that room save Maston himself was over thirty.

Maston said abruptly, "Were those barbarians Cain's?"

Tristan had seated himself to Maston's left, across the table from Solan and Rea. Solan pulled his chair out and sat before answering. "No, of course not. Cain's are better than that. I'd be dead now if that many of Cain's had gone after me alone. They were barbarians, silver-eyes it seems. I did something stupid, left Valley airspace on my way back—a shortcut over the Black Mountains. Someday we're going to have to do something about the barbarians, my lord Maston. They're getting too bold, and their ships get better every year."

Maston snorted. "I've greater worries. Between Cain and the Rulers and the Giants, the damn barbarians are far down on my list of concerns."

Solan shrugged. "Someday." From inside the vest of his flight jacket he withdrew a sheaf of papers which had been folded in thirds. "My lord," he said with obvious pride, "I have brought you the draft of a truce with Eastmarch. I believe it is quite fair."

Maston glanced at him from beneath bushy eyebrows, unfolding the papers. "I'd hope you believe it's a fair truce, having bothered to bring it back." He barely glanced at the text before tossing the papers back on the table. "So, he's agreed to come."

"Yes," said Solan eagerly. "A little friendly competition—my lord, it's just what you wanted. It'll be a good time to talk, with the atmosphere of festivity. If there's ever to be peace, we shall never have a better place to start."

"Don't repeat my own words to me, boy," said Maston sourly, and Rea Veramorn went as white as though Maston had struck her. "Tell me about your trip."

Solan sketched out the details he knew would interest Maston, the number of Eastmarch's slipships, the weapons he'd been shown at the weapons monger's. Maston interrupted him again. "Did he talk to you about the Ring?"

Every Commander there could see the Captain's temper stretching. Nonetheless he controlled his features and the tone of his voice. "My lord, he showed it to me."

"*What?*"

Solan was stunned by the force of Maston Veramorn's reaction; the man had come half up out of his chair. "He . . . showed it to me, my lord." Maston was staring at him. "My lord, I assure you it is true. What's wrong?"

"Nothing . . ." Maston sank back in his seat, his expression smoothing over. "I believe you. Now why did he do that?"

The question was hardly directed at Solan; he answered it nonetheless. "My lord, you know it is said that Lord Cain has the ability to touch thoughts, as the Rulers do."

"Besides being said, it's also true," said Maston absently. "So?" He still was staring beyond Solan, as though lost in thought.

"His thoughts touched mine, while the Ring was free of its enclosure. It was . . . a strange experience, my lord. I think he did not trust our intentions to observe the truce honorably and wished with the power of the Ring to probe my thoughts more deeply than he might have done otherwise."

"Describe to me," said Maston slowly, "how it happened, when he showed you the Ring. Do not omit a detail, no matter how minor you may think it."

It took some time; Maston kept interrupting him with questions to which Solan either did not know the answer or could not see the relevancy of. He finished simply: "I think perhaps he was as startled as I, my lord, at how it happened, though I would not swear so. It is difficult to guess at what Cain is thinking. At least I found it so. At lunch he said he trusted me, that he would come to the Games, and that we should make peace."

Maston said, dangerously gentle, "And you believed him?"

"Yes." The word was clear, flat; the other Commanders in the room glanced uneasily at Solan, but his gaze was directed only at their lord. "My lord," he said evenly, "I believe him. That does not mean I trust him."

"So," said Maston Veramorn, speaking for the benefit of every person in the War Room except Commander Captain Solan, "you have seen the Ring of Light, *felt* its power as though you were yourself a Ruler, in control of the Light. Do you, Commander Captain Solan, believe you might control this Ring yourself?"

Around the table, men were fingering the knives that were all they were allowed, by custom, to carry in their lord's presence. Four years ago an audience that this one was coming to resemble had ended with Maston, in a fit of rage, beheading a Commander First atop this very table; and though no man there knew how Captain Solan might react, there was no chance whatsoever that Solan would die as easily as that barely remembered First.

For that matter, Maston's own daughter might well cut his throat did a melee occur; she was known to love her husband better than her father.

"My lord," said Solan directly, "I have not said that I think I might control the Ring, and I do not believe so." He paused, held Maston Veramorn's eyes in clear challenge. "All I know is that Lord Cain wants me there when we negotiate a lasting peace, and my fellow Commanders agree."

The silence that followed was so still that a chair scraping on the flagstones of the floor might have set off a bloodbath. Finally Maston Veramorn, eyes glittering, laughed a hollow, jovial laugh. "And I, too, agree," he said loudly, good humor in his voice: "Let us have the Games and join forces with Cain. Perhaps together we may throw off the yoke of the Rulers from the rest of this Valley!" He came to his feet quickly, so that he might look down upon the seated table. "Tonight," he shouted, "we will feast!"

The cheers that followed sounded particularly halfhearted, and the meeting broke up more quickly than was usual. Solan bade his lord a quiet, civil good-bye and left with his wife once again on his arm.

In the hallway outside, Rea said quietly, "It looks to be a lovely evening. Let's take Orion and Pinch, some food and wine, and ride out for a picnic."

Give Maston a chance to calm down, Solan thought wryly. At times it was almost as though he knew, without words, what his wife was thinking. Teasing, he said thoughtfully, "Depends. How *much* wine?"

Half a dozen Commanders were walking the same way as Solan and Rea—though now that the potential danger in the War Room was over and the man was reunited with his wife, most of them were content to wait until later to talk with Solan. One Commander, however, Second Anders of the noble family Rivera, the closest thing to a good friend Solan had among the Warriors, passed them in the corridor, moving at a trot on the way to his duty post. He stopped beside them for just a second, walking backward, and said briefly, "Well done. Don't walk alone down any dark corridors, my friend," turned and continued on his swift way.

Maston Veramorn and Tristan d'Volta were left alone in the War Room.

Tristan said quietly, "You wanted Cain alone. Have you really changed your mind?"

Maston paced back and forth across the length of the rectangular War Room. The rage he had carefully controlled while the other Commanders were present was plain on his features. "Nothing's changed," he snarled.

Tristan watched him but a moment longer, then sketched a bow himself and let himself out of the War Room.

Had he ever really doubted, Maston Veramorn doubted no longer. The mad Giant Riabel had told him the truth.

The girl Rea, whom all the world thought his daughter, and the bastard from Westmarch, Commander Captain Solan, the man and his wife—were Rulers.

And brother and sister.

Twins.

The twin children of the Ruler Loden.

"Kavad?"

"My lord, I have brought you the materials you requested."

"Play them for me."

The holos flickered through the black space in front of Cain. "Stop." The woman in the holo had blonde hair and Loden's pale blue eyes. "Amazing. Kavad, you see it?"

"My lord, it might be a holo of the Ruler Selene."

"What an astonishing resemblance. Rea, her name is? I do not think I have seen a holo of her since she reached adulthood—surely I would have known. And Solan. Now that I have seen Selene's image in Rea, I see that family resemblance in Solan as well. Loden must have looked very like this as a young man, long centuries past."

"They are—man and wife."

"Does this disturb you, Kavad? It should not. Ken Selvren morals are not the morals everywhere."

"Among my people, my lord, the man's throat would be cut, the child drowned, and the woman"—Kavad almost, though he caught himself in time, said *exiled*—"sent to walk in wilderness."

"It is likely, Kavad, that they do not know they are related, except perhaps as closely as half brother and half sister. Solan thinks himself a bastard, and in fact was raised in Westmarch without parents. It will be no great stretch for him, or others, seeing his wife's features in his own, to imagine himself Maston's bastard. They cannot help but see their own resemblance, I would imagine. But Kavad, in Eagles even a full brother and sister may marry without shame. It's considered foolish, but not shameful."

"I am only a barbarian, my lord."

Cain laughed. "Meaning you think civilized morals are barbaric yourself." He sat silently, the holofield frozen on the image of Rea Veramorn. "Kavad."

"My lord."

"Get Doctor Denahi; I wish her nearby if I need help."

"My lord?"

"I am going to put the Ring on, Kavad."

Morning had worn into afternoon. Evening was approaching, and tempers flared short.

"Look," said Loga impatiently, "nobody promised you anything at all except the city of Parliament and our absence. These you will have. It's not our concern, once we have left, what problems Giants have with Cain, or Maston either." He shrugged and added, "I'm sorry Cain's going to make it harder for you to conquer the Valley, but, you know, I don't really think you should try to anyhow."

The Giant Laar fixed Loga with a fierce, hostile stare. "Hypocrite."

Loga looked startled, then thoughtful. "I suppose I am, at that. We have governed here against the wishes of the Workers for quite some time. I must admit, on the evidence, Rulers are as subject to rationalization as any other supposedly sentient life form I've ever met." He smiled at the Giant.

Laar snorted in disgust and did not address Loga. "Loden, Tribunal Elder, we were promised your position of power. It is splitting hairs with an ax to say that we were promised the *chance* at power. The agreement was clear, is clear, and if you do not aid us in retrieving the Ring, you are, all of you, forsworn. Discuss the ethics of *that*."

"I am the only living Ruler," said Loden, wishing desperately that he did not sound as tired as he felt, "who has ever seen the Ring. Giants, the secret of the Light is not in the Ring. It is hidden in a place where Cain, embittered man that he is, will never think to look. We have no secret, Laar, because there is none. Once the wars were done, we sought peace and harmony, and with the time developed the gift within ourselves; it was not always so strong as it is now. There is no barrier to prevent anyone—Worker, Giant, *anyone at all*—from taking the same approach. If we have learned better the control of the Light, perhaps it is only because we have worked at it longer."

"Brilliantly spoken," said Loga loudly. *Bullshit, alas.*

Not all of it, Loden replied tiredly. "Giant, consider peace. It is not such a terrible thing. Cain does not, yet, hate you as he hates us. Make peace with Cain and Maston and break the circle of hatred. Trust . . . can be."

The lungs of a Giant are an awesome thing. *"No!"* bellowed Laar. He came to his feet, towering high above them all. "Your agreement was to leave control in our hands! If Cain unites Maston and the other Workers behind him, with the power of the Ring, they are a threat to us! *We will burn this Valley clean of life before we allow that!"*

The silence that followed was broken by a low, warm chuckle. "Ah, Giant." Loden's daughter Selene, who was the fourth eldest Ruler in that room, older than Loden's current wife, said gently, "Be calm, Laar. I have known Cain. He will not master the Ring. Living with the Light is rather more difficult than wearing it on your finger."

Several of the other Rulers chuckled in turn, the tension somewhat relieved.

"Guys," said Loga abruptly, "we're wrong, and I've just changed my mind."

There was another long silence. Finally Loden said with a quiet that was almost anger, "Is this another joke, my friend?"

Loga was very still, eyes dropping shut. His voice came with effort. "He's putting it on. He's putting the Ring on. Close your eyes, and listen."

The Giants stared at them in bewilderment. Quiet descended on the Rulers in the Chamber. The breezes of the approaching night blew cool among them. "Yes," the murmurs came, and "Yes, I feel it," and "The Light is being raised."

The Ruler Elyssa said distantly, "He will not succeed. He cannot, the Light is not within him. You know what happened to him last time."

The Ruler Gabriel shook himself slightly, looked about, and said dryly, "The last time was damn near eighty years ago, Lady Elyssa. People change."

Loga did not move, but sat motionless with his eyes shut. He said quietly, "We have not much time left to decide. There is a power in the east, my fellows."

"Yes," said Loden after a heartbeat. "I feel it."

"If it is to be done, it must be done now." Loga exhaled slowly and opened his eyes to find Loden looking at him. "You and I, sir?"

Loden looked slowly around the amphitheater; at the Giants, standing impatiently and awaiting an answer; at Elyssa, shaking her head *no* with mute pleading in her eyes. He turned back to Loga. "He is our mistake, is he not?" There might have been no one but themselves in all the world. "You should have taught him better, and I should have killed him while I could."

Loga shrugged. "Perhaps. And perhaps we should have raised him up to join us, eh?"

The old Ruler bowed his head. His thought touched Loga privately. *I know you loved him, once.*

Once, said Loga, *there was that within him which could be loved.*

The Ruler Elyssa said, through frozen lips, "Loden, don't go. Please."

The two men stood with the glow building between them. Neither even looked at Elyssa. Loga said silently, *Do you suppose Cain has ever loved anyone?*

Loden scowled at him, fiercely. *How the hell would I know?*

I've thought about this a long time, you know. The radiance built slowly around them. *I think perhaps Cain loved Artemis.*

Loden shrugged. *Perhaps.*

Loga's thought was almost appealing. *He must have. Artemis gave his life for Cain.*

Loden Almandar said softly, aloud, "Perhaps."

Their forms vanished in the gathering Light.

The Sickness

The Year 1284 After the Fire

• 1 •

"My lord?"

Cain did not hear the barbarian guard's words. He was walking, placing his feet with great care. He passed through a blur of encroaching corridors and somewhat more open work areas, though never once did he come to the surface; he could tell.

The echoes were always wrong to the boy from the hills; the sounds of enclosed places.

Cain did not look behind himself. He did not see the shadow that followed him everywhere he went. Scalding-hot sweat ran down his body. There was no wind, only the gentle hum of the ventilators. His breath came sharp and shallow. The corridors grew dimmer once, and he knew that outside, on the other side of the Shield that protected them from the Rulers, the sun was setting. The fact filled him with a terrible, desolate grief.

Then he forgot about it. There were Workers around him, Workers all around. He had the distant impression of gaping, confused faces. The world turned around him once, and then there were gentle hands reaching for him, to help him up from where he lay, stretched flat on the ground. He fended them off, brushed their hands aside, and sat up himself, sat with his back resting against the trembling wall. The Workers' barracks filled his vision. Some wavering harsh light flooded the barracks, made the Workers expand and recede in his vision. Cain was not certain whether the silence was absolute or whether his mind had ceased registering the sounds his ears recorded.

From somewhere in memory, the voice came to him. *Control yourself! If you were not taught the proper breathing exercises at Academy, you surely learned them from me.* The meaning of the words was difficult to encompass, almost as though something did not *want* him to understand.

The Ring pulsed, a raw, hostile power, somewhere in the distance. On his hand.

They appeared on a dirt road leading to the Caverns.

At Parliament, high up in the Black Mountains, the sun would be visible for another twenty minutes. Here, in the shadow of the Gray Mountains, it was already dark. The road was empty this time of night; there was nobody to see the Rulers Loden and Loga sparkle into existence.

They began walking. There were few enough people, anywhere in the world, who, overhearing their conversation, could have understood it.

How badly, Loga wondered, *do you think he hates us?*

What makes you think he does?

We killed Artemis. We tried to kill him.

The Ruler Loden chuckled aloud. *It amazes me, at times, how poorly you have understood the men who have been your friends, Loga. You give them too little credit. I doubt Cain hates us, though I do not doubt he would destroy us if he could. And as for Artemis; we did not kill Artemis, my friend. He killed himself—he merely used us to do it.*

Do you suppose he'd guess we're coming?

If he does not suppose someone will come, he is a fool. Loden trudged along the road, eyes down, not looking ahead. *Cain is not a fool.*

Cain's breathing slowed, deepened. *Control does not come from strength, and strength does not come from anger; how, then, shall control come from anger?*

The dull throb eased slightly, the red heat that flickered around the edges of his mind cooling into, if not obedience, then a wary sort of truce. The blurred haziness before his eyes faded into a dim picture: the

Workers' barracks, and hundreds upon hundreds of Workers. There was a fierce pain in his chest, as though he'd had a heart attack; as he sat, it gentled slightly. It was, Cain thought, a damned undignified position for the lord of all Eastmarch territory, sitting slumped against the wall with his subjects staring at him in plain horror. The thought brought a dull glimmer of humor: what might Eric Malachor, simple lord of a small village, have thought of the preeminence of Eastmarch today, or of the man who ruled it?

He struggled back to his feet, leaning heavily against the wall. One of his ken Selvren was standing at the entrance to the Workers' barracks, watching him in obvious indecision. Cain staggered by him, and despite Cain's orders the guard came forward to help. One hand came down on his lord's shoulder. With perfect coordination Cain grasped the barbarian's forearm, touched the ken Selvren's chest with the outspread fingers of his right hand, and threw the man into the corridor wall.

An instant later the Ring *screamed*, a soundless white shriek that pierced like an iron spike straight down between Cain's eyes and into the depths of his brain.

They had nearly reached the first Shield pylon when the scream came. The Shield itself, stretched so large, was all but invisible except at its edges, where light from the stars was refracted slightly.

The scream struck them. Loga staggered, went down to one knee.

Loden Almandar swayed, very slightly. *He hurt someone,* he said flatly.

The shriek reverberated in Loga's mind. A more sensitive telepath than Loden, or any of T'Pau's People, he barely heard Loden and could not reply mentally. "Not with the Ring," he gasped. Loden helped him back to his feet, steadied him until the redhead was able to stand on his own again. "He's wearing it, but he didn't use it."

Through the Shield they could see, not a hundred meters away, one of the aboveground buildings that allowed entrance into the Caverns. They did not need to use that entrance. All they needed to do was get through the Shield.

They could not simply transfer through. The attempt alone would destroy them. In transit they were nothing more than transfer particles in n-space; self-aware, and with a degree of control over themselves, but massless energy nonetheless.

The transit of the Shield, as energy, would shred them into their component quarks.

As men it would merely be very, very painful, and more so for a sensitive telepath such as Loga.

When Loga was ready, without hesitating, they walked into the Shield.

It was like walking into molasses. The air grew ionized about them, and sparks like lightning flew from their hair and fingertips. The genie and the mutant pressed on against the building resistance.

"Denahi?" Cain's private doctor looked up at General Mersai's peremptory tone. Mersai was hunched over the lead workstation that monitored the protective Shield. "We're getting some really bizarre readings from the Shield. It's sucking better than four hundred megawatts and asking for more. What Cain's doing with the Ring, can it effect the Shield?"

Valri Denahi, the doctor whose only duty was attending to Cain, merely shrugged. She was sitting at one of the unattended workstations with her kit, waiting for the call that was sure to come once Cain had abused himself beyond even his remarkable physique's ability to compensate. "How can I say? I've never been comfortable with Cain's fits of mysticism, Commander General. I don't understand the Light, nor how my lord Cain manipulates it, nor how this damned Ring is supposed to aid either him or us against the Rulers." She shrugged again. "If Cain doesn't kill himself tonight, let's ask him, shall we?"

The question was rhetorical, of course, and Mersai turned back to his work. Lord Cain was known not to hear questions he did not care to answer; and if he had to not hear them twice, he was known to have a temper, and indulge it.

"Commander First," said Mersai, "what is our current power output?"

"Sir?" The First looked down at his workstation. "Sir, the power grid's current load is holding steady at twelve hundred fifteen megawatts; if I divert from the Worker quarters, I can about double what we're giving the Shield."

Mersai nodded. "Notify Worker quarters it's going to get dark," he said finally. "More power to the Shield. Give it what it's asking for."

Danger. The thrill of certainty shot through Cain, struck him like rain on the coals of a fire. Suddenly the whirling universe steadied around him and he was dead sober. The Ring was a far-distant problem, a thing that would not kill him nearly so fast as . . . as *what?*

He was standing on a catwalk, in one of the Caverns' large natural caves, not one of the excavated enclosures. It was . . . the observation walk above the Weapons Monger's production floor. One of his Warriors—no, a Commander, there was a starburst on her shoulder—was standing next to him at rigid attention.

There was a crumpled form on the floor, thirty meters beneath them.

"Commander First, what's happening here?"

The girl was trembling, and her voice shook. ". . . my lord? I don't understand your question."

Cain looked around the empty cavern, turning slowly in place. "They've come. Where are they?"

"My lord, I don't understand."

Cain turned on her suddenly. "Who is that down there? How did he fall and what was he doing in here this time of night?"

The Commander stuttered. "M-my lord, Teador, my lord, the Worker Teador. I d-do not know how he fell, sir. Is that correct?"

"What?" Cain looked around slowly. At that exact instant the lights flickered around them. "Did I throw him down there? I did, didn't I?"

He could barely hear her answer. "Yes, my lord."

"Oh." The sense of imminent danger was all around him. He was suddenly aware he did not have so much as a variable laser with him. Mind on other matters, he spoke without thinking. "That's not so bad, I was going to have him executed eventually anyhow. He's been spying for the Giants, and they're starting to mistrust the information I've been feeding him. Look, I've got to go. I think . . . somebody's waiting for me." It was the first time Commander Mielo had ever heard Lord Cain speak except in formal circumstances, and even through the mask of her fear it struck the daughter of Land'ners that he talked like the Steader he was reputed to have been. Cain patted her on the shoulder. "Look, it's all right. Don't worry. I've got to go." And the High Lord Cain left at a trot.

Moments later, while Commander Jana Mielo was still standing motionless, shaking with fear, Lord Cain's barbarian manservant walked out of the darkness at the south end of the catwalk and looked at the Commander First and the still form of the Worker below. Kavad merely shook his head. "One of his own bodyguards and one of his own Workers," he murmured. "I hope it is worth it."

The barbarian bodyguards were not, properly speaking, in the chain of Command at all. Nonetheless, when Kavad said gently, "Remain at your post, First Mielo," the Commander felt nothing but a rush of gratitude. She was not even surprised he knew her name. "I shall have the barbarian Jimal retrieve the body. Fortunately Teador is a known troublemaker."

"Sir, yes sir." She started to salute, sheerly by reflex. The barbarian caught her wrist in an iron grip. The silver eyes touched hers.

"Don't do that," he said simply. "I must go." Without hurrying, he turned and strode after his master, with long, swift strides.

"If I live to be *two* thousand years old," said Loga, wheezing slightly, "I *never* want to do that again. That last surge from the Shield nearly killed me."

Loga was lying on the floor in the building overlooking the landpads, where Cain and Solan had eaten lunch together only the day prior. The two Warriors posted to that building were unconscious, lying in heaps where they'd fallen. Weak-willed men; he had succeeded in bringing them both down with only a gentle suggestion. It brought home to him strongly the vast gulf that existed between himself and the average Worker; they were, indeed, different orders of beings.

Loden nodded. "No hurry. These two won't wake up anytime soon, and Cain will wait." Loga nodded, still shivering slightly. "Does Cain know we're here?"

"Probably." Loga pulled the cloaks Loden had taken from the Warriors more tightly about himself. "He's at least as good a telepath as I am, maybe better. Unless the Ring's taking up too much of his attention, he knows."

"Very well. Will he talk to us, first, or simply attack at the sight of us?"

"I don't know," Loga admitted. "It depends on how well he remembers what he learned in Academy."

The Ruler Loden had, in all his years, never paid much attention to the Academy, until it was too late to matter much either way. "I don't understand."

"If I were in Cain's shoes," said Loga, "I'd talk first. He can't lose anything that way, and might gain. But it's hard to predict what he'll do. He's awfully damn smart. Talking makes sense, so he might just attack, figuring we'll expect him to talk. He thinks I'm smarter than he is, and that scares him. If he's afraid enough, he'll simply flip an estar to decide."

Loden stared at him. "Are you out of your mind? He's a Worker."

"No, he's not. He's Cain."

Loden thought the subject over. The thought disturbed him; reflex so old it was almost hard-wired prompted him to dismiss any Worker as less than a fit opponent.

"Think of him," said Loga, "as the smartest Ruler child you've ever met. You won't be far wrong."

"The smar—" Loden nodded abruptly. "Perhaps there is some hurry, then. We will move as soon as you are ready."

"That's going to be a couple of minutes." Loga paused. He still felt very cold, as though that last surge of power from the Shield had ripped every last calorie of warmth from his body. "At least. Did I ever tell you the one about the cowboy who . . ."

They saw the blaze of the Ring first. It was like a wavering searchlight, bobbing up and down with the movement of Cain's hand. He entered the Command Center and paused for a second. In that second Doctor Denahi had time to be shocked by how very bad he looked. His normally pale skin was flushed, and his black robes were plastered to his body with sweat. But he was walking steadily, and contrary to the reports that had been reaching her, he seemed clearly aware of his surroundings.

"Everyone," he said, without raising his voice. "Out. I want this Center evacuated within the minute."

They stood without moving, the dozen Warriors, three Commanders, and Doctor Denahi. General Mersai said finally, "My lord, have—"

Cain turned on the old man, stared him down. "Did you understand that order, General?"

"Warriors!" said Mersai sharply, not looking away from Cain. "Dismissed! Regroup in Command Debriefing, at the double, *move!*" His Warriors did, shutting down terminals and turning control of surveillance and the Shield over to the distributed computer net. Within twenty seconds the Command Center was empty except for Cain, Mersai and Valri Denahi. Cain brushed past them, to the terminal where Mersai had been monitoring the Shield only moments before.

"Computer," said Cain, "screen only, Shield power requirement curve for the last hour." He only glanced at the resultant display. "Damn, two at least, and that's assuming one of them is Loden. Could be three smaller Rulers." He turned away from the terminal and saw the two of them standing there. A pulse of anger touched Cain, and at the anger's presence the Ring burned on his hand like an ingot of molten metal. His muscles tensed at the sudden surge of the pain, but he did not let it reach his face. "Was my order not clear enough?"

"My lord," said Doctor Denahi, "look at yourself!"

"My lord," said Mersai softly, "you're hurt."

The thought that reached for Cain's lips was, *Not as hurt as you're about to become.* Something prevented the words from being spoken, and he said only, "Yes, I know. And you're not helping. *Now go.*"

The tone of voice reached Mersai. "My lord." All of the acceptance in the world was in those words. He took Doctor Denahi, still protesting, by the arm, and led her from the Command Center, and left Cain alone.

Cain sank into one of the empty chairs, the Ring pulsing on his hand. The power was there, waiting for him, if only he could reach out and encapsulate it, bring it within himself.

And the Rulers knew that, of course; and the Rulers had no intention of giving him the time he needed.

He took long, slow breaths, trying to calm himself, to center himself for what was to come. If the Rulers had done what he would have done in their place, then the two Rulers who were coming would be Loden and Loga. But that was only a problematical proposition, at best.

The Ruler Loden was at least as smart as himself, and Loga was smarter; it made it hard to guess what they were going to do.

"Damn," Cain whispered, "I wish I had time to take a shower."

" . . . and the cowboy grabs his horse by the ears, stares it in the eyes, and says, 'Read my lips, damn it! I said *posse!*' "

Loden chuckled. "Not bad, my friend. Are you ready?"

In the darkness Loga let the cloaks he'd been clutching slide from his shoulders. He was still cold. "I suppose I am," he said finally. "With any luck, Cain won't be in any better shape. He felt sort of wavery for a second there."

"What?" Loden looked around at the quiet room. "He can't be near?"

"No." Loga came to his feet. "Let me navigate, if you would. We're going to go down a level, and several hundred meters away. Cain's waiting for us."

How do you know?

Engraved invitation, my friend, Loga said briefly. *He's already found us.*

There was a moment of warmth and safety.

Cold matter enfolded them.

The lights in the Command Center were dimmed; they could not see Cain well at all. His hands were folded in his lap. The light from the Ring, casting upward, threw Cain's features into shadow.

Loga was certain Cain had not missed the momentary dizziness that had touched him upon their appearance, nor the seemingly innocuous touch with which Loden Almandar helped him regain his balance.

Cain's voice, when it came, was strong and confident. "Please forgive me for not welcoming you, my lords Loden and Loga." Loga felt nothing behind the glare of the Ring, only a tightly held control that yielded him no information. "I have, sitting here, been thinking about what to say to you, or indeed whether to *say* anything."

Loden Almandar relaxed very slightly, without dropping his guard a centimeter. So, it was to be talk, at least first. "And what have you decided to say, Cain?"

His hands unclasped. Cain's left hand gestured to the chairs near where they had materialized. "Please, seat yourselves. We need not maintain the charade that Loga is not hurt, and I've no desire to see him suffer." His voice held honest admiration. "Did you really walk through my Shield?"

Loden answered. "Yes. Sit down, Loga." He was barely shaken by the passage through the Shield himself; he remained standing, for whatever psychological edge that might give him.

"The strength of an ox." Cain smiled at him. "And the sensitivity of a rock."

"I will not bandy words, Cain. I've come for the Ring."

"I've got the Shield running at double strength at the moment," said Cain. "You won't get out again as easily as you got in. As to the Ring . . . let us," he said softly, "talk with one another about the Ring. I've told my people to stay out. We won't be disturbed." The Ring brightened slightly, beat back the darkness. An island of light formed in the midst of the Command Center. "Perhaps you can take the Ring from me. Perhaps not. But I know you, I know how you think. Uppermost in your mind is the hope that, all our recent history to the contrary, I'm going to listen while you reason with me. Bearing in mind, as I must, that your people reasoned mine into a thousand years of slavery because we could not control the Light—nonetheless, Tribunal Elder, I am going to surprise you. And listen while you attempt to reason me into giving up the Ring of Light."

Loden glanced at Cain from beneath bushy eyebrows. "How old are you, Cain?"

"I haven't counted recently. Nearly a hundred, something like that."

"As I recall—forgive me if I do not remember your arguments exactly, Cain, it has been almost eighty years since your famous speech —one of your major grievances with the Rulers was that we denied youthbooster to the Workers and that we ruled them without giving them choice in how they might live their lives."

"As I recall, I was also upset because you were planning to fry my ass in the Glowing Desert."

The Ruler Loden actually smiled, one of the three or four smiles that Cain had ever seen from him. "Touché. But, Cain, look around you. You've lived the lifetimes of any two normal Workers. You rule a huge kingdom covering nearly half this Valley, and in that kingdom your word is law. Workers live and die at your Command. How are you different from us, Cain? You don't share the secret of youthbooster, any more than we ever did. You don't give your subjects leave to question your decisions. It seems to me, Cain, that you have become very like us."

"Insulting me," said Cain dryly, "is not going to help you convince me to give you the Ring. Besides, you're wrong. I don't know how to synthesize youthbooster; if I did, I would share it. I found a cache of the drug in Donnertown, that's all. There's not really enough to make a difference for any very large number of people. Once I've dealt with you, I fully intend to redevelop the science of genegineering and recreate youthbooster. Loga," he said, raising his voice very slightly, "my friend, if you don't stop probing my defenses I'm going to turn your brain to jelly."

Loga relaxed, very suddenly, almost slumping in his chair. His laugh was untroubled. "Worth a try, eh? How have you been, Cain?"

"Well enough, I suppose. It's been an interesting few weeks. Dropspace . . . have you ever gone through dropspace?"

"Many times. The first," said Loga without even searching his memory, "when Donner was still building his fleet, one trial run. It was a fascinating experience. It took forever, and it was over in an instant."

"Yes," said Cain slowly. "It was like that."

"I see you are still wearing Artemis' bracelet and buckle."

"Why not?"

There was no answer to that question, and so Loga countered with another question. "Have you made the jump yet?"

Cain was silent for a long moment. He made no attempt to hide the pain in the smile. "I haven't tried." He returned his attention to Loden. "I'm still not hearing any good reasons to give you the Ring. The women I stole it from swore it wasn't a weapon, and I might almost believe them—except that you're here. Why are you here if the Ring is not a weapon?"

"The Ring is killing you, Cain."

Cain spoke with terrible serenity. "Yes, I know. It's fighting; it does not care to be controlled. Whether it continues to kill me is entirely another question—I think I am beginning to understand it—and in any event, if you try to tell me you braved the transit of my

Shield to keep me from killing myself, you're a liar. And a poor one. Null argument, therefore. Try again."

"The Ring is not a weapon, Cain. It is not yours."

Cain smiled quickly. "I know. That's why I stole it. If it'd been mine the theft wouldn't have been necessary."

"I have come," said Loden inexorably, "to take the Ring because of a bargain entered into by myself for the Rulers. Keeping it will probably kill you, and if it does not kill you, even if you learn to control it, it will not aid you. At worst it is your doom, and at best it is not the weapon that will aid you in defeating us."

"You are still," Cain said softly, "not convincing me to give you the Ring."

Loden spoke as though distracted. "It's hardly yours to give, and is not yours to have." Loden's mind touched Loga's, thoughts exchanged with tight intimacy so that Cain could not overhear. *Loga, suppose we tell him we are leaving Earth?*

No help there. Even if he believes us, he will know we are doing so for reasons that existed before the Ring was stolen. The Ring's theft will not have changed them.

Let him know of our bargain with the Giants?

He might give us the Ring in exchange for the annulment of that agreement, Loden. He will not do so for the mere news of it.

Suppose I swear to him, by the Light, my mind to his, that we mean him no harm? Tell him that, in exchange for the Ring, we will swear to leave Earth and never return?

Try it.

The aside had taken only an instant. Loden saw Cain had caught the passage of thoughts taking place, though surely not the content of those thoughts. "Cain," he began, "let me offer you this bargain. If you will give us the Ring, I will swear to you, my mind to yours so there can be no lies, that the Rulers bear you no ill will; that we mean you no harm; and that, in return for the Ring of Light, we will leave Earth, every Ruler now alive on this planet, in voluntary exile to some other world, and swear never to return to Earth."

The words took time to penetrate. The black pools of shadow that held Cain's eyes stared at them. "You can't mean that."

"I do. But say the word, and I will join minds with you. You are a more powerful telepath than I. It is not one of the ways I can harm you."

Aside from the single gesture, inviting them to sit, Cain had not moved once since their appearance.

He leaned forward in his seat.

The word was long, drawn out into softness.

"No."

"Why *not*, damn it?"

Loga could see the thought move, the only visible thought Cain had allowed him yet; *Center, and quiet in that place, and in that deepness strength.* Loga knew, without knowing how he knew, that the thought was not directed at him, but at the Ring; and to his horror the glow from the Ring grew and steadied.

"Because you wish it." There was a tension within Cain, a tension balanced by . . . something, Loga could not place it. "My lord Loden, I don't trust you."

"Cain, by my grandmother's name, the offer is an honest one."

"I don't doubt." Cain searched the broad, open face. "You're an honest man, Loden Almandar. You've never in your life had to lie to avoid the wrath of someone more powerful than yourself. The only one who ever even tried to dictate your actions was your father, and you killed him."

Loden Almandar's features did not even flicker. "If you speak of my father again, boy, I will kill you. You will be the first man I have killed since killing my father."

Cain did not look at Loga. "Shut up, Loga." Loga, drawing breath to speak, was momentarily startled. "My point, Loden, is that I believe you. I don't need to touch your mind. You'd no more lie to me than kneel to me." He grinned suddenly, the grin of the wolf. "I, on the other hand, am a liar. It's helped keep me alive. And that part of me that scents a lie cannot help but suspect anything you tell me will not be more than a partial truth."

"I think," said Loga suddenly, "we are wasting our time here." Cain still did not look at him. "Cain's good at word games, Loden; he'll sit there and play at reason until he's screwed up his courage enough to attack."

"Play, yes," said Cain slowly. "Play as the Rulers have always played, in the tame garden with the tame Workers to tend the garden."

He was silent for a moment, and then chuckled. "You'd be surprised, gentle Rulers. I *am* learning. It was a nice try, but you're not going to make me angry." Cain's eyes moved over to where Loga sat, the faint luster of the Light visible like an aura around the redhead, a mere flickering glance before his gaze returned to Loden. "The Ring's tried that trick already tonight. It didn't work. I am *waiting*, Loden."

A peaceful hum seemed to touch the air.

Sheer self-control; deep within himself, a still cold pool of exhaustion waited for Loden. The words Cain was waiting for tasted like gall on his tongue. "What," said Loden Almandar, "do you want for the Ring?"

Cain was studying him curiously. "That was hard, wasn't it?"

"*What do you want?*"

Cain waited until the echoes of the bellow had faded. "Anger is counterproductive, Loden. It makes it *hard* to control the Light."

The Ruler Loga actually chuckled. "First point to the home team."

Cain snapped, "This is not a game, Loga. Tribunal Elder, I know something you don't."

"I do not doubt it. That is the natural condition of the world. There is not, I suppose, a child alive on Earth today who does not know *something* I do not."

"I know where your son is."

For the second time in as many minutes, a silence grew that threatened to engulf them.

Donner Almandar had left Earth in the year 271 A.T.F., at the end of the Great Schism, and taken most of the technical prowess of the Rulers with him. He was Loden Almandar's only son, and to sire Donner, Loden had required his grandmother T'Pau's aid; a flaw in Loden's genetic makeup prevented him from siring sons naturally. After T'Pau's suicide, and the loss of her genegineer's skills, he sired no more sons, but only, for over a thousand years, daughters.

Donner Almandar had not ever returned. His fleet, consisting of over five thousand vessels, made the Drop into subspace at the edge of the solar system.

Nobody had ever seen them again.

"That is not possible."

"Oh?" Cain studied him. "Why not?"

Loden's features were growing red. "Donner is dead. If he were not dead, he would have returned."

Control yourself! said Loga sharply. *We came here to manipulate him. Remember?*

Cain said smoothly, "What makes you think I'm talking about Donner?"

"If there was ever," said Loden slowly, "a Worker who deserved to be killed, you are he, Cain."

"It's hard, isn't it, dealing with somebody who might hurt you, who isn't afraid? It's very easy, isn't it Loden, to cry peace, to swear you will never kill, when there was never any chance you could be hurt in the first place? So easy," Cain whispered. "His name is Solan, Loden, he's a Commander in the service of Maston Veramorn. He's married to his twin sister, Rea, whom Maston has passed off as his daughter by a serving woman; they are both twenty-three years old. Were you, by any chance, attempting a parley with Maston Veramorn twenty-three or -four years ago?" Cain *felt* the first flicker of doubt and pressed on. "Were you, in proper Eagles fashion, given a woman for the night, Loden? Did you sleep with her, in proper Ruler fashion? Do you remember the reports that there was a Giant in the employ of Maston Veramorn and would you care to accept a wager that the Giant was the genegineer named Riabel?"

"The name . . . is familiar."

"It should be," said Loga thoughtfully. "He was the Giant who gave youthbooster to the Workers of Erebion. I think Cain's telling the truth."

Cain was staring at Loden, manner intent, like a falcon about to drop for the kill. "My proposal to you, Loden, is this: let me enter your mind as you suggested, and you mine. As a token of my good faith, I've given you the existence of your children, and I guarantee you what I have told you about them is the truth."

"And?"

"My condition is this; that you do not attempt to block away any part of your mind from me, on *any* subject. If you will agree to this, and if your offer is real—that you will, in exchange for the Ring, leave Earth, never to return—then I accept, and it will be as you have suggested. If the offer is not true, I'll kill you if I can. Are you prepared to join minds with me?"

"Are you willing to extend the same courtesy to me?"

"Free access to my thoughts?" Cain smiled. "Of course."

Can you hide the fact that the Giants plan to rule this Valley from him?

I don't know.

It's worth a try. Go. If he tries anything, I'll be right there.

Loden said without words, *Come to me, Cain.*

There was absolute silence, except for the breathing and heartbeats of the three men. Absolute stillness, except for the rise and fall of their chests.

When it was over, Cain was sitting motionless. "The truth, aye, but not all of it. Did you really think I'd tolerate the Giants as overlords?"

Loden's voice was very tired. "You locked me out of your mind. You said you would not."

Finally Cain looked up at Loden Almandar. He stood. There was not the slightest trace of uncertainty in his movements. "You incredible fool," he said simply. "I *told* you I was a liar. Don't you ever listen?"

And he attacked.

In battle, they were called the Terror: Loden, and Donner, and Loga. Together they defeated the Giants, in a battle that cost both sides dearly; together they defeated the White Flame Tribe, and together they sent fleeing the barbarian silver-eyes from whom Donner had, decades earlier, rescued the child Loga before the silver-eyes could kill him.

And then Loden killed John Almandar, his father; estranged himself from his son Donner; and, uncontested lord of all Earth, set himself to a life of quiet and harmony. Donner left Earth. Loga could not, and so stayed, and in the fullness of time his spirit grew with a wild restlessness.

THE RING

Donner was gone; and for a thousand and thirteen years, there was nothing to challenge their strength; nothing to test them.

The blaze came out of nowhere, a blistering-hot glare that bloomed in the Command Center like the birth of a sun. Cain *flared*, his body shimmering and writhing in the center of the firestorm.

The blow struck Loden Almandar like the end of the world. He was vaguely aware that Loga was gone, vanished into the blaze of light in that first instant. His knees buckled, and he fell like a Giant, the shape of space warping, closing, to pull him down with half a dozen gravities of acceleration. He felt bones crack, ribs shatter. Cain was all around him, a vast hatred so cool as to be nearly dispassionate, grinding his life down into the darkness.

In the last instant before the blackness would have held him forever, Loden was suddenly released. In what was very nearly the last instant of his life, he reached out for the Light, brought the white fire inside, and loosed the cold bonds of matter.

Loden hovered over an infinite shining black plain, across which the pale blue sparks of consciousness were scattered like stars through interstellar space. In the great distance, lights flickered, moving to and fro in purposeful patterns, on errands inexplicable to the human mind. All of near space was inundated with the faint glow produced by the massed minds of Earth. Very nearby indeed, two novae extended prominences of scintillating fire toward each other, flooding the otherworld with the force of their struggle.

The otherworld was not the home of the Light, merely the place through which the Light must be reached. As always, the Light beckoned to Loden Almandar, calling to bring him home. For a long time he balanced upon the point of the decision. He was distantly aware that Loga was dying. Loden's body was gone, stored as information for future retrieval, somewhere in the depths of his consciousness. It would take little enough effort to simply let go and find the peace that life had never brought him.

But there were responsibilities . . .

. . . promises to keep.

Bones had shattered in the fall, tissues ruptured. Loden reached into the pattern, reordered the information until all was well, and with an aching regret, allowed himself to be caught up in cold matter.

Loden Almandar appeared standing right behind Cain. Loga was only a few meters in front of Cain, standing motionless, eyes closed, arms at his side, wavering in and out of existence under Cain's assault, growing at times virtually transparent.

With the oxlike strength Cain had mocked, Loden Almandar struck Cain with his fist, just above and behind Cain's ear. Bone cracked, in his hand, and, Loden hoped, Cain's head.

The darkness was almost instantaneous. Loden felt, rather than saw, Cain fall, facedown. *Loga?*

"Yes," his friend's voice gasped in the darkness. "I'm all right. What the hell happened to you?"

Loden's eyesight adapted rapidly to the dim light from the workstation instruments. Already he could make out the dim shape of Cain, at his feet, and Loga, collapsed in one of the chairs. "I am not sure. I think Cain shaped space so that gravity was increased. An astonishing achievement, if so. Whatever he did, my body was severely damaged. I am sure Cain thought he had killed me. He almost did."

"You're not the only one. After taking care of you, he *pulled* me out of the otherworld. I didn't think that was possible." Loga sighed. "Wanna go through his pockets? He probably has a couple stars on him, maybe some jewelry worth stealing." Loga was silent for a moment. "By the Light, Loden, I can't *move.*"

Loden glanced at him swiftly. "You are going to have to. And to do so, we must find the power supply for his Shield and destroy it. I do not think either of us is in any shape to walk back through it." Loden knelt and put a hand to Cain's shoulder, to roll him over.

A voice said, "Lights up."

Standing in the entrance to the Command Center, the barbarian Kavad said quietly, "Please, take the Ring." He was pointing a rifle of some sort at them. Loden, who had seen many, many weapons in his life, knew only that it was some type of projectile weapon—which was all he really needed to know. "Possession of it has brought my master no joy."

Loden glanced over at Loga, sitting at the workstation. Loga shook his head *no*. Loden tried it regardless. "Do you know who I am?"

"Loden, only son of John, only son of the Creator T'Pau. I am Kavad, eldest son of Caria, only daughter of the Eldest Hunter Sheáll. If I were a woman, I would have led our Ken." Kavad moved, slowly, lengthwise across the Command Center. "Take the Ring; I will drop the Shield for two and one-half seconds, and you may leave. Commander General Mersai, whom you know, has, during your conversation with my lord, scrambled slipship fighter craft to Parliament. Take the Ring, now, and leave; and we will not bomb Parliament."

Loga spoke almost without pause. "Terms accepted."

Loden did not look at Loga. Kavad had reached the workstation that controlled the Shield and was watching, not Loden, upon whom his rifle was trained, but Loga. Loden said, "You must be joking. You're not suggesting we take terms from this barbarian?"

Loga stood, making no sudden movements. "I'm afraid so. Transition takes nearly two seconds for a jump, and I rather expect Kavad's an excellent shot. Most of my people are."

"We are not your people," said Kavad flatly.

"The same comment holds true for any attempt to harm Kavad mind to mind. The attempt takes a finite amount of time, and again we get shot. So Kavad throws the Shield open, and perhaps we vanish and appear elsewhere in the Caverns and cause the considerable havoc of which we are capable."

"And Parliament," said Kavad, "is touched by the sun. You have the right of it, Trickster."

"Take the Ring, Loden." Loga glided across the floor, tall and young, graceful and somehow wild. The barbarian faced him with the rifle. " 'Trickster'? You guys still call me that?"

A single sharp crack echoed through the Command Center. The glow building around Loden Almandar faded, and the warning shot echoed away into the distance. "That was foolish," said Kavad. "Trickster, I have not seen my home since I was a very young man. But the name of the *degunji* who betrayed us, who made war upon us so that he might become a god, has not been forgotten."

"That's not exactly how it happened. Ken Selvren drown their mutants, or they used to. Has that changed?"

Kavad ignored the question. "Take the Ring."

Loden said quietly, "The Ring will glow when I touch it."

Kavad shrugged. "Perhaps I will not shoot you."

A glare of light rose around them the moment Loden touched the Ring to pull it from Cain's hand. With an act of will nearly as difficult as the one that had brought him back from the edge of the Light, Loden put the Ring into a pocket, to break the bright singing contact with his flesh.

Kavad touched a switch. "The Shield will go down in fifteen seconds. It will stay down for two and a half seconds. If the glow of your departure touches my lord's form you will both *die*. Three, two, one, *now*."

Not quite two seconds later, they were both gone.

Kavad touched the stud that brought the Shield back up, and keyed the intercom. "Send Doctor Denahi in, quickly." He crossed to where his lord lay and examined him. Cain's pulse was thready, and his breathing shallow. His skin was so pale that Kavad's, against Cain's, looked little different. When he looked up again, Doctor Denahi was there, and so he relinquished his master into her care; Cain would live.

All considered, he was well pleased with how the night had gone. The Ring taken, his master still alive; had they killed Cain, Kavad would have been vastly displeased.

If for no other reason, tracking down Loden and Loga, to kill them, would have been—difficult. Not impossible, but difficult; and Kavad, by his own standards, was an old man. A few years' further service to Cain, and then death; a good life, one he would be well content with did it come to pass.

Kavad left the Command Center to General Mersai and his Warriors and went to Cain's quarters to prepare them for Cain's convalescence.

It was difficult, getting the Trickster's bright blue eyes out of his mind. People should not have eyes that color.

Even Cain's were better.

THE RING

The morning of Summer 5, 1284, was bright and cool, the air sharp and clean. There was dew on the hundreds of square kilometers of lawns that surrounded and permeated the City of Parliament. Fog crawled down off of the Black Mountains and only burned away as the day wore on, to reveal the quiet streets of Parliament to the sun—the white and silver spires, the sweeping terraces. Flowers bedecked the upthrusting towers of the city, roses and hyacinth, and everywhere the yellow daisies that symbolized the presence of the Light.

Above the rest of the city, the Chamber looked down upon the dying streets, the emptying buildings. Hardly a minute passed when some Ruler did not dissolve into Light, jumping up to where the Rulers' desperately small fleet of starships waited, never to return. In the Chamber itself, Rulers came and went the morning long, Rulers by the hundreds coming to see the Ring before it was returned, as Loden had decreed, to the Sisterhood. Near noon, as the Giants had been instructed, they left *Arskyld* and climbed the steep slope to the Chamber.

Not alone did the Giants Rome and Laar come this time. A small party of Giants made the climb, to claim Parliament. Two polar bears with pristine white pelts accompanied them, pacing unleashed, with jewel-studded collars at their throats.

"It is not mine, it is not yours, I will not give it to you and you cannot have it." Loden stared the Giants down. "Need I be any clearer? Can I be?"

The Ring pulsed atop the pedestal of black marble. Rage suffused Laar's features. Even seated he towered above any of the Rulers. His mood transmitted itself to the bears. They crouched, one to each side of the two chairs, as though they might spring at any moment. The Giant Rome, normally a serene individual—as Giants went—sat with his lips tight, the muscles of his forearms cording as his fists curled open and closed. The five young Giants behind them, by appearance closely related to the two brothers, were no less grim.

Loga, sitting as far away from the Ring as he could get, had a splitting headache. There was an uneasiness, a tension, that permeated the Chamber. There was no Ruler in the room, not one member of the full Tribunal, who seemed wholly at ease. Most of them were holding up well enough; but in the presence of the Ring, Loga felt as though his skin had been scraped entirely from his body. Everything—the sunlight, the wind, the angry thoughts of the Giants—struck him painfully, amplified to the point where the least, most vagrant thoughts touched him like shouts.

Loden had actually *carried* the thing, even touched it in the moment when he had taken it from Cain's finger. Loga could not remotely imagine what that must have been like. Loden had been behaving strangely, even more distant and withdrawn than was usual for him, ever since.

The Skaald Laar leveraged himself to his feet. They'd been there for fifteen minutes already, without any progress on the question of the Ring; his sons, and Rome's, standing behind them, would not tolerate the situation much longer. The same thought was apparently in Rome's mind; he followed his brother. Laar crossed the distance to the podium in two strides. Loden stood behind it, looking up at the Giant without any apparent emotion other than a certain weary courtesy. "You have seen the Ring. You know now Cain does not have it. You have fulfilled your bargain, we have fulfilled ours, and we are leaving. What happens now is entirely your concern, Giant. You will not see us again."

"Kera, Aline, the rest of you; go back to *Arskyld.*" Laar stood, towering above the pedestal. "I will have private word with the Tribunal Elder." The younger Giants stood motionless for a moment, and Laar growled, "Go now."

Rome did not move. Laar turned to his brother, intending to order him out with their sons, but something in his brother's expression stopped him. Laar waited then, patiently, until his sons and his brother's sons were out of earshot. "I cannot be seen," said Laar, "to ask permission, by my subjects. Now they are gone, and I do ask permission. May I hold the Ring, Loden?"

"You'll be sorry," said Loga aloud.

Loden shook his head slowly. "I think not, Skaald. It might harm you."

It happened so fast there was no way anyone could possibly have stopped it.

Laar reached for the Ring. Loden Almandar merely shook his

head; the Giant ignored him and brought his huge hand to close on the Ring. The glow dulled immediately, and Laar's eyes widened in shock. His mouth worked briefly, and Rome's hand closed on the wrist of the hand with which Laar held the Ring.

"Put it back, Laar," Rome said gently. "Are we common thieves, no better than a Worker such as Cain?"

The Skaald Laar ripped his hand free from his brother's grasp, pulled his arm back, and with the hand holding the Ring struck his brother in the side of the neck.

The sound of vertebrae cracking was clearly audible. Rome made an ineffectual grasping motion toward his throat.

And fell.

His fall seemed to take forever, and the sound of his bones snapping when he struck the hard stone floor echoed after Rome's body had settled. Blood poured from his mouth.

Laar stared, wild-eyed, at his brother's motionless form.

There was not even a glimmer from the quiescent chunk of crystal within his grasp.

Laar took a step backward, circling around Loden on his way to the exit. Some of the Rulers stirred as though considering action. Laar froze, seemingly waiting to see what they would do, trembling with what might have been rage, or perhaps fear as it came to him what he had done. Loden made a restraining gesture with one hand. He looked unutterably tired. "Let the Giant go."

The silence stretched; Laar took another step backward, turned, and fled the Chamber.

The Ruler Elyssa knelt and put a hand to Rome's neck, for his pulse. It only confirmed what every Ruler there had already been sure of. She stood, shaking her head.

Loden Almandar made a comment that showed his age as nothing else could have; the deity whom he named had not been legally worshiped since before the Great Schism. "Thank God," he said quietly, "we are leaving. I am so tired."

Their words moved around him, the placid, serene speaking of the consensus.

Gabriel said softly, "Cain started this. Let Cain and Laar finish it."

There was no pause. Julian said, "We have been true to our agreements, Loden. Faithful in our dealings."

Loden's daughter Maria said simply, "Leave the problems to time. Cain and Laar will be dealt with."

Elyssa went to her husband and held him tightly. "There's nothing we can do now. You've done more than you needed to; their problems are not ours any longer. Let's go home, my husband."

" 'What is truth,' asked Pilate, and washed his hands." Loden saw that many of them did not understand the reference. "We can pretend not to be involved. But we are, my friends. We are tied by deeds and by blood."

There was a moment of silence.

Rulers began vanishing, in gentle flares of light. Loden Almandar and his wife were two of the last to go.

Loga sat quietly, alone, with the body of the Giant Rome.

"If the kriss are right," said Loga at last, speaking to a being whom Loden Almandar had been raised to worship, a being whose existence Loga did not credit for an instant, "and You exist, and You created a world where events of this sort might happen—why, You, sir, are either a sadist or an incompetent."

The Rulers were leaving Earth.

The news was simply too stunning to assimilate quickly.

Near the day's end, Solan and Rea packed themselves a dinner and with their son rode away from Eagles, rode for half an hour down the stony paths away from the town, until they came to the small plateau where they usually picnicked. It was a wilder, less tended clearing than those to be found closer to Eagles; perhaps twice a year the Land'ners who owned that territory sent parties from Eagles to clear brush. The Killing Creek, where Lord Veramorn had killed the shrike in 1212, ran across the clearing's south end, and became a waterfall, cascading down the steep cut stone of the cliffs overlooking the Valley proper. The Valley narrowed here, at its far west end; Eagles, nestled in the foothills of the Black Mountains, was nonetheless on a clear day within view of the Great Dam.

Orion rode out ahead of them on his pony. They kept an eye on him and spoke as they rode.

"I can't believe," said Rea as her horse picked its careful way down the path, "that they're just *leaving.*"

Solan nodded thoughtfully. "I'm not sure what Maston thinks at the moment. Tristan is of the opinion it's all some dastardly trick to get us to lower our guard."

"My father," said Rea derisively, "is hysterical. Cain steals the Ring, the Rulers go to treat with Cain, *something* happens, and the Rulers announce they're leaving Earth." She shrugged. "And now Cain won't speak to him. It wouldn't surprise me if father has a stroke."

"Won't speak to Maston? Or can't? Tristan thinks Cain's dead."

Rea shook her head slowly. "If Cain's dead, nothing makes sense. The Lords Loden and Loga would have had to kill him during their visit—and you know how the Rulers are about killing. Or at least about doing it personally."

Solan nodded in agreement. "Killing by proxy is, of course, different."

"My point exactly. Maybe they're a little squeamish, but they're not above fighting when they must. *I* think Cain must have bargained them the Ring for their agreement to leave Earth. You don't think the Rulers are leaving because they're—well, I think the phrase was, 'just basically nice guys'?"

Solan laughed. "Close enough. Orion! Not so far!"

Forty meters ahead of them, almost out of sight from the curve in the path, the boy wheeled his pony and called in protest, *"Father!"* His voice was as high as a girl's.

"No!" Solan lowered his voice. "That boy's getting to be as spoiled as . . . well, as spoiled as all the other children in Eagles."

"Not everyone, my husband, has the advantage of growing up an urching—"

"The word," said Solan, "is urchin."

Rea shrugged. "I don't really care what the bloody damn Westmarcher word is. Do you seriously suggest we put Orion into an orphanage so he'll grow up to appreciate the advantages you can give him?"

Solan laughed at that, touched the spurs to his horse, and went to retrieve his son.

Twilight gathered.

Loga walked to the north end of the Chamber and looked out across the Valley. *Arskyld* was motionless. *What,* Loga wondered, *is Laar telling them?*

Surely not the truth.

He stood next to the podium, looking away, watching the sun set. Behind him the Giant's body lay motionless on the marble floor. He could not count the number of dead he had seen in his life—thousands, certainly, perhaps scores of thousands. His earliest memory, now so faint with time he was no longer sure whether it was true memory or just a ghost, was of the death of the silver-eyes girl Siedah. She'd struck him for some reason, and then she was dead. Long centuries after the fact, Loga simply could not remember how she had died.

He hoped he had not been the one to kill her. There was a good chance he was, at least, innocent of *her* death. He'd only been five when Siedah died.

No matter how many bodies he had seen, he never quite got used to it.

In the dying light of the sun, the white and silver spires of the empty city of Parliament turned the color of blood.

His parents lay together in the clearing atop the big blanket they'd brought. Wine, bread and sausages were perched in a basket atop one corner of the blanket. Orion was lying on his belly at the end of the clearing, as close to the cliff's edge as his father would allow. From where Orion lay he could see the entire length of the Killing Creek's waterfall as it tumbled down the stones. Down and to the north were the fields where the Summer Games with Eastmarch were supposed to take place. Some kilometers beyond the Games' fields was the sprawling city of Westmarch. Westmarch was, Orion knew, the third largest city in the world after Parliament and Singer, unless there were cities in the North Lands, where the Giants lived, that Orion did not know about.

Snatches of his parents' conversation drifted over to where he lay. For the most part Orion simply ignored them. They seemed determined not to talk about anything interesting. Politics Orion had no time for; why, in only a few weeks he would get to go to the Summer

Games with his parents. It would be the first time he had ever left Eagles, or been further away from Eagles than this very clearing where his parents went for picnics.

With the wonder of that fixed firmly in his mind, Orion could not for the life of him understand why his parents kept talking about the deeds and words of people whom Orion had never even met.

"It makes sense of a lot of things," said Solan, flat on his back, looking up at the darkening sky. His right arm was under Rea's neck, hand curling down to tickle her breast. "All the Workers who were taken from Turrin and Semalia; all the traffic in orbit. If they actually terraformed a planet . . ." His voice trailed off. Finally he simply said, "That's an incredible accomplishment."

Rea rested with her head on his shoulder. "Thankful we didn't have to go back to war, eh?"

"As the Light shines on my words," said Solan simply. "At least not with the Rulers. As for Cain . . ." He shrugged. "I'd rather not go to war with him either. Fortunately, Maston to the contrary, I don't think we'll have to."

Rea looked at him curiously. "Why are you so sure Cain is sincere?"

"Well . . . you'll laugh, but you had to see his face, the way he looked at me after we saw the Ring together . . ." Solan was silent for a moment. "Like . . . I don't know *what* like," he said in sudden exasperation. "Damn if I understand the man."

In the Weapons Monger's at Eagles, the senior monger, a brilliant technician who'd been trained by Cain's engineers in the days before the split, demonstrated the device Maston had requested.

They were alone on the Mongers' Floor, late at night. The work had been done secretly. Aside from Maston himself and the monger who'd done the work, there was nobody in Eagles who knew about it.

The monger, a man named Bassen something-or-other, handed Maston an apparently normal lance. "What do you think, m'lord?"

Maston hefted the lance. The balance was right; it felt correct. He removed the guard at the lance's tip and examined it—smooth metal, no break to show the lance had ever been altered. He put the guard back on. "It looks correct," he said mildly.

Bassen nodded eagerly. "Should, m'lord. My family mongered swords and lances for hundreds of years before Cain brought these modern weapons to the Valley. I grew up making decent weapons, not these—"

"Yes," said Maston coolly. "Show me the rest of it."

The man caught himself in midsentence. "Yes, m'lord. The control's in the remote, like you asked, just one button. Small enough for your pocket." He showed Maston the device, a small box with a single button on it. "This releases the guard at the tip. Watch." He pressed it.

The guard at the tip of the lance simply fell off. Maston nodded thoughtfully. "Bear in mind, m'lord," said Bassen, stooping to pick up the tip guard, "you need to use *this* guard on the lance; there needs to be a south monomagnet in the guard for the lance to knock it off. Use another guard, and the guard'll just sit there, snug as you please."

Maston said quietly, "There's no way of detecting it?"

"No, m'lord, not without breaking open the lance. It's a simple south-pole monomagnet near the tip."

Across the room a single mail shirt hung on a wooden post. "And the mail?"

"A little tougher, but I think you'll be pleased. The mail's been artificially aged to look like it might well be thirty years old, as you requested. Superconductor rings pulling nearly three hundred kilowatts; it produces a north-magnetic field to attract the south-magnetic monopoles in the lance. Touch the switch again . . ." The spear in Maston's hands shivered as though it would tear itself from his grip. "The mail is on the other side of the room. Attraction drops with the square of the distance; if you were ten meters closer, that spear would fly." The technician chuckled and turned off the remote. The spear ceased vibrating. "And take you with it, if you didn't let go."

Maston nodded again. "Very well, then. Two pushes of the button, eh? First to knock the guard off and then another to activate the superconductors in the mail?"

"Exactly," said Barren, beaming, "you've got it exactly."

"Well." Maston grinned at the man. "You've done a fine job." He clapped the tech on the shoulder. "Come here," he said genially, leading the man over to the side of the room. "One final question, just idle curiosity. This huge thing here, what is it?"

"M'lord?" Barren looked at him in confusion. "It's a laser cutter, sir. We use it to trim sheets of ferrocrete; it's the only thing'll do it."

"How do you turn it on?"

The monger went absolutely white. "M'lord? Why would you want to do that?"

Maston smiled at the man, but the smile never went anywhere near his eyes. "Show me how to turn it on, Barren."

"Yes . . . yes, m'lord." The man reached over and touched two switches set into the frame of the device. Lasers leapt into existence, brilliant ruby beams set at distances of two centimeters from one another. "It's not hard."

"So it's not," said Maston. The man's muscles had gone absolutely limp with fear. With one hand on Barren's shoulder, Maston quite gently propelled the man the two steps forward necessary to bring him into the curtain of light.

All that emerged on the other side were chunks of bloody meat and bone.

Maston cleaned the mess up himself.

Loga watched the sun touch the horizon. That the Earth *moved*, turning beneath the sun, was a thing Loga had, as a young man before his first trip into space with Donner Almandar, found some difficulty believing.

Standing there, at the edge of the Chamber, high above empty Parliament, high above the world, Loga watched the sun go down. He could smell the faint tang of blood from Rome's body. Once the sun had touched the horizon, far to the west, and there was some mark by which to measure the sun's passage through the sky, the sun seemed to gain speed, dropping swiftly. Loga could almost *feel* the Earth spinning beneath him. Cold, gentle winds touched his face.

As a child Loga had been told, by one of the men who watched the Silver-Eyes children, that sometimes when the sun set, it did so with a green flash.

In all his long life Loga had only seen it happen twice.

It did not happen that night. The Earth merely turned its back on the sun, and night descended around the only Ruler left on the face of the Earth, the mutant named Loga.

Their conversation was interrupted when their son dive-bombed them. They'd seen it coming. Orion had taken a good five minutes sneaking around behind his parents, preparatory to leaping upon them. Rea insisted that Solan let Orion think he'd succeeded, and so they merely continued their discussion of Cain and Maston, until Orion came rushing up to surprise them.

He hit rather harder than his mother had been expecting; Rea kept forgetting how fast the child was growing. She tumbled with him, rolling across nearly a meter, before coming to a rest on her back with Orion held over her head. "Surrender," he demanded.

"Nope." Rea tossed him instead to Solan. Solan grabbed him out of the air with every bit as much nonchalance as he'd shown walking away from his injured slipship the day previous. He slung Orion over his shoulder.

"Rea," Solan said in tones of concern, "have you seen Orion?"

Orion pounded on his father's back. "Let me down!"

"Why, no," said his wife. Rea brushed a strand of blonde hair back from her face and glanced around the clearing. "Why, where is he?"

Solan tickled his son with one hand, and Orion began giggling helplessly. *"Please* let me down!"

Solan shook his head. "I really have no idea. I haven't seen him in a while now . . . he was looking down over the edge a while ago." Solan came to his feet and walked over to where Orion had been lying.

"Daddy!"

Solan looked back and forth across the small clearing and came back to where Rea was sitting. Orion was laughing so hard he was shaking on his father's shoulder. "Rea, I can't find him!" With one hand he gathered up Orion's feet and held the boy, swinging slightly, upside down off the ground. "Perhaps he fell over the edge? Could that be?"

Rea sighed, perplexed. "Oh, I hope not. I've told him and *told* him to stay back from the edge."

Solan began swinging the hand that held Orion's ankles. Orion moved in slow arcs, back and forth with his face only centimeters above the grass. "Well, I certainly hope he turns up soon. By the Light, how will we explain having misplaced our son? Who would understand?" He released Orion's feet at the end of one swing and tossed Orion to his wife.

Rea picked him out of the air and held him up with both arms. "Well, here he is! Where have you been?"

It took several seconds before Orion had ceased giggling to the point where his words made sense. "You know! Daddy was carrying me."

Solan dropped down to the blanket next to them. "That's true," he admitted. "Son carrying and throwing, it's one of the events at the Games, and I've been lacking for a chance to practice." He took a healthy swig of wine from the neck of the bottle and offered it to Rea, who did likewise and who then gave Orion a small sip.

After they'd all caught their breath, Orion sat contentedly in Rea's arms. Rea whispered to him loudly, "I'm going to be jousting against your father in the Games. Who do you think will win?"

Orion considered the question. "Father," he said finally. "He's stronger."

"And in the archery contest?"

"You," Orion said instantly. Solan opened one eye and looked at them. "You're straighter."

Solan propped himself up on one elbow. "Oh, really?"

Rea grinned at him. "Steeplechase, Orion?"

"You're faster." Orion looked over at his father and could not prevent the delighted grin from breaking out. "Because you're smaller."

Solan showed his opinion in a loud snort of disgust. "By that logic, boy, you should be able to beat me in the steeplechase."

The boy sat up in his mother's arms. "I'll race you! I'll beat you!"

Solan shook his head in what Orion must have thought was displeasure, although Rea could tell the boy's instant response had pleased Solan well enough, and sank back to the ground. "It wasn't an offer," Solan said.

Standing alone in the dark, Loga brought the Light to surround himself.

The horrible foreboding that had touched him, after he and Loden Almandar had taken the Ring from Cain, had not gone away.

Arskyld simply sat there, motionless.

And Loga vanished.

"Look!" Orion cried in excitement, pointing up. "Bright lights! Lots of bright lights!"

The northern sky was glowing with a faint ghost light, and higher yet, in the star-filled sky, sparks of light were moving.

Rea said softly, the words not meant to reach Orion, "The aurora is supposed to be a blessing if it dances over you."

Solan shook his head slowly. "That's not the northern lights, Rea. Giant ships, I'd wager, taking off from the pole, are what caused that." He came to his feet and stood looking up into the moving sparks of light, high above his head. Rea stood and hugged him from behind, chin resting on his shoulder. "But it may be a blessing. The challenge is ours now, Rea. Just us and the Giants." He looked back over his shoulder at her, and she stood on her tiptoes and leaned forward to kiss him.

The starships glowed above them like stars.

Among those few humans in all the Valley who did not know of the abdication of the Rulers was the man who had caused it.

Cain lay in a deep coma.

The Games

· 1 ·

On the plains below Eagles, preparations for the Games continued apace. Tents sprouted like daisies across the vast clearings as men came from places as far east of Eagles as the city of Singer itself. With the abdication of the Rulers from Earth, the Games took on a significance entirely unanticipated when Cain and Maston had planned them. They were not the only Games to be held across the Valley. Down the length of the river Almandar, in the territory that the Rulers had controlled until their abdication, the traditional Summer Games were held in the traditional locations.

But the Games between Eagles and Eastmarch, the two centers of power left in the Valley, became, with the abdication of the Rulers, not merely a ceremony of reconciliation between two factions of rebels, but the meeting place where the future of the Valley would be decided.

And so they poured west down the Traveler's Road, and overland from the river Almandar, on foot and by carriage and on horseback, noble families both large and small, Land'ners from as far east as Allietown, and Merchants from every quarter of the Valley. They came bearing weapons both old and new: lances, swords and longbows, crossbows and crude rifles. From the territories of Eagles and Eastmarch came men with handguns and light knives. Two different families of Merchants arrived in carts that moved not by the straining of horses, but by the action of fusion cells turning crude electrical motors.

For the moment all was peaceful. The Rulers were gone from Parliament. Observers from Eastmarch and Eagles had verified that for their respective masters, but thus far neither faction had attempted to send forces to secure the city, empty now of all but Workers.

For the moment.

Eastmarch, in a swift move that Eagles was already protesting, extended its forces to engulf the city of Singer, the second largest city in the Valley, the very day after the announced abdication of the Rulers. The fact was that Eagles was overextended already and had neither the manpower nor the firepower to govern the new territories.

Maston Veramorn, in a bitter rage, sent a slipship to Eastmarch with the message that he *demanded* to speak to Cain, and was told by Commander General Mersai, politely and with great force, that nothing of the sort was possible at the moment; but that, Maston was to rest assured, their discussions at the Games would go on as scheduled.

With less than a week before the Games were scheduled to commence, Eastmarch had not sent a single Warrior to contend against the Warriors of Eagles in the Games.

Cain awoke on the Day of the Dead.

It was Summer 22, the day on which T'Pau Almandar had killed herself; by the celebratory calendar employed by the Church of the Light, it was the day on which the honored dead were remembered. In the traditional church ceremony, the first prayer was for the memory of T'Pau Almandar, with prayers thereafter for the memories of recently departed loved ones.

Mersai was kneeling in the chapel reserved for use by the Warriors, on Level Two just above the Weapons Monger's floor. He had just lit a candle for the memory of his elder brother, when a Commander First whose name he did not know entered the chapel and knelt next to him, murmuring, "Commander General, Lord Cain is awake."

Jarad had been a Warrior; he would understand. With a brief mental apology to the memory of his elder brother, Mersai ran.

Cain was sitting propped up in his bed, with a thick, pale blue robe wrapped around him. An IV was dripping into the vein in his elbow—his best bed robe had been sliced open to expose the inner surface of the arm. Doctor Denahi was standing next to him looking fiercely displeased.

Despite the fact that he'd been to see Cain every day since his battle with the two Rulers, Mersai shivered slightly when he saw just how bad Cain looked. In repose, the weight he had lost was not particularly obvious; sitting up, moving, Cain looked like a victim of transform fever in the last stages of desiccation before the changes began.

He looked *old.*

Mersai thought he controlled his face. "My lord," he said, saluting. "How may I serve you?"

It did not matter whether Mersai's expression revealed his dismay; Cain did not look at him. His head rested against the pillows. His voice was horrible. Mersai hardly recognized it. "Mersai . . . it's the Day of the Dead."

"My lord, it is."

"Siva of Eastmarch, no surname; and Barra Lusende; and Artemis of Erebion, no surname. Say for them the Requiem Prayer for the Dead, Orrin. I can't."

"My lord?" Mersai stared at the prone form. "My lord, I thought you didn't believe in the Church of the Light?"

"Orrin . . . ." The word was harsh, almost a whisper. Cain raised his head and fixed Mersai with burning eyes. "I do not. They did. Do it before night falls." And he fell back in exhaustion.

"My lord." Orrin Mersai saluted, turned, and left.

Cain sank back into the warm darkness.

They lay tangled together in each other's warmth.

"By the Light," Solan murmured into her ear after he had caught his breath, "you never cease to amaze me."

Rea's voice was sleepy and slightly breathless all at once. "That's good."

"And your father," he continued a moment later, "never ceases to amaze me."

Lying nude on the soft carpet before the dying fire in the fireplace, skin alight with the flickering scarlet gleam of the red embers, Rea murmured, already half asleep, "You're such a romantic."

Solan chuckled and bit her earlobe gently. "I suppose."

Rea made an indistinct sound of approval. "Mmm . . . do that some more . . . so, what'd he do now?"

"Oh, I was talking to Tristan earlier today. Tristan prayed today at the Warrior's Chapel for the memory of his parents. He told Maston about it, and Maston ridiculed him for it." Wide awake, Solan propped himself up on one elbow and ran his left hand in a slow stroke across her body. Her skin was still slick with sweat. "I thought Maston liked Tristan."

"My father doesn't *like* anyone." Rea yawned, stretching. Hard muscle moved beneath the sheath of her skin. "He just finds some people useful. But he *really* doesn't like the Church. Says the Rulers used it to keep us enslaved. Could be he's right, too. When the Rulers settled the Val—"

Solan groaned and rolled over on his back. "Enough! I didn't ask for the history of the Church, love. Remember I'm a poor ignorant Warrior."

"Ignorant? You?" The sleep had entirely left her voice. Rea sat up cross-legged next to his prone form. "My husband, if you'd been ignorant, I'd never have married you." She placed one hand on the hard flat stomach, and his skin seemed to jump beneath her touch. "You need to learn to be more subtle, and to keep your mouth shut a bit, but . . ." Rea looked down in mock surprise. "What's this? Are you ready again?"

"*Yes.*"

"Well," she said quietly, "I suppose we could do it again, but only if . . . if . . ."

"If what?"

"Only if you promise to be quiet and not wake up Orion with your bellows."

"Ha!" Solan practically whispered the word. "The door's closed, and anyway, you're hardly one to be talking, the way you scream."

"What? Are you dissatisfied, then?" Moving slowly, Rea moved over him and lowered herself until he was entirely within her.

Solan reached up and placed both hands on her rib cage, steadying her, thumbs just touching the swell of her breasts. "I'm a lucky man," he said softly, not joking at all.

Eyes closed, Rea began moving against him. "Yes . . . and don't you forget it."

THE RING

Kavad was serving his master breakfast when Commander General Mersai knocked for admittance. Kavad opened the door for the Commander and offered him coffee and breakfast. Mersai took a chair, accepted the coffee, and declined breakfast. The sunpaint in the room was turned very low, and the glowfloats were lying motionless and dark in a corner.

Cain nodded at Mersai and continued with his breakfast without pausing. Mersai watched with approval as Cain downed four large eggs, a slice of beefsteak, fried carrots, bread with jam, and half a jug of milk with cream, a bowl of shark soup, and a pair of apples, before going on to his coffee.

This was, according to Doctor Denahi, the third such feeding Cain had gone through since awakening, just after midnight. He should, she insisted to Mersai, be dead at this point, and if not dead, then in a coma—and even if he *were* alive and awake he should not be eating his third breakfast in less than three hours.

Mersai simply waited until Cain was done eating. "You're looking more yourself, my lord."

Cain nodded. "And feeling so, my friend." Cain waited while Kavad took away the tray and said, "It's good being back. I didn't like where I was."

Mersai said incautiously, "Where?"

Cain looked at him oddly. "Walking on a beach, Orrin." His manner changed somewhat, and he gulped down the remains of a cup of coffee and waited for Kavad to refill it. "Which is neither here nor there. Tell me what's been happening. Kavad told me what happened after I was knocked unconscious, how he gave the Ring to the Rulers." Cain's words were uttered without any particular emphasis. "I may execute him for that, I haven't decided yet."

Kavad, standing beside Cain's bed, did not even blink.

Mersai did. "My lord? You're jesting."

Cain shook his head. "I'm not. He disobeyed my wishes. For all he did it in what he saw as my best interest, nonetheless he bargained the Ring out of my grasp. My friend, I would have bombed Parliament to have kept that Ring." Cain sighed. "Orrin, listen. I've not quite been myself of late. Perhaps I've been a bit mad. But in the territories of Eastmarch, Orrin, the voice of authority is mine. You may advise— no, you *will* advise me, for I need your opinions. If you feel fitter to rule in my stead, kill me. The Warriors are loyal enough to you, you probably could."

Orrin Mersai knew better than to even speak.

Cain adjusted his robes around himself and placed his cup on the rest at his elbow. He looked back to Mersai. "If," he said softly, "there is a man or woman in all this Valley fitter to lead Eastmarch, tell me. I would know the name."

"My lord," said Mersai stiffly, "my life is yours."

"And I may take it," said Cain steadily. "Tell me what has happened while I have slept, Orrin." The terrible black gaze held Mersai fixed. "Tell me what you have done."

"My lord, the Rulers have left Earth, have left it forever. They have settled a planet called New Parliament, some forty light years away. Parliament stands empty but for Workers; Singer likewise." To his credit, Mersai did not hesitate. "My lord, I took Singer."

"Why?"

"My lord, our forces were ready. The city holds considerable machinery and resources that I thought might be of use to us."

"Indeed? You committed the forces of Eastmarch to an act of war over 'considerable machinery and resources'?"

"Yes, my lord. Essentially."

Cain nodded. "Did it occur to you that there was no hurry? Maston is no position to take control of the newly freed territories."

"My lord, I thought he might take Singer. It's of strategic importance, unlike anything else in all the free territories. From a military viewpoint, Parliament is useless. Singer has the largest waterlock in the Valley, the only large lake, and is, further, the source of the river Almandar. It would have strained him, but he could have taken it."

"Could he have kept it?"

"From us? No, my lord."

"Orrin, you have two great responsibilities. The first is to carry out my instructions. The second is to anticipate my instructions when possible. Was it possible for you to anticipate my wishes regarding Singer?"

"Yes, my lord."

"How is it you did not?"

"My lord," said Commander General Orrin Mersai, "I did not stop to consider what your wishes might be. I simply acted."

"Tomorrow morning," said Cain quietly, "I'd like a list from you of the Commanders whom you consider capable of assuming your position. I don't care about their current rank, simply their capabilities. Kavad, I would like the same from you, as to which of your barbarians might best assume your post."

Mersai and Kavad said almost as one, "Yes, my lord."

"Very good. Whatever my decision regarding you gentlemen, I will not implement it until you have, at least, trained your successors. For Kavad that will take less time than for you, Mersai. In the meantime," said Cain, "we have, I think, three days until the Games are scheduled to begin?"

Mersai said, "Ten, my lord. I postponed them by a week."

"Oh?" Cain considered that. "Well done," he said finally. "What does Maston think is happening?"

"It's hard to say, my lord. He's lost his temper in public on a number of occasions of late. The gossip in Eagles is that he's convinced you're either dead or preparing to invade him. We've had slipships here demanding he be allowed to speak to you three times since the abdication. The last time he sent Solan again, and I spoke to the boy at some length."

Cain actually smiled. "He's a good man. What sort of shape is Parliament in?"

"Fair. I'd hate to have to defend it against attack, I tell you true—stretching a Shield across an irregular shape like that would be hell. We'd have to build at least two fusion generators to do nothing but generate the damn thing."

Cain merely nodded. The major reason Eastmarch territory was ruled from the Caverns, rather than from some aboveground city, was that the Caverns could be protected by a Shield that was almost perfectly flat, bending only to touch the pylons that generated it. A small Shield could be bent with little effort; indeed, a small personal Shield was malleable enough that it tended to follow the shape of a human's nerve network with little encouragement. But the larger the Shield got, the more power was required to warp its shape. The Shield at the Caverns was the second largest in the world; only the Shield the Giants had warped to cover the entire North Lands was larger, and Cain's spies reported that maintaining that Shield required something like two thirds of the Giants' total energy output.

Cain did not understand the theory behind the Shields at all, but he understood them empirically, and that was enough.

"The Workers were," Mersai continued, "left entirely behind. Apparently the Rulers took no Workers with them when they left Earth."

"That makes sense," said Cain thoughtfully. "We outbred and outfought them on one world, they wouldn't want to take us with them to another. Doubtless the Giants automated things considerably. They could, they've the skill. I wonder what they did with the Workers they took from Semalia and Turrin?" The question did not seem to require an answer; Mersai sat silent. "How's the Library?"

"Stripped. Computers gone, shelves emptied. We used sonar to find the hidden room you've spoken of and dug through to it, but it was empty also. The most interesting thing we found, my lord, was in the Chamber, where the Rulers met, it seems, with the Giants."

"And that was?"

"Blood. Liters of blood, it must have been. The debating floor, it's called that on the maps you drew, it was covered with dried blood."

"But no bodies?"

"No, my lord."

"What news from the North Land?"

"They are in considerable turmoil. We have one report, unconfirmed, that the Giant Rome was slain by the Rulers before they left."

"Rome?" Cain looked interested. "The Senior Engineer? Why would the Rulers kill him?"

"I don't know." Mersai shrugged. "Assuming the report's true. Our sources in the North Land are quite poor. But there was blood on the floor of the Chamber."

"We've heard nothing else from the Giants since this happened?"

"No, my lord. Should we have?"

"I have no idea." Cain seemed to grow aware that his cup was empty. "More, please, Kavad. Mersai, the Rulers made a deal with the Giants, that the Giants might rule in their place after the Rulers abdicated."

"Rule?" Mersai looked as startled as Cain had ever seen him. "The *Giants?* Rule *us?*"

Cain nodded. "So Loden admitted before cracking my skull, and he was telling the truth. I'm not an easy man to lie to, even for a Ruler.

It was the payment the Giants requested for building the Rulers their retreat. But it sounds like something went wrong somewhere along the way—the Rulers didn't announce that they were abdicating in favor of the Giants?"

"No, my lord. Only that they were going and not returning. The simple folk have been in a panic, up and down the length of Almandar. Maston and Cain are names they use to terrify their children with, my lord."

"Yes," said Cain absently, mind elsewhere. "So Maston doesn't know why the Rulers left, eh? He probably thinks I reached an arrangement with them and the Giants." A smile twitched across his lips. "I warrant he's not sleeping well. We meet in ten days, then. The rescheduling was truly well done, Mersai. I'm not as displeased with you as I am with Kavad; I'll probably not kill you. How are we set for competitors in the various events?"

"Well enough. Some events we'll sweep; others will be close. The horseback events we're likely to be decimated in, for all we've far more Warriors to choose competitors from than Maston has. They *live* on their horses, up in Eagles. One suggestion Maston made was to let Land'ners and Merchants from the newly freed territories compete with Eagles and Eastmarch. A fair number of the highborn families have come to the Games grounds, to treat with you and Maston. Their sons will need something to keep them busy."

"If we throw the lists open," said Cain mildly, "we'll throw them open to everybody, not just the highborn. Make Maston that offer and see how he likes it."

Mersai, himself the youngest son of a highly placed family of Land'ners in old Telindel, nodded. "Yes, my lord."

"How many craft do we have capable of reaching orbit without being detected?"

The sudden change of subject did not throw Mersai; he answered instantly. "Six, my lord. With some refitting, perhaps eight."

Cain said slowly, "Orrin, this is critical. The orbital factories the Rulers abandoned because they'd broken down—they never let the Giants into them, and it may be the Giants feel, now, they have no need of them. I want to find out what condition those factories are in, but the Giants *are not* to know we are scouting them. You've a list of the various factories. If you have any questions about getting into any one of them undetected, leave that one be and discuss it with me. *Don't* try to scout any of the factories that are not dark; the Giants will surely have Workers aboard them, studying them under the supervision of Giant engineers."

Mersai looked puzzled. "Why would the Giants have Workers aboard the factories?"

Cain was silent a moment. "Mersai, *think.* The factories were built by men of a size with you and me. A Giant could hardly fit through the airlocks."

Mersai nodded. "My lord, it will be done."

Cain sighed. "Two more things, and then you may leave me. I've need of rest. Have an emissary fly to the North Land tonight. Somebody whose good sense you trust, who doesn't know too much. I'll write a greeting to the Skaald Laar for him to carry."

"Yes, my lord. And the second thing?"

"Misha?"

Mersai swallowed hard. "My lord . . . we went to the hospital your brother was in and found the plot he'd been buried in. We could bring the body back to Eastmarch for proper burial if you'd like."

Cain's face was very still. "Proper burial?"

"My lord, he was buried in a garden." *Like fertilizer,* the thought came to Cain.

To Mersai's surprise, the still expression left him and Cain smiled again. "Ah. No, it's okay. Leave him there. He doesn't need to be moved. Was there a stone?"

"A small one, my lord, it's how we found him."

"The year?"

"1231."

Cain sat, drinking his coffee. His gaze was fixed on something far away. "Misha," he whispered at length. "Good-bye."

Two days before the Games commenced, Eastmarch came to Eagles in force.

Exactly a thousand slipships—not quite two thirds the number Eagles could muster in total—with the blue starburst of Eastmarch on their hulls, escorted half a dozen larger craft, two of them personnel carriers, and brought them down to a gentle landing on the empty fields to the north of the Games grounds. From where they landed, a man could, looking up, see both the nearby town of Eagles and the far distant glint of the city of Parliament.

Eastmarch decamped from their ships, pitched tents, and waited.

At the far south end of the Games fields stood three pavilions, with the pennants of Eagles rippling in the breezes above them. They were the quarters of Maston Veramorn and his two Captains; Tristan at the east pavilion, Maston's—the largest—in the center, and Commander Captain Solan's, which he shared with his wife, to the west. Perhaps five hundred tents of varying size and quality were pitched behind them. The number was so small only because many of Maston's Warriors were making the ride down from Eagles each morning and riding back up each night.

In his pavilion, alone, waiting, Maston Veramorn sat glowering at the empty walls of the huge tent. Two score of his bodyguards stood before the tent's entrance, and Maston's manservant stood immediately to Maston's right, waiting for some instruction from his master.

Cain's ships had landed earlier that day; and thus far nobody, not even a lowly Warrior, had been sent to give Maston the greetings that, as host of the Games, were due him.

The message was clear enough.

Cain expected Maston to come to him.

Tristan d'Volta sat atop his horse at the edge of the lists and watched the riders prepare for their approach. He tried to ignore the babble of voices from the crowd around him, and the wafting smell of the roasted sausages the hucksters were selling.

The Workers who'd leveled the ground hereabouts had done a fine job, he thought. The terrain was flat and well packed. Though the days were dry, the ground had been wetted recently enough that there was little dust in the air.

The warmth was welcome enough. Tristan did not wear armor that morning, only a light tunic with an embroidered eagle on the breast, for he had no intention of practicing either jousting or swordplay that day. It was a pleasant day, and the mood of the folk in the crowd as the practicing took place for the Games proper was good: easy and even jubilant, for all it was slightly uncertain. There was not, Tristan suspected, a person in all that vast crowd who did not dream of the youthbooster Cain had promised when the Rulers were at last overthrown.

If most of the scores of thousands present for the Games were looking forward, no small number were looking back as well. Tristan had lost track of the number of old folks who'd tried to tell him about the Games of their childhood, before the days of slipships, laser rifles and slug-throwing handguns. Tristan was not sure who'd made the decision to include only the traditional events in the current Games, Cain or Maston or both, but the choice was going over well. Tristan made no secret of the fact that he was more at home with a variable laser in his hand than a sword, nor of the fact that his control of a slipship was better than his mastery of a horse.

Not, he thought with some complacency, that his horsemanship was all that bad. Among the younger Warriors, he was as good as many and better than most. Some of the old Warriors—none of them Commanders, as paranoid as Maston was about men his own age—who'd practically been born atop horses, could ride Tristan into the ground. That didn't bother Tristan much—not nearly as much as the fact that both Rea Veramorn and Solan could damn near do the same thing, and both of them with less years' training in horsemanship than Commander Captain Tristan d'Volta.

The two riders rode down the lists toward one another, horses gathering speed as they neared. When they made their final pass, they were not moving as fast as they'd be during the actual contests, but fast enough; the shielded lance took one of the riders up off his horse and sent him backward into the dust, to a roar of approval from the watching crowd.

At the ends of the list Tristan watched with a wistful expression of which he was utterly unaware as Rea Veramorn took her place at the north end of the run. Her long blonde hair had been cut short for the tournament; with her small breasts covered by carballoy armor, she looked less like a girl than like the prettiest boy he'd ever seen. Solan, at the south end of the run, looked like her elder, rather more masculine brother, and not for the first time Tristan wondered whether the rumors about Solan being Maston's bastard might not be true. It would explain a great deal, for all Solan and Maston didn't look much alike.

But then, Rea didn't look much like her father either.

From the corner of his eye Tristan saw a phalanx of men, in the black of Maston's bodyguard, moving through the crowd. He turned his horse slightly; Maston came forward to stand beside him, and put one hand to the bridle of Tristan's horse. "Tristan," said Maston by way of greeting. "How is practice going?"

Tristan turned back slightly to watch. "Good, my lord. They're both very good. Solan's been through three times, and Rea's been through twice now. They've put down everyone they've ridden against, and they're going against each other now."

They might have been alone together in the crowd, with Maston's bodyguards around them; none of the crowd were close enough to hear them. Maston scowled at Tristan's answer. "Could you beat either of them?"

Tristan looked down at Maston in surprise. "My lord? At what? The joust? Rea, certainly, if I rode against her with my full weight and speed. Solan, perhaps. In other subjects, it varies. At short range, where her lack of pull counts less, your daughter is, my lord, the best archer I have ever seen. They have, each of them, their strengths."

"They're idealists, unfortunately."

Tristan was disturbed by the tone of Maston's reply. Clearly Lord Veramorn was upset about something. "So? My lord, there are worse crimes."

"No, there are not," said Maston grimly.

A sudden roar went up from the crowd and cut off abruptly. Tristan swore at having missed the pass, and then checked himself in midoath when he saw what had silenced the crowd; one of the two riders lay on the ground inside the lists, writhing in obvious pain. Tristan spurred his horse forward and found himself restrained by Maston's hand on his bridle. He looked to Maston in disbelief. "My lord, let—"

"Shut up," said Maston. "Wait a moment."

The other rider dismounted swiftly, pulling her headgear off, and Tristan saw with a wave of relief that he did not stop to analyze that it was Rea. Rea ran to where her husband lay on the ground, knelt and helped Solan remove his headgear.

From thirty meters away Tristan heard the passage of words clearly, as did everyone else in the now-silent crowd of spectators.

"Rea," Solan whispered, face contorted in pain.

Rea was obviously frantic. "What? Where are you hurt?"

"Next time . . ." Solan swallowed, and coughed hackingly.

"What?"

"Next time," he said, in a voice suddenly strong, "I'm going to knock you on your ass. No more head starts."

The roar of the crowd's laughter drowned out Rea Veramorn's furious reply. Tristan laughed himself, until he looked down and saw Maston's expression. Solan and Rea walked arm in arm off the field, to scattered applause.

"The crowd seems to like them, eh, Tristan?"

Tristan shrugged. The comment seemed obvious enough. "Maston," he said gently, quite intentionally using his lord's first name, "they are both natural leaders. Is that bad?"

"Hmm? Yes," said Maston with a bitter laugh, "they are much alike. Breeding, it seems, does show." His lips twisted into an altogether unpleasant smile.

The comment made little sense to Tristan, unless Maston was impugning his own bloodline. He said carefully, "Solan's not after your position, my lord. And Cain trusts him, which, given the lay of the land, is no bad thing. Why don't you trust Solan, sir?"

Maston exploded. "Because he's a naive dreamer! Cain will cut us to pieces if he has the chance. The man wants power, Tristan. *He threw down the Rulers!* By the Light, do you know how long they ruled this Valley? This Valley was *built* for them by the Giants. If Solan gets the others to follow him, we'll be vulnerable . . . and I won't let that happen."

Tristan said nothing.

Maston Veramorn sighed at length and motioned to his bodyguards. He was not incapable of a certain rough charm when it suited him; he used it now. "Tristan," he said quietly, "you're a good man. I value your service to me. But you need to be less trusting; the world can be a treacherous place. Witness, I'm going to see Cain now." Maston saw by the look on Tristan's face that the implication was not lost on him. "Aye. Think on that while we negotiate our peace with this man Solan trusts."

And Maston and his bodyguards moved on, toward the north clearing where Cain's ships watched the practice of the Warriors of Eagles.

Seeking through the crowds, Tristan found the two blondes, man and wife, walking away together toward the three private pavilions at the south end of the field. He searched his soul for some hint of jealousy or envy toward the Warrior who had, seven years ago, walked out of Westmarch and taken his childhood sweetheart from him.

He was unable to find any.

In large measure, if not entirely, that pleased him.

Forty light years away, on a planet whose cycle of light and dark did not match that of Earth, the suns had just set.

Loden Almandar walked alone through the dark and empty gardens on the outskirts of New Parliament. His eyes were closed. Even with the artificial suns set for the night, he saw well enough by other means. Though native to the Earth, the blossoms were nonetheless of varieties he had not seen before; truly, the Giants had done well in their planning for this world.

The night sky was clear; the stars blazed overhead, shining brilliantly through an atmosphere somewhat thinner than that of Earth. Loden Almandar, walking beneath the stars, stopped for a moment and said aloud, "Senta."

On the path before him, a dot of light appeared, stretched up and down to become a brilliant line, stretched again to become a wavering sheet of yellow-white Light. The sheet coalesced suddenly into the transparent golden form of a fat woman wearing dancing veils, swaying seductively in the silence.

The rhythm of the dance intensified, and as the fat woman shed veils, she shrank, until there was nothing left of her, and the youngest of Loden's nine daughters emerged from the Light and flung herself into her father's arms. "Hello, father."

Loden held her out at arm's length, and looked her up and down. His smile was rather weak. "That was . . . new."

"Did you like it?"

"It is," he said, after apparent grave consideration, "the first disgusting thing I have seen in this paradise. Therefore, I suppose I do."

Senta grinned at him. "Loga's been teaching me. He's really amazing." She linked her arm through his, and together they continued down the dark path. "Did you know he can do sounds? And *color?*" she demanded. "I've tried and tried, but when I use the Light to create images, it always comes out sort of golden. Frustrating."

"The Light," Loden said mildly, "is the Light, not a bloody damn rainbow."

Senta shrugged. "Loga," she repeated, "does colors."

"Loga," said her father, "does many things sensible folk do not."

Senta's smile faded. "What's troubling you? You've turned entirely gloomy ever since we got here. I mean," she waved an expressive hand, "I prefer Earth myself, I admit it, if only because there's more people there my own age. Even if most of them are Workers. But, father, you know, it's not so bad here."

"I am plagued by memory," said Loden in a flat voice. "Ghosts," he said, using the Ruler word for a thing not remembered directly, but only in the memory of a memory. "I had hoped to leave them at peace when we left. Do you know why we left Earth, Senta?"

"Because Cain kept threatening to bomb Parliament," Senta said with simple practicality.

"No." Loden shook his head, and said again, "No. It was not that, my dear. We could have dealt with that, if only by having the Giants build air defenses around Parliament such as they have guarding the North Land. We left Earth . . . because Cain was right."

"Father?"

"Not the ruthless man you've known of all your brief life, my dear. A boy only somewhat older than yourself, before decades of war and preparing for war changed him. *Therefore,*" he quoted, "*there is some greater force than the force that you are capable of wielding; and if force is the only basis of law that you acknowledge then there is some higher law than the law of the Rulers of Earth.*" It was only a partial quote, but Senta recognized it as the conclusion of Cain's famous speech to the Tribunal, after having been condemned to exile in the Glowing Desert. "Seeing him stand before us like that—it was like looking into a mirror and seeing all your best parts brought out to stand by themselves. All the time we fought him, the Twenty Years' War, I held that image of him, of a man who was *better* than us; that image, it may be why he beat us. When we decided to leave Earth, I consoled myself that someone better than ourselves would be left behind to guide the Workers in their own path."

"But he's changed?"

"Aye." The word bore a vast load of despair. "Loga does not believe me even now, but—the man whose mind I touched briefly in our attempt to treat with him, and more deeply in the instant I took the Ring from his hand—the man is power mad. Cain's out for himself now, and Maston always was . . ." His voice held genuine sadness. "Even Laar now."

The thought flickered, just at the edges of her awareness; nonetheless Senta caught it. "You have a *son?*"

In the darkness it was impossible to read her father's expression; Senta had the impression she had startled him. "It seems so. A boy named Solan, and, in fact, another daughter named Rea. Twins, twenty-three years old."

"Father, I thought . . . I mean . . . I thought that was *impossible.*"

"A boy child, sired by me? It is, without aid of a genegineer. But they had a genegineer, a Giant named Riabel whom I slighted once long ago. But that small accomplishment—the changing of an X chromosome to a Y—is nothing as compared with what else this particular genegineer did, must have done: mirrored my twenty-fourth gene pair and brought the twins to term in the womb of a Worker. Some woman in the keep of Maston Veramorn."

"Maston?"

Loden Almandar sighed. "You're easily amazed, child. Please try to keep your voice down."

"I'm sorry, father," Senta said instantly. "It's just—the idea that I have a brother, and nine sisters rather than eight. It's an odd thought. What are you going to do about it?"

"I can't leave two of my children there." Loden shook his head slowly. "I can't do it. Donner . . ." He broke off and did not finish the thought aloud. "I can't do that."

"Father, it was the Tribunal's ruling that we were not to return to Earth, that our affairs and theirs were henceforth separate. Even you are subject to that ruling."

Loden grinned. "Aye, true enough. But I would advise you, my dear, to remember that the Tribunal members are merely men and women, no different from any other Ruler. To be sure, they're hardly likely to countenance deliberate disregard for one of their rulings—but I have known them for a great long while, Senta. There is not a Tribunal member alive whom I did not know when he or she was still a child. There is no ruling they have ever made that may not be disregarded under the correct circumstances. Presented with the accomplished deed, they will rethink their decisions."

"That seems rather . . . arrogant," said Senta.

He nodded. "It is. But it works. One does not do such things often; but when one can defend oneself eloquently, and justify one's actions ethically, it *can be* done."

Senta offered no reply to that, and Loden, who had not expected one, was content to walk with his daughter in silence. Senta walked beside her father, arm linked in his, thinking furiously. Part of the same Tribunal decision that had led to the creation of this retreat also stated that, once the Rulers had left Earth, they had truly *left* it, and no individual Ruler might return without the permission of the Tribunal.

The Tribunal issued rulings but rarely, and only on subjects of great importance. The penalty for disobedience to a ruling of the Tribunal was harsh, in reaction to the civil strife of the Great Schism, perhaps; it was, with murder, the only crime for which a Ruler who was signatory to the Covenant might be put to death. And her own father, the Tribunal Elder, was contemplating such an act. Senta said, some minutes later, "Father? What are you going to *do?*"

"Loga and I," he said quietly, "have been considering returning to Earth. To help them—the Workers, the Giants—where we may, now that our people are safe at last. I believe it is the correct thing for us to do."

"Loga's in on this—what shall I call it—conspiracy? You're telling me *Loga's* developed a conscience? Our Loga?"

Loden chuckled. "You may need to know him a few decades longer before you see it, but yes, there is a conscience there, and has been. What are you, about fifteen?"

"Sixteen, father. Almost seventeen." Senta was not insulted by the question; most Rulers, used to counting the long passage of the years by convenient fives and tens, guessed her age at either fifteen or twenty.

"It may take you a while, but you will learn, Senta, that behind that facade of hard cynicism, there is a fine spirit and a good man." The thought struck Loden hard. *A man,* it came to him, for perhaps the thousandth time, *with problems of his own.*

The Arcade stretched across eight and a half square kilometers. It was a larger copy of the Arcade in old Parliament on Earth, though with new attractions. There were less than a thousand Ruler children on all of New Parliament—judging, as Rulers did, that anyone under thirty was a child. And so the Arcade, and its rides and mazes and games, were nearly empty.

Senta's sisters were riding the ponies on the carousel.

"You don't really think," said Senta, "he would've told me all that if he didn't mean for us to *do* something?"

Three of her elder sisters, Tara and Jasmine and Lanie, bobbing up and down on the horses, listened to her with wide-eyed, apparently credulous solemnity. They were the four children Loden had sired by his wife Elyssa. After nearly a century of barrenness, both Loden and Elyssa had ceased hoping for children. And then, in one of the freaks of biology that sometimes came to pass among the Rulers, Elyssa began ovulating irregularly over a period of nearly two decades and bore to Loden Almandar four daughters during that time. Lanie was the eldest of Senta's full sisters, almost thirty; Jasmine and Tara were only a year apart in age, twenty-three and twenty-four. They were the two siblings closest to one another in age among all the Rulers, not counting the odd pairs of twins.

"Listen," said Senta, "you *have* to listen. See, the thing is, father was *right* . . ."

Elyssa was unusually quiet that evening as they were preparing for bed. Loden was not quite asleep when her voice roused him.

"I'm going to speak to Senta in the morning."

"I doubt that's necessary," said Loden quietly. "Love, the child's no fool. Young still, and headstrong, but amenable to reason. The trip she planned was criminally foolish, her sisters told her so, and if she has no respect for your opinion or mine, she *does* listen to what her elder sisters think."

"There's a piece of the truth, if you like," said Elyssa sharply. "No respect for *my* opinion, surely. She hangs on your words carefully enough."

Lying in bed with his hands behind his head, Loden grinned at her as she dressed for bed. Her hair was still wet from her bath. "Elyssa, you sound as though you're jealous of your own daughter."

Elyssa sat before her dressing mirror, features very still for a moment. When she spoke, her words were not quite bitter. "She's more your daughter than mine. They all are. In look and character they might as well not be mine, you are stamped on them so well. T'Pau wrought well in her children."

Loden sat up in bed and nodded, rubbing his temples wearily. "T'Pau was a brilliant genegineer. Something better than ninety percent of my genetic structure is composed of dominant genes. It is not surprising that my children resemble me."

"I did not say it was surprising." Suddenly Elyssa turned to face him. "Objectionable, perhaps. Loden, Senta's but a child. This morning she had no concern more pressing than deciding whom she was going to be in love with next week. This evening she's prattling of these children of yours, this Solan and Rea, to her sisters. Concerned about whether leaving Earth was the right thing for us to do. There are only two Rulers on this planet who would have discussed this with Senta, and I have already asked Loga. He assures me that it was not him, and I believe him; he doesn't respect me enough to lie to me."

"Ah." Loden was wide awake now. "So perhaps I did put the thoughts in her head. I did not mean to, and I do not doubt her sisters have put her straight. Where was the harm?"

"Whether you like it or not, whether I like it or not, the child is my daughter. Before even that she is subject to the rulings of the Tribunal. The fact that she tried to recruit her sisters to aid her in her foolishness has worried some of the members of the Tribunal, Loden, myself among them. Lanie says she nearly talked them into it, at that, and that scares me. You're too close to yourself to see it, and perhaps it's been too long now, but rest assured, my husband, Donner has not been forgotten. The arrogance that made him the leader he was is there in Senta, and at least some of the same charisma." Elyssa was silent a moment and then said carefully, "Loden, there are those who don't fully trust *you*. The Tribunal has thwarted your will so seldom, they cannot help but wonder what will happen if they feel they must. Are the rules really for everyone but Loden and his children?"

Loden said gently, "You don't need to worry about Senta. She's not going to Earth."

Elyssa stared at him, features twisting. *"Let* her," Elyssa screamed suddenly. "I don't *care* what she does! Senta can spend the rest of her life on Earth for all I care." She was almost sobbing. "Damn you, do I mean so little to you that you'd leave me forever to care for Worker rabble as though there were anything of worth in them? Without even *discussing* it with me?"

Loden kept his features composed and his thoughts stilled. "Elyssa, I will do what I must. I have never done more than that, nor less. Our people are safe here. There are two Rulers on Earth who do not know who they are or what their heritage is, and that is intolerable. That they are my children is irrelevant. Even if they did not exist, there are still areas where we can help them. Because we fought with Cain for twenty years does not mean that we are free of all obligation to them for the rest of time. We are *not.*"

"You can't change centuries of hatred and distrust." Elyssa stared at him searchingly. "You *can't.*"

"Not," said Loden steadily, "if we do not try."

Elyssa was silent for a long while before she said simply, "I don't want to lose you."

Loden lay awake in bed, unable to sleep. Elyssa was asleep at his side, chest rising and falling evenly. He was no Loga, whom Loden knew sometimes had premonitions, not even one such as Cain, whom Selene assured him had the same gift. It was not premonition of any sort which kept him from sleep, simply restlessness.

The restlessness itself was not hard to analyze. Most of the other Rulers were adapting to this new world well enough. There was some grumbling about the lack of servants, but the automated services the Giants had provided them were acceptable; in their way, better than the services of the Workers, because they were not fallible in the same ways. The controlling computer was very bright, though not self-aware, as some computers had been in the days before the Fire Wars. It understood with a reasonable degree of comprehension any commands meter west of the Games grounds, and would doubtless vanish when the Games were done.

"Those are the lists, are they?" Cain did not wait for a reply from Maston, but strode toward them. As had happened much of that evening, Maston found himself following the man, whether he would or no.

Cain stopped at the edges of the lists. Maston saw his shoulders jerk as though some attack of illness had struck him, and for a brief, pleasant moment he hoped it might be so; but the moment passed, and Cain ducked under the cords that separated the spectators' grounds from the run on which the joust would actually take place. He walked out across the packed dirt, to a spot near the center of the list, and there Maston watched him kneel down and touch a hand to the empty ground. The hand moved slightly, as though the man were searching for something.

Maston waited for Cain. It was all very well for a man who was, after all, only a Steader, to crawl about in the dirt if he wished, but a Veramorn had more dignity. At length Cain rose again and walked briskly back to where Maston waited.

"Did you see anything of interest?" Maston inquired with polite sarcasm.

Cain did not even glance at him. "Blood. Blood in the dirt. Come, let's go inside, it's getting cold out here."

. . . *For I have seen a coldness, and in the coldness a man* . . .

Cain did not know where the thought had come from; it was vaguely familiar, the echo of something he had heard or said long, long years ago; and then, at his elbow, Solan said proudly, "This is my son."

They were gathered together in Maston's pavilion, where dinner was being served. The tent was not small, but seemed crowded nonetheless with better than a dozen people between its walls. Maston Veramorn and his two Captains and four other highly ranked Commanders were there, as were Rea and her son, Orion.

Cain had with him Kavad and Kavad's eldest son, a half-breed silver-eyes named Jimal; Commander General Mersai and Commander Major Mondàl Dantes. The presence of the barbarians Maston had

given it in the common tongue, and was growing better by th€
interpreting Anglish. The Giants had not programmed it to und
Anglish, for it was a language the Giants themselves did no1
Before the Rulers had forced them to learn the common tongι
had spoken only old Russian, and today it was still the only tong
used besides the Valley's common tongue.

Still, the problem was not the computer, which was l
quickly, nor the robot servants, which were unobtrusive, nor the
which Loden hardly noticed. It was just this: in the time since tl
left Earth, Loden Almandar had not been *needed* for anything
were no threats to counter, no Workers to supervise, no Giants
with, no barbarians to wage campaigns against; simply nothing

In all his life that had never happened to him before.

Perhaps midway through the interminable night, a ι
touched his mind. *Loden?*

Gabriel? What is it?

*My grandson Edward just awoke me, Loden. One of our sι
has left orbit.*

· 2 ·

I should have known, thought Maston Veramorn, *that the
couldn't really have harmed him.* They walked together, late tha
noon, for the first time in nearly twelve years, with their two
bodyguards trailing behind them at a decent distance. Maston ι
Cain the facilities Eagles had thrown up to handle the crowds a
various sporting events. Cain looked, and acted, like a man in tl
of health; it was very much at odds with the reports Maston's ι
Eastmarch had given him only two weeks past, of a man in a co
the verge of death.

Like a cockroach, thought Maston.

"Hard to kill," Cain agreed smoothly. That late in the d
grounds were largely empty; most of the Warriors who would b
peting had either ridden back up to Eagles or else returned t
tents, and most of the spectators had done likewise, to their t
whatever crude structures they had constructed to shield themse
small town seemed to have appeared out of nowhere, not quite

protested with what was, for him, consummate grace, before agreeing to let them stay because he had no choice.

Cain was barely seated when Solan brought Orion forward. The child was dressed formally, as one might expect of the grandson of Lord Veramorn: an exquisitely tailored black Warrior's uniform in the cut that Eagles favored, without any insignia of rank, but with the silver eagle brooch that proclaimed him a Veramorn. Cain found that interesting; had Maston granted Orion the right to wear the signet of the Veramorns, or had Solan—or, likelier, Maston's notoriously strong-headed bastard "daughter"—simply pinned it on the boy without asking?

Maston Veramorn could hardly look at the child without broadcasting a flash of displeasure so sharp Cain found it almost audible.

Cain looked the boy over for a brief moment, after that brief moment of disorientation had passed—a likely enough child, for all he was quite young. He looked like his father, blond with blue eyes, which hardly surprised Cain; genetically there could be little variation between them. Cain's faith in T'Pau Almandar was complete; Loden would have no unpleasant recessive genes, and therefore Solan and Rea, his mirror images, would not either; and therefore they could not have been reinforced in Orion.

The boy's gene chart would be interesting.

With Cain seated, their eyes were almost at a level. Cain said, speaking as directly as to another adult, "Good evening, Orion. I'm pleased to meet you."

Orion's voice was as high and pure as a girl's, but his words were clear. "Lord Cain." He bowed slightly, stiffly.

"How old are you, Orion?"

"Five, my lord."

Cain nodded, distantly aware of Maston's eyes focused upon them from the other end of the long table. Rea Veramorn was watching them also. Something puzzled Cain about the child, for a moment, before he realized what it was: at the age of five the boy's mind already took more effort to touch than either of his parents. Cain glanced up at Solan, standing behind his son. "Why did you name him Orion?"

The question obviously surprised Solan. "Actually, I didn't. My wife . . ."

From her place beside Maston, Rea said across the length of the table, "It means star hunter."

Commander Mersai broke off his conversation with Tristan. "The boy's named Orion? Why, that's my name."

The first animated expression Cain had yet seen from Orion broke across the boy's face. "We have the same name?" he demanded.

"Aye." Mersai's broad face split in a grin. "It's pronounced a bit different—*Orrin*—because I'm from Telindel and don't have your western accent. But it's the same name, from the hunter in the sky."

Cain turned to Rea. "I know what it means, my lady." His use of formal address obviously pleased Rea Veramorn, Cain noted, though she strove to hide it. "I meant, why did you name him so?"

"Is it important?" Rea frowned. "Why did your parents name you for a kriss demon?"

Cain sat back in his chair, studying Rea Veramorn thoughtfully. "You're well educated, my lady. But wrong. My parents named me for the kainan."

Maston Veramorn chuckled. "Did they really? My grandfather," he said, "shot down a kainan and then killed it with his bare hands."

Cain was spared the necessity of finding a reply to that. Orion, who had not been dismissed, was still standing beside Cain's chair. "Is the kainan bird as big as an eagle, Lord Cain?"

Cain looked directly at Maston Veramorn. "Rather larger, Orion. The kainan is not a bird, but a shrike. Like other shrikes, it eats eagles. They are," he said evenly, "a great delicacy."

Senta had never been to the Worker-controlled territory around Eagles; she needed an image to work with.

From the bridge of the starship, Senta focused the ship's telescopes on the open plain beneath Eagles. At first the image wavered badly, but in the course of minutes the computer built up slowly, bit by bit, a true picture of the Games grounds. The fact that Earth had turned its back on the sun slowed the computer's construction of a working image considerably, but not fatally; the starship which was chasing her was still outside the orbit of Jupiter when the holograph the computer was building was completed.

The holograph hung, life-size, obscuring utterly one bulkhead of the bridge. It looked exactly as though the bridge had simply opened out onto a vast clearing, with tents thrown up in the distance and the town of Eagles visible high in the hills.

In nearly the same instant the Light took her, and the starship was empty again.

"You have Singer; I want Parliament."

The dinner platters were cleared away; they relaxed around the table with drinks and dessert. Orion had gone to bed, without complaint, only a short while ago, and with the aid of a map Cain and Maston divided the Valley between them.

Cain had to think for only a moment. "Very well. You're considerably closer to Parliament than I am; it's yours. If you need help getting their fusion generator running again, let me know."

The offer galled Maston. "That won't be necessary," he said shortly.

"It's an old generator," said Cain quietly, pausing while a serving man refilled his wine goblet. "It's not like the fusion machines I brought back from Donnertown."

"We'll manage." That was from Commander Captain Tristan, in a tone of voice near hostility; Rea Veramorn laid a hand atop his, in a placating gesture.

Cain did not appear to notice; he smiled. "On to Goldriver, then. I've no objection to letting you have Goldriver as well, but I want its gold and platinum production."

Maston stared at him. "Are you out of your mind? You've mines in Eastmarch; we don't. Do you know how desperately starved we are for industrial gold?"

"Almost as starved as Eastmarch," said Cain. "Goldriver's output will just about meet our projected needs. Need I remind you, Maston, our production facilities are far larger than your own? Our mines in Eastmarch are barely a tenth as rich as the mines in Goldriver. I'll run the mines, Maston, and if there is surplus—especially of platinum—I'll share it fairly, without even charging you for it. Further, any iridium is yours; I don't need it."

"That's not really acceptable," said Solan without even waiting to see if Maston intended to speak. "All night you've graciously granted

Eagles all those things you've no need of and refused to even bargain on subjects where we are both in need."

"In my place," asked Cain with honest curiosity, "would you?"

Solan started to snap a reply and then paused, seeing that Cain meant the question. He was uncertain for a moment how to answer and then said slowly, "I suppose it would depend on whether I intended a peace based on cooperation—trust, if you will—between our peoples. That's not impossible, Cain; we're more alike than different. If I intended real peace, a peace that would not need weapons to enforce it, I would, Cain, share even those resources of which Eastmarch does not have enough. If I intended a peace based on force—and, between us here at this table, Eastmarch can enforce such a peace, though you'll have Eastmarch Warriors die for it—I would not."

"Very well," said Cain after some thought. "Our manufacturing capacity outstrips yours better than three to one, but let's call it a three-to-one ratio for simplicity's sake. Let us, then, divide the gold and platinum, as it is mined, in that ratio. We will, then, in proportion, be equally served."

Orrin Mersai glanced at Cain quickly. Cain ignored him.

Maston said after a moment, "Are you serious?"

"Yes."

Maston stared at him suspiciously down the length of the table, obviously suspecting some trap. "Altruism is not like you, Cain."

Cain sipped at his wine, letting it sit in his mouth for a moment before swallowing. It was too sweet, as most Eagles wines were, but not bad for all that. "Gentlemen, my lady Rea, Commander Captain Solan has said what we all know, but which I have not, for politeness' sake, stressed. Maston, the Rulers are gone. Assuming the Giants are content not to interfere in our affairs, and the barbarians are unable, you and I are the only powers left in this Valley. Perhaps I am not an altruist, Maston Veramorn, but neither am I a monster, in proof of which you may witness the fact that these talks are occurring at all. Maston, if I wanted Eagles, I could take it from you, but see, I have not done so."

Maston's features drained of blood. "Are you threatening us, Cain?"

Cain cradled his goblet between both hands. The silver of the goblet gathered the light from the pavilion's glowfloats, and Maston found the winking light, reflecting from its surface, oddly distracting.

Cain let the goblet roll slightly between his fingers, back and forth, mere centimeters in each direction. "I see no need for threats," he said mildly, a faint smile playing about his lips, ". . . when one has superior firepower."

Their conversation, aboard the starship that had followed Senta back to Earth, was brief.

One day and then they're going to go down in force, eh?

So they say, my friend. Loden's thought was particularly empty of emotion. *It should not take us so long, however. Where Solan is, we will find Senta.*

Loden could almost hear Loga's grin. *No doubt. And then what?*

Loden paused. *I am not entirely certain. Perhaps we will take Senta home and pretend that none of this ever happened. And perhaps, my friend, we will decide she is correct, and we'll tell the Tribunal to go hell, stay on Earth, and teach this Solan the things he should know.*

Sounds like fun. Seriously, said Loga, *I've been bored.*

"So, Pinch," said Orion seriously, "what do you think of Cain?"

Pinch was lying on his back before the firepit in the center of Solan and Rea's tent, tongue lolling, as Orion scratched his stomach.

"I know you weren't there," said Orion impatiently. "But I told you about it. What did you *think?* He can't be as old as they say."

There was a sharp, flat crack, like the sound of a whip being wielded, immediately behind Orion, and for just a moment Orion's shadow, on the wall of the tent in front of him, loomed huge and black.

The voice said, "Who can't be as old as they say?"

Things had grown considerably more relaxed, as problem after problem was resolved.

"Good. So river access is taken care of. If we have . . ." Cain broke off in midword.

After a long moment someone at the table said, "By the Light, look at his eyes." Cain was not sure whose voice that was. After a moment he shook himself slightly and looked down into his wine. Looking back up at them again, Cain said simply, "Excuse me. I thought I heard something."

Pinch came up in an instant, with a low growl in his throat. Orion put a hand on his dog's shoulder to restrain him.

"What are you doing here?" For a moment Orion thought it was Cain; then the man came forward into the firelight, and he could not imagine how the idea had occurred to him. Though Cain and the intruder were of about the same size and height, Cain's hair was cropped short and his eyes were black; the intruder had eyes even bluer than Orion's own, and red hair that fell in rings past his shoulders.

"Looking for your parents. Shh," said Loga, speaking directly to the dog, and instantly all the tenseness went out of the muscles under Orion's hand. "What's your dog's name?"

"Pinch. He's a hunting dog," Orion said proudly, but did not add that his mother would not allow him to go hunting yet.

"When you talk to him," said Loga, "does he talk back?"

"No, that's just pretend."

"Ah. During the later Fire Wars, there were dogs that could talk, you know. T'Pau created them. I'd thought that breed was gone." Loga went down to one knee and held out his hand to the dog. Pinch crept forward, sniffed at the Ruler's hand for just a moment, and then his tail began wagging. "He's got good taste," Loga continued, scratching the dog between the ears. "What's your name, kid?"

Orion hesitated perceptibly. "Orion. Who are you?"

"Loga." Loga cocked his head to one side. "You're not afraid of me, are you?"

Orion hesitated again and then said, "You're not supposed to be in this tent, it's just for my parents. But no, I'm not afraid."

"Why not? Aren't I big enough?"

"I'm going to be a Warrior, so I wouldn't be afraid anyway," Orion said proudly, "but Pinch likes you. I like the people Pinch likes."

"There're worse ways to pick your friends," Loga conceded. "Are your parents coming back here tonight?"

Orion nodded. "After dinner with Cain."

Loga said sharply, "Cain's *here?*"

Orion grinned. "Yep. In the tent next to this one."

There was no way Cain would not have felt the raising of the Light that had heralded Loga's appearance. Loga used a word Orion had never heard before and added, "Great. Look, I've got to go, then. I'll try to come back to see your parents tonight, or tomorrow night if I don't make it tonight. Tell me, Orion, have you seen a lady, about your mother's age, who looks like her?"

Orion shook his head. "No. Who is she?"

Loga sighed. "An idiot who's led a sheltered life."

"What?"

"Nothing, kid. Time for you to go to bed."

"But I'm not sleepy," Orion protested instantly.

"Yes, you are," said Loga gently.

"No I'm . . ." The protest was cut off by a huge yawn. Loga walked the child, stumbling half asleep, over to where a pallet of stretched deer fur had been set up next to the firepit and tucked him into bed.

"Thanks," Orion mumbled, eyes already closed. "G'night, Loga."

Loga touched a single finger to Orion's temple. "This visit, child, it was just a dream."

"A dream," repeated Orion sleepily.

"Yeah," said Loga. "Just a dream, and you're not going to talk about it to anyone, especially your parents."

"Okay . . ." The child's voice trailed away into nothingness. Loga turned back to the dog, which had been watching the proceedings curiously. " 'Bye, Pinch."

Loga brought the Light to him and vanished.

Very nearby, the elusively familiar presence raised the Light once again.

Cain let nothing cross his face. Eastmarch Commander Colonel Mondàl Dantes was talking, sketching out a plan for a minimal degree of integration between Eastmarch and Eagles forces, largely for the purpose of policing the length of the river Almandar.

Cain leaned over and murmured to Kavad, "Loga's here." Kavad nodded, and though even Cain saw no signal pass, several minutes later Kavad's son Jimal excused himself, saying that he was needed back at the Eastmarch camp. Perhaps Maston found something suspicious in that, for he announced shortly thereafter that he was growing weary and wished to retire for the night. Cain agreed easily, and left the tent to wait outside while Mersai finished the details of his conversation with Commander Captain Tristan.

Solan joined him a moment later. It was chilly outside; even in Summer the Valley's nights were never warm. The stars above them were very bright. Solan said quietly, "You wanted to speak to me alone, Cain?"

Cain had; one of his first instructions to Kavad, that morning, had been to pass word to Solan that Cain wished to see him. Things had changed since that morning, however, and Cain said gently, "No, that's not necessary, Solan. Not tonight, at any rate. I'm rather tired and, like Maston, need my sleep."

The answer clearly disconcerted Solan. "Oh? Kavad seemed to imply it was . . . urgent we meet."

Cain laughed easily. "Kavad has a way of making everything I want seem urgent; it's part of his job." He clapped Solan on the shoulder. "Tomorrow will you and your wife have dinner with me? That's soon enough. Besides, I've the impression your wife would like to have you to herself tonight."

Solan chuckled. "Was it that obvious?"

"To the others at the table? Not at all, I'm sure. But she was thinking about something else for—easily—the last half hour there."

"You understand women, Cain."

Cain shook his head. "Not really. I understand people. Women are not so different from us. I mean it, spend the night with her; I can wait." Their conversation was cut off when Mersai and the other two members of Cain's party made their farewells and came out to join them.

Solan said, "I look forward to meeting your men in the Games tomorrow, Cain, Commander General. Good night, gentlemen."

Orrin Mersai nodded. "Good night, Commander Captain."

Cain said simply, "Good-bye, Solan."

· 3 ·

She stood in the trees, well back from the edge of the clearing. Her eyesight was good, far better than that of a Worker; nonetheless Senta was not certain at first that she had actually found them. The man and woman lay together on a blanket, flesh exposed to the cold night air, white skin bleached of color under the moonlight.

She was only seventeen years old. The things that Loga, or Loden, were capable of, were for her only vague rumors. But Loga had been teaching her; she thought she might attempt . . .

With great concentration, she reached out, found the glimmer of their thoughts. It was hard, far harder than the work of raising the Light. Her breath came short, and then . . .

It was as though she were *there* with them on the blanket, and the strength of the bond that existed between them struck her with dizzying force. Her knees grew weak, and she leaned against the gnarled trunk of an ancient oak.

"You'll be a good peacemaker," the woman said. Rea, it must be, though Senta felt in her a resolve the likes of which she associated only with Rulers hundreds of years old. "That was well done, how you talked Cain into sharing the mines at Goldriver." The simple touch of the woman's mind was almost more than Senta could bear, and she turned her attention to the man, her brother, Loden Almandar's son.

It was like grasping a white-hot spike of iron. At the surface of his mind the man was thinking, and the words echoed at his mouth, "Yes, it was, wasn't it?" An unbound strength took Senta, enveloped her in a single moment of brilliant intensity again, like the hard will Senta observed in her half sister Rea, but a broader, deeper strength, so essentially male that it took Senta a moment to recover herself sufficiently to make the comparison with what she had found in Rea.

It reminded Senta with a sudden sharp ache of her father—Loden's strength, but without the failings of her father's vast age; a clear, mature confidence that reminded her of Loga, but without any measure of the redhead's cynicism, and underlaid with the clearest conception she had ever encountered that there were actions correct, actions incorrect, and that all of life lay in knowing the difference between the two.

In that first instant of touch, Senta knew she had never met a better man in all her life.

The thought reached her from elsewhere, the thought of a mind so like that of Commander Captain Solan that for an instant the Ruler Senta thought it had come from him.

If he is at all like Donner, I do not doubt you have not.

Senta found herself elsewhere.

It was a dark place, without form or content.

Senta? The voice whispered through the edges of her mind. *Senta, where are you?*

Father?

In the gloom, Loden Almandar slowly shimmered into existence. He did not do so with the thunderclap of a physical transfer, nor even with the glow of the Light, and it came to Senta that they were in someplace that had no existence in the real world. His face was indistinct. *Senta, come back. The Tribunal is awaiting you in orbit.*

Father, I've found them, she protested. *Don't you understand?*

Senta, I did not mean for you to come here. You should not have come. I am sorry if you misunderstood me, but this is not a game. The Covenant is real, and the penalty for disobedience is great.

I'm not afraid.

You should be.

Father, if I have disobeyed the Covenant, surely you can understand. If it is right that we help them, then it is right. You were going to, she said, *and Loga, because you believed you should. And you were right; the Tribunal cannot be the keeper of my conscience. Should I have done less than you only because I am young?*

The despair rose up around Loden Almandar, a rising flood of hopelessness. *My child. Oh, my child.*

Father?

I am old, Senta. Being sent to the Light holds no fear for me. It will be a homecoming, not something I dread. And Loga was never in danger, for he never signed the Covenant. You are in danger, child, you must return.

Earlier, you spoke to me from your heart. Whose words are these? Yours, or Elyssa's?

There is an order to all things, said Loden Almandar, *a rule of law without which we are no better than barbarians. Donner thought as you did, and caused the Great Schism. Do not think the Tribunal has forgot-*

ten him, Senta; they have **not.** *The criticism has been leveled, correctly, that I have at times placed myself above the law; and it is the truth that Donner did so, and you are doing so even now. Senta, return to us. Do it now. You are in graver danger than you imagine.*

I must talk to him, father. He's one of us and he doesn't even **know.**

The power released her, and Senta came back to herself, standing, shivering with the cold, at the edge of the clearing.

Not twenty meters away, Solan and Rea lay together in the moonlight, the murmur of their voices only just audible to Senta. Senta stared through the trees at the two lovers, a look very like wonder in her eyes.

Occasionally, in the course of that long, long morning, Loga felt the restless sweep of Cain's mind, seeking through the crowd. Loga wandered through the scores of thousands in the crowd, in the dress of a Steader or entertainer, red hair gathered up under a cap to help disguise him, searching for Senta. Had Cain not been present, Loga might have found the girl in seconds, by searching for her in the way Cain was even now searching for him.

Alas, Loden had made him swear not to interfere with the Workers in any way other than that minimally necessary to retrieve Loden's daughter. In the instant Loga found the girl, in a telepathic search, Cain would likewise find *him.*

And that would, like as not, set off a bloodbath of considerable proportions. Loga was not at all certain Cain was above having slipships bomb as much as a hundred square meters at a time, simply in an attempt to kill Loga.

Searching the crowd by eye, damn it, took *time.* Loga wished for a vain instant that he might, just for a few minutes, mount the podium Cain was seated upon. From that vantage point he might have found Senta in only a few minutes. He cut the thought short; wishing for Cain's vantage point was no more fruitful than wishing for Cain's absence.

Loga knew for a fact that Senta was here. Loden had spoken to his daughter the prior evening.

The fool girl was putting them to all this trouble rather than coming home immediately because, Loden had said, she wanted to *talk* to Commander Captain Solan.

Loga had seen Solan several times that morning as the Eagles captain made his way through the crowds, smiling and joking with folk as he went. It had been a long, long time since Loga had last seen Donner Almandar, and even with the mnemonics techniques that the Rulers had developed from necessity, he was not entirely certain that his memory was not playing him false; but in Solan it was as though Donner Almandar had come again. He was not so hugely muscled as Donner had been, but besides that they might have been twins.

Rumor was that Solan was largely responsible for the current truce between Eagles and Eastmarch. He was clearly wildly popular and was, for a fact, quite handsome.

Talk, thought Loga cynically, *is not the word I would have used.*

Cain and Maston sat beneath an awning on a raised viewing platform and watched the Games and the teeming thousands of spectators who had come for them. Kavad stood alone, immediately behind Cain. Three of Maston's bodyguards held the same position behind his chair.

The archery competition was done with; Rea Veramorn, to nobody's particular surprise, had done very well, though in the end she took only a third. In long-distance target shooting, two of Cain's halfbreed Warriors, with eyesight better than that of any Worker and strength greater than that of Rea Veramorn, did well enough to take the first and second place.

Cain said conversationally, taking care that his voice did not travel beyond Maston to his bodyguards, "It's good to have a chance to speak to you privately at last."

"What do you mean by that?" Maston's voice was distracted; he radiated tension so strongly that he was giving Cain a slight headache. Though he had known it intellectually since childhood, it had taken Cain any number of years to *believe*, on an emotional basis, that other people could not sense emotion and thought as he did; Cain found it easier to ignore an overloud noise than the emotions of a disturbed man.

"I'm curious about your daughter Rea. Who was her mother?"

"A serving woman. I barely remember her name." Maston did not even look at Cain, but kept his eyes fixed on the field.

"Barely, or not at all?"

Maston turned on Cain suddenly, glaring. "What bloody concern is it of yours in the first place? You tend your house; I am well able to tend my own."

"Concern?" Cain lifted an eyebrow. "My concerns range into the unlikeliest of places, Lord Maston. For instance, did you know that Loden Almandar is here today? And at least one of his daughters, and Loga as well."

Maston Veramorn froze, midway into a word.

Cain nodded. "I assure you, they are. Loga I have felt, and Loden and his daughter I have seen. Loden is well disguised—he wears the dress of a Steader as though he were born to it—but few Workers are so large."

Maston came back to life and snarled, "You lie."

"Have you seen a woman who reminds you of Rea?" Cain saw the shot strike home. "One might ask, then, *why* are these Rulers here, after leaving Earth with such fanfare, having assured us one and all that their abdication is forever?" Cain spread his hands in a supplicating gesture. "Can you guess?"

Maston Veramorn turned away, as though he would not listen to Cain. He kept his eyes fixed rigidly ahead; his nostrils flared wide, but he did not reply.

"I think," said Cain, "that Loden is here because he knows his son is here. And his daughter as well, the child whom you have passed off as your own, the lady Rea. He must be asking himself, Maston, as I have asked myself, why have you done this? May I tell you my guess?"

"If you must."

"I think it occurred to you, Maston Veramorn, fool that you were and are, that if you controlled a child, and that child controlled the Light, then you might control the Light. And so, with the aid of the mad Giant Riabel, you arranged for this thing to happen. I can only imagine your rage when you found that the girl whom Riabel gave you could not control the Light, no matter what the inducement. Control of the Light, Maston," said Cain, so softly that the bodyguards only a meter away from them could not possibly have heard it, "is a thing that even Ruler children must be *taught*."

Maston's breath came very short. Cain could count the man's pulse in the side of his neck. "But what confuses me, Maston, is the boy. How did it come to pass that you did not know of him? Did Riabel produce one child, and one only, and say to you, *this is all that came of my work?* And knowing you, I presume you then slew him—perhaps before he had a chance to tell you of the boy, perhaps after he told you about the boy, but before he could tell you where he was?" Cain sat back in his seat, laid his head against the seat's back. In that position all he could see was the very edge of the canopy, and beyond it the blue, blue sky. Clouds moved across it in scudding slow tapestries. "Some mysteries, I suppose, will never be laid clear. Life is too short. And yet, Maston, I can look at you, at the age that overlays your features, and know that you have no access to youthbooster." Cain paused. "Maston?"

Maston Veramorn half screamed the words. *"What, damn you?"*

Cain's eyes were fixed on the distance; storm clouds were gathering, far to the west. "Did you know, Maston, that the engineer Riabel created a variant of youthbooster that works on humans?"

"No," Maston Veramorn whispered. "You lie."

"I've almost used up what I found in Donnertown myself, you know. You shouldn't," said Cain, "have killed him."

In their tent Rea helped her husband prepare for the joust, complaining all the while. "Did you know there are female Eastmarch Warriors who'll be in the joust? And I can't compete in the event because I'm not a Warrior."

Solan sighed. "It's a Warrior's event, love, always has been. Besides, you'd not make it more than one or two passes before getting knocked on your ass."

Rea frowned when she saw the armor he donned. "What's that? Why aren't you wearing your carballoy breastplate?"

Solan shrugged. He was pulling a thick wool tunic on, to protect his skin from the cold iron breastplate. "Maston asked that I wear it. He says it was his when he was a young man, and he wore it in the Games."

Rea looked at him sharply. "I'm surprised he didn't give it to Tristan."

"So am I," said Solan, buckling the straps that kept the armor in place. "But, with all the talk of peace going on, this could be such a gesture, from him to me. I wasn't about to turn it down."

"I didn't say you should." Nonetheless, Rea looked disturbed.

By what, she could not have said herself.

"When you were a child, Maston, did you look up into the sky and find shapes among the clouds?"

Maston did not reply. Cain looked away from the brilliant white clouds, back to Maston. Maston was clearly unaware of Cain's very presence. In the run immediately before the viewing stand, two contestants rode at one another. With his eyes fixed directly upon the contestants, the crash of their impact reached Cain only as a distant disturbance. Maston, watching the event, was literally quivering with tenseness. The pass was inconclusive, and one lance broke; the riders went back for another run.

Cain said quietly, "Have you seen the matchups for the joust?"

"What?"

"I said, have you seen the matchups for the joust?"

The words penetrated; Maston jerked visibly. "No . . . no, I haven't. Why do you ask?"

"Solan," said Cain quietly, "is to joust first against one of your Warriors, a First Jacobs. If he unseats Jacobs, he will then find himself contending against either Eastmarch's First Mielo, or Eagles' Captain Tristan."

Maston was perspiring visibly. "So?"

"I mean to mention," said Cain, "that if any one of my Warriors finds himself riding against Commander Captain Solan, that Warrior will slip and fall from his horse immediately upon entering the run."

Maston stared. "Why?"

"Further, we have strictly guarded access to the lances our Warriors will be using. The lances themselves, incidentally, are blunt at their tips. Even if a lance guard were to accidentally fall from one of them, the resulting blow could hardly be fatal." Cain smiled at Maston, a wholly dead smile that touched nothing but his lips. "I should hate to see Commander Captain Solan die, accidentally, beneath an Eastmarch lance. Or even, Lord Maston, beneath an Eagles lance."

"Why are you saying this?"

"Because, Maston Veramorn," said Cain, "I cannot change the future. Solan Almandar's death will not be laid at my door." Cain did not think he had ever seen an adult Worker, of whatever class, look so terrified. "Blood," he said. "There was blood in the dirt."

It became clear, in the course of the morning, that the Warriors of Eagles were the popular favorites with the crowd. Cain was hardly surprised, given that most of the Workers there would be from either Eagles territory or else territory considerably nearer Eagles than Eastmarch.

When Solan took the field against the Eagles Commander First Jacob, the screams and applause of the crowd raised up to a deafening thunder.

Cain simply watched, bleakly.

When Solan unhorsed the other Commander in a single pass, the roar, already deafening, grew awesome. Workers who had spent the entire morning sitting on the sides of slopes looking down upon the lists came to their feet, screaming their approval. Speech, even between two men as close to one another as Cain and Maston Veramorn, would have been impossible.

It did not matter.

Cain had nothing to say.

His attention was drawn to the private seats at the very side of the lists, shaded as was the viewing platform he shared with Maston; it was where the highborn were seated. In the very first row, Orion sat clutching his mother's hand, flushed with excitement.

What a beautiful boy, Cain thought, with complete irrelevance.

Maston was holding something in one pocket of his longcoat.

In the crowd, further back, among the common throng, Cain's eye picked out a blonde girl: Loden's, surely. He thought it was the same girl he had seen earlier that morning. She seemed very young, young even by the standards of Workers.

Cain thought, *Senta*. It had to be her, unless Loden had yet another child whom Cain did not know of. In that instant he knew he was correct. In the moment her name came to him, the girl turned and, across the great distance between them, met his gaze. Her eyes opened, very wide, but she did not look away. Cain did.

The crowd gave voice again; Commander Captain Solan entered the lists at one end, and Commander Captain Tristan at the other. Cain watched as the men prepared for their run. Tristan's aide examined the lance he had been using, and without explanation replaced it with another. Cain did not think Tristan even noticed the change. The man sat high in his saddle, eyes on Solan, clearly relishing the contest. From the other end of the lists, Solan nodded at Tristan, brought the visor on his helmet down, brought his shield up, lowered his lance and urged his horse forward. Tristan called something to Solan that the wind bore away from Cain, brought his own visor down and set his horse into a canter.

Cain sat and watched. Perhaps only Cain in all that vast assembly of humans truly saw what happened. As Solan and Tristan approached each other, Maston moved convulsively, shoulders twitching beside Cain. The guard cap on Tristan d'Volta's lance fell free, and the hardened sharp carballoy tip of the lance shivered slightly and then lunged forward of its own volition, almost tearing itself from Tristan d'Volta's grasp. Solan's shield took the tip of the lance full-on and simply shattered with the force of the impact. The lance sheared through the shield, through the weak iron of Solan's breastplate, through Solan and out the other side. Solan was torn from his saddle; the lance was ripped from Commander Captain Tristan's grip.

Solan did not scream; he never made any sound at all. He struck the ground of the run with a thud that Cain found clearly audible.

In that clear, stretching instant, the entire universe came into astonishingly clear focus for Cain. He had time to watch the expression of excitement on Orion's face turn to something else entirely, had time to see the glow of the Light touch the Ruler Senta. The roar of the crowd was fading, evaporating into silence. Solan arched his back, shuddered wildly once, and slowly began to grow still.

Among all the scores of thousands who were there that day, there was nothing but silence.

The blood blessed the earth, bright red in the brilliant sunshine of the day.

Senta's Star

The Year 1284 After the Fire

· 1 ·

"Now," said Cain to Kavad, "we salvage."

Ken Selvren did amazing things with knives; there was no living Worker who was the equal of even one of the half-breed silver-eyes. In the instant of silence following Solan's death, Maston Veramorn's three bodyguards died without noise, without notice. Throwing knives simply appeared in them without warning. Maston was standing, staring out onto the field where Solan lay. He did not even see his bodyguards die. Kavad left the platform without hurry, walking down the stairs and into the milling crowd surrounding the run. Quietly and without fuss, Cain's bodyguards began breaking up the still-shocked crowd around Solan's body, separating the Workers out into smaller, manageable groups. Cain sat, watching; Rea was at Solan's side, a sort of wild panic stamped upon her; Maston seemed transfixed by Solan's quivering form.

An Eagles Warrior whom Cain did not recognize was holding Orion so that the boy could not see his father's death, even as the Warrior himself stared in utter horror. The boy twisted and squirmed in the Warrior's grip, until, at last, the Warrior let him see.

Cain never saw where the first shot came from; almost certainly it came from one of Maston's men, panicked at the sight of Eastmarcher barbarians moving purposefully through the crowd. In that instant any hope of managing the crowd vanished. Someone, Cain did not see who, screamed, and the crowd became a mob. Cain came to his feet slowly, unbuttoning his vest and withdrawing his handgun. He stopped on his way down from the viewing platform to strike Maston behind the ear with the butt of the gun. Maston pitched face-forward off the platform, down two meters to the ground. Cain followed him less quickly.

Kavad was calling out with an amplified voice, "Treachery, treachery! Eastmarch! To me, Eastmarch!" Despite the confused resistance by Eagles Warriors, Cain's silver-eyes had largely stabilized the small pocket surrounding Solan and Tristan and Rea. Cain could not even find it within himself to be angry. He touched the microphone at his collar. He could barely hear his own voice over the rising screams of the wounded. "Mersai, this is Cain. It's gone up. Can you . . ." Cain shot an Eagles Warrior in the back of the head at point-blank range as the Warrior struggled with one of Cain's barbarians. A laser warped past Cain's ear, singeing his hair. Cain did not turn but continued without hurry and without pause toward the knot of folk around Solan.

Mersai's voice clicked in on his earphone. *"I see it, my lord. I'll be there within a few seconds."*

The crowd parted before Cain. From out of nowhere a form cracked into existence immediately beside Rea and Solan, and Cain knew before the glow of the Light had faded sufficiently to make out the man's features that it was Loga. In the midst of what was rapidly becoming a pitched battle between Eagles and Eastmarch, the Ruler's appearance produced a notable effect. A local hush descended around Loga, and Warriors backed away from him; nobody but Cain even shot at him.

Cain did, twice, and struck him both times. The glow of the Light had never left Loga. He stared straight at Cain, with a puzzled expression, as the slugs took him in the abdomen. He did not stop either of the slugs; they tore straight through him and out the other side. Loga had not even begun to sag when he flared like a living sun, and was gone.

Cain touched the microphone at his collar, striding forward into the mess. "Kavad, pass the word, if you see a Ruler, if somebody appears out of nothing, shoot to kill."

A scream that might have been rage or pain or joy for all Cain knew came from somewhere off to his right. He had no warning; because she was a poor telepath, he did not feel her raising of the Light as he had felt Loga's. With a blinding speed that left him amazed, the

Ruler Senta flickered into existence standing next to her sister Rea. Cain had never seen a Ruler come out of the Light so quickly.

From the fields where the Eastmarch fleet had landed, from the north, the slipships came, and the large personnel carriers.

Through the crowd, Senta's eyes locked with Cain's for just a moment. Cain had his handgun up, pointing at her. Rea was in the line of fire, and Cain hesitated. A moment of disbelief touched Senta's features, and then the two women were gone.

There was a moment of blinding light, and then a cool black darkness. Rea Veramorn felt herself in some way change in that instant, as the first touch of the Light awakened an ability that had always been latent within her.

A quiet, gentle voice was saying, *Be calm. We will leave the other-world shortly.*

The disturbance widened away from the run and grew more vicious as brief peace settled around the scene of Solan's death. Eastmarch troops had perhaps a dozen Eagles Warriors facedown on the ground with their hands laced behind their heads, Commander Captain Tristan, still in his mail, among them. Mersai's voice came to Cain again. *"Sir? Retreat or dig in and take the territory?"*

Bullets sang in the air around Cain. Lasers flicked wildly; one touched Cain momentarily, but against the heat-resistant cloth it was hardly noticeable. "Retreat," said Cain without needing to think. "If I choose to take Eagles, it won't be like this."

"Yes, my lord." The personnel carriers came to gentle landings approximately a hundred meters from where Cain stood, in the clearing immediately to the north of the run. Only one of the Eagles Warriors was still on his feet, the Warrior who had been holding Orion. One hand still gripped the boy's shoulder. Orion was staring unblinking at his father's form, not ten meters away.

The Warrior standing behind the boy made as if to reach for a weapon. Cain did not see a weapon upon his person, but did not wait to find out if he was wrong; he shot the Warrior once. Cain was not aware of Kavad's presence until that moment, when the silver-eyes said, "My lord? Take the child?"

Cain stood watching Orion. In the midst of what had become a pitched battle, the boy did not seem to be aware of anything but his fallen father.

"Yes," he said. "Take him."

Hands aided Maston Veramorn to his feet, brushed dirt from his clothing. Voices babbled at him. ". . . taken your *grandson* . . ."

Maston lashed out blindly. "Take your hands from me!" he screamed. His eyesight was clearing slowly. Nearly thirty of his Warriors were clustered around him; only about half of them even had weapons. He became aware, suddenly, of the presence of three of Eastmarch's huge personnel carriers in the clearing immediately to the north. Eastmarch slipships by the hundreds hovered overhead, and perhaps three hundred Warriors, in the black uniforms of Eastmarch, were backing off the field with their weapons at the ready, retreating in order to the carriers. Scattered fire from Eagles Warriors followed them, and Maston saw two among the Eastmarch number fall as he watched, to be picked up and carried by their fellows. The Eastmarchers returned fire carefully, aware as Maston's own Warriors did not seem to be that there were still Workers in the line of fire.

Cain was among them, reloading his handgun as Maston spotted him. "Hold your fire, damn it!" Maston yelled across the field.

The sound of his voice drew Cain's attention. Cain touched a stud at his collar, and his voice boomed amplified across the field. "Eastmarch! Cease fire!" Another Eastmarcher fell after the order was given, but the order held, and the Eastmarchers retreated to the carriers without further death. Cain looked toward Maston; at the distance, Maston could not make out the man's expression. He saw Cain give his handgun to one of his Warriors, and then turn his back on them all and walk away.

Maston snapped orders at the small group of Warriors near him and, with his Warriors surrounding him three deep, strode out the run, to where Solan's body lay. One of his Warriors had withdrawn the lance from Solan, and now the lance lay parallel on the ground next to him.

Though he did not let it show, Maston felt a brief twinge of satisfaction at the sight of Solan's still features.

Tristan was sitting only a few meters away from Maston, face buried in his hands. What little had been accomplished here had been done by a Commander Second whom Maston did not even recognize; Tristan did not even look up at the sound of Maston's voice, not until Maston came to him and addressed him directly, quietly. "Damn it, man, get to your feet. Have enough pride to wait until you've some privacy to do your grieving in." White-faced still, the Commander Captain nodded jerkily and came to his feet, somewhat shakily.

There was a sharp crack, followed by a gust of wind.

A sudden silence descended immediately behind Maston, and Maston heard a snatch of speech. ". . . dar, and you will get out of my way."

There was only one living creature in all the world whom Maston Veramorn was truly afraid of, and he recognized the man's voice instantly. There was a weakness in his knees as he turned, and even as he despised himself for his fear, he knew that he would do nothing to offend Loden Almandar.

H er body was returned to her, and with the resumption of its form, the body's emotions struck her like a hammer.

"What *happened?*" Rea screamed at the girl.

They had appeared in a gorge high in the Black Mountains, looking down upon the Games field. From this height men were only specks, and larger items such as the personnel carriers and pavilions were only small, brightly colored markers on a war-games board. The girl said quietly, looking down, "I wish I could tell you, but I don't know. I wasn't looking for something like that to happen. I only came to tell you who you were."

The words meant nothing to Rea, and the girl was not even looking at her. "Who are you?" The girl did not answer her, and Rea said desperately, "Listen, Orion. My son. *My son is down there.* He needs me. You have to take me back."

The girl turned suddenly. "I can't, my lady. Did you see how it happened? The lance, it *moved* of its own accord, as though some person controlling the Light had taken hold of it. I think Solan was murdered, my lady." A disturbed look crossed her face. "Though who with such mastery of the Light might have done so—I do not think Cain has such skill, and surely neither Father nor Loga—"

"*Who are you?*"

"My lady?" The girl stood silently for a moment, looking at her. When she spoke, Rea saw her awkward for the first time. "I'm sorry. My name is Senta. I am the Ruler Senta Almandar, daughter of the Tribunal Elder Loden." Senta paused, and added simply, "I'm your sister."

"It is too late," said Loden aloud. He withdrew his hands from Solan's temples and rose slowly. The mud he stood in was a mixture of blood and earth. The wound was too vast, and the boy had been dead too long for even Loden's vast skill to resurrect. Loden turned slowly, scanning the faces of the Eagles Warriors surrounding him. It had not even occurred to him that he was in any danger; surely no Worker would dare to fire upon him.

His eyes locked with Maston's. "Worker," he said gently, "do you know who this was?"

Maston stood as though transfixed. He forced his mouth to work. "Commander Captain Solan." He was distantly aware of his own Warriors around him, but despite himself the words left his mouth. "My lord."

Loden Almandar did not even notice the honorific. "He was my son, Worker." Standing in the midst of Maston's Warriors, Loden Almandar said simply, "I should kill you." The glow of the Light came down to enfold him.

Not one of Maston's Warriors so much as moved to defend their lord. Years later that fact brought Maston nightmares with horrid regularity.

"I should kill you," Loden repeated, "and perhaps I will."

The Ruler stood looking down upon Maston Veramorn and finally sighed, a deeply weary sound, and vanished.

Maston Veramorn stood shaking after he was gone, absolutely unable to move.

Senta said directly, *Can you trust me?*

The touch of her thought jolted Rea as nothing else had. "Can I? Yes. Should I? I don't know."

"Fair enough. *Think*, though," said Senta urgently. "Somebody killed Solan. I am almost certain; and if your husband was murdered, might you not also be in danger?"

Rea Veramorn stood as though struck. All color had drained from her face. "Oh no," she whispered. She sat down on the ground abruptly. "That damned iron breastplate Maston gave him. If he'd been wearing carballoy he'd never have been in any danger at all. Maston killed my husband." She looked up at Senta. "I can't go back. He'll kill me too, he'll have to."

Senta shook her head gently and knelt next to Rea, shivering slightly in the cold winds that moved through the high gorge. "I don't think so, my lady. The way the lance shivered and then leapt forward—someone took control of that lance with the Light."

Rea did not even look at her. "You damn fool. Have you never seen a monomagnet in use? It behaves exactly as you describe, moving slowly at first, and then with geometrically greater speed as it approaches its opposite pole." She turned slightly until her eyes met Senta's. "You've got to go get my son."

"This boy, Orrin you called him . . ."

"Orion."

"Orion," Senta said precisely. "Very well. If—" Senta broke off, and then continued more slowly. "If Maston knows you are Loden's children, and it seems to me he must, then he will recognize me for what I am. We look too much alike, you and I. And my accent is too obviously that of a Ruler; I could not pass for a Worker in Eagles, to ask about your son's whereabouts. Do you think the boy would be in any immediate danger?"

"Danger?" Rea said slowly, "No. I don't think even Maston would dare harm the boy publicly. He's only five. After a year or two he might have a fatal accident, but for now I think he is safe."

"Good. Now listen, I must take you somewhere safe. Do you see this?"

Rea nodded. "Yes. Yes, I do. Where are you thinking of?"

"The safest place of all would be New Parliament, but—I think not." Senta ran through her options at a furious rate. "A Worker by raising, you are nonetheless a Ruler by blood. They might not let you come back here. Eagles is simply not safe for you, and no more so are the territories of Eastmarch. I think . . . Parliament. It's the only place you'll be safe."

The Light descended around them.

They appeared in a small room without windows, dimly lit by a dying fire. An old woman was dozing in a chair before the fire. The crack of their appearance did not rouse her, though the sudden wind nearly killed her fire. "Her name is Farina," said Senta. "She was my nurse when I was a child; she's a bit simple, but you can trust her."

Rea only nodded, looking around at the old woman's cramped quarters. Senta knelt next to the old woman and shook her gently awake. "Farina? Farina, it's me, Senta." The woman stirred slightly, and opened her eyes slowly.

"Senta?" she said sleepily. Her wrinkled features broke into a delighted smile. "Is it you?"

Senta smiled back at her. "Yes, Farina. It's me."

"Well." The old bright eyes glanced at Rea and then back to Senta. She sat up somewhat straighter. "Would you like some wine?"

"No, Farina. Farina, I need you to do something for me."

"Surely," said Farina instantly. "But why are you here at all? We were told you would never return." Her features lifted slightly. "Are you coming back, then?"

"No," said Senta gently, "I'm not even supposed to be here now. I suspect I've angered the Tribunal rather a lot."

Farina gestured to where Rea stood. "Why have you brought her here?"

"This is one of my sisters, Farina. She needs somewhere to stay. There is no other place; I know she will be safe in your hands. You must tell no one she is here." Farina nodded, and Senta hugged the old woman quickly, stood, and turned to Rea. "Will you be okay?"

Rea said slowly, "Yes. Yes, I will."

"I'm going back to face the Tribunal and ask their aid in rescuing

Orrin—*Orion*—from Maston. . . . What I said, about how they might not let you come back to Earth, if you journeyed to New Parliament with me?" Senta hesitated. "The same is true for me as well. I'm here on Earth against the wishes of the Tribunal. After I've gone to New Parliament to plead my case, it is possible they will not let me return here."

Rea bit her lip. "I see."

"The journey to New Parliament is two days, so we have four days' travel time there and then back here again. If I have not returned before the passing of a week, you must, my lady, assume I will not return, and you are on your own."

"That," said Rea evenly, "is the truth whether you return or not. My husband is dead."

"I must leave." Senta said with some difficulty, "I know . . . the depth of the feeling you had for him. I am sorry."

"I will wait for your return," said Rea. "One week."

Senta did not reply; the Light of her passage left an afterimage burning on Rea Veramorn's retinas like a hole in reality.

She appeared on the bridge of the starship she had stolen.

They stood waiting for her, stood motionless as though they had been waiting so for all of time and were prepared to wait another eternity if they found it necessary. Gabriel and Calandra, Michael and Senta's sister Selene; four of the eleven members of the full Tribunal.

She had no time to say even a word. The Light touched Senta in a way she had never known before, in a cold and invasive fashion, took hold of her and wrenched her out of the world.

Senta found herself floating immobile in the midst of a great vacuum, immediately above the surface of a small asteroid. There were stars all around her, blazing with the brilliance given them by lack of atmosphere. Her body was held in a distant n-space pattern. In some fashion she did not understand, the Tribunal had taken her very body away from her.

They shimmered into existence before her, ten of the eleven Tribunal members; only Loga was not present. Like Senta they did not become fully corporeal. The Light sheathed their forms, protected them from the hard vacuum and solar radiation. Her father spoke quietly, formally, the pain in the words obvious even to Senta, like a drumbeat underlying the surface of his thoughts. *Senta Almandar, you have been brought before the Tribunal of the Rulers. You stand accused of rebellion; that you knowingly and willfully disobeyed the ruling of this Tribunal. You are signatory to the Covenant; how say you?*

Senta said quickly, *The Tribunal? Ten of you? Where is Loga?*

We believe he is dead, a victim during the battle following my son's death, said the whisper of Loden Almandar's voice. *He must at the very least have been grievously wounded, for we have had no word of him since. We have retrieved Solan's body, and if we find Loga's as well, which does not seem likely, they will be buried together on New Parliament.*

Even lacking her body to provide any glandular response, the words struck Senta hard. *Loga's dead? How?*

Selene answered her. *Cain shot him, in the battle between Eagles and Eastmarch after Solan fell, and he vanished. Such a thing has happened only rarely in our history. We do not know if he could have survived. It seems unlikely.*

Loden waited until it was clear that Senta would make no response to Selene. *Ruler Senta, you have heard of what you are accused. How say you?*

A lightning-swift thought, Senta did not know where it came from, or even whether it was male or female, touched her and was gone. *Apologize.* Despite the grim demeanors facing her, then, there was at least one Tribunal member who held some sympathy for her. Her father, surely. And perhaps others? *How do I say? I say that, among other things, you are behaving with astonishing speed. Need this be done this instant?*

Loden said grimly, *Senta, answer.*

Why do you ask what you already know? I do not deny what I have done. But it is only what Loga and Loden planned to do themselves; you must know that. Was it wrong for me to do what my elders planned to do themselves?

Elyssa's thoughts touched her. They held a pain, and, in the same instant, a cold determination Senta did not understand. *You have bro-*

ken the Covenant. *You're no fool, girl; have we so many laws that you could not abide by the most important of them?*

It doesn't matter what I say, does it? You've made up your minds already. You're all afraid—terrified—of what will happen if you don't purge my rebellion. Look at yourselves, Senta pleaded. *Where is the compassion you're so proud of? Where are the ideals? Live them, you have the power. There is no one who has more.*

Gabriel said slowly, *You are very convincing, child. And indeed, so was Donner. You are much like him, both in demeanor and in arrogance.*

Senta slowed her racing thoughts with an effort of will. *Very well. I broke the Covenant, an agreement I signed when I could barely hold the scriptor. I did what I thought correct, no more and no less. If that is a crime, then it is a crime and I do not dispute you. Let me then request my own punishment. Return me to Earth. Let me stay on Earth, breathe the air of Earth, and die when old age takes me, as though I were a Worker myself. Let me stay and help them. There is a child named Orion; he is Loden's grandson, the child of the Rulers Rea and Solan. I swore to Rea I would bring her son to her.*

Her father's visage turned away from her, without answering and it came to Senta then that they were discussing her fate. Their demeanor was hard and cold; there was not one of them there who did not remember that it was another of Loden Almandar's children, and one not unlike to Senta, who had occasioned the creation of the Covenant in the first place. The thought struck her as grimly humorous: to the extent that she had pleaded her case convincingly, she had perhaps acted as her own best accuser.

Donner had been convincing.

Senta reached out then, as Loga had taught her, and as much as she was able searched their thoughts, and found no hope there, no hope in any of them. Her father's thoughts she almost could not bear to touch, they were so burdened with the pain of his despair. Even Elyssa and Selene and Maria, her mother and sisters, returning their attention to Senta, did so with an utter rigidity that reflected the finality of their judgment, a finality with its root in nothing more complex than fear of a universe that had spun out of control.

Loden seemed almost unable to say the words. *It is our judgment that you be imprisoned here, upon this asteroid, and think upon your arrogance.*

Elyssa added swiftly, *I leave you with this thought, child; is the judgment of a seventeen-year old girl truly better than that of ten adults, not one of whom is less than half a millennium old?*

Once, said Senta, *humans did not believe there was anything immoral in the taking of a human life. Even those who were quite old, by the standards of their own society, did not believe so.*

Such eloquence. . . . We will return for you, said Gabriel simply, *in fifty years.*

Loden Almandar never turned his attention away from where Senta waited defiantly. *Give me your power.*

The Light descended like a storm upon the small asteroid, swirling boles of yellow radiance that blasted out of nowhere and down into reality. The illumination gathered around the ten forms, gathered and built, and then was channeled in a single instant into the form of the Tribunal Elder Loden. Loden's form blazed incandescently. Before him, Senta felt the world grow very still and distant. The last sensory input she received for a vast time was the sight of her own father moving forward to bring, with the power of the Light, a great darkness down upon her.

There was a vast silence when the thing was done, and one by one the forms of the Rulers flickered away. Loden Almandar remained, and the Ruler Gabriel, and the Ruler Elyssa, when all the others had gone.

Gabriel said softly, *Loden, there is work to be done.*

Loden Almandar nodded silently. Senta's presence was gone from among them, and even when he reached for her, as powerfully as he might, there was only the merest hint of her thoughts to be found.

It is time to go, my husband.

I think I shall remain here, said Loden . . . *for a while. I have done my duty.* He was aware of Elyssa and Gabriel conferring privately, but he paid them no heed. Try as he might, with only his own strength there was no way to break through the barrier the full Tribunal had built around Senta.

Loden, said Elyssa finally, entreatingly, *my love, we must go. You know her punishment is merciful. Fifty years is not so long.*

Indeed. Loden turned to Elyssa, and the woman flinched at the touch of his thoughts, at the acrid taste of the man's despair. *I shall wait.*

I . . . don't think we can let you do that, said Gabriel carefully.

I do not think you can stop me. Elyssa, I enjoin you, remember this when I am gone. I have loved you.

Elyssa could not speak for the horror that had come upon her. Finally she forced the words out: *Loden, please don't.*

I have loved you, and deeply. But my spirit is here. It belongs here with my daughter, whose only crime was that she believed I was still the man I once was. I belong here. I shall, he said simply, *stay.*

For the rest of their lives the two Rulers who watched Loden Almandar's death could not forget it, though they tried, and tried. It was not spectacular; the Light-bounded form grew hazy, not with the suddenness of a jump, but simply lost resolution, spilled away from itself into the quiet equilibrium of death, as all that was mortal of Loden Almandar tore itself into nothingness.

There was a moment, Senta never knew how long, when there was simply nothing, and then slowly she came back to herself. The Rulers were gone; the asteroid was gone, and the stars and her body.

The universe was gone.

The asteroid swung through its orbit; and Senta waited, awake and aware, cut off from any sensory input whatsoever, in utter dark and silence.

The remnant of what had once been Loden Almandar settled in place around the asteroid that held his daughter imprisoned. It would not be correct to say that it was Loden Almandar, only some small part of what had once been the man; for Loden Almandar was dead, and his essence was gone from the universe.

That remnant did not think, did not reason. It could not have communicated with any living human well enough to explain its actions coherently. But from some far distant realm, through the otherworld and down into reality, a thought came, and the thought was made real.

Across the surface of the asteroid, quantum probabilities altered, electrons fell down atomic orbital shells, and threw off photons as they fell.

In that instant, the asteroid blazed like a second sun.

· 3 ·

They strode through the empty streets of Parliament.

The Worker chattered away excitedly. "At first I couldn't believe it myself, my lord, she looked so like the Ruler Loden's daughters, but then I heard you were looking for her, or for one so similar it must be the same—"

Maston interrupted the man brusquely. "You are sure the woman is the same you have seen the holograph of?"

"My lord, certain."

They came to a small cottage at the south end of the city. Though Maston could not have known it, it was one of the cottages that had once been set aside for the use of the students at Academy.

The first Warrior to reach the door tried the handle. It did not move, and Maston nodded at the Warrior's look. The Warriors broke the door down, and Maston stepped through, inside.

Rea was sitting at the edge of the bed, and at Maston's appearance she stood slowly. Her eyes were red from crying, but she was not mourning now. "Father?" She looked from Maston to the faces of the Warriors with him. "She told the truth, didn't she? You're not my father." Rea took a step forward. "You know, I never really believed you were. Not deep inside I didn't."

Maston glanced through the small cottage and gestured one of his Warriors to check the room adjoining.

Rea said softly, "Where's my son?"

Maston chuckled. "The brat? Cain took him. As I have taken Parliament, as I have taken you." He gestured to the Warriors he had brought with him and said shortly, "Get her." The Warriors standing behind him hesitated, and Maston snapped, "Now!"

Five of his Warriors moved forward, cautiously; they had seen Rea practice with her husband at hand-to-hand combat.

Rea lifted a poker hanging on its thong from a hook next to the fireplace, and a bitter smile came to her. "Come on, then," she whispered. The Warriors slowed again, and then went at her in a rush. Maston was never sure afterward exactly what happened in that instant. One of his Warriors came stumbling backward instantly, clutching his throat; and another screamed, a high womanish sound, and went to the ground clutching a shattered kneecap. The third lasted a moment longer, and then a swing of the poker broke his collarbone, and another stove his skull in. The remaining two Warriors crashed into the woman in the same instant and smashed her down into the room's wooden floor. One of them stamped on the hand that held the poker, bones snapping audibly, and Maston waved forward another pair of Warriors to aid them. It took all four of his largest Warriors to finally immobilize her.

One of his Warriors lay dead on the floor with a cracked skull, the other dying with a crushed throat.

Maston stooped and picked up the poker she had killed two of his Warriors with, stuck the tip into the coals of the fire, and left it there. A movement back at the door caught his eye, and Maston turned to see his informant backing away from the cottage. "Where are you going?"

The man froze. "Nowhere, my lord."

Maston made a gesture with one hand. "Hold him," he commanded the two Warriors, and they did, one grasping each arm to hold the Worker fast. The man's feet did not touch the floor firmly.

"My lord," the man babbled, "I am your servant, you know that, I am your faithful servant, I brought you the—"

Maston looked at the man thoughtfully. Behind him he could hear Rea struggling quietly with the four Warriors holding her. "*My* servant, as you were the Rulers' servant, as you would be Cain's did he pay you enough." The Worker stared at Maston in abject terror. "Kill him," said Maston simply, and one of the Warriors forced the man to his knees while the other withdrew a light knife; and it was done.

Maston turned away from the man's twitching corpse and walked back to where Rea was being held. When he touched the handle of the poker, the handle was distinctly warm. He used the poker to stir some of the brighter embers with and said very quietly, without looking directly at Rea, "Hold her tightly. I saw a man once had this done to him, and when the iron touched his eyes he broke the ropes that bound him." He did then look at her, at the terror with which the woman was struggling, waited until she met his gaze. "You're fond of pokers, eh?" he said, very softly indeed. The tip of the poker came up out of the coals, glowing dull red. "Have one, then."

She began screaming the instant iron touched her eyes, and was still screaming when Maston hung the bloody poker neatly back on its hook and snapped at his Warriors, suddenly irritable, "Clean up this mess and have her confined. I'll decide what to do with her later."

Rea was still screaming when he left.

The boy was pale with shock. Orion had not said a word the entire trip back to Eastmarch. Cain waited all that night, and through the full day following, before he took any drastic measures. When, that evening, the child still did not even answer to his own name, Cain made his decision.

Mersai and Kavad were with him; Cain sent them from the room, and prepared to descend into madness. He sat cross-legged at the foot of his own bed; Orion sat in a large chair immediately before him, clasping his knees with his arms, the pale blue eyes open, fixed on the floor, staring sightlessly. Occasionally his stare wandered, to Cain, to the room's furnishings, and then back to the floor without focusing on anything at all. The child reminded Cain, with an intensity that disturbed him, of his brother Misha as he had been during that week between the time his brother had gone mad and the Ruler Elyssa had come to take Misha away to the hospitals at Parliament.

"Orion," said Cain, "look at me." He pronounced the boy's name correctly, with the western accent.

Orion's eyes came up slowly, and met Cain's.

"My name is Cain," Cain told him, "and we're going to be friends, you and I."

Cain touched the boy's temple, the flat of his hand clasping the side of Orion's head. The maelstrom of the boy's thoughts leapt out to envelop him, fiercely and with a flat horror as finely etched as anything Cain had ever found in the mind of an adult. For a single moment he lost touch with his own body, and in an instant of sheer terror he *felt* the flicker of the Light being raised. He forced Orion's thoughts away, took control back from the child, and waited until he was sure that the mind he held within his own would not flare out of his control again. *Sleep, Orion,* he said then, with a gentleness that would have astonished every human being who had ever known him except, perhaps, Loukas of Semalia. *Forget.*

The boy shook his head slightly, irritably, as though he had not entirely heard Cain, and the his eyelids drooped, and within instants he was asleep. Cain delved into the depths of Orion's mind, seeking through the child's near-term memories of the last few days. He jerked once as though he had touched a live wire; the boy had talked to Loga briefly. Cain scanned through Orion's memories of the conversation, ending with Loga telling the boy it had all been only a dream, and then continued with his own work. He sectioned off entire chunks of the boy's memory, then picked him up and carried him over to Cain's own bed, laid him down, and covered him with blankets.

Cain sat with Orion, while the boy slept, all that night. Cain had not slept himself since the night before Solan's death; and he had been ill recently enough that the passage of the night left him feeling empty, light as a feather, as though all his reserves were gone. The boy slept the deep sleep of exhaustion, nearly a full five hours, and then, just before dawn, stirred slightly and sat up, rubbing his eyes to get the sleep out of them.

Orion blinked, and moved slowly. He looked around, with a clear, innocent, curious awareness in his eyes, and then turned to Cain. "Who are you?"

"I?" Cain found his mouth was dry. "Orion, I'm your father."

"Oh." Orion looked at Cain sleepily for a moment and then grinned. "That was a silly question, wasn't it?"

Despite himself, Cain found he was smiling back at the boy. "I have," he said gravely enough, "heard sillier questions in my time."

Cain took breakfast with Orrin Mersai, in the dining room that looked out over the landpads; he left Orion with Kavad.

"What a hideous disaster these last few days have been," said Orrin Mersai as he sipped at his coffee. "You say Maston planned that mess at the Games? It seems unlike him, my lord. Clumsier than he usually is, I mean."

Cain nodded. His eyes were half closed; he had barely touched his breakfast. "I regret Solan's death. I might have made peace with Eagles through him, if Maston had been willing to let him live." His breathing was slow, untroubled, near sleep. "But I am not dissatisfied, Orrin. Not at all."

"Begging your pardon, my lord," said Mersai grimly, "I fail to see anything good come of these last few days."

"I have got me someone who can wield power, Orrin. And I will teach him how, and why."

"My lord?" said Mersai with some incredulousness. "You can't mean that boy in there?"

"But I do. You will recall, Orrin, before we went to the Games, I asked you to find yourself a successor. I approve of your choice. Dantes is an ambitious man, yet sufficiently bright that I doubt he'll be fool enough to try to assassinate me. Commander General, in your opinion, is Dantes ready to assume your post?"

Mersai put his coffee cup down on the table. "Sir—my lord—if we do not go to war within, say, the next quarter, then yes. Dantes is not ready, even under your direction, to lead our Warriors in a war, even against Maston. He's an excellent tactician, but only an acceptable strategist. Oh, we'd not lose, not against Eagles, but we'd have more casualties than if I were leading our Warriors."

"That's an acceptable risk," said Cain without pausing. "Mersai, you are relieved of duty."

Orrin Mersai's face was very still. "Yes, my lord."

Cain studied the man seated with him and, after a moment, smiled. "Mersai, you and Kavad are perhaps the only friends I have in the world. The only reason I've allowed it is that you both understand that it is always secondary to your duty, and mine. Mersai, your only duty, from now until the day you die, is to teach Orion. That's all, that's everything. You are going to teach that child everything you have ever known and point him in the direction of subjects you were never able to master. You will never fail to answer any question he ever has on any subject, as honestly as you are able, except as it relates to myself, and even on those subjects you will remain silent, you will not lie to him. The only one who will ever lie to that child is me; I've already begun."

Mersai said slowly, "You place considerable importance upon the boy, it seems."

"What do you know of silver-eyes ways, Mersai?"

"A little, my lord."

"Kavad," said Cain quietly, "gave Orion one of his knives."

Mersai nodded after a long moment. "I see. Cain—my lord—he's only a *child*, damn it," the man burst out.

"No, Commander General," said Cain, "he's not." His smile was thin, precise, and exhausted. "He's clay."

With the thin orange line of a personal Shield surrounding him, sitting atop a black spire of rock named Despair high above the Glowing Desert, Loga watched as the Light took the shape of the Ruler's Tribunal, near the edge of the spire. The nine of them stood there with the Light glowing about them, and finally it was the Ruler Elyssa who spoke when it became apparent that Loga was not going to.

"Do you know," she said quietly, "we almost gave up looking for you?"

Loga lifted an eyebrow. "A shame," he observed, "that you did not."

"You must return to New Parliament with us, Loga."

"I must?" Loga grinned at them, and directed his words to Loden Almandar's widow. "I cannot, my dear, think of anything in the world which I *must* do at this particular moment."

The Ruler Elyssa said dangerously, "Do you dispute our authority?"

"If by authority," said Loga softly, "you mean power, surely I do not. If you mean, do I acknowledge the legitimacy of the Covenant, why, I don't for an instant deny that those few Rulers still alive who actually signed the thing as adults, rather than as children, are indeed bound by the agreement if they are honorable. If on the other hand you mean, do I think I am bound by the Covenant to do whatever it is the nine of you have decided I should, why, no, I don't think that at all."

"I do not think it will be easy," said Elyssa, "for I know how great is your mastery of the Light; but we are prepared to enforce our will."

Loga nodded. "One thing you don't know."

"What?"

"The Covenant."

"Yes?"

"I never signed it."

"*What?*"

"I never signed the silly thing. I was still with Donner at the time it was drafted, and nobody thought to ask me to sign it when I returned to Parliament after Donner had left Earth. Pure oversight, I think. Or possibly Loden suggested that if I did not leave with Donner, we might neglect the minor detail of putting my name down on the rolls." He grinned again. "You won't believe this, but I honestly don't remember exactly. It's been a long time, don't you know."

Elyssa was staring at him. Loga knew her well; she wanted desperately to disbelieve him, but could not. "You lie, Trickster."

"Quite the contrary," he said dispassionately. "I was still with Donner when you folks decided you couldn't face the horror of dissension in your ranks again. It's easy enough to check, if you like. Go look at the rolls from 240 through 300, and try to find my name there." He stood, in a single smooth flowing motion, and faced them down. He did not even raise his voice; Elyssa took a step back from him at the very tone of his words. "And in the meantime, this is *my* rock. I've named it Despair, in memory of the disease that finally killed Loden Almandar. And I, madam, am not a love-struck child still uncertain of her powers, nor yet a weary soul-sick father to listen to the poison in your tongue and not know it for what it is." Though he had not moved, Elyssa took yet another step back. "And I say this to you; get off my rock before I blast you off it."

Elyssa could not control her incredulity. "You'd fight against the will of the Tribunal?"

Loga screamed the words at her. *"The hell with the Tribunal and the hell with you and get off my fucking rock!"* The Light blasted down between them at his call, danced like flame against the rage in Loga's eyes.

The Rulers fled.

Loga calmly returned to his place and reseated himself.

"Thank the Light they left," he said aloud. "I thought I was going to have to get nasty."

He calmed his breathing and sat in the midst of the great cold desert. It was very dark, and the stars above him blazed with an inhuman bright splendor.

There was a new star in the sky.

Orion

• ——————————————— •

The Years 1284 to 1299 After the Fire

• 1 •

The day was cold.

Gray clouds scudded across the sky. Freezing winds gusted across the landpads above the Caverns, and a thin layer of ice covered the landpads themselves. Cain sat in the dining room overlooking the landpad, sipping at coffee that grew cool too quickly. Even in the dining room it was not warm; the long window panels that looked out over the landpad were nothing more than ordinary glass, and only a single layer at that. Cain knew of a way to make glass in a double layer with a think vacuum between the layers, to produce windowpanes that insulated both heat and cold with equal effectiveness; but it would have required retooling the machines that made glass, and there was never enough time or engineering expertise to do even the things which they knew how to do already.

There was never sufficient time for research.

Cain listened with half an ear as Jimal read reports aloud to him.

Jimal was one of Kavad's eight or nine children; Cain was not sure of the exact number. Like the other half-breed silver-eyes in Cain's service, his skin was nearly as dark as Cain's own, though his eyes were as silver as those of any other ken Selvren. He had been raised in the silver-eyes fashion, but in civilization. He was in many ways—socially, certainly—more an Eastmarcher than a ken Selvren. He was somewhere in his mid-twenties, well educated and sharp enough that Cain had at one point considered asking him if he were interested in becoming an engineer. He'd abandoned the idea reluctantly: while Eastmarch had, at least on the surface, broken through the old lines of caste that

the Rulers had imposed on Worker culture, there were still some preju-
dices that even Cain did not tread on lightly. While his engineers
would have taken Jimal into their ranks without a moment's visible
hesitation, they would have been unhappy about it and would have
made certain Jimal knew it.

Jimal was, Cain suspected, even more intelligent than his father,
though lacking his father's depth of experience.

"Instructor Mersai," said Jimal, "reports that Orion has been asking about his mother, and once about a dog."

"About his mother? Does he ask about her often?"

"Yes, my lord."

"Has he asked about his father?"

"No, my lord. To all appearances, he considers you his father. He
does wonder why you don't see him more often."

Cain nodded. "I'll take care of it. Go on."

Jimal scanned down the printout he was carrying. "The balance of
the report concerns subjects we have no good information on. Our spies
in the North Land haven't learned anything of note; they're not,
frankly, very good spies."

"We've hardly spent the same sort of resources spying on the
Giants we've spent in other areas. I'm afraid that's going to have to
change."

Jimal continued. "There's some sort of stink about the Senior
Engineer Rome's death, but it's being hushed up. No more on that.
The only other news from the North Land is that the Giants are as
concerned about the new 'star' as we are, perhaps more so; they're not
as used to being presented with things they don't understand as we are.
We don't have the faintest idea ourselves what the thing is; spectral
analysis has been useless. The spectrum doesn't match anything we've
seen before. It's somewhere out in the Belt, and it's awfully cold for
something as bright as it is. It's got to be emitting energy almost entirely in the visible spectrums. Commander Colonel Dantes suggests we
send a probe. The ship you took to Cassandra is in acceptable shape for
such a journey."

Cain nodded. "Do so. But yank the subwave motors. The ship we
can rebuild if something goes wrong; the subwave motors we can't."

"Yes, my lord. We've explored in their entirety three of the dark
orbital factories. The Giants seem uninterested in them, my lord.

Though they've a considerable amount of orbital traffic of one sort or another, almost all of it centers around their own factories. We haven't enough of an analysis yet to know exactly what we've got in the three factories we've explored."

"And we still don't know exactly where the Rulers went?"

"No more than we did. They are 'forty light years away.' Assuming they told us the truth, which I am inclined to doubt."

Cain chuckled. "You're almost as cynical as your father, Jimal. I approve."

Jimal bowed slightly. "Thank you, my lord. I treasure your compliments."

Cain glanced up at the man sharply; Jimal's face was perfectly straight. Cain himself had what the Ruler Loga had once called 'a nearly perfect poker face'; Loga had never met Kavad's son. "Yes," said Cain after a moment, "I do not doubt it."

The Giant ship *Arskyld* came just before noon.

Cain watched it descend from the sky with plain admiration; despite reports and holographs of the vessel, its sheer size was almost beyond belief. It was not really intended to operate in atmosphere, although Cain's spies at Parliament, while the Rulers were still there, reported that the Giants had assured the Rulers that the vessel's fusion engines were perfectly clean; and indeed, as *Arskyld* sank to its landing, the radiation counters Cain had planted around the landpad's perimeters hardly noticed the huge vessel's presence.

The ship was nearly a kilometer in length along its greatest axis; when *Arskyld* touched the ground of the landpad, there was a sudden sharp cracking sound as the roughened plastisteel covering the stonesteel base actually split apart in places under *Arskyld*'s vast weight.

Perhaps ten minutes passed after *Arskyld*'s landing when nothing happened. A squad of Eastmarch Warriors trotted out across the landpad and stood waiting in the chill winds while the Giants prepared to descend from the ship.

To Cain's surprise, the Skaald Laar arrived alone except for a pet, a polar bear on a leash that was chained to a bracelet on Laar's wrist.

He was lightly dressed despite what Cain considered an extremely cold day and was not in formal Giant attire. Cain knew enough of Giant etiquette to find a bad omen in that. He bore no weapons Cain could see, only what Cain recognized as a Giant-fashioned computer/communications device hung at his belt. Laar had to stoop slightly to enter the dining room, even though Cain had ordered the room's ceiling raised and had a new door installed with, supposedly, sufficient head clearance for a Giant to enter with ease.

The Skaald Laar settled into the specially constructed chair Cain had provided for him with a grunt of relief. With both Cain and Laar seated, the Giant's head was still better than a meter above Cain's. Cain'd had the foresight to seat Laar at the opposite end of a fairly long table; nonetheless he had to tilt his head slightly to meet the Giant's eyes.

He did not rise upon Laar's entrance.

"May I offer you refreshment?" asked Cain courteously.

"If you have sivka, surely," Laar rumbled.

"I'm afraid not, Skaald. I do not know the—food, or is it drink?—you refer to."

"It is a mildly alcoholic drink, very hot."

Cain nodded. "We here in Eastmarch know very little about the North Land. We hope to change that, but for today, I fear I can offer you nothing but native Valley foods and drink. We have mulled wine, beer, hard alcohol of various sorts, and an Eastmarch drink called coffee that acts as a mild stimulant."

The Giant shook his head. "I think not. If you would, however, I find this room too warm. I would appreciate it if we might lower the temperature somewhat."

"Certainly. Jimal, see to it, and bring my coat."

Laar settled into his chair more thoroughly and clasped his arms across his chest. It was an impressive sight; small mountains of muscle guided even casual movement. "Shall we begin?"

"Certainly. I confess, I am somewhat curious, Skaald, on a number of fronts. Try as I might, I have been unable to make sense of much of what has happened in the last quarter." Cain grinned suddenly. "Actually, make that the last decade and we'd be a little closer to the truth."

The Giant did not smile back. "I am not here, Worker, to discuss your need for education."

"Please," said Cain easily, spreading his hands, "I'm not looking to aggravate you, Skaald. Can we not have a civil discussion?"

Laar said without inflection, "You are a wise Worker, Cain, as Workers go. In your place I also would refrain from aggravating the Skaald of the Giants."

Cain bit back a reply and let nothing show in his features. "I am sure you know, Skaald, that the Rulers took the Ring of Light from me."

The Giant's lips twisted into a huge grin. "The Ring? Of course I know you haven't got it, Worker." If possible, the grin grew even wider. "I do."

There was a single moment of utter stillness, deep inside Cain; the entire universe seemed to freeze around him for one eternal instant. His features did not even flicker, and his reply came quickly. "I suspected they took the Ring from me at your urging, for it was your bargain with them, was it not, that if you terraformed their retreat for them, you would in return inherit their place and their power in this Valley?"

"This was our agreement, yes. There was a disagreement, the details of which need not concern you, in which the Lords of Light killed my brother Rome."

Cain nodded thoughtfully. "Skaald, this is what I do not understand. With rare exceptions—and those exceptions have been criminals, the likes of the Giant Riabel—the Giants have never shown any great interest in the affairs of Workers. You must know, Skaald, that we will fight to preserve our freedom. I do not say we will win such a battle, but assuredly we shall wage it. What is there in all this Valley that you find worth the certainty of Giant deaths in such a battle?"

Laar chuckled, a low, rumbling sound. "That, Worker, is another of the subjects I did not come here to discuss. Our motives need not concern you, only how our desires affect you. Accept our decision. We worked ten years, labored as we have never labored before, for the right to rule this Valley once T'Pau's People were gone. You ask if the deaths of Giants is worth the prize; Giants have *already* died for it, Worker, hundreds of them, in falls and accidents that occurred while terraforming a planet with gravity even greater than that of Earth. The only subject we will discuss, Cain, is how we will implement our rule. If you will cooperate with us, we will be merciful, and impose upon the life of Workers no more than our needs dictate. We will need the aid of Workers in ruling, as the Lords of Light did."

"It may be," said Cain patiently, "that battle between us is not necessary. I've seen enough war, Giant. We Workers have an opportunity to build something for ourselves for the first time in ten and a half centuries. We can't do that if we're slaves, and we can't do it if we must fight against the Giants. Skaald, we are willing to compromise. Surely you don't want this Valley simply for some abstract prestige; surely there is a *reason* why you wish to rule here. Skaald, if you will merely explain that reason, we may be able to prevent bloodshed." Cain held the Giant's gaze. "If you will not explain yourselves, there will surely be war between us."

Laar looked at Cain curiously. "You will fight a war you cannot win? I do not think so."

"Jimal," said Cain without raising his voice, "what time is it?"

"Five twenty-two, my lord."

"Sometime in the next five minutes or so, Skaald, three meteors will strike in the waters surrounding the North Land ice cap. Your missile defenses, even if they are employed, will be of no use to you; the meteors are just big rocks with some iron wrapped around them. A direct strike against one of them with a fusion weapon might—I say might—deflect it slightly. Alas, you do not have the ability to deliver such a warhead against a moving target. You are, I think, essentially helpless."

The Giant simply stared at Cain as though the words had made no impact at all. The bear at his side sensed something of its master's mood and growled, a deep low sound.

Perfectly collected in the face of the Giant's stare of disbelief, Cain said, "I think we can wait while you check to see whether I am telling the truth or not. Jimal, freshen my coffee, please." Cain leaned back in his chair and simply watched Laar.

Laar did not move for another several seconds and then touched a single finger to the device at his belt. "Kera."

"Skaald?" The voice issued from the device with as much fidelity as though the deep-throated Giant from whom it issued were there in the room with them.

"Kos estevchi dla ir'gon Cain. Ca senvet kentralli dokumen. Si-mat." The Giant Laar turned to Cain, and with the glare not lessening for an instant, said, "We shall wait."

Less than four minutes later, a babble of voices exploded out of the device Laar carried. Cain's command of the Giant's tongue was poor; with so many voices at once, speaking so quickly, he did no better than to pick out a word here and there. Laar spoke with his underlings for nearly ten minutes, without interruption, while Cain waited patiently.

Perhaps a minute into Laar's discussion, Jimal leaned over beside Cain and murmured in his ear, "Forgive me, my lord. Shall I summon a specialist in the Giant's tongue to examine the recording of this conversation?"

Cain nodded after a moment. They were recording his talks with the Skaald Laar for later analysis; that he could have those who *did* speak the Giant's tongue examine the recording before Laar had even left had not occurred to him.

He was beginning to develop a real appreciation for young Jimal.

Cain felt the room's temperature dropping as they waited, and donned the coat Jimal had brought him. Once he had finished speaking with the other Giants, the Skaald Laar lapsed into a moment's silence, thinking. The glare had faded, and when he finally spoke, his voice, though light years away from civility, was more puzzled than angry. "You put a mass driver on the moon. As long as we do not find the base from which you launched, there is no practical way for us to defend ourselves. You cannot destroy us with such weapons, I think, but you can damage us badly."

"I was expecting," said Cain, "that the Rulers would have you build antimissile and antiaircraft defenses around Parliament for them. We prepared for that eventuality. As it happens, our preparation against the Rulers was wasted." He shrugged. "I thought we might use it against you instead." Cain sighed. "Laar, listen. I'm no Ruler, but I'm still better than twice as old as you are. Will you please listen to me?"

"It seems I must." Laar looked down broodingly upon Cain. "The obsession that the Lords of Light developed over you—perhaps there was some reason to it."

"Perhaps," agreed Cain. "Laar, you wish to rule us. I understand that. I do not understand *why*."

"The terraforming of New Parliament," said Laar softly, "was a—dry run, I believe is the term slipship pilots use."

"I see." Cain's breath plumed faintly in the cold of the room. "Twenty-four thousand Semalians and eighteen thousand Turriners, taken from their homes and families for a dry run."

"What do you know about Giants, Cain?"

"Less than I'd like. A bit about your history and origins, almost nothing about your internal politics and customs."

"I was only a young man when you returned from your infamous Exile, Worker, and started the Twenty Years' War. Already at that age I had broken most of the major bones in my body on one occasion or another. In the course of your war with the Lords of Light, I fathered seven children. Despite medical facilities that surpass anything you have ever dreamed of, only three of them made it to adulthood, and the seventh killed my wife in the birthing. All of this, Cain, because we mass too much."

Cain said slowly, "In . . . Earth's . . . gravity."

Laar looked briefly startled. "You *see* it, then? The solution?"

"The moon? No." Cain looked down at the table before him, at the steam rising from his coffee, and then straight up at the Giant. "Mars. You're going to terraform Mars."

"Yes . . . yes," said Laar, "you do see." Wonder touched his voice. "Cain, you amaze me."

"Kavad, that's cold enough," said Cain absently. "You needn't drop the temperature any further."

Jimal lifted an eyebrow at the use of his father's name, but said nothing.

"You'll need Workers, of course," said Cain. "How many?"

"If we use Workers to do the delicate labor that we find difficult, we can complete the terraforming of Mars within twenty to twenty-five years. If we must do all the work ourselves, the job will not be completed within my lifetime, and perhaps not in the lifetimes of my children."

"How many?" Cain repeated patiently.

"Over the course of the first fifteen years, one hundred fifty to one hundred seventy-five thousand Workers between the ages of fifteen and forty."

Cain did not hesitate at all. "If you will agree to take Workers only from the territories that the Rulers recently abandoned, and none from Eastmarch or Eagles, I will not interfere with you."

The Giant's eyes closed for a moment, and when they opened again he said simply, "Done."

Later that evening, as the sun fell away beneath the edge of the Earth, and Eastmarch rolled into the planet's shadow, Cain emerged from the seclusion he had entered after speaking with the Skaald Laar, and called for Colonel Dantes.

The man came promptly and stood waiting while Cain paced like a caged animal across the short length of the outermost room in his quarters. Cain wasted no time with him. He stopped pacing only long enough to snap at the man, "Dantes, have you seen the transcript of the negotiations between myself and the Skaald Laar?"

"Yes, my lord," Dantes said instantly.

"He claimed that he possessed the Ring of Light, Dantes. Find out if he told the truth, and do it quickly."

"Yes, my lord."

Cain faced him suddenly. "I want it back, Dantes. And I'll have it, too."

Cain's new Commander Colonel eyed his lord for a long second. "My lord," said Commander Colonel Mondàl Dantes, "I do not doubt it for an instant."

Just less than a quarter later, the refugees began arriving from the banks of the river Almandar, pouring into Eastmarch; old folk and children, for the adults in their prime had been taken by the Giants.

The refugees came by the thousands, and in the years to come, by the scores of thousands. The old folk Cain did not care about; he left them alone, to make their way or not as they were able.

But the children; the children came also, came with a terrible and deep-rooted hatred for the Giants that made every child a potential

Warrior. A family that had once been highborn, or at least well off, could count upon some degree of welcome in Eagles or Eagles-controlled Parliament; the vast majority for whom that description did not apply had only one place to turn for aide: no child was ever turned away from Eastmarch. The trickle of refugees became a flood, and as the years passed and the pace of terraforming accelerated upon Mars, the flood became an ocean, an ocean of humanity pouring into Eastmarch, a process as gradual and, in its way, Cain found reason to hope, eventually as significant as the rising of the One Ocean in the Valley's early history.

· 2 ·

When he did not have to study, Orion wandered through the Caverns. He was watched constantly, although at first he was not aware of it. He had to go slowly, because Pinch was only a puppy now, and the puppy could not walk very fast. When it trotted, it could keep up with him for a while, but it kept tripping over its own legs.

He did not mind the fact that he had to move slowly; the Caverns were fascinating.

There were four levels to it. Level Four, the bottom level, was where the Workers—laborers, engineers and Warriors alike—lived, where they slept and ate; it was also where Orion's quarters were, and his father Cain's. Though he had not seen them yet, the fusion power generators were also on the bottom level. The third level was where the Mongers were—where the weapons were constructed—and the second level was where the Warriors trained in hand weapons and simulators for the slipships. Though it seemed to Orion that the Mongers' Floors were always humming with the sound of the Workers and their machines, there were never enough slipships for all the trained pilots to actually fly.

He found out later, when he made a comment about it to Kavad, that the Caverns were laid out so that the Workers, at the lowest levels, would be as safe as possible from aerial attack. The slip ships were at the top level so that they could get out to return an attack as quickly as possible. At the time he did not even think about it. It was his new home, and his concept of time was shaky enough that "last year" was a time as far away as the time of Cain's return from Exile. The idea that somebody had thirty years ago *designed* the Caverns in which he now lived was utterly foreign to him.

The thing about the Caverns that made the greatest impression upon him was that, for the first time in his life, he could go anywhere he wanted without anybody ever tying to stop him.

The freedom, false though it was, was exhilarating.

He spent some of his time in the Workers' barracks on Level Four. In the first few quarters he spent in the Caverns, before the refugees began arriving, it was the only place in the entire Caverns where there were any children at all. There were not many of them even so, and most of those were the children of Cain's Warriors. Despite the constant construction and tunneling, space was limited in the Caverns, and except for those of Cain's Warriors, and a very few of his engineers and silver-eyes, there were not many families in the Caverns. Most of the adult Workers in the Caverns visited their families in nearby Telindel briefly every third or fourth week, and for two weeks twice every year. If they felt that was not enough time, they were free to leave the Caverns and find work in Telindel or Saerlock, or any of Eastmarch's territories. Few did; pay in the Caverns was good.

Despite his status as Cain's son, he made true friends quickly. There was a dark-haired girl named Lisa who was slightly older than he was and tough and smart and knew the Caverns—both the natural caves and the huge, complex network of tunnels and corridors—better than Orion had ever known Eagles. And a popular boy whose name Orion did not learn for a long time because everyone called him Bellows on account of the fact that he could hardly speak a sentence without shouting some part of it. At first the children had asked him about his father Cain, but Orion would not answer those questions and sometimes got angry when they asked, so in the end they just played together as if he were no more than a Warrior's child himself.

He spent hours at a time up on Level One, where the Command Center was, and the slipships. The Command Center interested him, and the Warriors there were nice to him, answering any questions he had as clearly as they could.

The slipships fascinated him. His mother had promised him that when he was old enough, he would be a Warrior and fly a slipship the way—the way somebody else had.

And now Cain was promising him the same thing, and with better slipships than anything Eagles had on top of it.

In those first few quarters after Cain brought him to Eastmarch, Orion acclimated slowly. If he did not take to the life of the Caverns instantly, neither did he reject it. He was used to open skies, the hill country around Eagles, and at first he was troubled by claustrophobia; but talking to Cain about it made him see that it was silly to be afraid just because there was a roof above him most of the time.

He came to enjoy talking to his father, when Cain had the time to spare him. When things troubled Orion and his instructors Kavad and Mersai could not help him with them, Cain always could. There were curious blank spots in Orion's memory after some of those conversations, but the blank spots were not themselves frightening; Orion was not old enough to be frightened simply because he could not remember something. For a while it upset Orion that his father did not have more time for him, but slowly over the course of the passing weeks, without ever bringing up the subject with Cain, he came to realize that whenever there was something important that he needed to talk to Cain about, Cain was there.

It was comforting.

He had been in the Caverns for barely two weeks when Cain explained to him one morning, as they took breakfast together, about his mother.

They were seated before a scarred low table of some black wood, taking a breakfast of sausages and bread and cheese. It was the only time of day when Orion always saw Cain. Though the rest of the day might vary wildly, Cain was always present for breakfast. (The food was not as good as what Orion had been served in Eagles, and he said so even though nobody paid him any attention; but it was good enough.) Pinch ate with them, which delighted Orion—he remembered how in Eagles his—somebody had refused to let Pinch eat at the table with them.

"I know you want your mother, Orion, but the Giants took her away before I could stop them. You've heard, from Mersai, how the Giants are taking adults to make them work on the terraforming of Mars. Your mother was one of those whom they took."

"Oh." Orion did not look up at his father. Sometimes his black eyes were very hard to meet. "Can we get her back?" he demanded.

"We'll get her back soon, Orion."

"Soon?" The word had only one meaning for Orion. "Today?" he said eagerly.

"Not today, Orion, but very soon. You and I, we'll beat the Giants together and we'll get your mother back."

Orion worked his way through the sentence, and then said hopefully, "Tomorrow?"

Cain smiled at him. He had a good smile. "We'll start making plans tomorrow, son. Tomorrow." He cocked his head to one side. "The Giants," he said, "have the Ring of Light. What we must do, Orion, is get the Ring from them. When we have the power of the Ring the Giants will not dare to keep your mother."

"Where's the Ring?"

"It's in the North Land, Orion. Where the Giants live. To rescue your mother, we're going to have to go and get the Ring, take it back from the Giants."

Orion grinned suddenly. "Okay," he said simply. "We'll get the Ring."

His father smiled back at him and said very quietly indeed, "Yes, we will."

"Do you know how to ride?" Mersai asked him one morning.

They were in Orion's room, where they usually studied academic subjects, just down the hall from Cain's suite of five rooms. There was a bed in the room, a huge desk, and several chairs, one of them sized so that Orion could reach the top of the desk. Orion even had his own toilet and shower and fireplace. The walls were simple shaved stone, cut with a laser and then reinforced in places with stonesteel.

They had been working on reading and writing that day. Orion knew a little bit already, because his mother had thought it important, but he had already realized that there was no subject in the world about which he knew enough to satisfy Kavad and Mersai. Some of the things they taught him he very much enjoyed—Kavad was teaching him to throw knives, for example, and Mersai had shown him how to read a battle map and how to command the Caverns' computer system to do what he desired of it. Other things did not particularly interest him, though he did not find them difficult, and reading and writing fell into that category. Still other subjects he could not see the reason for at all and disliked intensely. His head for mathematics was, Cain commented once, abominable. (Orion had never heard the word before, and once Cain had explained it to him, he fell in love with it and used it frequently in the following weeks.)

"Of course I can ride," said Orion instantly. "I had a pony when I was in Eagles. His name was Terry."

Mersai nodded. "Good. The thought's taken me, I'm not sure why, but I've a mind to see some open skies today." Something flickered across his features. "Well, it's been nearly a quarter since I've been aboveground. Reason enough, to be sure. *Command*, what's the weather like outside?"

The computer's voice issued from a panel in the wall next to the door. "Warm at midday, temperatures dropping to several degrees above freezing by sunset. Overnight lows at minus ten degrees. A light coat or undress uniform jacket is indicated."

The old man was visibly disturbed for an instant and then threw it off. "Good enough," he decided, and grinned down at Orion. "Grab your coat and let's go."

They rode out from the northern edge of the Shield; only there, at the northern and southern edges, had Cain bothered to install Gates through which people might pass from one side of the Shield to the other. The Warriors on duty at the Gate passed them through without any fuss. Orion was unaware of the murmurs that passed among them over his presence. There was likely not a person in the Caverns but knew of the kidnaping of Maston Veramorn's grandson, and how the child called their Lord Cain "father." It was ridiculous on the face of it that dark Cain might have fathered such a fair child, and the Workers commented on it among themselves.

After the two had ridden out together, one of the Warriors turned to another. "First time I seen 'im," the man said, his voice thick with a Saerlock accent. "Fair as a Ruler, eh? If that's Cain's get, *my* father was a silkie."

The Warrior addressed spat contemplatively. "Best learn to sweat poison," she said mildly. "If the boy calls Lord Cain father, and Lord Cain don't stop him, it's good enough for me."

It was the first time Orion had seen the territory surrounding the Caverns.

They rode steadily all that morning, north toward the Great Dam, across the long flat fields that surrounded the Caverns. It was all farmland, corn and skipper-wheat, and where they could find them Mersai led them along what few straggling roads there were. Sometimes there were no roads or paths and to continue in the direction Mersai was leading them, they had to ride through some poor farmer's crops. That they destroyed crops did not bother Orion; in Eagles they had ridden so all the time, unless the land they rode across belonged to some powerful Land'ner family, and then they had ridden around even if it meant a long detour. In Eastmarch, Orion had been told, there were no Land'ners, so Orion did not really understand why it bothered Mersai when there was no road in the direction he wanted to go in, and they must ride over crops to continue.

They saw almost no people as they rode, only farmers at a distance. Once Orion saw a shrike wheeling about in the sky far above them. It thrilled him, for he had rarely seen a shrike before; they had been hunted in Eagles until they were almost extinct.

Mersai was actually not much of a horseman, Orion observed. He remembered being told by . . . (the process of avoiding this particular thought was growing much easier; Orion's thoughts hardly paused) by someone back at Eagles that Eastmarchers, living as they did on the flatlands or even underground, some of them, had little occasion to ride and did so but poorly. Mersai sat astride his horse just a bit too stiffly, and his stirrups were higher than Orion would have tied them. If he had to ride more than maybe half a day his upper thighs were going to get sore.

Near midmorning they crossed the closest thing to a real road they had seen since leaving the Caverns, and even it was overgrown with weeds. "It's the old east end of the Traveler's Road," Mersai told Orion in response to his question. "Used to be a village called Eastmarch out a bit east of where we are now, and nobody at all at the

Caverns. Though it's deserted now, your father grew up in that village."

They rode west down the remains of the road for just a short while, and turned off the road on a spot that looked, to Orion, no different than any other place they had been by.

They started up into the hills. Orion rode on ahead of Mersai, as far ahead as Mersai would let him go. It felt like a homecoming of sorts; although the hills were rounder and grassier than the rocky cliffs of Eagles, it was still highlands such as he had lived in all his life.

Mersai rode slowly, as though he were searching for something, and it was nearly noon when they reached the place where he called a halt and they broke for lunch. The clearing where they stopped was at the side of a small, nearly dry brook. Once, long ago, there had been a house in that clearing; Orion could see where the house's foundation had been. It was all that remained.

It was sunny in the clearing, and the air was very still, almost unmoving. The Great Dam rose high above them; treebunnies were visible in the tops of the trees, moving lazily in the heat of midday. Orion took his jacket off after tethering his pony to one of the pines at the clearing's edge, and Mersai did the same. They ate lunch together under the warm sun, and Mersai finished off most of a midsized wine bulb.

Orion found it interesting that he felt no need at all to mention to Mersai that there was a man, in the dress of a Trader or entertainer, standing at the edge of the clearing, watching them. Mersai did not seem to notice the man's presence, though the intruder should have been visible in his peripheral vision.

The old Commander yawned and lay down on the grass with his coat rolled up beneath his head as a pillow. "I'm for a nap, lad. You can wander about if you like, and then we'll head on back down."

Orion nodded, but said nothing, and in an astonishingly short time Mersai was deep asleep, snoring, and the man standing at the edge of the clearing came forward to join Orion.

Orion said, "Hello, Loga."

The redhead paused a moment, briefly startled. "Hi. You remember me, do you?"

"Yes," said Orion slowly, drawing the word out. "You were in a dream I had, but . . ." A delighted grin creeped out upon his features. ". . . it wasn't a dream, was it?"

"Nope." Loga settled to the ground next to Mersai, comfortably cross-legged. "I told you to think it was so you wouldn't tell folks I'd been there."

"Are you going to make me think today was a dream?" Orion demanded. "That would be abominable."

"Abominable?" The Ruler Loga chuckled and said, "Nope. I'm sorry I messed with your head last time, kid. I wouldn't have done it if I could have trusted you not to tell people I'd been there."

It was not phrased as a question, but Orion caught the implication. "I won't tell anybody you were here today."

"Good. You can tell if you want, you know—I won't stop you. But I'd rather you didn't, because if you do, Cain won't let you come up here to see me again."

"I won't tell anybody," Orion promised. He gestured to where Mersai lay snoring. "How did you do that?"

"What makes you think I did?"

Orion shrugged. "I don't know. Did you?"

"About ten years ago," said Loga, "we—the Rulers—were fighting a war with Cain. When the war ended, we all came together to sign a treaty. At one point Mersai and I were left alone together for most of twenty minutes. One of Cain's few mistakes. I'm what's called a telepath, Orion, as is Cain. It means we can touch a man's thoughts, put thoughts into his head. Mersai here is a pretty stiff-necked fellow; I couldn't make him do anything he really didn't want to. But when it's something he might do anyhow, I can—encourage him—slightly. I did that today because I wanted to see you."

"Why?"

"Wanted to let you know I was here, mostly. Let you know that if you needed help, I'd help you if I could." Loga shrugged. "When I was a boy, a man named Loden helped me when I needed it. If he was still around he'd like it if I could help you."

"You think I need help?"

"Oh, I don't know," said Loga mildly. "I guess the question is, do you think you might ever need help?"

Orion considered the question and then said shyly, "Yep. I guess so."

"Okay." Loga grinned at him. "You'll enjoy coming to see me," he pledged in return. "I have it on good authority that I'm the only person within riding distance of the Caverns with any sense of humor at all. Cain, and your tutors Mersai and Kavad—I tell you true, they're three of the gloomiest sons of bitches I've ever met in my life. It's a shame, you know; Cain at least used to be good company once, a long time ago."

The redhead's grin was infectious, and Orion grinned back at him even though he was not sure why. "Do you know my father Cain?"

"Your fath—" Loga stopped speaking abruptly, and the grin faded away in slow degrees. "Cain," he said, picking his words with care, "is your father?"

"Yes. Do you know him?" Orion persisted.

"I did once."

"Loga?"

Loga looked at the boy seated before him and said gravely, "Orion, can I touch you?"

Orion considered the request for a moment and then said, "Okay."

Loga leaned forward slightly, and a single finger made contact with Orion's cheek and stroked upward to his temple. Orion felt something like the touch of a feather tickling him in a part of his body that did not exist, and then the sensation faded. It took Loga barely an instant; then he whistled, a long low sound, and pulled his hand away. "This is a bad idea," he whispered to himself. "Damn it, Cain, this is *stupid.*"

Orion said, "Loga? What's wrong?"

"You're not Cain—" Loga bit the words off with a visible effort. "Damn, damn, *damn.*" The redhead came to his feet in a single flash of movement and then stood very still for a long time. "Orion," he said at last, "Cain told you he was going to get your mother back from the Giants?"

Orion nodded and said firmly, "Yes."

"The Giants do not have your mother, Orion." The fusion-blue eyes fixed on Orion. "All the other children you have seen, all the refugees from along the banks of Almandar, oh yes, they took those children's parents; but Orion, when your mother Rea vanished, there were no Giants anywhere in the Valley."

"Oh." There was a sudden sick feeling in the pit of Orion's stomach. "My father didn't tell me the truth."

"I think Cain has not told you the truth about a number of things, Orion," Loga said carefully.

"Should I ask him why?"

"If you do, Orion, he will want to know how you came to learn that he had lied to you, and then you will not be able to see me again."

"Okay." The boy's features were as grim as it was possible for the features of a boy who was not yet six to be. "I won't ask him." Orion looked over to where Mersai slept, oblivious in the bright warmth from the sun, and then back to Loga. "I have to go back now. Is this where I should come to see you?"

Loga nodded. "Yes. This is the place. It's a reasonable place for you to ride to—there's a waterlock above us here through which the Caverns gets much of its fish. Whenever you come, I'll be here." The Light came down to touch him then, and when the wind and thunder of his passage had faded, Orion shook Mersai awake.

"Come on, Orrin," the boy said with a completely unconscious familiarity. It was the first command he had ever given anyone in his life. "We're going back now."

The executions were to be held in Cavern Two, one of the four natural caves that had not been altered at all during the construction of the underground dwellings. Shaped like an amphitheater, with nearly six thousand seats lining its walls, it was the largest of the natural caves, and the second largest place in the Caverns. Only the shipyard where the slipships rested, on Level One, was larger. Cavern Two was nearly three hundred and twenty meters wide and almost forty meters high. Its base began on Level Four, and the rows of seats arrayed around it reached up all the way to Level Two.

In Eagles, when it was necessary to execute somebody, it was usually done by hanging them; public executions in the Caverns were performed by laser fire. They were rarer than formal executions had been in Eagles, Orion knew already. The only person with authority to condemn a person was Cain, and Cain almost never had the time to set aside for a public ceremony of execution. When Cain condemned somebody, the man or woman died right then, by handgun or light knife.

In this instance Cain wanted a public example. Three of the four people to be executed had taken money to spy for the Giants, and the fourth was a Commander Second who had plotted an assassination attempt against Cain. Normally the Commander Second would have been disposed of quietly, without fuss, but given that the three Giant spies were going to be executed regardless, Cain determined not to waste the occasion.

Loga was wrong, Orion came to realize as time passed, in saying that Cain had no sense of humor. Though there were subjects Cain never jested about, he explained his plan for the execution to Orion with what was, Orion thought, a joke:

"Spying for the Giants is a fatal mistake, Orion, and I intend to hammer the point home; but attempting to kill *me* is at least as bad." Cain looked thoughtful. "Maybe worse, depending on who you ask."

Orion was almost certain that was a joke.

The executions were set for 5:10, during the lunch break. Mersai took Orion, and they waited for Cain. They were there before most of the crowd. All Warriors who were not at duty post were commanded to appear for the execution of the Commander Second who had tried to kill Cain, and Warriors, most of them in uniform and some of them with their children, filed into the amphitheater in groups of fives and tens while Mersai and Orion waited. The seats in the amphitheater were arrayed around the walls in roughly three groupings, one for each of the three levels that Cavern Two reached up through. Orion saw his friend Lisa on the other side of the amphitheater, standing in the very front row opposite him with a female Warrior whom Orion assumed was her mother, and he waved to her.

Across the length of the amphitheater the girl simply stared at him coldly and turned away from him.

The bottom level seats, which were accessible only from Level Four, were entirely filled by Warriors when Cain, with Jimal a pace behind him, finally joined Orion and Mersai in the very front row of seats.

There were four posts erected in the amphitheater's sand.

At 5:05 exactly three men and a woman were led out to the posts and manacled there. While they were being chained into position, Orion felt a tug on his sleeve and twisted around in his seat. Lisa was standing in the aisle behind him with her chin quivering. Orion could tell she had been crying, and recently.

Cain had not even glanced at Orion; he snapped, "Get that girl out of here," without having looked to see who it was Orion was talking to.

Orion protested immediately, "But she's my friend."

That stopped Cain. He rose from his seat and turned to look at the girl standing in the isle. "Indeed? Jimal, who is this child?"

"Lisa Wanarè, my lord," Jimal said instantly. "She is the daughter of Commander Second Louis Wanarè and the Warrior Irina Chuft-Wanarè."

"Oh? We're executing her father, are we?" Cain actually looked at the child for the first time. "Lisa? Who brought you here?"

The girl bit her lip, but answered. "My mother, my lord."

"Your mother?" Cain stared at the girl. "By the Light, *why?*"

"My lord," Lisa said haltingly, "she said to—to see what happens to people who are stupid." She turned to Orion and said swiftly, "Orion, please ask him not to kill my father."

Cain glanced around; the tableau was beginning to draw attention. "Orion," he said quietly, "this child is a friend of yours?"

"I said she was."

Cain murmured to Jimal, "Bring me the girl's parents." Jimal nodded swiftly, and even as a troop of Warriors with laser rifles were taking their positions, twenty meters in front of the condemned, Commander Second Louis Wanarè was unchained from the firing post and brought, hands still manacled at his sides, before Cain. His wife Irina arrived immediately behind him, scowling fiercely at her daughter. The background noise of folk talking ratcheted upward as this was happening, until Cain had to call for silence. In the silence that followed the command, Cain's words to Lisa's parents, unamplified though they were, carried a great distance.

"I have only one question for you both, and if you attempt to lie to me, I'll know it. Did either of you ever suggest to your daughter that she become friends with my son?"

The Warrior Irina said softly, "No, my lord. I never did."

Commander Second Wanarè, face blotchy with sweat, was not even able to bring forth speech; after a moment he shook his head *no*, vigorously.

Cain said, so quietly the comment could not have traveled more than a few meters, "Commander Second, you are, I think, the most astonishingly lucky man whom I have ever met. You are surely one of the most stupid." He touched the stud at his collar, and his words boomed forth. "Commander Second Louis Wanarè, you stand before me condemned of treason. Because my son has interceded on your behalf, you are going to leave here today with your life." He removed his finger from the stud and said quietly, "Second Wanarè, turn around and observe. Observe closely." The finger touched the stud again. "The three prisoners remaining are guilty of accepting money to spy for the Giants. None of them actually did so. We caught them too quickly, before they had even time to collect their money. Warriors," Cain said formally, "target."

Utter silence descended upon the huge cavern, such silence that the sound of safeties on the lasers being unlatched was audible even at the highest tier of seats.

Cain said one word:

"Fire."

It did not last long, only a fraction of a second. One of the condemned screamed in a voice so high Orion thought it must have been the woman, and then there was silence again.

Lisa's father had fainted.

Cain did not close the circuit on his microphone. His words to Jimal boomed out across the cavern. "Take this coward to the North Gate and strip him of his clothing. Leave him naked on the Traveler's Road. He is not to be harmed by my Warriors or any of my subjects; he is likewise not to be aided. Post his features throughout Eastmarch territory with those instructions. Do it now."

It was done.

• 3 •

Orion's life took on a quiet rhythm with the passing of the quarters, with the slow turning of the seasons, with the wheeling procession of the Earth about the sun. His education continued unabated, subjects seemingly without end; geography and history, enough mathematics to plot a trajectory without aid from a computer. Military science he took to with fervor; before his tenth birthday Orion could have planned a battle to Mersai's satisfaction equally well with swordsmen and archers or slipships armed with lasers and missiles. They never practiced war games with thermonuclear weapons, though the Caverns had them. As Mersai put it, with Fire weapons you picked a target and detonated the device, and that was all there was to it. Orion suspected that Mersai disliked nuclear devices not because of their use in a disaster that had occurred better than twelve centuries before his birth, but because they took no skill at all to use, and thereby cheapened the Warrior's art.

He practiced flying slipships by simulator long before Cain was willing to risk his life in an actual craft. For several years that was Orion's chief unhappiness in life, that Cain refused to allow him to fly a real slipship.

He came to be aware that he was, at least most of the time, watched by either the silver-eyes bodyguards or by one of his father's discreet Warriors. Though nobody ever prevented him from going anywhere he desired, he was usually under somebody's supervision. It was worst while he was little; the only time he was certain he was free of them was when he went out riding with Mersai, because there was nobody in Eastmarch, Orion was sure, who could have trailed a person on horseback if their lives had depended upon it. (He was wrong about that, as it happened; he learned later that most of the silver-eyes, even the half-breeds who were actually raised in Eastmarch, could have done it with ease. Because he went riding with Mersai most of the time he was rarely followed; Cain trusted Mersai.) He did not go riding often; Mersai never did learn to sit a horse properly and was often too sore to walk after a day in the saddle. Besides, Loga, though Orion found him fascinating, rarely told Orion anything Orion did not already know from his lessons at Eastmarch, though occasionally the old Ruler corrected his history, from personal knowledge. On those rare occasions when Cain thought a visible bodyguard was necessary, it was always Kavad who played the part. Orion was not sure at what point it was that he realized that Kavad's first and most important duty with regard to Orion was not instruction but that of an exceptionally discreet bodyguard. He was good at it; Orion never chafed at Kavad's attentions.

As he grew and put on weight the supervision lessened considerably and finally, Orion judged, ceased entirely. He was in little real danger in the Caverns at any rate; he was well liked as a child, and by the time his duties brought him into conflict with the Workers whom he commanded, the idea that any of them might have harmed him was ludicrous. Had he not been raised as Cain's son he would have made an ideal bodyguard; like Solan, like Loden, Orion was destined to be a large man, and he received the same training in hand-to-hand combat that the silver-eyes children got. He was a Warrior in all but name long before he was old enough for the uniform.

There was one subject that he was never told he was studying, was never told to study, and was never graded upon by Mersai or Kavad or Cain; but had he done badly at it all the rest would have meant nothing.

He learned how to lead.

He was nearly seven when the refugee children began arriving in the Caverns proper. Those who made it as far as the Caverns were largely the orphaned children of Warriors from the territories the Giants raided for adult Workers. Most of them were at least somewhat older than Orion, and many had received some small degree of training by their parents before those parents had been taken. Cain's rule extended into those territories but slightly, and except for his stronghold at Parliament, Maston Veramorn paid them no attention at all. They lacked any strong government for the first time in the history of the Valley; and as a result, with the way things were along the banks of the River Almandar these days, the skills of a Warrior were practical, and practiced, to a degree those territories had not been since the rebellion of Erebion—and even that was an event lost in the mists of history to most Workers, merely something that had happened once upon a time to their great-great-great-grandparents.

At first it was not much remarked upon by the Workers, the coincidence of how most of those children who made it as far as the Caverns, past the refugee camps at Saerlock and Telindel, were the children of Warriors themselves.

Coincidence was one of those few words, Orion was learning, that his father spoke with plain contempt; *trust* was another. It was only after Cain was dead that Orion realized that his father had been swearing when he used those words.

Orion was not by nature a cynic; nonetheless he learned skepticism and learned it well, at the hands of the greatest skeptic he would ever know.

The day he met No-Name he was playing a board game with Lisa, sitting on empty crates in a corridor at the lower southwest end of Level Four. Pinch was at his side; the dog usually was, except when Orion visited the shipyards or Mongers' Floor, where animals were not allowed. The dog was fully adult now, with a surprising resemblance to the first Pinch whom Orion had been raised with in Eagles. Had hunting been as popular an Eastmarch pastime as it was in Eagles, Pinch would have been a fine hunting dog.

The corridor they were in connected a storage room with a row of Workers' barracks, and hardly anyone ever went there. It made for an excellent place for games.

The game they were playing was not a complex one, not as complex by an order of magnitude as the war games he played with Mersai. The game had two fleets of slipships, Giants and Eastmarch, attacking each other, with points awarded for destruction of enemy slipships or capture of enemy territory. Normally when Eastmarch children played such games, the wars were assumed to be between Eastmarch and Eagles; those who played with Orion learned quickly enough that the bad guys in *his* games were the Giants.

The game was essentially a calculation of odds, with a slight edge awarded to defensive postures (as, Mersai assured Orion, was true in real battles as well). Orion played conservatively and beat Lisa consistently. She had a gift for tactics better than Orion's own, but no patience; the idea of *waiting* for an advantage was foreign to her.

It did not occur to Orion to let her win, or even to explain to her why she was losing; Mersai and Kavad never did for him. She'd either figure it out herself or she didn't deserve to figure it out.

Bellows showed up as Lisa was proceeding to lose her fourth straight game in a daring do-or-die raid against Orion's Shield generator. Had it succeeded Lisa would have won the game easily, but the odds in the maneuver's favor were only, Orion estimated, about sixteen or seventeen percent, and the dice did not fall the way they had to for the maneuver to work.

The dice were a major reason Orion never played war games with Cain. Somebody named Loukas had taught Cain to cheat at dice with a perfection that astonished Orion.

"Hi, Lisa, hi, Orion," called Bellows as he came into sight around a bend in the corridor. He had with him a large boy whom Orion had never seen before, a dark-skinned child with a Semalian cast to his eyes. "What are you doin'?"

"Playing a stupid game," said Lisa sourly. "Who's he?"

"This is my new friend," said Bellows eagerly. "I just met him this morning and he was telling me about how the Giants took his parents away to work on the planet and they had to walk all the way from Turrin to Singer but they couldn't stay in Singer 'cause there's not enough houses to live in so they had to walk to Saerlock and from there a bunch of the kids got a ride to the Caverns."

Lisa looked the boy over. "What's his name?"

It brought Bellows up short. "Uh, I don't know." Orion snickered, and Bellows glared at him and turned to the boy. "What's your name?"

The boy said flatly, "I don't have a name," and Orion laughed at him.

He was not laughing at what the boy had said, though he did not understand it. But in Eagles, when somebody told a joke about lowlanders—who were known to be so dumb they were just barely smart enough to bury their crap downwind—the accent they used was the accent this boy had just spoken in.

"What's so funny?" Bellows demanded loudly.

"Him," said Orion, pointing. "He talks funny."

Bellows was silent for just a second and then, without warning, punched Orion in the face. Orion was still sitting on the crate, and the blow sent him sprawling. Pinch came up off the cold floor in a flash, fangs bared, and lunged at Bellows.

"Pinch, down!" said Orion sharply. The dog came to heel instantly, every muscle quivering, the growl still in its throat, and Orion climbed back to his feet and dusted his pants off where the corridor's dirt had gotten on them. Then he grinned at Bellows, who was still eyeing Pinch, moved in and kicked the bigger boy in the shin, stepped to the side and with the same foot kicked him again in the back of the knee. He took Bellows by the wrist of his right hand as the boy started to topple and went down to the ground with him, letting Bellows' bulk cushion his own fall. To the two who were watching it was all a confused blur of movement which ended with Bellows facedown on the ground and Orion perched on his back, with Bellows' right arm twisted straight up in the air behind him. "Do you surrender your knife?" he demanded. Bellows only grunted, and Orion twisted his arm further back. "Surrender your knife," he said patiently.

"*Ouch* . . . Okay, I surrender," Bellows yelled, and Orion let him go instantly, stepping back to where Pinch was sitting watching the entire affair.

"Do you want to try again?"

Bellows sat up with his back against the corridor wall and shook his head, grimacing with pain as he shook his arm. "No. But he doesn't sound funny, he just sounds like a Semalian. *You* sound funny."

Orion shrugged. "I didn't mean anything bad, Bellows. He just surprised me." He turned back to the Semalian boy and smiled again. "So you don't have a name? Why not?"

The boy stared at Orion with flat eyes. He had not smiled once yet. "The Giants took it. They took it with my home and my parents."

"Oh." Lisa looked at him curiously. "So what do we call you, No-Name?"

"If you like." The boy turned to Orion. "What you did to Bellows, the fighting trick—can you show me how to do that?"

The idea that anyone would *want* to learn the things Cain's bodyguards *had* to know surprised Orion for an instant. "Why?"

"I never saw anybody do anything like that before," the boy said simply.

"Really?" Orion grinned at him. "I actually did it wrong. Kavad would have criticized it."

"Doing *what?*" asked Cain.

"He was teaching them," said Jimal precisely, "hand-to-hand combat, my lord. The ken Selvren disciplines of kartaari and shotak.

And then they played a war game that involved an attack upon the North Land."

"Did they?" Cain actually smiled, something Jimal saw but rarely. "Did they indeed?"

"Yes, my lord. Do you wish to take some action?"

"No, no. Leave them be. Who were the children?"

"Lisa Wanarè—"

"Of course," Cain nodded.

"—Jackson, son of the Warrior Donali, no surname—they call him Bellows; and a Semalian child who just arrived in the Caverns, Kennian Temera."

"Temera?"

The tone of Cain's voice reached Jimal; he lifted an eyebrow. "My lord? Is something wrong?"

"The boy was brought here alone? Not with his grandparents or any relatives?"

"Alone, my lord. Most of them are arriving alone, as you requested. Without their families." Jimal tapped keys on the video tablet he commonly carried with him. "There were interviews and tests the children went through in Saerlock before we brought them here, and I think . . . here we are." Jimal scanned the interview and test results quickly. "Test results good to excellent; the interview seems to indicate some emotional problems, which under the circumstances is hardly surprising. The Temera family was fairly prominent in Turrin before the Rulers abdicated. Both of his parents were taken by the Giants and at least one of his grandparents. The child left Turrin with his great-grandmother, who died on the way to Singer. He's been alone since then." Jimal paused. "Would you like to see the child, my lord?"

She died on the way here, Cain thought clearly, and then, *It probably wasn't her.* She'd have been his own age, or pretty near. Workers just didn't live that long without youthbooster. Or not many of them did, at any rate. "No, no." He waved a hand at Jimal in dismissal. "The name seemed familiar for a moment, that's all." It would be easy enough to check—simply ask the boy his great-grandmother's name. Cain did not seriously consider doing so for even an instant. "You may leave me now, Jimal."

Jimal's expression did not change at all. "Yes, my lord."

THE RING

The conversation was quiet, the voices kept low. The recording was a poor one; most of the voices were indistinct enough that Cain referred to the transcript Jimal had prepared for him fairly often while listening to it.

There were at least seven different voices, marked on the transcript as Voice One, Voice Two, and so on. Only two of the voices had names assigned to them. One of them was a crank named Tolrin whom Cain had not bothered to execute because he attracted other disaffected Workers who were potentially more dangerous than he was.

The second voice belonged to Irina Chuft-Wanarè, Lisa Wanarè's mother.

"Face it," said a man's voice, "Cain's here to stay. You may not like his policies—I don't—but they make sense a lot of the time, and when they don't make sense it's usually because Cain doesn't explain himself."

Tolrin: "So why *doesn't* he explain himself? Damn it, we're not stupid, if there's reasons for the things he's doing, we have a right to know."

Irina Chuft-Wanarè: "There's only really one question, isn't there? Do we believe him when he says he doesn't know how to synthesize youthbooster or don't we? If we believe he's really researching the subject we're crazy to try to take him down; even a swift, successful coup would interrupt the research. If we don't believe him, we're crazy not to."

Male voice: "What about the boy?"

Chuft-Wanarè: "That boy is our way. He gives me hope."

Female voice: "I don't trust him any more than I trust Cain. He's no more Cain's son that I am."

Male voice: "Doesn't matter, does it? He's Cain's heir."

Female voice: "Heir to a man who doesn't age? I can think of positions with a brighter future."

Chuft-Wanarè: "He's just a boy yet, but he's a chance. Our children are his friends. Cain has no friends among us; how our lives run means nothing to him. It won't be that way for the boy."

There was a momentary silence on the recording. Then a male

voice said, "Cain has the boy here for a reason. His reasons, not ours. You've all seen the black-eyed bastard at work; you really think that boy's going to grow up with a mind of his own?"

Another brief silence.

Chuft-Wanarè: "Stranger things have happened."

Normally they would not have been consecrated together, but Orion requested it, and Cain assented though they were still, by normal standards, two or three years too young to become Warriors. The day after his tenth birthday, Fall 9 in the year 1289 After the Fire, Orion and his three closest friends, Lisa and Bellows and Kennian Temera, became Warriors together.

The ceremony was the same ceremony by which Warriors had become consecrated, bound to the service of the Light, for better than seven centuries. For two days the four friends did not eat; the second day was Fall 8, Orion's birthday. They did not celebrate Orion's birthday—that was an Eagles custom, and the children in Eastmarch had never heard of it. After his first birthday in the Caverns, four years ago, Orion had never thought about it again. He spent his tenth birthday riding with his friends, and in the evening of Fall 8 the four of them were outfitted with the formal dress uniforms of Warriors of Eastmarch and presented with the formal swords they would never, likely enough, have occasion to use in any but a ceremonial fashion.

They spent that night kneeling together with their swords, meditating in the Warrior's Chapel on Level Two, just above the Weapons Monger's Floor. There were no electric lights or glowfloats in the chapel, only the traditional wax candles, and they guttered low as the night wore away.

Sometime in the course of that night Orion passed out of himself, into a great darkness; and when he returned and the world grew firm about him again he was where he had been, kneeling before the huge altar of the Light. Lisa and Bellows and No-Name were kneeling beside him, and the sharp golden radiance was fading back into the nothingness from which it had emerged.

Orion could not remember where he had been, only a sense of warmth and security and belonging that he had never known before in Eagles or Eastmarch, and that much of what he had brought back faded swiftly, and left him kneeling, stiff and aching from the long vigil, on the cold flagstones.

They spent that first day in the duties of Eastmarch Warriors, were inducted in the morning into their squadrons; in the evening Orion found himself standing a watch at the South Gate with Lisa while No-Name and Bellows stood watch at the North Gate. For that watch they were, theoretically, the sole guardians of the approaches to the Caverns. They had not eaten in three days nor slept in two, and Orion made it through the day and the evening's watch with a wavering, giddy determination. He did not know how the others managed it.

Lisa was eleven that year, and taller than Orion. Years later Orion remembered looking up at her when she leaned over and whispered as though it was a great secret, "I think I like your hands, you know why?" She did not wait for an answer. "Because they were the only part of you that didn't shine when the Light came. Your eyes were the color of suns," and Orion did not know what she meant by that.

The next day Cain gave Orion a slipship as a gift.

A Warrior whom Orion did not know brought Orion's slipship up out of the shipyard; they did not trust Orion enough to let him do it himself. Orion waited on the landpads aboveground while the silo doors opened and the Warrior brought the slipship up and out of the underground shipyard, and set it down twenty meters from where Cain, Jimal, Mersai and Kavad stood. Lisa was with Orion, and No-Name; Bellows had picked up time on the always-busy simulator and had chosen to hone his own flying skills on the simulator rather than watch Orion make his first run with the real thing.

Orion buckled in under the Warrior's watchful eye, and after Orion had finished, the man reached in and without a word tightened the straps around Orion's hips until Orion could barely move.

Standing well back from the slipship, watching Orion, Mersai said softly, "My lord? Don't you think he's a little young for this?"

Cain glanced at Mersai and then at Kavad. "Kavad? Do you think Orion is too young to pilot a slipship?"

The old silver-eyes did not hesitate. "His reflexes are excellent, my lord, but he does not realize he can be hurt."

Cain smiled. "Then we are all in agreement. It's good to find

myself agreeing with men whose opinions I respect." He turned back to
watch Orion going through the power-up sequence.

Mersai traded a glance with Kavad and said, "My lord Cain, why
did you give Orion this ship?"

"Orion," said Cain, "disagrees with us."

Orion finished the preflight checks and scanned the instrument
banks. They'd taken the weapons out of the slipship which annoyed
him—on the simulators he was one of the best dogfighters in his age
group. Aside from that things appeared to be in order. The slipship's
Shield was at full strength, the fusion cells were ignited and the thrusters were hot. The lifeplant had been taken out of the slipship as well,
and Orion's "flight suit," though made of the same heat-resistant material as a real flight suit, had no attachments for an oxy-helium supply.
That limited the possible length of the flight drastically; there was only
enough air in the cockpit for about ten minutes' breathing for an adult.
Orion figured that gave him fifteen minutes, though he didn't for an
instant expect Cain would actually let him stay up even that long the
first time out.

The last thing he did was open the ship to ground channel. He
did not get the Flight Commander whom he expected; instead Cain's
voice came from the speaker. "All right, listen carefully. You mess this
up and you'll be thirteen—at least—before the next time you get to
touch a slipship. Up and around and down again; you land-gliding, nose
up. Don't try anything fancy. We're going to leave the Shield down the
entire time. If an Air Alert comes while you're up, don't panic. You
have at least three minutes after the Alert sounds before we have to
raise the Shield; in three minutes a blind man could land a slipship. Got
it?"

Underneath his helmet, Orion was grinning. Cain was worried, he
must be; he couldn't really believe Orion didn't know the most basic
things about combat flying. He kept the grin out of his voice. "Yes, sir."

There was a brief pause, and Cain's voice came again: "Shield
down."

Orion wasted no time; he brought the nose up with the attitude
jets and hit the thrusters at ten percent beneath redline.

The slipship went straight up.

Cain watched impassively as Orion took the slipship through half a dozen simple barrel rolls and then practiced banking, gently and then more sharply. Five minutes had not passed when Cain touched the microphone stud at his collar and said, "Okay, Orion, bring it down now."

The slipship was in the midst of a long circling curve around the landpad when Cain said that; the slipship completed its turn and came about for what looked like the landing Cain had told Orion to take.

At the last possible instant the slipship scooped air, steadied itself on attitude jets, and brought its belly jets up until it was hanging, almost stable, forty meters above the open silo doors.

Cain touched the stud of the microphone. "Orion," he said calmly, "don't try it. It's harder than it looks."

The slipship hung an instant longer and then dropped like a stone. It did not even slow as it dropped beneath the level of the silo doors.

They heard the sound of the crash through the silo doors, and Cain said simply, "Let's go below."

Orion was actually at the silo doors when he realized he was in trouble. He was moving fast, and on the simulator all he had to do was pull the belly throttle up in synchronization with the attitude jets.

In the simulator there were no gee effects. When the belly jets cut in Orion was slammed vertically down into the pilot's seat and the throttle didn't come up nearly as far as it should have; suddenly it was four times heavier than he'd been expecting. A grown man would have had the muscle to compensate; Orion pulled wildly and still the throttle did not come up far enough.

The slipship touched.

One landjack crumpled under the impact, and the entire slipship canted to one side. The slipship's wing touched the floor of the ship-yard and bent with a sound like nothing Orion had ever heard before—metal screaming like a living thing. The slipship made a slow, majestic half turn about its axis before coming to a stop.

He was still adjusting to the fact that he was alive when the flight crew popped the canopy, cut him out of the seat webbing and helped him down out of the slipship to the flight deck. It took him a moment to get his bearings, and then the lift from the surface opened and Lisa and No-Name came running to where he was standing. Cain followed them less quickly, and after assuring his friends that he was all right Orion turned to face Cain with more composure than any ten-year-old boy in the world could have been expected to have after crashing a slipship on his first flight.

"It was a good takeoff, wasn't it?"

In front of his friends and instructors and the flight crews and all of the Warriors who were present on duty, Cain struck him. It was the first time Cain had ever struck him, and the only time Cain ever did.

It was the only time Orion ever saw Cain angry.

The blow staggered Orion, but did not knock him from his feet. The voice said silently, cutting straight through the pain so that nobody heard it but himself, *A slipship is not a horse, boy, and it's not a simulator either. You can die in one when you make a mistake.*

Orion was searching for a reply when Cain turned and swept off the field, Jimal keeping pace with him.

Immediately behind him, Mersai's rough voice said, "You scared him, lad."

Orion came out of his shock slowly, and then turned on Mersai in a sudden burst of fierce anger. "I'm a Warrior now, Orrin, I'm not a child. Does he think he can protect me from danger forever?"

"Could be," said Mersai simply. "I stopped trying to decide what Cain was thinking a long time ago, Orion." Mersai paused, and then grinned easily. "That was some damn fine flying."

The hurt fell away from Orion's features in an instant. There was still blood trickling down the corner of his mouth from where Cain had struck him. "You think so?"

Mersai nodded. "Yeah. But it was pretty stupid."

Orion froze on the verge of saying something and then relaxed after a long instant and sighed. "Okay. I get the point."

Mersai patted him on the shoulder. "I thought you would."

"But, Orrin?"

"Yeah?"

"It was worth it."

Orion lay silently in the sweat-soaked bed, clutching to himself Cain's assurances that he was going to live. It was hard to be sure, for

Orion was coming to know that he did not, and probably never would, understand the complex man who was his father. Cain had lied to him so often, with such an obvious lack of guilt that Orion never knew how to take the things Cain told him, not even such a simple things as an assurance that Orion was not going to die.

Bellows and No-Name came to visit him in the afternoon, but Orion was still delirious from the poison and did not know them, and so they went away. He was aware of Lisa's presence, briefly, but then she too was gone, and as the afternoon faded away to night and Orion's head cleared somewhat, he realized that Cain was sitting in the chair next to his bed, and once that Cain was holding his hand. The fever came and went unpredictably, and once Orion heard himself asking in a very rational-sounding voice for his daddy, and distantly was disgusted with himself for the use of the word. It was what babies called their fathers, and he knew he had never addressed Cain so before. If Cain made a response to that, Orion did not remember it the next time his head cleared. He was vaguely aware of the soothing, almost hypnotic murmur of Cain's voice, of the distant chant of forgetting.

Jimal came in while Orion was sleeping fitfully, and Cain said, "Where is Kavad?"

"My lord," said Jimal, "my father has confined himself to his quarters until you decide what to do with him."

"Did he find the woman who gave Orion the poison?"

Jimal hesitated. "My lord, he did. She's dead. She killed herself."

Cain looked up quickly and nodded. "Pity. I'd have enjoyed doing it. Go, now." He turned back to Orion.

Cain sat with the child all that night. The fever finally broke just after midnight, and Orion awoke weak but clear-headed. There were odd images dancing at the edges of reality, a blonde woman who looked like the way he remembered his mother except she was too young, and she was calling to him. Another was the striking, almost aesthetic parallel alignment of the body of the fallen Warrior and the lance that had taken his life.

"I hate it down here, you know," he whispered to his father. "You can't see the skies at night, you can't see the Star."

"The Star?" Cain said quietly.

"*Art wondrous things,*" the boy said suddenly, clearly, "*renowned, unknown . . .*" The words were spoken in the Old Tongue, a language

Orion had never been taught, and they went through Cain with a thrill like an electric shock; they were the opening lines of a poem the Ruler Loga had been fond of quoting. "It's wonderful out there, isn't it?"

Cain shook his head slowly. "I don't know what you mean, Orion."

"I feel . . . funny . . . when I look at the stars," Orion whispered.

"Funny how?"

"I don't know . . . that I belong there, too."

"Do you?" There was nothing intimidating in his father's black eyes, only a troubled look. "Anywhere in particular?"

"No." The boy's voice was harsh, strained. "Just out there . . . to go places the way Donner did. When I'm older I'll do that, won't I?"

Cain stroked a loose strand of the boy's hair away from his hot forehead. "You'll do many things, Orion." Cain waited with the child patiently, and not long after that boy descended into true sleep, his breathing even and untroubled.

Cain knew for a fact that no one in the Caverns had ever told Orion about Donner Almandar.

They executed Kavad two days later, as soon as Orion was strong enough.

It was a private thing, quietly done late at night on the Second Level, in a large auditorium where war games were staged. The only folk present were Cain and Orion and Jimal, Kavad and a firing squad of three other silver-eyes. There was no ceremony to it; a post was erected hastily before Kavad was brought in, dressed in a simple white tunic, and came to stand before Cain and Orion.

Cain said simply, "I'm sorry it's ending this way, my friend. You've made two bad mistakes in not quite six years. That's too many. One would have been too many for anyone except a friend."

The barbarian bowed low to Cain for the very last time. "Yes, my lord."

"Kavad."

The old barbarian straightened and met Cain's gaze without flinching. "My lord?"

"They tell me, Kavad, that the silver-eyes hell is a place of ice."

"Yes, my lord."

Cain nodded. "Appropriate." He said no more, and it was Kavad's own son who took him to the post and manacled him into position.

Cain did not draw it out; the instant Jimal was out of the line of fire Cain said flatly, "Fire."

Three brilliant emerald lines of light touched the bound form for a fraction of a second and then ceased. Kavad spasmed in that instant and then sagged against his bindings. Raw seared flesh showed through the barbarian's tunic. Several seconds later a low moan came from him.

A muscle twitched in Cain's cheek. "Fire again," he said loudly.

The lasers reached out a second time, and this time the man did not even twitch, but merely went limp.

Cain watched the limp form a moment longer and turned to Jimal. "Bury him with honors in whatever fashion ken Selvren find appropriate." Cain was distantly aware of Orion, at his side, trembling visibly. "Go," Cain murmured to Jimal, and the silver-eyes bowed, a harsh expression upon his features, and withdrew.

The smell of burned meat wafted to where Cain and Orion stood, and Orion said stiffly, "Father? May I be excused?"

Cain nodded. "Yes."

Orion left with his spine and shoulders straight, without looking back at the people watching him leave, and did not vomit until he reached his quarters.

So did Orion's childhood end.

· 5 ·

They rode out from the Caverns late on the afternoon of Fall 32, 1293 After the Fire, four young Warriors atop the best horses to be found in all of Eastmarch territory. They rode steadily north in the fading light, Orion enjoying the crisp feel of the air in his lungs, the scent of the pines once they had left the farmlands behind, the grace and power of the gray stallion he rode. Kennian, whose horsemanship was very nearly as good as Orion's own, rode at his left hand, and Lisa and Bellows brought up the rear. Kennian rode silently—he never talked much—alert to his surroundings in a way Lisa and Bellows were not. Though Orion still called him No-Name, his name was Kennian; and if in speech Orion used their childhood nickname, nonetheless Orion did not think of him so, and had not for many years.

Lisa and Bellows didn't stop complaining once all the way out to the campsight. The campsight Orion had chosen was not far distant, only two hours' ride. The day following was Fall 33, the nineteenth anniversary of the signing of the Treaty of Eastmarch, and none of them wanted to camp so far away that they got back too late.

Orion paid Lisa's and Bellows' complaints little attention; they were not serious, and after nine years together he knew it.

"Why can't we fly the new stuff?" Bellows was demanding. "I can handle a standard slipship as well as anyone, I know I could handle one of the new jobs. Falcon class isn't so different." He was silent for a moment and then burst out, "Cory's squadron took Falcons up to the orbital factories last quarter and they won't even let us fly the damn things in atmosphere!"

"Train, train, train." Lisa repeated the litany with the perfection of long practice. "Careful, careful, careful. Too young, not enough muscle. Slow down and think about it real careful before you do it and then don't do it anyway because you're too young."

"We became Warriors three years younger than anyone else in our squadron," said Kennian softly. He did not raise his voice, but the words carried. "Of course the image has stuck with them, that we are young. Orion crashed the first slipship he ever flew and you, Lisa, have come so close to cracking up so many times that nobody wants to be on your wing except us."

"My scores are better than yours, No-Name," Lisa shot back.

"True. You fly closer to the edge than I do. It looks great. If we ever end up in combat it may be useful. But we're at peace right now, with Eagles, with the Giants, and the way you fly scares the other Warriors."

Lisa was silent for a long moment, riding thoughtfully. Finally she said, "I don't notice you ever hesitating to fly with me."

Kennian twisted in the saddle to look back at her and smiled one of his very rare smiles. "Sure. Everybody dies sometime. I guess I won't mind being killed so much if it's by one of my best friends." He turned back and rode ahead without waiting for a reply.

Bellows nudged his mount over closer to Lisa and murmured, "Someday you're gonna learn not to argue with him."

Lisa sighed and spurred her horse forward after the big gray.

They camped that night in a clearing not far south of the old village of Eastmarch, tethered their horses and built a fair-sized fire with deadwood from the forest's floor. They were beyond the furthest reaches of the farmland that fed the Caverns. The Great Dam rose high above them, a monstrous structure of stonesteel that shone pale gray in the light of the crescent moon.

They shot a pair of treebunnies for dinner, skinned the animals and roasted them over their fire. Had they not hunted successfully they would not have eaten, for they had brought no food with them, only beer bulbs and wine. After dinner they swapped stories and sang songs. Bellows was actually a fair harpist, though he had not brought the instrument with him, so they sang with just their voices. Lisa's voice was fair, as was Orion's; Bellows' was really quite good, and Kennian could have made a living as a musician; he had the best voice of anyone whom Orion knew.

Kennian sang them a classic Semalian song called "The Diamond of the Day." Orion had never heard it before and liked it instantly. Kennian said it was a ballad from the days of Artemis the Liberator; supposedly, said Kennian, Artemis himself had actually written it. "I don't believe that myself," said Kennian mildly. "To have done all the things that were said in Semalia about the Liberator, the man would have had to have been—well, like Cain, I suppose. He was a Worker who controlled the Light as if he were a Ruler, invented a kind of youthbooster that performed properly on Workers and Giants alike. And he was the finest musician of his day, with a magic harp called a guitar, and the greatest Warrior in all the Valley. The only part of it that's true for sure is about the youthbooster; it's what caused the Erebion rebellion." He smiled rather absently. "Not a lot of heroes in Semalian history; I guess folks made a lot out of what they had."

Orion lay flat on his back on his bedroll. It was after midnight, but he was not sleepy. Kennian was snoring very quietly not far away from him, and Bellows' chest rose and fell evenly on the other side of the fire. Lisa's breathing was irregular, and Orion was not at all surprised when she finally got up from where she lay, brought her bedroll over and laid it down beside his. He rolled over and kissed her without hesitating, pulled her to him and ran his hands down her back, over the swell of her buttocks. She moaned into his mouth and squirmed up against him more fully, one hand snaking down to rub him between his legs, touching him gently and then with greater urgency. Finally the tension left her in a single instant, and she took her mouth away from his and rolled over on her back next to him.

"Didn't you feel anything?" she asked.

"No."

Lisa sighed. "Bellows keeps asking me, you know."

Orion nodded. "I do know." He was silent for a moment. The Star, high above them, was very bright, almost beckoning. "You could do a lot worse."

"I love you, you know."

"I know." He spoke with perfect honesty. "I love you too."

"I suppose." Orion could almost see the gears turning in the back of her mind and did not interrupt her thoughts. "Why can't you? Is it just me or is it something else?"

The Star gleamed in the sky above Orion, the only thing in Orion's field of vision. He could not take his eyes from it. "I don't know," he said honestly. "I wish I could; you're as pretty as any girl I've ever seen and you're one of the four people I care about most in the world. There's just . . . I don't know."

"Oh." She was not really angry, Orion saw, merely upset and puzzled and distantly sad. "Do you think maybe you like boys instead?"

Orion winced at the question, though she had asked it without any hostility at all; it was a thought that had not left him alone for most of the last year. There was no real prejudice in the Caverns against men who slept with other men, but it was not common, and people made jokes about those who did. "I don't know," he said finally. "I don't think so."

"Oh." Lisa sighed and snuggled up against him, and brought her bedroll up to cover them both against the cold night air. "Good night, Orion," she said, very quietly.

"Good night, Lisa."

When they left to return to the Caverns the following morning, Orion still had not slept.

On Fall 80 of that year, two days before Year's End, they sat together by the fire and the snow fell gently around them, Orion's gray tethered loosely behind him. A half-empty container of wine bulbs rested on the ground next to him.

"He's dragging you all off to war with the Giants, Orion, and he's doing it because he wants the Ring."

Orion shook his head. "You're wrong. If he wanted war with the Giants, we'd be at war now. There's a lot of sentiment in the Caverns to wage war upon the Giants, and Cain simply won't. Politically it may be the worst problem we have."

Loga chuckled. "I enjoy talking to you, Orion. It reminds me of how Workers actually think. If they're not doing something now, why, it must mean they're never going to do it. Orion, listen, Cain's an old man by Worker standards. I know he doesn't look it, but believe me, he is, and I believe he's finally learning to take the long view. You haven't gone to war with the Giants only because Cain's not ready yet. But you will." His voice was suddenly different, lacking the overtones of humor that was nearly always there. "I've seen it."

Orion nodded thoughtfully, sipping at his wine. He did not agree with Loga, but did not know how to argue his point; instead he changed the subject. "Did you know one of Cain's silver-eyes tried to trail me out here?"

"I was watching. If you hadn't lost him, I'd not have appeared when you got here." Loga grinned easily. He was lying flat on his back, chewing on a stem of grass. "Do you know, you're probably the only person in this Valley who would have lost one of Cain's silver-eyes? Not counting me," he amended. "But I have an unfair advantage."

Orion shrugged, poking into the fire with a stick. The snow was too light to put it out, but still the hiss, as snowflakes vanished into the heat, was constantly audible. "They taught me themselves. Or Kavad did, at any rate." The burning branches collapsed in upon themselves, and a shower of sparks leapt up from the fire, flashing yellow and orange. Orion lifted a wine bulb in a toast. "To Kavad; may he have a better master in the next life than he had in this."

"Ken Selvren don't believe that the wheel turns, Orion. They believe in an afterlife, but it's a cold place, a frozen hell."

Orion snorted. "They must find dying a particularly unpleasant prospect."

"Don't we all." Loga examined the stalk of grass he had been masticating, tossed it away and began anew on another half-frozen stalk. "But I wouldn't make fun of their religion if I were you. At least it's their own. The Church of the Light, or at any rate most of its tenets, was designed as a tool to keep the Worker population subject to the will of the Rulers. And it worked, too, for a long time. Oh, there's something real at the center of it, some very real power, Orion, but I don't know if that means that the religion is particularly worthwhile. That is the essential fallacy the Rulers refused to see—this desperate assumption that there is more moral being—or at least some moral *force*—from which the Light emanates. Be damned if I can see it."

"I think he knows you're out here," said Orion suddenly. "It's strange, but he's never asked me about it and I can tell it's in his thoughts."

Loga did not need to ask who "he" was. "You're likely right. He's a smart man. I don't find much of a trace of him in your thoughts, so he's probably been leaving your mind alone; and if he has, then he won't know for certain I'm here. But you know, I don't think he cares very much either way. I can't really harm you—or won't, which is the same thing—and he knows that. The worst thing I could really do to you, by his standards, would be to tell you some stuff he's not ready to let you know—and I'm starting to think he may even be right on some of those subjects, at least at the moment."

Orion laughed loudly, not without bitterness. "Hoo. By the Light, Loga, you don't talk like my father's worst enemy."

The Ruler sat up, dusting flakes of snow off his sleeves. "I'm not his enemy," Loga said simply. "Sometimes I think he's starting to understand that."

"Fine," said Orion instantly, with a hard grin. "Come back to Eastmarch with me."

"Not a chance. I *could* be wrong."

Orion laughed at that, too, and sank back another slug of the wine. The wine warmed his insides, made the world a far friendlier place. "You're a sensible man, or Ruler, or whatever you are."

"A man first, and after that—hell, I don't know. Once I was ken Selvren, and once I was a Ruler, but I don't think I'm either of those things any longer. What I mostly am is very old, and kinda tired."

Orion sank back into the snow, held the wind bulb upside down and squeezed it dry, let the wine flow down his throat without ceasing until there was no more to be had. "At least you're a man."

"What do you mean?"

Orion said the words in a rush, before he could lose the courage to say them to the only person whom he knew who might be able to help him. "There's something wrong with me, I don't know what. I've tried to sleep with two women in the last half a year, and nothing, there was just nothing there for either of them. One of them I liked and the other one I love, and there was just nothing." His pause was almost imperceptible. "Nothing at all."

"And are you thinking about the Star when this happens?"

Orion sat up again slowly. The universe wavered around him. "That's crazy. How the hell could you know that?"

"Do you?"

"Yeah. Pretty bizarre, isn't it?" Loga did not answer him, and Orion said again, "How did you *know* that?"

"Fascinating," Loga murmured to himself. "I wish I could talk to T'Pau again. I wonder if she had any idea what she was doing when . . ." He broke off, and said almost clinically, "Did you know that the Rulers, for all the Workers in Parliament were available for their lusts, rarely bedded Workers? They found one another attractive."

Orion stared at Loga in bewilderment. "So?"

"The Star," said Loga. "I've been there, kid. Took the Light into myself and made the jump. It's an asteroid, nothing more. A man who's dead now, Loden Almandar, set it alight with a cold fire as a beacon, to tell people it was there. His daughter is chained to it. I tried to free her, but I can't. She was bound there with a greater power than I can raise alone. Whoever unties her is going to need more power than I've been able to raise alone." Loga smiled up at the cloud-covered skies. "Senta's been calling for help for a long time. I think you must hear her. You're not the one she's calling, but you're very like that person."

Orion said drunkenly, "Say again?"

"Her name was Senta, and she came to Earth to help the Workers after the Rulers had abdicated. She meant well, for all the damage that came of the attempt. You'd have liked her," Loga said softly, "for you and she are much alike."

"You've got to be kidding."

"Nope."

Orion said very carefully, "Slow down a second. Let me check this and see if I have it right. I'm in love with a Ruler who I never met because she's calling to me because she thinks I'm somebody else. And because of that I'm not enjoying it when I try to sleep with somebody else?"

"That's basically it."

"Oh." Orion was silent for a moment. "Well, this sucks."

Some forty senior Commanders sat together in Command Debriefing, what would have been called the War Room had the Caverns been the holdings of some old-fashioned lord from the days of the Rulers. Among them were Cain, Jimal, Commander Colonel Mondàl Dantes and Commander First Orion. Jimal stood, a pale-skinned man with a bearing as rigid as though a pike had replaced his spine.

Dantes was speaking.

"They've overtrained, my lord. You can't keep a standing army of this size without some hope for battle. Better than half your Warriors are under the age of twenty, and they're hungry for their first battle. We've been taking them out across the Glowing Desert, violating ken Selvren flight space, merely to give them some taste of blood." Commander Colonel Dantes spread his hands helplessly. "My lord, you've saddled me with what's got to be the youngest army since . . . since . . . since the bloody Fire, at any rate. It's all very well to give them supervision of the laborers and such, but a Warrior who's content with the likes of that is a Warrior I don't want covering my back. Even without the use of Fire weapons we could conquer Maston in two or three years, the silver-eyes in perhaps two. We'd be ready for the Giants, then."

"You think they won't be ready for the Giants if we don't blood them first?" Cain's voice was even, features composed; in better than ten years service as Cain's senior Commander, Dantes had never managed—as the late General Mersai had—the fairly difficult task of reading lord Cain's demeanor for the subtle clues that were all he ever gave a man to go by.

"My lord, I do."

"Orion, what do you think?"

The youngest Commander in the room by full four years, Orion had already the full height of a man; he did not hesitate to speak his mind. "Sir, I think the Commander Colonel is correct. You've built up a fine war machine; it aches to be used."

"Do you think we should attack Eagles, Orion?"

They were seated across the table from one another. Orion had arrived at the meeting fresh from standing watch and had taken the only free chair left. Though he had not been late, he had been the last person there. "Sir, I should prefer not to attack the place of my birth. That's a personal preference. Should you decide otherwise, I will of course perform my duty."

Cain nodded. His thought reached Orion privately: *I know that, of course, but it needed to be said publicly.* He said aloud, "Well, I'm afraid I've bad news for you, ladies and gentlemen. We're not going to war with Maston, and we're not going to war with the barbarians. We're going to war with the Giants. . . ."

The sudden round of spontaneous applause from the Commanders cut him off, and the applause changed as the Commanders withdrew their knives and pounded the knife butts on the surface of the long conference table. Cain waited, with a gentle smile, until the reverberations of the knife butts had died back. "I'm afraid you're not listening carefully. We will go to war with the Giants, but we're not going to do so for another seven years."

The silence was sudden and absolute.

"Worse yet, we're not going to war with either Maston or the barbarians. Maston will be our ally when we bring the war to the Giants, and though I suspect that none of you really believe this yet, the fact is we need him. The barbarians are irrelevant; I refuse to embark upon a war simply to provide some amusement for my troops. The Giants," said Cain persuasively, "are a greater foe than the Rulers ever were. There is no assurance at all, Commanders, that we will even survive the coming war with the Giants, much less prevail. Though our forces outnumber theirs, their weapons are, simply put, superior to our own. I've had our strategists prepare an analysis of the Giant defenses and munitions, with our own strike capabilities shown in contrast. You'll each be given one copy; you're to read the document and then destroy it. Dismissed."

The nearly shocked silence prevailed as Jimal distributed the bound documents to the Commanders and dissipated only as the Commanders were leaving the room. Cain did not pay particular attention to their murmured comments to one another on the way out the door; their real opinions would not come out until they had a chance to read the analysis and talk the subject over with other Commanders whose opinions and discretion they trusted. Cain glanced at Orion as the boy was rising from his seat; Orion interpreted the glance correctly and stayed. Dantes never even left his seat. Shortly there were only the four of them left.

"Your honest opinion, Orion?"

"It seems a mistake, sir. Seven years is too long for them to wait."

Cain glanced over at Dantes, then back to Orion. "I think I'd have to agree with you, Orion. May I ask you a question?"

That was not the response Orion had expected. "Certainly," he said cautiously.

"How well, Orion, do you think forty Commanders can keep a secret of this magnitude?"

The thought had not occurred to Orion. "Poorly, sir." He thought furiously. "I'd wager the Giants will have a copy of that report, verbatim, within a quarter."

"More like a week," said Cain. "We'll make sure they get one."

"So when are we really going to attack?"

"In three years, Orion."

"Oh." Finally Orion said with a perfectly straight face, "That's much better, sir."

"I thought you might think so."

At the far west end of the Mongers' Floor, Bellows complained.

"Seven years! I'll be *twenty-three* in seven years! Seven more years of *this* and I won't be fit to fly a slipship or a Falcon to a picnic, much less into battle."

"Mm-hmm," said Orion without any particular sympathy.

This was one of the worst of the supervisory tasks that had been assigned to the Warriors in the last few years: at the west end of the Mongers' Floor was a waste dump where the useless slag the mongers produced was disposed of. The smell was horrid, acid and cloying all at once. Though the slag was useless, of utterly no value in and of itself, procuring samples of it was, paradoxically, one of the highest priorities Giant spies had. From a single piece of slag, the Warriors were assured by Cain's engineers, a Giant engineer could deduce an absolutely remarkable amount of information about the alloys and plastics the Worker engineers were developing.

It was boring duty. One stood upon a catwalk overlooking the waste dump, a huge hole greater than a hundred and sixty meters deep and some eighty wide, and made sure, as Bellows put it, "that nobody makes off with any of the precious garbage."

Orion was paying attention to Bellows' complaints with only a portion of his mind and running over the details of a simulated dogfight he'd had that morning with Lisa with the rest. There was a sound like a twig snapping in the forest, sharp and thin but still clearly audible over the omnipresent hum of the machines on the Mongers' Floor, and suddenly the world turned on its side. Orion's first clear awareness that there was anything wrong came when he found himself thrown against the catwalk's guardrail with such force that he heard the bone in his left arm pop even over the sound of the tearing metal. Far away, Bellows was shouting at the top of his lungs, and it occurred to Orion, irrelevantly, that the nickname he had been given as a child was eerily appropriate; Orion did not think he had ever in his life heard anyone make so much noise with just his lungs.

There was a sudden clear calm moment in the midst of it all, and Orion found himself facedown on the surface of the catwalk, right hand clutching the gridlike surface of the walkway. The moment ended and the catwalk continued its almost majestic tumble, folding down toward the depths of the waste dump until the slow drop ceased with a sudden jar. Orion found himself hanging above a lethal drop with the strength of only one hand, feet swinging free as the catwalk strained against its few remaining ties to the superstructure that had, moments before, supported it.

Orion's left arm was entirely devoid of feeling. He could not move it at all.

He hung above the void, clinging to life with three fingers of his right hand.

"Say again?" Commander Captain Mielo shouted into the microphone. *"Damn it, Warrior, slow down. I can't make heads or tails of what you're saying. West end of the Mongers' Floor? Is he still there or did he fall?"*

The Commander Center's lights flickered suddenly, wildly. "Captain?" One of the Warriors on duty looked over to where Commander Captain Mielo was standing. There was rising panic in his voice as he continued. "Captain, the power feeds to the Shield have shorted. We've got"—he paged through screen after screen of displays—"nothing. Captain, the Shield is down!"

Orion's perception of the world had narrowed down to the line of fire that ran through his arm, connecting his hand and the grill upon which he hung to the rest of his body. After some interminable time he became aware that the sunpaint flickered as though it were going to go out, and then it did so. He never knew how long he hung so, feet swinging slightly above the dark abyss, when the Light came and illuminated the pit like a small sun, and with it the silent voice. *Sorry I took so long. Want a lift?*

Yes, Orion remembered saying later, *yes, please.*

The Light took him.

When Cain arrived, a squad of armed Warriors at his back, Orion was sitting on the deck of the Mongers' Floor, holding his broken left arm with his bloody right hand. His friend Bellows was standing next to him, a projectile handgun drawn, looking fiercely protective. There was a crowd gathered around him, Warriors and laborers and engineers.

No appearance of concern touched Cain's features. "How are you?"

"I'm fine," Orion said shortly. "Father?"

The boy almost never called him that these days. Cain was momentarily startled, and it was visible to every person in the crowd that had gathered around Orion. "Yes?"

Orion looked up at him, and in the pale blue eyes Cain found no fear, no reaction to the death he had so narrowly avoided except for a certain drawn grimness that reminded Cain, for the very first time, of Loden Almandar.

"You have to drop the Shield, Father."

Cain glanced around at the watching crowd. Most of them were puzzled by Orion's comments, but there were at least a few of the engineers who clearly understood him and were watching Cain to see what he would do. Cain thought about the armed Warriors at his back. Trapped inside the Caverns on Cain's own territory, even with the power of the Light at his command, how long could Loga possibly last?

"The Shield came up again too quickly," said Orion patiently. "He didn't have time to get out after saving my life."

As if of its own accord Cain's hand came up and touched the stud in his collar. "Commander Captain Mielo."

"*Yes, my lord.*"

"Did you find out what caused the power supply to the Shield to fail?"

"*Yes, my lord. Pylon Eight's casing was opened from the side that sits outside the Shield, and something like laser fire was directed into it. The engineers say you're not supposed to be able to crack the casing without setting off all sorts of alarms; it looks as though whoever did this knew what he was doing.*"

"He did. Commander, drop the Shield for fifteen seconds, and then bring it back up again." Cain cut the connection and found himself ridiculously looking around the Mongers' Floor, as though Loga could conceivably have been fool enough to have secreted himself somewhere on that Level. He did not see the Light of Loga's passage, nor hear the crack of the rushing wind; but then the thoughts of his old friend, the feel of the thoughts so like his own, touched him as though they had not been enemies these eighty years.

Thanks, Cain. Much appreciated.

You're quite welcome. Thank you.

Any ti— The rising Shield cut the thought in half, and Cain dismissed the Ruler from his thoughts with a palpable effort. "Jimal, find out what happened to that catwalk." He raised his voice. "The

Workers who did this will wish they had never been born." It was not an empty threat, and the far edges of the crowd that had gathered to watch began fading away. Cain paid them no attention. He turned to Orion, who was watching the scene with eyes too grim and world-weary to belong to a sixteen-year-old boy. "Where's Doctor Denahi?" Cain scanned through the rows of Workers in vain.

"I don't think anybody called her," Orion said. He grinned shakily, but the grin was merely the movement of his lips, no more. "They were too worried about what they were going to do about Loga."

"Well, that's taken care of, isn't it? Come on," said Cain, "let me give you a hand."

The discussion, held late at night, was long and acrimonious; Orion was not entirely certain why he had been invited to it.

A sign of trust, perhaps?

There were some thirty Workers at the secret meeting, held in a tunnel that descended roughly sixty meters beneath the lowest depths of Level Four. About half of them were Warriors, the other half laborers; only one was an engineer. Orion was armed—he was always armed, these days—but even so, if he had not had Lisa and Bellows and Kennian with him, Orion thought he might have been somewhat worried (not afraid, no, never afraid), for the Workers were angry, and it showed. Orion had been the subject of one assassination attempt, and his left arm still ached occasionally where the bone had not knit properly; he was not anxious to submit himself to a second attempt.

". . . and not a word about youthbooster in eleven bleeding years. 'We're working on it,' he says, working on it and working on it— well, *he* ain't getting no older, is he? Wasn't that what we fought against the Rulers *for?*" The speaker, an older Warrior named Tolrin whom Orion knew only vaguely, continued, "I don't mind telling you lot, I'm not a young man any longer. They say as how youthbooster doesn't make you younger again, just keeps you from getting old—listen to my words, I don't want to be sixty when I get to stop aging. Living forever don't sound so bloody appetizing when you got to do it without no *teeth*, does it?"

There was a general murmur of agreement to Tolrin's statement. Unexpectedly, the lone engineer there spoke up. He spoke with the almost stilted correctness that bespoke high birth. "It is out of my division, and yet I know for a fact that Lord Cain donated six of his youthbooster tablets to research. I have heard, however, that duplicating them is harder than you might think. They are not chemical drugs, but are actually transform viruses, which are quite difficult to work with." The point hardly needed pounding home; an outbreak of transform fever the summer prior had killed nearly three hundred Workers, including two of the Warriors in Orion's own squadron.

Lisa's mother, the Warrior Irina, said suddenly, "Orion, how old are you?"

"Sixteen, Warrior."

"I think we can cease worrying about the youthbooster," said Irina simply. "If Cain's not telling the truth, then Orion will continue to age for another ten or fifteen years and then stop. I can wait that long to find out for sure. I doubt Cain'll let Orion die of old age."

Orion became aware of the group's attention shifting to him. He shrugged. "I believe him myself on that subject, and he's lied to me more than he'd bother to lie to any of you."

Irina smiled at Orion. She was an attractive woman, a bit sharper-featured than Lisa, a bit more worn down by time, but otherwise very similar. "You realize, Orion—you must—that the world you've grown up in is not the world that we've known. You've had the best of what Cain's had to offer you, the very best. I'm not saying that it's been terribly bad for us—there's a reason we get refugees here, and it's not because the Caverns are such a grim place to live—but it's not been as good as it could be either. We discussed you before you were invited to meet with us, you know. We remember what you've done for us over the years, beginning with the time you saved my fool of a husband from the consequences of his own stupidity and including the friendship you've shown us and our children. There were others who didn't feel we should trust you—including the man responsible for sabotaging the catwalk—and they've been taken care of."

" 'Taken care of'?" Orion smiled thinly. "You killed these people as a service to me?"

A Warrior whom Orion did not know said simply, "Yes. Those of us who are here are here because we trust you, and we no longer trust the Lord Cain. We're here because we're willing to follow you." The man paused and added directly, "My lord Orion."

Orion turned to Lisa, with an eyebrow lifted. The girl simply shrugged; she knew nothing of this. Orion nodded, accepting it, and turned back to the crowd. Brief as it was, the interplay had not gone unnoticed. Wondering what Cain was going to say to it all, Orion said flatly, "I accept your fealty. And if you will follow me, then I will tell you this: you can serve me best by continuing in your present places, but redoubling your efforts. You want to make things better for your-selves? Very good, that's admirable. I understand it. But before we can do anything for ourselves, we must be safe, and to be safe we must defeat the North Land." Orion took a deep breath; he was reaching them, he could feel it. He spoke. Watched his words striking them. "You've all heard how we'll attack the Giants in seven years; if you do as I say, work and work *hard*, that battle will come much, much sooner than you can possibly imagine."

"Not bad, Orion," said Kennian on their way back through the tunnel after the meeting. By a silent common agreement, they did not discuss the meeting they had just left, except for that one oblique comment. "I'm for bed," Kennian said a moment after that. "I've a watch to stand first thing in the morning and time on the Falcon simulator at midday."

"Not a bad idea, bed," said Bellows cheerfully. He and Lisa were holding hands, and Kennian snorted at the comment, and then split off from them at a cross-corridor without even saying good-bye. Bellows looked after him in surprise. "What's got into him?" he demanded of Orion.

Orion patted Bellows on one shoulder, consciously avoiding Lisa's eyes. "Used to be four of us, my friend. Now there's two of us and a couple. I guess he misses the way it used to be."

Bellows looked disturbed for a long moment. "What about you?"

Lisa echoed the question. "Yes, what about you?"

Orion hoped he kept the storm of conflicting emotions from his face, and thought he might even have succeeded. "I used to know that if I dealt fairly with all whom I met, then they would deal fairly with me. I used to know that Cain wanted something beyond simple power. I used to know that if I spoke my mind to my friends, we'd fight, but stay friends." His smile was melancholy. "Things change, don't they?"

Orion turned from them and walked away down the corridor, alone.

· 6 ·

They were playing a board game called chess in Cain's suite the following evening. Cain was winning—he always won—but with Cain, at least, Orion found no shame in that. The chamber was that which had once held the Ring; usually it was empty save for its rugs and the table that held Cain's various board games. Today there was something different, a computer workstation such as Orion had never seen anywhere else in the Caverns, a machine that radiated a tangible age. Orion knew from a comment Cain had made several years ago that it was one of the few pieces of technology Cain had actually judged worth taking with him when they abandoned Donnertown just before his return from Exile. Orion had never seen the machine before outside of his father's most private quarters, the fifth of the five rooms in which he lived. Until that night Orion had seen the machine only two or three times before at all.

Orion did not comment on the machine's presence, though he was sure it was there for some reason; if Cain wished him to know the reason, Cain would tell him, and if he did not, asking would be of little use.

Jimal served them as they played, milk and coffee for Cain, hot mulled wine for Orion. Cain's quarters were, to Orion's tastes, rather too cold; he kept his uniform jacket on as the game progressed.

". . . so they pledged you their fealty, and you took it?"

"Yes, sir." Orion moved a Warrior, and Cain took it en passant. Orion moved his Lady's Prelate in to take the Warrior that had taken his. He was playing more aggressively than usual tonight; though his Lord and Lady were still back behind the front row of Warriors, both of his Prelates and both of his Commanders were out in the field of battle.

"Will you tell me their names, Orion?"

"If you request it of me, sir." Orion studied the board carefully.

"Your game is off tonight, Orion." Cain castled and watched Orion study the board. "You directed them to increase their labors, but gave no specific time schedule for the attack upon the Giants you promised them?"

"No, sir, I did not."

Cain tasted his coffee and nodded. "This may not turn out badly at all." Orion looked up at him sharply, and Cain smiled. "What were you expecting?"

Orion said slowly, "I thought you might kill me, actually. Accepting an oath of fealty while you live is treason, isn't it?"

Cain chuckled. "Well, let's say that in your shoes I'd have done the same thing. Your choices weren't great, son, once you'd made the mistake of going without telling me. You could have shot your way out of there with your friends at your back and probably died in the attempt; you could have turned them down flat and waited to see if you were allowed to leave alive; or, you could have killed me yourself, in which case accepting their oaths wouldn't have been treason."

Suddenly it came again, that same bright, hard, joyless grin Cain was growing to find so disconcerting. "That, sir, had occurred to me already."

"Oh?" Cain sat very still for a long moment as the hard grin faded. "Orion," he said quietly, "you are at this moment the only person alive whom I am at all afraid of. You're also the only one whom I love." The words disconcerted Orion, and then Cain brought the black Lady's Prelate across the length of the board and, holding it by its tip, knocked Orion's Lord's Commander clean off the board. "Your Commander," he said quietly, "is down."

The Commander . . . is down. "Yes," said Orion vaguely, "he is, isn't he?" The board was suddenly hazy before him, and he had to shake his head to clear it. He looked up at his father, and Cain's face was vague, indistinct. Even the black eyes were fuzzy, without the clear sharp presence that usually imbued them. His skin felt flushed. "Excuse me," Orion said after a moment, "I'm . . . having difficulty focusing on this."

Cain waved a hand at him. "Forget the game. You're playing abominably anyhow." Cain leaned forward slightly. "Abominably, Orion."

Abominably? The word had associations for Orion, some flavor of youth and innocence that was gone from the world entirely these days. Cain was talking, and Orion had missed the first part of what his father had said to him. ". . . and the better you see those things, Orion, the better you develop that skill to see in the dark, the worse the Light, when it comes, burns your eyes. In Donnertown it was like that, trapped between the Glowing Desert and the barbarians; so I took in the barbarians and taught them and trained them until they became my hands. Donnertown changed me in ways I cannot even describe, taught me truths you cannot communicate to one who has not lived them. Donner Almandar, who left this world better than nine centuries before I was born, thought as I did, Orion; and I know this, for I have *been* Donner Almandar, and I have been Loga. You, Orion, are going to become me."

Orion became aware that his hands were shaking. It felt as though some restraint deep within him had suddenly snapped. "Father," he whispered, "I feel ill." Images flashed through his mind, strangely compelling, the man with the lance through him, back arched up away from the packed earth of the run; a woman beckoned him, a woman with short blonde hair and Orion's own pale blue eyes.

"You've been ill for a long time," Cain agreed, "and some of it's been my fault. Stand up." Cain helped him to his feet, though Orion almost fell and staggered once as Cain walked him to the computer workstation and seated him before it. "The contacts go so, here and here." Cain touched the contacts to Orion's forehead, and the metal contacts grew instantly, strangely warm.

· 7 ·

The world fell away from Orion, and the blistering cold of the nighttime desert took him.

It was late at night, and the stars blazed down on the Glowing Desert, unbearably bright. The air was extremely cold, and struck into Cain like a razor. At the guard post at the edge of Donnertown, before a bank of instruments that scanned the Glowing Desert, and northward from there to the home of the Rulers of Earth, Kavad looked up from his post. He nodded to Cain, and Cain raised a hand to the young barbarian and continued on.

He ignored the cold and walked across the landing field to the hangar. In the hangar he ignited the fusion generators and rode the lift down to the vault that held the youthbooster.

"Command," he said without raising his voice, "lights."

And the lights came on.

He made a slow circle, looking up and around at the vast-ness of his surroundings. The torches they had carried down into its depths over the course of the last five years had given him a hint, but only a hint.

He was in the largest artificial structure he had ever seen, a hangar so huge that Cain was not even certain whether the far wall was really there, or just that his eyes were insisting that it must be.

Cain brought his attention back down to the door before him. The pointboard was still there, and Cain had to fight down a strong urge to refrain from touching it. That pointboard was older than most of the Rulers, older than Parliament itself. Electric fire danced over his skin as he reached out for the pointboard. Be-cause he was not sure of any other way to do it, he said again, "Command, open."

The soft, inhuman voice said, "Please enter the password."

Cain's hands seemed very far away. A point at a time he struck the letters to shape the words that would give him the tools to bring a war home to the Rulers.

There could only be one answer. The words had been quoted twice in Donner's writings and underlined in Donner's book of religious writings:

Let there be Light.

It was dark.

Orion ripped the contact away from his skull and sat in the chair, gasping for breath as though he had just run ten kilometers. For an enduring instant it had seemed as though he had *been* his father. The room's glowpaint was extinguished. Orion sat breathing heavily, the sound of his laboring lungs harsh in his ears, and then suddenly, there in the gloom, stood Cain. Orion said through a dry mouth, "Father? What is this?"

"Truth." Cain was only a darker blackness in the chamber's murk. "A diary. A machine I found in Donnertown. Memories, Orion, the memories of seven different men and women, among them mine, and

Donner Almandar's, and those of the Ruler Loga when he was no older than myself."

"I thought . . . Father, for a moment I thought I was you."

"For a moment you were. You know, this should be interesting, seeing what happens to you when you've learned how I think."

The words were spoken in such a flat tone, with such an utter lack of inflection, that for the first time in his life Orion was, for just a moment, afraid of Cain. He was suddenly sharply aware of the acrid smell of his own sweat. "Father . . . you can't really be afraid of me. You brought me to this, there was a reason for it."

"You're learning, child." There was something in Cain's voice Orion could not identify. "I'm sorry, Orion. I really am."

"Sorry for what?"

Cain shook his head. In the dimness Orion could barely make out the movement. "I'm sorry for the times I've lied to you. More specifically, I can't tell you. But . . . perhaps you will remember that I said it."

"Father, I don't understand you."

Cain turned to leave, and stood indecisively in the doorway for just an instant before turning back.

"You're about to."

Hidden inside his church, Preacher Jack watched the pilgrim come in off the Glowing Desert.

He rode a horse, the pilgrim did, a big healthy black with a white star over its right eye, coming out of the desert on the eighth day after the new moon. The town the pilgrim rode into was an old one; some of the buildings were built of the feather-light, almost indestructible ferrocrete that no man today knew how to make. The rest of the buildings were adobe, less than a hundred years old, from the days when the old priest had given the sermons that kept the Church of Donner alive. Now the town was empty, except for Preacher Jack. Jack was almost certain that it was the eighth day; the old priest, before he died, had taught Jack to count all the way to ten. Sometimes these days Jack couldn't remember for sure whether six came before seven or after, but he was certain that it didn't matter once you got past them; eight was eight, and nine was nine, and ten was ten.

Straight enough, that.

Jack came out to meet the pilgrim himself. The old priest would never have done that, but the stream of pilgrims had pretty much dried up since the death of the priest, and Jack had gotten to where he enjoyed the odd pilgrim. Well, most of them. There'd only been one in several quarters now, and that one hadn't been pleasant, going on and on about the youthbooster, until Jack had been forced to kill him. Jack had never been able to find the priest's cache of youthbooster, the same cache that Saint Donner had left behind when he left Earth, and without the lure of it the pilgrims—or at least the pilgrims who were worth having—just weren't going to come.

He had pretty much reconciled himself to that.

Jack came out onto the porch in front of the church and called out to the pilgrim as the man led his horse toward the well in front of the church. "Hi there, pilgrim," he called out cheerfully. "Be welcome."

The pilgrim took a moment before replying, bringing the horse to a halt. He did not have the look of most pilgrims; a large man with black eyes and a grim set to his features that, along with the sight of the ken Selvren laser rifle tied down at the back of the saddle, made Jack uneasy enough to turn off the safety on the Westar laser strapped to his left wrist inside the flowing sleeves of his priest's robes. Jack was not good at guessing age; the pilgrim was perhaps twenty-five, he thought, perhaps somewhat older. Other things were out of the ordinary as well: the pilgrim's horse did not have the look of an animal that had been ridden across the Glowing Desert, and the pilgrim himself looked, impossible though it was, as though he had bathed recently. Though he was pale-skinned—perhaps the fairest-skinned man Jack had seen in his entire life if he did not count the ken Selvren, who sometimes came over the mountains—the desert sun did not seem to have touched him much. "Hello, old man," the pilgrim said finally. "May my horse and I drink from your well?"

Jack nodded. "Use the bucket by the side, and don't put it back down in the well after your horse drinks from it. Let it cook itself clean in the sun." The man dismounted and lowered the bucket into the well, brought up a single bucket. At first Jack was not sure his eyes were not fooling him, when the pilgrim's hand went down into the well, an orange rim of light seemed to follow it. The pilgrim pulled up the bucket and drank most of its contents and then lowered it again. Jack squinted more closely; the gleam remained.

Shivering slightly, Jack brought his hands back together before him in what he hoped looked like a priestly gesture and, under the cover of his robes, turned off the safety on the small automatic strapped to his right wrist.

The second bucket the man put down in front of his horse. He turned to face Jack and came right up to the porch of the church. "What's your name, old man?"

"I'm the Preacher Jack," said Jack with all the dignity he could muster.

"My name is Cain," said the pilgrim, speaking evenly but without apparent anger, "and in addition to the Shield I'm wearing impact armor; so, if you would, take your hands from your sleeves and bring out the laser and the handgun with them. And give them to me."

Jack stood frozen in place, grasping the Westar laser at his left wrist with his right hand, and the holy Smith & Wesson handgun with his left. He wasn't sure what "impact armor" was or how that was supposed to stop the impact of a properly blessed ferrocrete-jacketed slug from scrambling a man's insides. . . .

The pilgrim who called himself Cain was . . . looking at him. A single drop of sweat was trickling down the pilgrims' temple, but otherwise he seemed calm, almost unconcerned. Aside from the laser rifle, which was still with the horse, he carried no weapons Jack could see.

"Give me the weapons," the pilgrim repeated, with a strange intensity. The pilgrim's eyes never left Jack's, and he was beginning to tremble.

"I can't . . . my hands have gone to sleep," Jack whispered. The pilgrim came up the steps swiftly, pulled Jack's hands apart, and relieved him of his weapons.

So did Cain of Eastmarch take Donnertown.

It was in the days of the Reconstruction that Donner left Earth and took most of T'Pau's People with him. His attempts to convince Loga to join them were many. One night they stood together, two days into what became a week-long drunk, overlooking the Mojave Spaceport Donner had commissioned the workers to build for him. "Damn it, Loga, where's the challenge left here? We could freeze the ice caps again, we've the skill to do it, though my thought is that the Giants would have little liking for such a plan. But did we do so, reclaim the land that lies now beneath meters of water, cleanse the radioactive poisons from the world, slay the mutants and the monsters that have arisen in the world, in which the all of it there is no challenge for the likes of us, still this world would not be what it once was. Too many of the old species have passed away and will not return. It is in my heart that our days on this planet are not many."

Loga shrugged. "Your days, perhaps." He paused. "Where will you go?"

"We'll fare forth, explore . . . conquer. What better destiny for men? For despite Loden's propaganda, we're hardly gods, at least yet." Donner stood at the edge of the balcony, the large, competent hands gripping the steel in frustration. "And I confess, I think this business of playing the god—of nursing the damn barbarians on their way to civilization—damn it, Loga," he exploded suddenly, "it's a bad idea. We'll but make them into a mirror of ourselves and tear down their strengths with nothing to give them to balance the loss. We've strengths of our own, yes, but our strengths are not theirs." He was silent for a moment, then added, "And lacking as we do T'Pau's skill at genegineering, giving our strengths to them becomes rather a moot point."

Loga moved restlessly across the balcony, looking out over the great fields where actinic sparks of light flew away from scenes of construction. Too many things at once, the redhead thought. The starships in orbit were only half done, and here on Earth Donner was squandering vast resources in his drive to complete them—and as many extra as might turn out to be necessary to accommodate as many of T'Pau's People as cared to join them.

Loga did not doubt that Donner would complete his fleet of starships and, as Donner put it often and loudly, fare forth, explore, and conquer.

Donner Almandar was the first, and still the best friend Loga had ever had; still he could not find words within himself to describe for Donner how boring it all sounded.

Orion did not knock, entering Cain's quarters. Cain was seated cross-legged before the breakfast table, reading a sheaf of reports as he ate.

"Cain?"

Cain took one look at Orion and said quietly, "Jimal, leave us." The silver-eyes bowed slightly, picked up Cain's half-finished breakfast tray, and left with it.

Cain did not rise. "Good morning, Orion."

The boy took two steps forward. His voice was trembling. "The machine—your memories were not all there."

"Nor were Donner Almandar's, you will note. A wise man does not expose himself in that fashion. There will always, Orion, be things I will not wish you to know."

Orion's chin quivered as though he was going to cry, but he did not. "You've lied to me."

"Aye. Constantly. What's new about that?"

The boy blurted the words. "Who am I?"

Cain's face went very still. "You are my son." The dark eyes held Orion. "Is that not enough?"

"You told Commander Captain Solan you could not sire children, that they would be monsters." The words came in a rush. "And I have been so blind, never to have seen that a man of your coloring could not have sired a son with mine. Damn you, Cain, *who am I?*"

Cain looked away from the boy, toward the sunsilk hanging of the Glowing Desert, and sat for a moment watching it, motionless. "Your mother was Rea Veramorn. She was the adopted daughter of Maston Veramorn. Her true father was Loden Almandar. Your father was a man named Solan who was a Commander in the service of Maston Veramorn; if you have been in my memories, you will have seen something of the sort of man he was."

Cain heard the desperation in the boy's voice. "You've lied to me and lied to me and *lied* to me! Why should I believe you now?"

"Orion?"

"*What?*"

The word was only the merest whisper; nonetheless it reverberated through the empty chamber like a shout. "Remember." Cain turned slowly and saw Orion standing frozen in shock. He repeated the word once.

"*Remember.*"

Orion took a stumbling step backward and then another, staring at Cain with utter horror.

He turned and ran.

"Lord Cain?"

The outspeaker blared suddenly, interrupting the smooth procession of Cain's thoughts.

"*The word you are looking for,*" Loukas had said, so very softly, "*is guilt.*"

"Yes?"

"My lord, this is Commander Captain Peralt, Flight Commander on duty. Commander First Orion is demanding that a Falcon be released to him. He's not scheduled for flight time. He seems—disturbed, my lord."

"Hold him," said Cain with instant decision. "I'll be up shortly."

He was standing there in his flight suit when Cain reached the shipyard, standing patiently but with something burning sharp in the deceptively innocent blue eyes.

"Where are you going, Orion?"

For the first time the boy no longer seemed a boy to Cain. The person standing before him at the edge of the shipyard, the rows of slipships and Falcons at his back, was a man, holding himself with iron self-control. "Does it matter? I'll be back."

"Where?"

"I don't know yet!" Orion shouted at him. There was not a person in the shipyard but had found some excellent task to be engaged in at that moment, except for the unfortunate Flight Commander, standing at rigid attention, features utterly drained of blood. "Damn you, let me go!"

Cain did not look away. "Surely." He could not recall having felt so strange in many years. "Flight Commander, drop the Shield at his command."

Orion turned without replying and strode out to where his slipship waited.

Cain said so softly that no one heard the words but himself, "Let him go."

He took the slipship west. He broke through the sound barrier while crossing Almandar and soared past Eagles within minutes after that. He was hailed by silver-eyes craft once and did not even bother to reply, but climbed until their ships broke pursuit and turned back.

Orion chased the sun across the world, tears streaming down his cheeks, crying for his dead father Solan, looking for the green flash that comes in the millisecond before the sun blows out.

Cain sat that night out on the catwalk at the top of the dome in Cavern Three, within earshot of the Mongers' Floor, listening all night to the quiet murmur of the machines.

The Ring

The Year 1299 After the Fire

· 1 ·

Cain dreamed.

In his dream, the water rose and covered him, and in the depths of that water he drowned.

The morning of Winter 8, 1299, dawned cold and clear and brilliant.

On that day, Cain observed his one hundred and twelfth birthday.

On that day Cain arose out of a dream of his own death.

He slept alone, and he had slept nearly all his life, without a wife, without a companion. Sitting up in bed, alone in the darkness, there was no one to hear his words but himself.

They were dead on schedule. "The time is here," he whispered aloud.

In the decade and a half since Cain of Eastmarch's taking of the child Orion, Maston Veramorn had grown old.

He felt it most in the mornings, when he must rise from the warmth of his bed, and his bones ached. As a young man it had worried him that he would, as he aged, lose his teeth and his hair, that wrinkles and liver spots would cover him. Now he chided himself for those small fears; they were, he had come to learn, only the smallest and least significant part of growing old. The cold cut him more deeply than it had in his youth, and his blood took longer to get moving. He could not move so fast as he once had, nor work so long nor so hard. Emotionally he found himself changing as well. He clung to Commander Colonel Tristan these days with a sort of palpable desperation. Tristan was surely the only living human being whom Maston held any faith in, and Tristan's immediate subordinate, Captain Bordine, was gunning for Maston's position. Bordine reminded Maston of himself as a young man. Maston knew he should have Bordine assassinated, and it was the final proof of his growing age that he did not quite hazard to order the assassination made.

He was entirely uncertain as to which of them would survive the attempt.

His forces now kept Parliament, rather than Eagles; it was closer to the mines at Goldriver, the mines from which Maston Veramorn had, every year since 1284, sent a full three quarters of the mine's production of gold and platinum to the territories of Eastmarch. They had never even attempted to cheat on the count; Maston had not dared.

In the fully fourteen and a half years following the disastrous assassination of Captain Solan, Maston had never once spoken to Cain. Far too late, when faced with, in Bordine, the sort of viper he had imagined Solan to be, Maston Veramorn came to understand his mistake, and almost to regret it. Bordine was not as charismatic as the still-remembered Solan, not quite, but he was more cynical and far more ruthless.

Had Solan still been alive, Maston was sure, the likes of Bordine would have, of necessity, remained eclipsed by the man's sheer brilliance at everything he had ever turned his hand to. So he was the Ruler Loden's son, or so mad Riabel had claimed; it hardly mattered. In Solan there had been a real loyalty, though strained at times; he might have quit Maston's service, but he would never have led a coup.

Perhaps it was coincidence, and perhaps not; Maston thought about the events of 1284 rather often, and with a regret that mounted with the passing of years.

Perhaps it was coincidence, and perhaps not; Maston was not in deep remembrance on the evening of Winter 9, 1299, when the messenger from Eastmarch touched down in an old slipship at the private landpad Maston'd had built outside his home, the estate that had once belonged to Loden Almandar.

The messenger was a woman, a Captain Mielo, who wore the severe black uniform of an Eastmarch Warrior as though she had been born to it. Among Maston Veramorn's green-clad Warriors, the sternness of her dress and demeanor stood out sharply. He kept her waiting while he checked whether she had come in one of the new Falcon-class slipships Eastmarch was building; Maston desperately wished to have the opportunity to tear one of those new vessels apart.

She had not, he was informed; the craft Mielo had come in was a slipship that looked to be some twenty years old. Maston took the information without outward sign of displeasure and bade them send the woman in to him.

When he finally received her, he did so with no one but Tristan in attendance.

The chamber in which Maston Veramorn received her was designed to intimidate, and did so most of the time. Maston sat in a large chair just to the right of a panoramic window that looked down over the city of Parliament and past the circle of Parliament to the Valley beyond and below. The view, though not as stunning as the view from the Chambers further up the mountain, was sufficiently impressive for one who had never seen better. The deep white carpet was lush enough to muffle footsteps, and there was some sort of soundproofing in the walls which Maston's engineers had not been able to duplicate yet, and might never. The total effect was to shut down most of the senses a Warrior lived by and dazzle his eyes at the same time.

The chair to which Captain Mielo was shown was extremely soft, so that the woman had difficulty keeping her spine straight, and was subtly but distinctly lower than Maston's own.

With all the advantages Maston Veramorn had engineered for himself in that interview, he found himself lost almost instantly.

Captain Mielo wasted no time whatsoever. She refused, politely, offers of food and drink. "Lord Cain," she said flatly, "desires your aid in making war upon the North Land."

The week following Cain's hundred and twelfth birthday, Orion felt as though he had been born again. Most of that week he spent working in the saddle, under open if often snowing skies, riding through Eastmarch territories with Kennian. Orion rode a vicious gray which fought him for two solid days before submitting to his will. The horse had been sired by a big gray Orion had occasionally ridden as a teenager, and it had inherited its sire's speed and endurance. The temperament must have come from its dam, for Orion could not recall the old gray having been so hostile. He'd actually named the brute at last— Kurda, from the name of a bad-tempered species of grayish-white hawk common in Eagles—despite his wish to refrain from growing emotionally attached to an animal that he could not care for as a horse's owner should.

The work was tedious and cold, and at times frustrating, for there was no way for them to tell the Workers of the territory exactly what was going to happen, or when; but Orion thought the warnings they gave were clear enough.

"When you receive the warning," was the message Orion and Kennian gave at steading after steading, house after house, "you'll seek high ground. You won't get much warning, for the Giants will be watching the Valley with their observation satellites, and if there's any significant movement before the warning is given, it'll be a tip-off to them." Some of the folk they gave that message to shrugged it off, and for them there was nothing Orion or Kennian could do. If the Giants nuked the Great Dam, as Cain expected they would when they were attacked, most of Eastmarch territory except for the hills, everything that was actually within sight of the Great Dam, was going to end up under eight meters of water.

They worked their way up and down the length of the Traveler's Road, from Eastmarch to Saerlock and back again. Other messengers covered the territories that were too far south from the Traveler's Road for their route to cover.

The only thing north of the Traveler's Road, along its entire length from Singer to Eastmarch, was the Great Dam itself.

Still other messengers covered the territories between Singer and Saerlock. Towns to the west of Singer they did not warn, and had no plans to. Orion detested the logic behind that, but could find no flaws in Cain's reasoning: warning Eastmarch territory, where Cain was reasonably certain they knew every Giant spy, was safe enough. The same warning in those territories that Eastmarch did *not* control—the length of Almandar except for Singer itself, most of the central Valley, and everything west of Singer on the Traveler's Road—would be suicide.

They slept at night in the open, camping at the edge of the Traveler's Road, taking turns at the watch they kept. The watch was probably not necessary; the Traveler's Road, where it passed through Eastmarch territory, was far safer than it had been at any time since Cain's birth. The stability of Cain's rule, these last twenty-five years (forty-five if one counted the time of the Twenty Years' War) had counted for something.

It was an odd journey for Orion. Though he had never been to Saerlock before at all, and only a few times to Telindel, strange flashes of memory struck him, memory that came not from experience, but from Cain's life.

He scared Kennian half to death at least once. They were riding back to Eastmarch, to the Caverns, after completing their assigned route, and Kennian was singing him, as Kennian put it, "a classic Semalian ballad written after the rebellion at Erebion."

At the song's conclusion, Kennian paused. "Hate to say it, but there's a verse missing here my great-grandmother didn't know. It's been lost a good while—"

He broke off in midword: Orion was singing, an even tenor holding the tune of the song more perfectly than Kennian had ever heard him sing a song before, as though some true musician sang through Orion's throat.

Say I don't look like what I look like
Say I don't sing like what I do
Did you think I didn't know that
Know my own guitar was through?

Tell me what it is you want
What it is you want from me
Tell me what it is
And I will tell you
What I think that it can be

"Two verses missing, actually," said Orion when he finished, grinning. "You need to practice up on your Semalian history a bit, No-Name."

"Where did you hear those verses?" Kennian demanded.

"Loukas sang me that song a dozen times when I was a boy," Orion said absently, and rode on without thinking about the comment. It did not strike him what he'd said until he realized that Kennian was not at his side and turned back to find his friend staring at him, plainly frightened. Orion tried to pass it off as a joke and claim the verses for his own, but Kennian did not believe him, and Orion did not blame him.

He wouldn't have believed it either.

They neared the Caverns late on the afternoon of Winter 16, a TwosDay. There was snow slush on the Traveler's Road, but the sky itself was an aching clear cobalt blue, and the sun's warmth was such that Orion had thrown back the hood on the parka he had been wearing.

They stopped at the North Gate and waited while the Gate was widened to let them through, then rode on in. They rode to where their horses were stabled at the edge of the landpad. It was one of the limited aboveground buildings that the Caverns boasted, a single long barn where the few horses the Caverns needed were kept. The kennels were there also, and bays for pigs and cattle destined for the dinner tables in the Caverns. The kennel master spotted them riding in and called out for them to come by the kennels before they went below.

Orion left Kurda with the stable boy, Kennian did the same with his own mount, and together they went down to the kennels. Orion saw immediately what the kennel master had called them over for; the pregnant bitch had given birth while Orion was on the road, and there were four puppies, still almost blind, in the pen with her. Orion picked up one of the puppies carefully; a male, it was the only one that was even on its feet, wandering with wobbly legs around the small confines of the pen. The kennel master grinned at Orion, obviously pleased with the animals. "Will that be the one, Cap'n?" (Though the title was in fact correct and had been for most of a year, Orion suspected the man did not know it; the kennel master called everybody that—even Commander General Dantes—except for Cain, who was "My lord.")

"I think so," said Orion, holding the squirming pup up to look it in the eye. Pinch the Second had sired the pup's mother in his last year of life before old age had taken him, and this puppy resembled him closely enough. Orion scratched the puppy just above the eyes, smiling. "Yes, of course, Pinch. Call him so when you train him; I want him to know his name."

"Orion!"

Orion's expression did not change, did not so much as flicker. He handed the puppy to Kennian and turned to face Cain. "Sir?"

Cain was dressed formally, in a shining ebony Eastmarch uniform without insignia. Orion could not recall ever having seen it on Cain before in real life, and not otherwise except in the sunsilk hanging that portrayed the signing of the Treaty of Eastmarch. "They told me you'd ridden in. We're due to meet with Maston, Orion, tomorrow if possible. How soon can you be ready to travel to . . ." Cain broke off and lifted an inquiring eyebrow. "Is something wrong, Orion?"

Orion had not realized he was staring. "Sir . . ." He laughed suddenly. "I've never seen you in the dress uniform of a Warrior before. It . . . suits you."

"I take it that's a compliment?" Cain did not wait for an answer to that question, but continued. "Leave the dog, if you can tear yourself from it, we need to talk a bit. First Temera, you're welcome to join us."

Orion outlined their travels as they took the lift down into the depths of the Caverns. They used Cain's private lift. It let them out in the corridor immediately outside Cain's quarters, with only a pair of silver-eyes to get by before they were actually inside. Cain sent Jimal out for undress uniforms for both Orion and Kennian, and quizzed Orion while Kennian showered and changed, then did the same to Kennian while Orion cleaned the grime of the road from himself.

When both of them were clean and fed, Cain outlined his plans for the following day. "Maston's balking somewhat, unfortunately. Bombing the North Land, as he's pointed out, is hardly a productive plan of attack while they've got their Shield up, and he doesn't believe me when I tell him we've a Falcon-class ship that can make it through the Shield protecting the North Land. So we're going to show him. The largest Shield he's got is the one protecting his own estate—not much, but it'll drive the point home when you go through it."

"Wait, wait." Orion put down the glass of mulled wine he was using to warm his insides with. "You've lost me, sir. My ship's not ready to fly?"

"Of course it's ready."

"Sir . . . the engineers had barely finished the penetration device when I left. It's only been a week."

Cain said mildly, "They worked day and night, quite hard. It got done."

"Day and night?" Orion blinked; the engineers were legendary for their pigheadedness, even with Cain. "I have difficulty picturing the engineers doing that willingly."

"Willingly?" Cain said gently, "Orion, we're preparing for a war. They've had good treatment for so long they've forgotten somewhat that they exist to serve Eastmarch and not the other way round. I worked the engineers until they complained and then I had one shot. It got done."

Orion swallowed the last of his wine. "I believe you," he said rather blankly. "So my ship's ready, the squadrons are ready, we've prepared folk to evacuate if the Great Dam gets nuked. What's left?"

Cain shrugged. "Say good-bye to the Caverns. If the Great Dam goes, you'll never see it again. Take whatever you think is important with you when we go to Parliament; the odds are excellent we'll never be back."

"That's it?"

"Essentially."

"And we attack when?"

"Dawn on the twenty-second."

Kennian choked on his coffee. Even Orion stared. "You're joking."

Cain shook his head. "No. Now that we're committed, we're going to move fast. The Giants aren't expecting us right now; we give them another week and they will be. Would you like to see the ship, Orion?"

"My lord," said Kennian almost warily, "you know, I'm sure, that you're considered somewhat too cautious by many of your Warriors."

"First Temera," said Cain, "there is a time for caution and a time for action. The man who mistakes his time is a fool, and a short-lived one. It has been twenty-five years since Eastmarch last went to war, and it may be that our Warriors have in some measure forgotten how it is done. I am," he said evenly, "about to remind them. Gentlemen?"

The craft sat in the center of the shipyard. It was unlike any other ship Orion had ever seen. Every other slipship was black, for night work, or else brown on top with a sky-blue belly for day work.

This ship literally took Orion's breath away. A brilliant, mirror-silver sheen covered the craft's surface, to reflect away as much laser fire as possible. It made the craft easy to spot from a great distance, but that hardly mattered. If things went as planned, Orion would be flying it *inside* the Shield covering the North Land. It didn't matter much, in that instance, how the damn thing was painted, Orion thought to himself; he intended to be very hard to ignore.

There were other significant differences between this craft and a normal Falcon-class slipship. The wings were swept back further, to allow the craft to reach higher speeds than a normal slipship. It was shaped more like a needle than a standard slipship, though its tail was notably more bulbous. The thrusters were forty percent larger than normal thrusters, and there was a corresponding increase in the number of fusion cells driving them. There were trade-offs, of course, for the greater speed; the ship had no room for lasers, and only a pair of fusion-tipped missiles destined for what Eastmarch's spies had determined was the power supply for the North Land's Shield.

There were hooks driven into the silver skin of the slipship, where the superconductor skin would be attached. Orion looked a question at Cain, gesturing to the hook he was touching, and Cain shook his head. "The penetration sleeve was completed at one of the orbital factories. We could have brought it down, but it seemed just as easy to send the ship up to get it."

Orion raised an eyebrow. "Penetration sleeve?"

Cain glanced over at Orion and withdrew his hand from the shining silver hull. "It's what it is, Orion. Is there a problem with the name?"

Orion glanced over at Kennian, who was having difficulty keeping a straight face. "The name seems a bit—suggestive, sir."

Cain actually chuckled at that. "For all of me," he said mildly, "they can call it the Eastmarch Love Glove—and some of the engineers have been—as long as it works."

Finally Orion took a step back from the craft and simply stood, looking at it. Though there was perhaps no one in the world except Orion himself who would have caught it, Orion saw Cain watching him, taking his own very distinct pleasure from Orion's. "I like the ship, sir," he said at last.

Cain said with perfect seriousness, "I thought you might."

"Well, when do I get to test it?"

"Save the show for Maston. Tomorrow's soon enough."

Orion nodded. "What's the mood like among the Workers? Do they know yet how soon we'll attack?"

"No."

"May I tell them?"

Orion saw Cain considering the question, and finally Cain's features relaxed into a gentle smile. "Certainly. I see no harm in it now. If there are any Giant spies left alive in the Caverns, I've been negligent."

"Thank you," said Orion simply. "They've been waiting for a long time."

They stood at the edge of what had once been Loden Almandar's estate watching the sky. Earlier that day it had snowed, but just past midday it had ceased, and though the skies were slate-gray, the weather looked unlikely to worsen.

There were some thirty of them all told waiting at the edge of the landpad, Eastmarchers and Maston Veramorn's men alike. Perhaps they could not properly be called *Eagles* Warriors any longer—not since their industrial base and mainstay of their striking forces had moved to Parliament. Maston himself had not even visited Eagles in over two years.

A thin and almost invisible orange haze colored the sky above them.

"The science is actually quite old," Cain said conversationally. "I'm surprised the Giants haven't thought of this already. A Shield is

essentially a quark discontinuity that produces an intense, highly local-
ized magnetic field at the atomic level. That's why it works so much
better against metal than against flesh—all those free electrons." Cain
grinned at Maston, who was not following the explanation, and at
Commander Colonel Tristan, who was, and carefully. "Superconductors, on the other hand, are perfectly diamagnetic; they've known that
since before the Fire. A superconductor sheath, Maston, produces an
equal and opposite reaction to any impinging magnetic field." The grin
grew quite wide. "We put a laser inside a small bag woven of superconductor cloth and tossed it through the Eastmarch Shield while the
Shield was running at full power. The laser still worked when it came
through the other side. Empirical research, you know. We do a lot of
that in Eastmarch."

There were a pair of outspeakers set up at the edge of the field;
they came to life suddenly. "Commander Captain Orion here. I'm in
orbit, linking up with the penetration sleeve. Give me twenty minutes
and I'll be downstairs."

Tristan d'Volta moved closer to Cain and said privately, "He's
starting his run from orbit? Is that safe? Do Falcon-class craft really
have that sort of range? Reliably, I mean?"

Cain said dryly, without even looking at Tristan, "Low orbit, in
this instance, but because the engineers took the sheath into low orbit
to save us time, not because the ship couldn't make geosynchronous
orbit. Yes, it's safe. You'd be amazed at a Falcon class's range; I doubt
you'd believe me if I told you what it is. They are quite reliable." He
half turned to face the man. "Is there anything else I can tell you,
Commander Colonel?"

Tristan was surprised to find himself flushing; he was better than
forty years old, and even Maston was unable to do that to him these
days. "No," he said shortly, and retreated back to the company of his
fellows.

They waited, and before the time Orion had promised them had
quite elapsed they saw the distant glimmer of the modified silver Falcon. The ship grew swiftly, and the boom as it dropped below the speed
of sound reminded Tristan eerily of the sound a Ruler made, appearing
out of the Light. More than one Warrior, even among the Eastmarchers, cried out as the slipship scooped air and dropped like a stone
straight toward the Shield. A slight insubstantiality around its edges was

the only visible sign of the superconductor sheath that made the maneuver anything other than a particularly elaborate form of suicide. The ship's belly jets cut in as it sliced through the Shield, and the ship finally came to a halt hovering on belly jets less than half a meter above the ragged ground of the landpad.

Orion's voice issued from the outspeakers. "We don't recommend that anyone but properly trained Eastmarcher Warriors try this. It's harder than it looks." The ship walked around its axis, slowly, until Orion, looking out through the canopy, met Cain's eyes. Orion grinned at Cain, flashed them all a thumbs-up sign, hit the nose jets, stood the ship on its tail, and took the craft straight back up through the Shield.

It was gone within instants, with no trace that it had ever been there except the expressions, grim and stupefied all at the same moment, of Maston Veramorn's Warriors. Where the ship had balanced for a moment on its tail, the thrusters had fused the ground into glass.

Cain passed by Commander Colonel Tristan on his way off the field. Tristan was staring at the spot where, a moment before, Orion had been sitting in his slipship. It was probably, Tristan thought, his imagination, but even through the canopy, from thirty meters' distance, the man had looked the very image of his father.

"Well, Tristan," Cain said politely, "any worries now?"

The ships from Eastmarch, iced down before their flights to present the smallest possible infrared signature to the Giant observation satellites, landed one by one all that night.

Though none of them had looked forward to it, eventually it was inevitable. The morning of the day before the attack on the Giants, Winter 21, Cain and Maston and Orion and Tristan met privately.

They met in Maston's War Room, better than an hour before the debriefing of the general forces was to take place. Cain was sourly amused to find that the building that had been set aside for the purpose had once been a part of the Academy.

It was a "private" meeting, meaning that there were three of Maston's retainers present to serve refreshments if anybody required any and that both Maston and Cain had brought their bodyguards along with them.

Even with the holos their spies had brought them over the course of the years, Maston was not prepared for the shock of adrenaline that ran through his system when Cain and Orion finally joined them. It was like seeing a ghost; for several seconds Maston simply could not get over it. Tristan was staring at the young man in disbelief. There was a brief and very awkward moment before Orion, after glancing at Cain, came forward to where Maston and Tristan were seated. The two men came to their feet, and Orion said, without any hint of uncertainty, "Maston Lord of Eagles and its territories; Commander Colonel; I am honored to make your acquaintances." Tristan reflexively reached forth and clasped the forearm Orion offered him, and Orion grinned suddenly. "Again. Do you know, I remember you, Tristan? You sat with me on occasion when my parents were occupied."

Tristan said softly, "By the Light, do you know how you resemble him?"

Orion nodded easily and removed his arm from Tristan's almost painful grip. "You are, I think, the seventh Eagles Warrior to comment on it." He turned then to the old man who was, it seemed, Maston Veramorn, and said rather more formally, "And of course I remember you as well, Lord Maston. I could," he said with mild understatement, "hardly have forgotten."

"I don't trust you, Cain," said Maston Veramorn flatly. "My Warriors don't trust you. You can use Parliament as a staging area—because I can't stop you—but our forces will not work together."

Cain nodded. "I hardly thought they would. As long as your forces don't get in my way, that's fine."

Maston nodded jerkily. He was, Orion saw, nervous about even being in the same room with Cain. *Or could it possibly be me?* Orion wondered.

"Very well, then," Maston said. "There are two rumors I would like to question you about. Our spies in the North Land have verified that in late 1284 you struck the seas around the North Land with three meteors. Why aren't you prepared to do this again and save yourself some of your resources, and us the chance of being destroyed by the Giants after your failure?"

Cain shrugged. "We sent up a suicide team to the moon in 1280 and had them plant a mass driver on its surface. They died there; we had at that time insufficient skill to return them safely. The 'meteors' were simply chunks of rock with iron bands around them so that the mass driver could grab them. We only ever had three; the mass driver was intended for use against Parliament, not the Giants. Three such missiles would have destroyed Parliament even if they'd installed the sort of antimissile defenses that protect the North Land. When we found ourselves in the position where we had to have a credible weapon against the Giants, that was all we had. We used it and then bluffed them that we had more missiles available to continue to use it. We didn't and we don't, but they bought the bluff."

Maston was nodding slowly. Tristan said suddenly, "Perhaps in 1280 you did not have skill to resupply that mass driver. Today that is not the case. Why don't you?"

Orion answered him. "We'd love to, Commander Colonel—but the Giants are watching the moon very carefully. If you will only show us how to send a craft to the moon without betraying the position of the mass driver to the Giants, we will do so in the very instant."

"It makes sense," Maston agreed, "clear-cut sense, until I add in another datum. Cain, I am told the Giants have the Ring."

Orion was certain that he let nothing show on his own face. Cain made an appearance of nodding reluctantly. "I've had that report myself. If true, it's unfortunate. I expect the Ring will perish in the attack."

"Attacking the Giants with this mass driver of yours," said Maston, "would destroy the Ring for sure."

Cain smiled. "If," he said softly, "I had the missiles to send against them. Unfortunately, I don't." Cain changed the subject in a way he knew was sure to disconcert Maston. "This Bordine who's been scaring you—would you like me to kill him for you?"

The general briefing went smoothly; Cain had not expected otherwise. The briefing was largely for the benefit of Maston's Warriors. Though they would not be involved in the attack except in support positions, there was powerful interest on their part about the details of how the attack would be waged.

If the attack failed, there was little question but that the stronghold at Parliament would fall, perhaps within as little as a few weeks. The Giants did not field slipships of the sort that the Workers had built; they massed too much to fly such craft. Unfortunately with their skill at cybernetics the Giants hardly needed to risk their own lives in battle; they possessed small, robot-controlled fighter craft that were very nearly the equal of a single slipship of traditional design. Even a Falcon would be hard-pressed to handle more than two of them at any given time—and the Giants had such vehicles by the tens of thousands.

"In a drawn-out battle," said Cain, "we don't stand a chance. So we're not going to have a drawn-out battle. Period. Most of the Giant defenses are planned around their Shield; if the Shield goes down, we can concentrate on bombarding their communication centers. We don't know, unfortunately, the exact nodes that process the control signals for the drone slipships. So we're going to hit everything. Their perimeter defenses are formidable, but we can handle those; we'll hit the perimeter while Orion penetrates their Shield, and hopefully we'll create some confusion that will aid Orion in knocking out the Shield's power supply. Once the Shield goes down—well, they've built over the centuries in a fashion very like the Caverns; most of their building has been done underground, because of the temperatures aboveground. If we can open up any of their underground passageways to the One Ocean, I'll count it an added bonus."

"What about the Workers left at the Caverns?" demanded one of Maston's Commanders. Orion recognized him as the Captain Bordine who was, Cain told him, giving Maston nightmares these days. "Flying iced slipships out of there under cover of night is one thing; evacuating seventy or eighty thousand Workers is another entirely."

Cain shrugged. "I'm letting them evacuate just before we begin our attack."

Bordine said clearly, voice pitched to carry across the War Room, "That might alert the Giants."

Orion stood slowly and waited until all eyes were upon him. "I hardly care whether it does or not. You've more faith in our counter-intelligence efforts than I do if you think the Giants don't have some vague idea about what's happening already. Hopefully they're off balance enough that they're not actually expecting an attack tomorrow morning, but I wouldn't even count on that. We're *going* to evacuate." He paused, let the words sink in, and added, "It will be well timed."

There was a moment's silence, and then the briefing moved on to cover other subjects.

Maston and Tristan d'Volta spoke quietly together while Eastmarch's General Dantes held the center stage.

"Did you see the way he talked to them?" Maston knew Tristan was not referring to Cain. "Even Bordine knew better than to push the point. Our own Warriors," Tristan whispered, "were hanging on his words."

"Solan's son," said Maston flatly. "I'd be careful, if I were you. He can't bear you much goodwill."

Tristan d'Volta nodded slowly. "The way Solan died . . ." His voice held a trace of roughness. "He must know that was a mistake."

Maston looked across the room to where Solan's son and Cain's pupil sat, observing the proceedings with an attentiveness that was eerily reminiscent of Commander Captain Solan and with an occasional cynical smile that was pure Cain. "An accident, surely," said Maston. "Do you think that's what Cain's told him?"

The woman sat alone in the dark.

She did not know it was dark, for she was blind.

There was one window in the cell Rea Veramorn had been imprisoned in all these years. It faced east, so that, in the mornings, for a brief while, the bright warm sunlight flooded in upon her. By noon the cell had grown cold, and by afternoon it was usually quite chill.

Rea had difficulty, at times, remembering that her life had ever been any different at all. This dark cell, with its hard bed and the single chair beside it, had been all her world for a very, very long time. She did not know what year it was for sure; she thought at times that it might be 1300 already, for all anyone ever spoke to her. Her two guards did not even seem to be aware she existed. When they let Farina—who brought her meals to her—through and then let her leave again, this was the only time Rea heard them speak at all; the rest of the time they were silent.

At times Maston himself came to see her—to question her about the Light, about her dreams, about her son. Upon those occasions Rea feigned madness, calling him Father and babbling unceasingly about Solan and Orion. In the early years that had seemed to put him off, and eventually he had gone away again. Of late when he visited her, she could hear the occasional quaver in his voice, as he rattled on about a Commander Captain Bordine or sometimes Cain. Apparently the years of feigned madness had convinced him; he did not seem to expect a response from her, and did not get one.

At times during those years she *was* mad, at least somewhat, drifting in the memories of brighter times, of the days when the sun was something more than a simple warmth upon her skin. It was not a great madness, more something she allowed herself than something she could not prevent. If that child, Senta, had spoken to her truly all those years ago, that the Tribunal Elder Loden was in truth her father—and with the passage of time Rea had come to believe that Senta had, indeed, spoken as truly as it was in her to do so—then it was probably, Rea thought, that she could not go truly mad. T'Pau Almandar's skill at genetic engineering was legendary even among the Workers with whom she had been raised.

Rea had a servant, of sorts, during those years of imprisonment. At first Maston had planned to kill Farina, but in the end did not—if only because she was so patently harmless. After he had ascertained that she could neither read nor write, he had her tongue cut out and gave her to Rea as a servant.

On the evening before the very last day of her imprisonment, Rea had a dream of a great darkness, and in the darkness a golden radiance came and touched her briefly. The voices in the light murmured words to her that she did not entirely understand. She woke the next morning as clearheaded as she had been at any time since her blinding.

On that, the very last day of her imprisonment, Maston Veramorn came to see her again. He was clearly disturbed; though he did not speak to Rea as one might to another individual, the picture came clear slowly nonetheless.

Cain had come to Parliament, preparatory to waging war upon the Giants.

Orion was with him.

Cain and Orion took their dinner—rolls filled with sweet beef and black coffee—as the shadows lengthened through the city of Parliament, and as they ate, pored over their own plans together in the War Room after all the rest of them had left, again and again and again until Orion was sick of it. "You have to have this down perfectly," Cain stressed. "You don't have any margin to speak of at all; once that Shield goes down the Giants aren't going to last long, and if you're trapped in there when that happens you're not going to make it. So," he rolled the maps out across the tabletop again, "let's run through it one more time."

Orion sighed. "Okay," he said quietly. "Once more. I hit the Shield and go after the power supply." The map they stood before flickered and gave them a view of Skaald's Plaza, the square that was the seat of Giant government, from which the Janter clan had ruled the North Land for better than two hundred years. "The Ring is in a vault in the Janter estate; I come in through their Shield, target *here* and *here* and blast the power supply to hell. Back to the Skaald's Plaza, along the *prikazyvat*"—he mispronounced the Giant word badly, but Cain hardly cared—"and put down in the center square. I'm to be met by one of your spies, guided to the Ring, kill anybody who gets in my way, take the Ring, and come home." Orion spread his hands. "Well? It's not that hard, Cain. Basically a smash and grab."

"Basically," Cain agreed. "Eat your roll before it gets cold. What's worrying you, Orion?"

Orion was standing before the map, one hand cradling a cup of coffee. His shoulders were tense. "Do I really look so much like him?"

The question startled Cain for just a moment. "I suppose . . . it's been a long time, but I suppose you do."

"And Maston really killed him?"

"I said I would not lie to you again," Cain said flatly. "He did." He examined the coffee left in his cup and lifted it to his lips to finish it.

Orion found himself chewing on his thumbnail and stopped. "It's just—I've heard things since I've been here—I'm not sure we should trust Maston, sir."

Cain went utterly rigid and swallowed the coffee already in his mouth by sheer willpower. Then he took a deep breath and burst out laughing. "Maston? *Trust Maston?*" He barely got the words out between clenched teeth, shaking with the laughter. After a while the laughter trailed off into weak chuckles. Cain wiped tears of laughter from his eyes, looked up at Orion and saw the expression of concern in his eyes, and was off again. Finally he succeeded in calming himself and waved at the chair beside his own. "Sit down, son. Believe me, lad, I don't trust Maston. The man takes to treachery the way silkies take to water. Why, I'd *kiss* a red silkie before I'd trust Maston; my chances of survival would be better. But . . ." He took a final deep breath, and his features stilled, "I believe I'm smarter than he is."

Orion had no idea how to take Cain's sudden explosion of laughter; he did not think he had ever seen Cain laugh before. "That's not saying much."

Cain's gesture of dismissal was tacit agreement. "True enough, in a way. He has blind spots. Did you hear, when Commander Mielo was explaining to him why we needed Parliament as a base to strike from, she had to spell it out for him? It had simply never occurred to him that the Great Dam might be destroyed. He could not have done so himself while we were at war, those ten years following his rebellion against me, for he had no Fire weapons, but he could have destroyed the Great Waterlocks to much the same effect. The water would not have come so quickly, but it would have come just as surely. It pains me to think of the precautions I took protecting those damn waterlocks, only to find that it never even occurred to Eagles to blast them open." Cain shrugged. "Still, he's a bright man, Orion, for all his blind spots. He's betting our forces get stomped badly enough by the Giants tomorrow that when we're done, he'll find himself in a better position to tell us to go to hell. He's a good chance of winning that bet, too."

"Is all this worth it, sir? Just for the Ring?"

"It's not just for the Ring, son. The Giants are afraid of us, and rightly so—they've enslaved enough Workers over the course of the years, I think they must know there can never be peace between us. When Mars is sufficiently terraformed they can live there, I think they'll destroy us with thermonuclear weapons. Unless they can't any longer." Cain was silent a long while, staring sightlessly at the huge map of the North Land that covered the War Room. "And even if there were not that to consider, if it were all just for the Ring of Light —it would be worth it.

"Don't ever doubt that, Orion. Never."

THE RING

Halfway across the city of Parliament, in Maston Veramorn's home, Maston sat in quiet conversation with Commander Captain Bordine.

"When the attack starts, the Warriors still in Eastmarch will lead the other Workers aboveground. There are three lifts by which they can exit the Caverns; I want those lifts destroyed."

"When the flooding comes," observed Bordine laconically, "there'll be an awful lot of drowned folks."

Maston Veramorn nodded. "His industrial base is the only thing he has left after his Warriors. If his Warriors are decimated in battle against the Giants, and his laborers and engineers are lost to the flood, he won't be nearly so powerful."

Bordine leaned forward and said softly, lips very close to Maston's ears, "Can't understand how it is you find yourself the guts to go up against Cain when he scares you so bad." Maston did not reply, and chuckling to himself, Bordine left to see that what Maston desired was done.

Maston Veramorn sat alone in the dark after he was gone. His face was pasty gray. His hands trembled, and he could not stop the trembling no matter how he tried.

Cain sat alone in the control room of an Eastmarch personnel carrier. It was the only place in all of Parliament where he knew for a fact he was safe to relax and let his guard down.

Something was happening even as he waited, watching the glowing instrument panel of the personnel carrier. Cain was not sure what; breathing deeply, slowly and evenly, with all his guards down, mind open to the vagrant thoughts of the humans around him, he sat and waited.

Orion wandered alone through Parliament's twilight. He was not concerned for his own safety. He was armed, and there was nobody in Parliament with any particular cause to harm him on that night of nights. He was one of only three pilots with any flight time at all using the penetration sleeve. Lisa and Kennian were the other two; Lisa was still back at the Caverns, readying the evacuation, and Kennian, though he was here at Parliament, was with their squadron and would have required debriefing before he could fly Orion's mission.

Therefore, thought Orion mockingly, *killing me—tonight—makes no sense.*

The thought of the squadron, billeted at the low north end of the city, made Orion briefly lonely. The gap between him and his friends had been growing ever since Lisa and Bellows had become lovers, and had accelerated when Orion was made a Commander three years before any of the rest of them. Lisa and Bellows were still only Commander Seconds, and even Kennian, who was, in the mechanics of it, a better pilot than either Orion or Lisa, had only reached Commander First.

He threw the loneliness off with a concrete effort and started paying attention to the city through which he was roving. Even after fifteen years of Maston Veramorn's neglect, the city still showed its origins clearly. The home of the Rulers, even with the Rulers gone from it, was an evocative place, with streets lined with shade trees and more estates of various sorts than Orion had ever even imagined could be found in a single city. In places now the marble facing had been torn from the buildings, or else merely cracked and not repaired, and the streets were filthy along long stretches. With Cain's memories floating through the back of his awareness, Orion had glimpses of the city as it had been in Cain's youth, and the disparity saddened him. Orion knew intellectually that he was, genetically, of the breed that had designed this city; emotionally he was a Worker, and the damage that his people had done to the finest city on Earth shamed him in some measure.

At the south end of the city he found himself following a bobbing, weaving light. When he had first become aware of the light he was not certain, but he had already been following it for some time when that happened. A thrill of warning touched him, but the glow paused, waiting for him, and so Orion continued after it and came to the southern border of the city of Parliament, where the streets ended and the forest came right up to the edge of the ferrocrete. Looking further up the mountainside, Orion saw the distant glow of the debating Chamber, separated from the rest of Parliament by a stretch of empty mountainside.

He saw their movement through the trees, the shifting of the Light among the tree trunks and branches and leaves, and then they came out to where Orion waited, the likenesses of three women, ethereal and unreal. Their presences swirled about him, their thoughts reached in to delve through Orion's own . . .

He was walking down a street in Parliament he did not know, with a splitting headache. He could not remember where he had been, nor with whom, nor what they had spoken of. He was not watching his heading, was not paying attention to where he went. His thoughts were . . .

The presences hovered at the edges of Rea's perception, three women who, like herself, had lost something very precious to them. *Orion,* Rea thought with a sudden sharp hurt that transcended all the years since she had last seen him.

"Orion," she whispered aloud.

Farina came to her that evening. The guards let her through with a sort of bored tension that was, to the blind woman waiting inside, almost palpable. The tension had nothing to do with Rea, or Farina; the pair on duty at the end of the hall that led to Rea's cell was the same pair that had been guarding her in the afternoons and evenings for, Rea thought, three or four years now, and though they had been told otherwise, after all these years they did not believe—could not believe, no matter what Maston told them—that there was anything dangerous about the crazy blind woman.

"Farina," said Rea very quietly when the old woman was finally let through, "come sit by me." Farina had no tongue; she made a distant murmuring sound of agreement, and Rea smelled the warm spicy scent of her and heard the creak of the chair settling under Farina's weight. "Maston said today that Cain was here in Parliament, and a man named Orion is with him. Is this true?"

The murmur of agreement again.

Rea let out a long breath she was not even aware she was holding. She considered briefly attempting to send Farina with a message to Cain's camp, and discarded it; Rea understood Farina well enough, but she'd years of practice at it. The chance any of Cain's Warriors would pay any heed to an ancient woman whose tongue had been plucked was near to nonexistent. The chain of thoughts took little time to complete.

Rea said quietly, "Farina, can you do as I instruct you even if it will be dangerous?"

There was a moment's silence and then the simple sound of agreement again.

Rea said very quietly indeed, "Call one of the guards inside. Tell him I am very ill and require a doctor."

The woman's dying scream was pure and wordless, a ragged mixture of hatred and triumph, without any fear in it at all.

Across the world itself that scream echoed, as one of Loden Alamandar's blood was dragged near the precipice of her death. A man sitting atop a spire of rock, in the midst of the Glowing Desert, simply closed his eyes and shook his head in long regret. Cain of Eastmarch, alone in his personnel carrier, winced suddenly as though a pain had touched him briefly and shivered quietly at the thought of his own death; he did not know where the thought had come from.

Orion, standing in the deserted streets of Parliament as the gentle drifting snow gathered about his shoulders, came back to himself, abruptly aware of his surroundings for the first time in—he did not know how long it had been. It was entirely dark; the last thing he clearly remembered was looking up toward the southern slopes of the Black Mountains, up toward the Chamber, as the sun set beyond the tips of the southwest peaks.

There was an old woman in dirty clothing trotting out of the darkness toward him. He took a step back from her almost reflexively. She was panting from her running, and she had no tongue. She seemed alarmed that he was backing away from her and tugged at his sleeve furiously until he understood that he was to come with her. Once the thought had come to him what it was the old woman desired, it was suddenly perfectly obvious to Orion; of course he was to go with her.

You are the one, they said quietly in the darkness at the back of his mind. Orion followed the old woman through the empty streets, and for the first time was struck by what an alien city Parliament seemed, the architecture so very different from anything he had ever seen at Eagles or Eastmarch. It seemed odd to him that he should find the city strange now, when it had not seemed so before, and they had nearly reached their destination before Orion realized why this was so.

Cain's memories were gone. Where they had been, he could now find nothing.

The building he was brought to was ancient indeed. It reeked of age like few things Orion had ever seen. That it was one of the original buildings of Parliament, more than a thousand years old, was immediately apparent. It was a thin, two-story structure, large enough for only a single room. Orion smelled the blood before he reached the doorway; there was a man in the livery of an Eagles Warrior sprawled just inside the doorway, bleeding profusely from a cut just above his forehead. He had not, Orion judged, died of the cut, but from the broken neck he had received tumbling down the stairs. Orion's handgun was in his hand, safety switched off, though he could not recall having drawn it. The old woman seemed less concerned about her own safety than Orion was about his own; for someone so very old she went up the stairs with remarkable alacrity.

Orion followed her. At the top of the stairs was an old, wavering glowfloat illuminating a door that had been half torn from its hinges and, lying in the doorway, a very dead man, also in Eagles livery. He had died neatly, the bone in his nose jammed up into his brain. The stink of blood did not come from him, though it was even heavier in the air than it had been at the building's entrance downstairs.

The woman was lying propped up in the bed, hands folded across her stomach, and at first, in the dim radiance of the glowfloat, Orion thought she was dead too. She wore a plain dress of some dark brown stuff, with a spreading stain of black blood in it. Then her head shifted slightly and the dark holes where eyes should have been turned toward him. Adrenaline ran through him like a knife. He holstered his gun slowly and glanced around the rest of the small room—no, the cell, for there were bars on the window.

Orion found his voice at last. "Madam? Did you—" He rephrased the statement. "You killed those men."

The whisper was so faint he barely caught it. "Yes."

"You're a prisoner here?" Orion took a step closer to her. He felt very distant from everything that was happening, as though it were some show being staged for his benefit. The woman's hands were covering the wound she was bleeding from, and he could not see how bad the wound might be.

"Yes," she whispered again. "It is you?"

"Is it who? My name is Orion, madam." Orion glanced over at the old woman, standing patiently beside the door. *One without a tongue,* he thought irrelevantly, *one without eyes.*

The blind woman seemed to smile at that. "Ah. I had hoped to hear your voice again. Only a day ago I had no hope of ever doing so."

Something almost prevented Orion from saying the words. There was something about the whispered sound of her voice . . . "Hear my voice again? Do I know you?"

"I am Rea Veramorn."

The words struck Orion with numbing force. "Rea . . . *Veramorn?"* He was aware how his voice was rising. Oddly he seemed to be observing it all from very far away at the same time. "Madam, do you claim to be my mother?"

"I claim nothing." Her voice roughened on the last word, and she coughed, a wet sound. "I ask nothing. The one thing I desired most in the world has been given me. Senta was supposed to bring you back, and she didn't. But you came, Orion, you came at last."

The storm of thoughts would hardly settle in Orion's mind long enough to assemble words from them. "Senta? You are speaking of Senta Almandar?"

The woman did not answer his question. "Orion," she whispered instead, "hold my hand, please?"

Orion stood frozen before the woman's deathbed. "Madam, I must try to get you a doctor. You're very badly wounded."

"No!" The word sent her into a spasm of coughing, and when she finished her voice was even weaker. "I'd sooner die than face another of Maston's doctors."

"Then I'll take you to the Eastmarch camp! It's only a short way, madam."

"I do not think I will survive the journey, Orion," the woman said, very, very clearly. "I do not think . . ."

He never did find out what she thought. Her voice trailed away, and the movement of her chest stilled, and Rea Veramorn died without speaking again.

Orion buried her in the forest at the edge of the city of Parliament, thoughts increasingly dissociated from the reality of cutting chunks of earth free with his light knife and lifting the chunks until he had excavated a shallow grave for the woman. By the time he was done his uniform coat was filthy, so he took it off and laid it over the dead woman's face before filling the grave back in with the lengths of cut sod. The flickering forms of the women came as he worked and danced high above him, the murmur of their voices filling his ears.

When he was done he cleaned his hands as well as he might with the snow, and got most of the dirt and blood from his hands. He was only vaguely aware of what he was doing. The power of the Light flickered at the edges of his perception, and the thoughts of the women touched him deep inside.

He stood quietly when he was done, trying to decide what to do next; and the shimmer of the Light descended to cover him.

He found himself sitting on the stairs outside the War Room, head cradled in his hands. He stood slowly, looking up toward the sky as though there were something there of concern for him, and stood so for a long time with the gentle snow drifting down to kiss his face. The Star was invisible, of course, with the sky so overcast. Finally he looked away, distantly puzzled by his own thoughts, and continued up the stairs into the War Room to speak to the man who was inside.

He was not sure how he had known that it was Tristan d'Volta inside, even before he wandered into the huge room where the holographic map of the ice cap was erected. Tristan was sitting before one of the workstations, fighting a mock battle with the computers that controlled the simulation of the North Lands. Orion joined him without a word, and wordlessly Tristan handed him the bottle he had been drinking from. Orion sniffed at the bottle and smelled something like vodka inside; he took a long draught of it and sat considering while the slug of liquid burned a trail of fire straight down into his stomach. After a moment he nodded and handed the bottle back to Tristan.

"This stuff is awful."

Tristan chuckled, and Orion saw he was half drunk already. "Yes, but there's lots of it." He upended the bottle and drank deeply, then handed the bottle back to Orion again. "How about a game? I can't seem to beat the computers. Damn computers are convinced we're going to lose tomorrow."

"Sure." Orion powered up the workstation he was sitting at and glanced over at the map showing Worker and Giant forces. "Will this simulation let me send a ship inside their Shield?"

"Nope. Computer's no fool," said Tristan grimly. "I tried to tell it you could do that, but my programming syntax is pretty bad; it wouldn't listen."

Orion nodded. "Blue Giants against red Workers? I'll take the red."

"You're on," the old Warrior said simply. "Prepare to die."

Sometime after midnight a quiet thought came to Cain. *Hello, Cain.*

Cain had an impression of a cold blackness. Loga was somewhere out there in the night, alone in the cold winds. "Hello, Loga. I'm surprised to hear from you."

There was a distant chuckle. *Why? Because you haven't heard from me in the past? It's hard sending a thought past that damn Shield of yours.*

"I know. That's actually what it was put there for, among other things."

Something is moving tonight.

"Yes, I feel it. It's damn familiar, Loga, but I can't quite place it."

Perhaps it does not matter. We are on the cusp of great events. Someone died tonight, I do not know who, but I felt the tremor of her passing. She did not die easily. And there has been more. I have seen the flood come, Cain.

"Is that all? I've got a better one than that."

What have you seen, Cain?

"My own death, Loga."

There was a very long silence, and Cain thought Loga had withdrawn into himself, though he still had a sense of the old Ruler's presence. Finally Loga said, *Alas.*

"My feelings exactly. I don't want to die. Did you know we synthesized youthbooster at last? In a plant that grows like a weed. If you can grow the damn plant, you can live forever." Cain sat alone in the darkness, brooding. "I've been sitting on the announcement, waiting until after the attack on the North Land has succeeded. I thought about it for a long time and finally concluded that telling the Warriors that they might live forever—if they survived the attack—was not the proper way to convince them they should fight with wild abandon."

Yes. That was the problem that finally felled the Rulers, you know. They loved life so well they did not dare to risk it. Loga shrugged. *We all die sometime.*

"True enough. I've had a good run. I don't really regret anything I've done. It hurts, though," Cain said, "having given my life to see that the Workers would have a chance to own themselves, to make some future for themselves, and to know now that I'm going to die before I find out how it all turns out."

Cain was silent a moment. He could feel through their link the cold wind of the Glowing Desert as it touched Loga, swept across the black spire of the rock Loga had named Despair. "How many times did I try to kill you?"

Cain felt Loga shrug. *Three times, four. I've forgotten. Fortunately your heart wasn't in it.*

"You don't think so?"

I could be wrong, Loga admitted. *I prefer to think otherwise.*

Orion gave up after the second successive game in which the Giants had whipped the Worker forces without any trouble at all. Tristan accepted his decision without argument and offered Orion a swig from the bottle he had just opened.

Orion was tempted for a moment, but then shook his head. "I'm not going to get any sleep as it is. I have to fly first thing in the morning. I can't drink any more, I'm afraid."

Tristan turned to him suddenly and said fiercely. "I want to fly with you tomorrow."

Orion looked at the older man critically. "I'm not sure that's a good idea. You've had a fair amount to drink."

Tristan snorted. "By the Light, you're a strange one. You've your father's looks, and at times I hear him in your voice. Other times"—he shook his head—"you'll say something, make some gesture, that couldn't come from anyone else in the world except Cain."

Orion could not think of what to say in response.

Tristan looked at him. "I'll be sober come morning. I've been handling my morning-afters longer than you've been alive. Damn it, I'm serious, Orion. I'm a hell of a good combat pilot, and I don't want to miss this fight." He was silent a moment longer, judging how Orion might take his words. "Besides," he said finally, "I'd like to see you fly."

Orion closed his eyes for a moment and sat in the midst of a great floating darkness. He opened his eyes and found Tristan staring at him with naked hope. Orion said quietly, "I'll talk to Cain. I think he'll let you."

· 2 ·

"I don't *believe* this," Lisa shouted in fury above the general roar. They were in the Command Center at the Caverns, and Lisa had just received their final orders from Commander General Dantes. "They gave Tristan d'Volta, Maston's bloody second-in-command, an entire Eastmarch *wing* to command!"

Bellows shrugged, listening on his earphone as the reports poured in throughout the Caverns. The fusion generators would be shut down within another fifteen minutes, and after that the Shield would go down, and the Cavern sunpaint would run on battery power until their reserves went dead. Every Worker still in the Caverns was accounted for and in position to make the trek to high ground when the time came.

"Bellows?" Lisa shook him by the shoulder. "Aren't you listening? With a pair of Commander Seconds stuck here at the Caverns, Cain gave one of Maston's Warriors a wing—not to fly with, but to command!"

"D'Volta's known to be a top pilot," said Bellows practically, "and with battle experience as well, which is something you can't say about most of our own Warriors. Cain would know if he could trust the man."

Lisa simply turned away from him in disgust, and Bellows touched the microphone at the workstation he stood before. "Commander General? Is the Command given?"

"The Command is given."

"Second Jackson out," said Bellows evenly. He turned to the Warriors in the Command Center. "It's time. Evacuation begins, let's *move.*"

THE RING

Tristan was surprised at how *good* it felt to be going into battle again, and amazed that he was going in leading one of the eight attack wings. Maston had been furious when he was told about Tristan's request, raging and screaming like Maston of old; but, Tristan was pleased to find, he could not find it within himself to care, or be afraid.

Perhaps that was part of what had left him feeling so euphoric.

He was flying his own slipship, of Eagles construction. Cain might trust him enough to command a wing, but not enough to let him inside a Falcon. It wasn't entirely distrust that motivated that, though Tristan suspected that was most of it; better than two thirds of Eastmarch's forces were still flying the oldstyle craft.

Tristan and his wing of six hundred and fifteen slipships were third to launch. He sat in his ship and watched as a single silver needle took to the sky, half an hour before dawn. The sky was lightening by the time the first full wing launched, six hundred and fifteen slipships launching in waves of twenty at a time, one wave every fifteen seconds. It took just better than four and a half minutes for the entire wing to launch. Tristan called the role of the Commanders who were to report to him and then checked on the private circuit for the aide he'd been assigned, a Commander First Temera. Temera confirmed the count was correct. There was a break of not quite two minutes before the next wing launched, and six and half minutes after that Tristan lifted in the first wave of his wing and flew north, toward the far-distant line of the Great Dam.

The attack was a fairly simple one; the slipships would leave in eight wings, the earliest launching wings looping around to strike the North Land from the ice cap's far shore as the last wings were reaching the near shore. If things went well, the ice cap should be struck, at one instant, by fighter craft on all sides. Slower bombers would launch shortly after the last wing of slipships left; again, if things went according to plan, which Tristan knew they'd a tendency not to, the Shield should go down at just about time the bombers arrived.

They passed the Great Dam, dropped slightly to hug the surface of the One Ocean, and flew north.

Laar Janter did not know, when he awoke that morning, that he would be dead before the day had passed. When the warning came that the Workers were attacking, it was near midday by the clock the Giants lived by. Free of the cycle of day and night due to the fact that they lived near the planet's rotational north pole, the Giant society had, over the course of centuries, evolved a cycle of day and night that had no connection whatsoever to the one that ruled their Worker neighbors to the south.

The day was a pleasant one. Laar found the ten degrees Centigrade of the Skaald's Plaza pleasantly invigorating as he made his early morning rounds, stopping in to discuss progress and problems with his aides. The Skaald's Plaza was huge, nearly five kilometers in diameter. The ceiling, two hundred meters overhead, was a ten-meter-thick layer of reinforced ice. The air in the Plaza was the blue of deep ice. It was, to Laar Janter's way of thinking, one of the few truly beautiful pieces of architectural work he had ever seen.

A public holograph showed temperatures hovering around minus thirty degrees Centigrade outside the Skaald's Plaza and nearly eight degrees Centigrade inside the dome. Most Giants kept their home quarters heated to exactly twelve degrees Centigrade, the Skaald Laar among them. With the thick subcutaneous layer of fat the Giants had evolved since the first of the Fire Wars, temperatures that were comfortable to a Worker or Ruler, Giants found sweltering.

There was a corollary to that, of course, and Laar could not help but be reminded of it as he made his slow way through the morning's meetings and consultations, as the authority of the Skaald produced consensus after consensus on any number of subjects. The Worker slaves whom the Giants had been keeping since the abdication of the Lords of Light found the ambient temperatures the Giants enjoyed far too cold. Even in their own quarters, which the Giants allowed them to heat somewhat hotter than the warmest Giant rooms ever got, they kept most of their clothes on. In the corridors they were bundled as though temperatures were actually down below freezing, and not in fact a brisk ten degrees above the point where water solidified.

The Workers annoyed Laar, when he admitted it to himself. He did not think they should be necessary—they had not been when he was a child—for such simple things as caring for one's own home or making sure the streets were kept free of ice. The necessity for paying attention to things happening down around his belly button also annoyed Laar. The Workers were fragile and fast moving; occasionally, once a year or so, one forgot himself and actually *ran* through corridors. Workers caught making that mistake never made it twice; they were executed before they could present a bad example for Giant children.

The only time a Giant ever ran, anywhere, was when his life was endangered. The dangers of falling were simply too great.

He ate the midday meal with his wife Rushada. She was his third wife; his first and second wives had died in childbirth. Though Laar was often too busy to spend much of a day with Rushada, he made a point to eat with her whenever possible. Giants took only one meal a day, and at that meal they ate hugely. Their Worker slaves served the meal with a reasonable degree of unobtrusiveness. Laar hardly had occasion to be displeased with them, though they had still not made enough progress in learning the Giants' tongue, and occasionally he had to prompt them in their own language.

A red panel, recessed into the wall of the dining room, lit suddenly before they had even finished the third course. Laar rose to answer it without haste. Usually the warnings concerned nothing more severe than warnings of minor earthquakes, so that Giants might secure themselves before the tremblers struck. He touched a stud in the monitor that tied him to the central Giant infobase, and before the system could even come up the image of one of Laar's subordinates appeared before him in a fifteenth-sized holograph. "Skaald," he said without appropriate salutations, "observe the scanner feed." His image vanished and was replaced with a graphic indicating the North Land ice cap. There were thousands of dots converging slowly upon the North Land in a tightening circle. At first Laar's eyes refused to make sense of the image being presented him, and then suddenly he understood what he was seeing.

"They're actually attacking," he said to nobody in particular. "Fools." He cleared the graphic, and his subordinate's form reappeared. "Either Cain alone or Cain and Maston together. It hardly matters. They must believe we haven't noticed them yet or they would not be holding such tight formations. Let them in closer to the Shield, and then bring the drones up outside them. We'll annihilate them upon the Shield." Laar was silent for a moment. "We have a strike force in position to destroy the Great Dam?"

"Of course, Skaald."

"Do so," said Laar simply.

They were moving the Workers out through four different exit routes, the three lifts and straight up through the silo doors above the empty shipyard. The silo doors were nearly fifty meters above the floor of the shipyard. The Workers had labored through the night building a rough scaffolding to reach the silo doors. Already Lisa was wondering what they would have done if one of the engineers had not, the prior night, had the idea for the scaffolding; by her rough count they were evacuating nearly a thousand Workers a minute through the silo doors, as opposed to only about six hundred a minute through the three lifts. They looked to cut their estimated evacuation time down to just about half an hour, rather than the hour and a third that would have been required using the lifts alone.

There was a sudden stillness in a group of Warriors over at the other end of the scaffolding, and Lisa Wanaré clicked on her earphone just in time to hear that, for the first time since the end of the Fire Wars, a nuclear weapon had been employed in a battle. Saerlock had been touched by the Fire. The news brought a strange sensation to Lisa's stomach, which surprised her; she didn't even know anybody in Saerlock.

Perhaps it was simply the realization, on an emotional level, that one could kill a city in war just as if the city had no better defenses than a single Warrior.

Only an instant after that the voice continued. *"Spysats report that the Great Dam is breached in the vicinity of Saerlock's waterlock. Rate of flooding is not accurately known yet. Expect the first flooding in the vicinity of the Caverns within half an hour. Total immersion will occur in not less than two hours.*

Lisa stood stunned for a moment. The Workers were going to be wading through rising water on their way to high ground; there was no way they would reach the foothills in less than an hour and a half.

The dazed sensation lasted only a second, and a powerful fury was born within her to burn it away. She turned on the Workers, who were passing the news to one another, withdrew her handgun and fired it straight up into the air twice. They were silent for a brief startled second. Into the momentary silence she screamed at them, her rage at the universe plain in her voice, *"Move,* damn it! You stupid bastards want to *die* down here?"

They moved.

THE RING

Orion came straight down from orbit, in a free-fall parabolic descent no different from that of a meteor. He would be running on instruments until he hit the Giants' Shield, because the penetration sleeve, though it was as nearly transparent as Cain's engineer's could manage, still cut off sixty percent of the light that would otherwise have reached him; it made his optics unreliable. The ship's systems were entirely shut down at the moment regardless; on far radar the craft should look like a shiny chunk of nickel-iron to the Giant computers, just another piece of cosmic debris that would burn up in the atmosphere. By the time it became apparent that he was not burning up, the slipship attack should have their air defenses so busy that they would have no time to fire upon a single suicidal pilot who was diving on their Shield.

That was the theory, at any rate.

The thing that warned Lisa first was the sudden dimness on the floor of the shipyard. The silo doors were closing, so silently that it took Lisa a moment to connect the sudden darkening on the shipyard with the fact that the pale sunlight was actually reaching them through the silo doors. She stared up at the doors in horror as they swung slowly shut and then clicked on her comm channel to the Command Center. "Bellows? Is some fool there closing the silo doors? Bellows, damn it, use the override on Workstation Three. Do it fast!" There was no reply from Bellows. Lisa did not waste time waiting for one, but turned to the rapidly panicking group of Workers. "Calm down, it's all right. It's all right!" she called more loudly. "Commander Jackson will have the override in just a minute. Don't panic, we're all going to get out!"

In the Control Center a pair of Warriors were sprawled dead at their posts. Five Warriors and a Commander in the uniforms of Eagles stood with laser rifles leveled at Bellows. "You realize that at last count there were still sixteen hundred children who had not been evacuated? Are you prepared to kill the children?"

The Commander, a Captain Bordine, clucked sympathetically. "Your own Lord Cain's orders, I'm afraid, direct to us from Commander Captain Orion. I guess he figures to get rid of some rebels this way."

"That's not even a very good lie," Bellows spat at the Captain. "You're really prepared to keep these Workers trapped in here until the floodwater reaches the Caverns?"

"I wish I could let them go," said Bordine seriously, "for I'm a kind man at heart. Alas . . ." He let the words trail off and shrugged slightly. "Such is life." He grinned suddenly with true amusement, and it was one of the most horrid things Bellows had ever seen. "And death."

"*Bellows?*" Still there was no reply on the earphone, and the closed silo doors were not budging. Swearing, Lisa Wanaré left for the Control Center at a dead run.

Orion keyed on the comm channel for his squadron, the wing Tristan d'Volta had ended up commanding with Kennian as his second. "No-Name?"

"*Here.*"

"Orion here. I'm coming down over the ice cap. Spread a gentle reminder, No-Name, torpedo strikes kept below the waterline, and no torpedo strikes at all until I'm on my way out again . . . please."

"*I'll keep an eye on it. Good luck.*"

Sitting alone in the dead slipship as it plummeted toward the North Land, Orion had to smile. "Luck? What for? Just because I'm flying into the North Land half blind, without lasers, and once I make it inside the Shield I'm going to be outnumbered about four million to one?"

There was a brief pause before Kennian's reply came. "*You're right, and I take it back. When you're done, the Giants aren't going to know what hit them. First Temera out.*"

"I don't need luck," Orion murmured to the dark instruments as he started the procedure to bring the fusion cells up and the thrusters on-line. "Just a miracle."

THE RING

The One Ocean reached the Caverns as Bellows stood trying to decide what to do about the Warriors who were pointing laser rifles at him. Through the one-way observation windows that opened onto the shipyard, he saw the salt water spray forward over the edges of the nearly closed silo doors and fall like rain upon the upturned faces of the waiting Workers. He appealed to Bordine again in desperation. "They're going to die if you don't let me open the silo doors again."

Bordine shook his head slowly. "I'd like to. I really would. But— you see, we *promised* Lord Cain we'd take care of this for him. You wouldn't want me to break a promise, would you?"

A laser-thin beam of scarlet light appeared immediately behind Captain Bordine, widened and spread into the shape of a blazing ruby king cobra nearly eight meters tall, its head brushing against the ceiling of the Command Center. Bordine whirled about in the instant of its appearance and was looking almost straight up to where the cobra's head reared above them, when the image suddenly vanished and the Ruler Loga appeared in its place. The glow of the Light never left him. "Hello," said Loga. "I have some bad news for you." Bordine lifted his handgun, and Loga took it away from him and buried it in the man's sternum up to its hilt. The five Warriors whom Bordine had brought with him were standing bravely, keeping the beams of their lasers focused on the incandescent Lord of Light in their midst. Bellows took advantage of their preoccupation to drag one of them down to the ground and snap his neck, and when he looked up again from that task, the forms of the four remaining Warriors had been spread across the Command Center with various lethal wounds to keep them occupied. Bellows looked back and forth from Loga to the dead and dying forms of the Warriors.

Loga shrugged and looked almost embarrassed. "You do enough of anything over the course of the centuries," he explained, "and you get to be good at it. Anyway, listen. You going to let those folks in the shipyard out? I would myself except, from a strictly ethical point of view, I'm not sure I'm really supposed to be getting involved here."

"Yes," said Bellows slowly. "I suppose—" He broke off without finishing the sentence and ran to Workstation Three, slapped a pair of switches, and listened intently to the reports flooding in on his earphones. When he rose up again from the terminal, Lisa had appeared standing in the entrance to the Command Center, watching the tableau without comprehension.

Loga glanced over at one of the fallen Warriors, who was clutching a shattered windpipe, legs drumming against the floor of the Command Center in the last stages of asphyxiation. "Brutal," he murmured to himself, "but then, he probably . . . deserves it." He looked up to meet Lisa Warnaré's gaze, said cheerfully, "See you," and vanished.

Orion had not expected to be afraid.

He had not been afraid in the carefully staged battles with the silver-eyes, though Warriors did indeed die in some of those skirmishes. He could not, at that particular moment, recall ever having been afraid of anything in the world except, sometimes, Cain.

There were butterflies in his stomach as he brought the thrusters up. The Shield protecting the North Land was so huge that its refraction effect—the only thing that made a small Shield visible—was negligible. He did not know except by instruments when he had actually passed through the Shield. A heatseeker exploded near him in that instant, buffeting the ship wildly, and Orion blew the penetration sleeve free of the craft with a sensation of violent relief.

He could *see* again. He was traveling across frozen tundra, devoid of either civilization or life. He shot a glance at the monitor in his control panel, orienting himself against the map of the North Land displayed there. Three solid dots glowed on the map display, two red dots showing both the fusion generator and, if Orion could not reach that, the power lines branching out to the Shield pylons. The third dot shone blue, the place where Laar Janter kept the Ring of Light. A single white spot pulsed twice a second, showing Orion where he was. One red spot was very close, and Orion adjusted course slightly and relaxed in the pilot's cocoon as the slipship leapt forward at better than five gravities' acceleration.

They sat on the high bluff and in utter exhaustion watched the water rise. Lisa's uniform was entirely soaked, rimed with salt. The last twenty minutes of their march had been through waters high and swift enough to drown an adult Worker. "How many did we lose?" asked Lisa finally.

Bellows sat down beside her and tried to take her hand. She snatched it away. "It's just a raw estimate, but somewhere between fourteen and fifteen hundred Workers. A lot of them were children." He sighed and sat rubbing the back of his neck. "By the Light, Lisa, it could have been a lot worse."

"Could've been better," she said distantly. "You don't think Cain really sent those Warriors?"

"No," he said quietly. "That doesn't make sense any way you read it."

"Do you think Orion would do something like that?"

Bellows struck her before he realized what he was doing. She rolled with the blow and came to her feet with her handgun out, but pointed at the ground. "I guess you don't," she said after a moment. A trickle of blood ran down from the corner of her mouth.

Bellows' shoulders sagged. He had not even come to his feet. "I'm sorry," he said quietly. "Sit down again, or hit me back if it'll make you feel better. I don't know why I did that."

The woman stood there clutching her handgun as though it were the last object in her world that made any sense at all. "Did you know there was a little girl who was walking next to me most of the way here? Her mother's been looking for the girl ever since we made high ground and hasn't found her." Lisa stood, shoulders shaking. "I remember somebody screaming next to me, and I didn't even look around."

Bellows looked up at her. "Lisa . . . please, stop crying. It doesn't help them any."

"I'm not crying for them," she said fiercely. "They couldn't take care of themselves, it's their own damn fault."

Bellows knew she did not mean that, but knew also not to say so. "Then what's wrong?"

"Orion's damned puppy," said Lisa bitterly. "I promised him I would take care of it." She stood watching the rushing flood waters rise, covering the farmlands that had once fed the Caverns. "I don't think anybody even opened the kennels. They must have drowned in their cages."

Tristan d'Volta was fighting for his life.

Nearly a third of the wing he putatively commanded was already destroyed as slipship after slipship met with destruction under the fire from the Giant drone. Most of the Falcons in his wing had not been damaged; most of the normal slipships, except for those in the very center of the wing, were in serious trouble. He rolled his slipship over and then took it momentarily straight up. It was one of the few maneuvers he had found that the drone ships did not respond well to. The drone that had been on his tail was suddenly underneath him. Tristan scooped air to slow himself and destroyed the drone with a single line of laser fire. The instant he saw the laser touch, he keyed open his comm. "First Temera, what status?"

The Eastmarcher's voice reached him calmly. "Two hundred twenty-seven, make that twenty-eight, ships down. Nine of them are Falcons. Two-twenty-nine. Orion's been inside the Shield for nine minutes. Second Fogan requests—"

Tristan never found out what it was Fogan requested; the ionization trail of the shot that nearly destroyed him half-blinded him. He snapped "Out," and returned to the immediate task of staying alive.

Orion was barely able to see in the first instants after the acceleration cut back. Red spots danced madly before his eyes as the blood flowed back into them. His first thought, when he saw the power supply station he was supposed to destroy, was that he was hallucinating, that his brain wasn't getting enough blood.

The fusion generator that supplied power to the North Land's Shield was, it seemed, very similar to the fusion generators Orion was familiar with. Its principal waste product was—must be—simple hot water. Fusion power was clean; the water would be hot, but not radioactive.

With that hot water, some brilliant Giant had decided to construct hot springs. Scores of Giants, both adults and children, lounged in the springs in the shadow of the fusion plant, some of them staring up at Orion's ship in mild curiosity.

Children, thought Orion clearly.

Bathing in the shadow of a prime military target.

In his slipship, two hundred meters above them, Orion screamed at them. *"Don't you bloody fools know there's a war going on?"*

Evidently they did not.

Orion brought his ship about and began his run from better than two kilometers distant. Somewhere deep inside he was aware that he was very, very grateful that he did not need to see the Giants he was about to kill when he killed them.

He released a single thermonuclear missile while he was half a kilometer distant, and both he and the missile arrived at the fusion plant at approximately the same moment. There was an instant of blinding brilliance, and then Orion was outrunning the wavefront of the explosion at better than twice the speed of sound.

There was no triumph within him.

In the War Room at Parliament a sudden cheer went up from the technicians monitoring the workstations. Cain did not even have to ask them what that meant. He keyed open the comm line to Commander General Dantes, aboard the lead bomber that was even now approaching the North Land. "Commander General," he said with a sudden surge of almost aggressive elation, "the Shield is down."

Dantes' voice returned to them immediately, boomed out across the War Room. *"Yes, my lord."*

"Communication nodes first," said Cain evenly. "I want that drone fleet out of the air. After that, you may destroy to suit yourself."

"My lord, it will be a pleasure."

An aide Commander whom Cain did not know, in the emerald uniform of Eagles, said quietly, "My lord? Better than half your slipship fleet has been destroyed already. Lord Maston has volunteered to reinforce your ships if you have need of it."

Cain glanced around the room; he did not see Maston anywhere. He turned and smiled at the Commander, and the man actually flinched. "Tell Maston I give him my thanks for his generous offer to aid the Workers of the Valley in their time of need, but that his aid is, now, hardly necessary." The Commander stood there, frozen, and Cain said softly, "You go tell him that, wherever it is he's hiding from me."

Laar Janter sat alone in his cubicle and, on the private monitor that was the prerogative of a Skaald, watched his dreams die under the Workers' bombs. Most of the bombs were chemical, and even so the toll was devastating. The few nuclear weapons that the Workers used were directed against purely military targets. They did bomb the civilian complexes, but not with Fire weapons.

Even as he made the distinction in his mind, the floor he was seated upon shook beneath him.

Briefly, he considered the Giants on Mars. His son Aline was there, in charge, and Laar was almost certain that Aline would do what Laar, in his place, would have done. The Mars colony was very nearly self-sufficient and more than able to defend itself against the Workers for the forseeable future.

Aline would write the losses off. Laar could not even find it within him to blame Aline; it would be the correct decision for him to make.

He rose slowly, wearily, ignoring his wife's plaintive questions, and lumbered into the vault where he kept the trophy that had cost him his own brother's life. There was a Giant-sized safe buried in one wall. Laar ignored it and placed his palm against a scanner next to the vault's door. A portion of the wall itself slid aside, and an elevator lowered the glass encasement that housed the Ring. He was not entirely certain why he was doing this; it seemed to him, at that moment, that the Ring itself was calling him, tugging at him as it had not seen fit to do in the fifteen years since his taking of it from the Lords of Light.

He sat in the exact middle of the vault with the Ring of Light cradled in the palm of his huge hand. The pale, almost invisible glow of the Ring brightened for just an instant. A great peace swept through Laar Janter, a calm willingness to meet whatever fate the universe had in store for him, and then the ceiling fell on him.

Orion circled the Skaald's Plaza slowly.

"This isn't fair," he heard himself saying aloud. "This isn't *going* right."

On their maps the area below Orion—the Skaald's Plaza—was shown as an open square. Since the time their spies had smuggled out maps of the Plaza, the damned Giants had covered it with a dome of ice.

Orion was touched by a moment of wild, almost unreasoning panic. How was he going to meet his contact when the bloody square he was supposed to land in had been enclosed? The dome covering the public square looked fragile enough. Orion suspected it was only reinforced ice, thirty or forty meters thick. Had Orion been armed with even low-power lasers, the dome covering the Plaza would not have lasted long. He forced the panic down and thought about the subject as clearly as he could. If only his ship had been armed. . . .

Orion did not stop to think about it, or he probably would not have dared to do it. He scooped air until he was hovering on belly jets immediately over the thinnest section of the great dome, used the attitude jets to bring the craft's nose up, and walked the ship's thrusters across the surface of the dome. In the first instant the steam exploded upward in billowing great clouds, surrounding the ship on all sides until Orion could not see half a meter beyond his canopy in any direction. He kept at it, moving the ship with the belly thrusters, keeping the ship stabilized horizontally with the attitude jets and vertically with the ship's thrusters. The steam blasted up around him, an unending white cloud that had always been there and always would be, and then at last there came a cracking sound so loud that Orion heard it even over the sound of his thrusters. He boosted power to the thrusters, got the ship up over the dome, and inspected his handiwork.

Nearly a quarter of the surface of the dome, at its thinnest section in the dome's very center, was fragmenting as Orion watched, crumbling before his eyes. He waited until the wreckage of the dome had finished falling into the square below and took his ship straight down.

Cain sat watching the holograph of the battle as the Worker forces tightened their circle about the North Land. His chin was propped up on his fist. The only part of him that seemed at all alive were his eyes. Black is a dark color; nonetheless there was no Worker in the War Room who did not see how Lord Cain's eyes shone.

Maston Veramorn came and went several times as the battle progressed. Cain was never unaware of him, but had no time to spare the man just then. Occasional queries he disposed of quickly. General Dantes, aboard one of the bombers, reported that Giant spacecraft were launching from the North Land, and Cain said simply, "Let them go. You don't ever prevent your enemies from running away, Dantes. It sets a bad precedent."

"*Yes, my lord. Lord Cain, we've had no communications here from Commander Orion. We've refrained from shelling the Skaald's Plaza; shall we continue to do so?*"

Senses tuned tight and fine, Cain heard Maston Veramorn's sharply indrawn breath from across the length of the War Room. He did not waste time on regrets, but said merely, "General Dantes, send a small detachment to the Plaza. If Orion is not there, then he is dead, and you may destroy it."

Orion found himself in a vast underground grotto, nearly a quarter of a kilometer above the floor of the Plaza. He touched the thrusters lightly and drifted forward, dropping slowly as he coasted toward the far end of the Plaza, where the Plaza was still covered by the thickest section of the dome. There were only perhaps a dozen Giants that Orion could see across the entire Plaza, and about half of them were lying dead where chunks of the dome's ice had fallen on them. A Giant near the entrance to what Orion's map showed as Laar Janter's quarters was fighting wildly with something invisible that wielded a variable laser with considerable skill. Orion took the slipship forward and brought it to a gentle landing thirty meters from the building in which the Skaald Laar supposedly kept the Ring.

He cracked the canopy on the craft the instant he was down and scrambled down to the grooved ferrocrete surface of the Giant walkway, handgun in one hand and a variable laser in the other, prepared to kill any Giant who came within fifty meters of him. The nearest Giant Orion could see was better than two hundred meters away and moving at a swift walk away from the spot where Orion, and most of the roof as well, had touched down. Orion glanced about wildly, searching for the contact whom he was supposed to meet. He actually looked at the man once, standing next to the dead form of a disemboweled Giant, and then away, before glancing back at him and actually *seeing* him. Against the background of ice and pale white building stone, the man was next to invisible. He wore white clothing, and his hair had gone completely white since the last time Orion had seen him. His skin was paler than any Worker's could be, and his eyes were silver.

He was still gaping when Kavad said, "Master Orion, it is good to see you again. You're looking well." Orion's mouth opened and then closed again without any sound at all issuing forth. Kavad said gently, "Sir? Would you like to come with me to get the Ring?"

· 3 ·

"This isn't happening."

Kavad lifted a single white eyebrow. Orion stared at him. "Really, it's not. Kavad, do you know what a strange day this has been?" A building took a direct hit from a Worker shell not eighty meters away from them, and Orion did not even flinch. "For example, you're dead."

"No, sir," said the silver-eyes with the perfect composure that Orion remembered so well, "I am not dead. I am merely," Kavad explained, "in hell."

A structural beam was holding him pinned by the chest to the floor of the vault. Laar's right arm was shattered. With his left arm he strained against the spar and with a great effort raised it up several centimeters above his chest. He held it there, straining, and then suddenly the beam slipped and fell back upon him. He felt and heard ribs cracking, felt the sudden sharp pain as one of his ribs was pushed in and punctured a lung. Breathing suddenly became difficult, as the blood seeped into his lungs. His wife came and tried to help him, but simply was not strong enough; gasping, Laar told her to bring him help.

"I *can't*," Rushada said through her tears. "Everyone who can has been taking to the spacecraft and fleeing. The Plaza is near empty already."

Laar lay there under the beam, listening to the distant explosions, and finally said quietly, hearing the sound of the blood bubbles in his voice, "Can you make it to one of the ships yourself?"

She nodded convulsively. "There are still some left. I don't want to leave you, Laar!"

Laar closed his eyes and let the pain wash over him. "I'm afraid you don't have much choice, Rushada. Seal the vault and go." There was never any doubt within him; he felt her cool lips against his own, and waited there in the pain-filled dark.

When he opened his eyes again he was alone. The walls of the vault shook occasionally with the explosions. Laar composed himself, still clutching the dark Ring, and waited for his death.

There came then a blast so strong it lifted the girder that was pinning Laar Janter to the floor a full ten centimeters into the air. In strict accordance with the laws of gravity the girder came back down again.

Laar came back to awareness some infinite time later, floating awash in a crimson haze of pain. The pain did not lessen even for an instant; a spray of ice water roused him regardless.

High in the wall of the vault, a chunk of the wall about the size of Laar's fist had come free, and from the hole where that chunk had been came a spray of salt water. Laar stared up at it for a while without comprehension. He thought at first that he was in no danger from the water alone; it was not coming fast enough to swamp the vault in anything less than several hours. Then he noticed that the hole was widening, and the flow of water increasing.

He twisted his head as far as it would go to the side and saw the door to the vault, firmly shut.

To Laar Janter's utter horror, there was water coming under the seal at the bottom of the door.

"I am sorry," said Kavad as they slogged through the ice water filling the long, overarching corridors, "that I was unable to get a new map to Lord Cain before the attack began. The dome has been in place for three quarters now. Unfortunately, reliable communications with Eastmarch have been difficult to arrange."

"Difficult to arrange," Orion repeated numbly. "Kavad, how are you *alive?*"

"Lord Cain's mercy," said Kavad precisely. "He shot me with low-intensity lasers. I had a ham steak inside my tunic. A leader of Cain's status, Orion, cannot permit failure to go unpunished, cannot be seen to be weak, even to—perhaps especially to—his own son." They came to a cross-corridor and suddenly found themselves face to face with a female Giant. Orion had his handgun pointing at her, and Kavad stood with the three-meter blade of his variable laser extended, facing the woman. She turned away without ever making a sound and lumbered off in the other direction.

"I'm not his son," Orion said stonily.

Kavad merely glanced at Orion. "As you say, sir. We are nearly there."

The acrid scent of hot metal roused Laar Janter to full consciousness. He was very cold, half submerged in the glacial water of the One Ocean. His broken arm was numb. He twisted his head slightly to the side; had he turned it as far as it would go, both his nose and mouth would have ended up beneath the surface of the rising water. Out of the corner of his eye he saw the blade of the variable laser slicing slowly through the door of the vault, and when the section of glowing metal fell free into the water, it raised a scalding hot wave and sent it washing over Laar's face. When the wave subsided, a Worker stood above him, a Worker in a flight suit which bore the emblem of Eastmarch upon it. The Worker stood in the chill water above Laar, and Laar heard him say, "Kavad, go. Save yourself if you can; the slipship I came in can only take one person back out again." The Worker to whom the man was speaking must have left, for the Worker standing above Laar did not speak to him again. He knelt in the ice water next to Laar, and with one hand propped up the Giant's head above the level of the rising waters. Laar was suddenly aware that the Ring was pulsing sharply, literally burning in his hand despite the ice water in which it was submerged. Some radiance must have given the Ring's presence away, for the Worker smiled at him, a smile that seemed to Laar somehow mad, and said quietly, "I am Orion of Eastmarch, Giant, and I have come for the Ring which you are holding."

Laar's entire being was focused upon the variable laser in the Worker's hand. "Orion? Cain's child? Worker, I beg of you, cut the beam which holds me pinned."

"Give me first the Ring."

"Worker, Cain stole this Ring. I killed my brother for it, wasted my life guarding it. The Ring will do you no good. Let us leave it here, to be swallowed by the waters forever."

"Perhaps the Ring will do me no good, Giant. Possibly so. Still, I must have it."

Now that a chance at life had been presented him, Laar was surprised to find how badly he wanted not to die. "Worker, the water is rising! Cut me free and I will give you the Ring!"

"It sounds very much," said Orion mildly, "as though you are asking me to trust you? I have many reasons, Giant, not to trust you."

The Giant said desperately, "My spies have told us what Cain told you, that he has proclaimed your mother was taken by Giants. We did not take her. We never had your mother, Orion. There was no Giant in all the Valley when your father died and Rea Veramorn vanished." Despite it all, there was still hope in the Giant's eyes.

Orion said softly, "I believe you, Laar. Indeed, I do. I have known for a long time that Cain lied to me about how my mother met her end." An odd look crossed his face. "It may be that I do even know the truth about her death; and if so, then I know that Giants had nothing to do with her passing." Laar's huge form sagged with relief. Orion continued slowly. "There are many, many things which Cain has told me which I know are not true." The variable laser in his hand lit, and the blade wavered out to hover above the Giant Laar. Laar's eyes widened in fear. "Take a deep breath," Orion told the Giant, and when the Giant had done so Orion released his head, let it sink back below the levels of the water. He stood and the variable laser's blade dropped slowly, and bit into the heavy beam. A spray of sparks flew up from the point of contact. The beam was half beneath water; salt-scented steam billowed up as the laser dipped into the water to continue cutting. Though he had chosen a point as far from Laar as possible, Orion could see bubbles in the water as it began to boil at the point where the beam lay beneath the water.

The beam snapped suddenly, cracking under its own vast weight as the laser cut through its width. Orion lifted the laser from the water swiftly, and removed his thumb from the stud which activated the light knife. The two halves of the beam settled gently as they separated; one rolled completely off of the Giant's body, and the other sank down to pin one of the Giant's legs. Without stopping to think, Orion laid hands to that length of metal, well down from where the laser had touched it, and heaved once. The structural beam moved only a few centimeters, but it was enough; the leg came free. With a single convulsive movement, with the hand holding the Ring, the Giant Laar pushed himself back up above the surface of the water, drawing air in a huge gasp. Orion turned back to the Giant, breathing heavily himself from the exertion. Laar was moving back from Orion, moving slowly until he had his head propped up. Laar's eyes were fixed upon him, an unreadable expression in their depths.

Laar said softly, "I cannot feel my legs, Worker."

"I'm sorry," Orion said gently. "That's all I can do. You're too heavy for me to move."

"True. You are, after all, only a Worker." The Giant's eyes closed. Without any word at all, the hand which had held the Ring clutched so tightly simply uncurled, and the radiance of the Ring struck upward through the water, the light dancing beneath the water. Orion did not hesitate; he knelt, took the Ring from the unresisting Giant, curled his own hand around it, and his fist glowed red with the sudden flare of the Light within his clutch.

He rose and ran for his slipship.

Kennian Temera flew his Falcon above the tundra. The squadron was following him, but he had received the orders from Cain before any of the others except Tristan, and Tristan d'Volta's slipship was no match in speed for an Eastmarch Falcon. The map was transmitted to his slipship's computer from Commander General Dantes' bomber, and the instant he had the coordinates he brought his slipship round and sped away from the cleanup of the drones.

The other Warriors followed him, but Kennian never looked back. When he reached the Skaald's Plaza, not five minutes later, he was moving so fast that he could not even open his airscoops to stop; at that velocity deforming the ship's aerodynamic profile even slightly would be like running into the side of the Great Dam. He banked instead, to come back around, hitting the deep radar as he did so. There was a dome of some sort, two full kilometers in length, covering the Skaald's Plaza. That dome was not shown on Kennian's map. The deep-radar image built slowly as Kennian banked, and by the time he had slowed enough to eyeball the dome and visually make out the hole Orion had blasted through it, the deep radar had built up a picture of what things were like down below.

There was a slipship inside.

His thrusters were cold, and Orion sat impatiently in the slipship while they warmed again, almost unable to ignore the brilliant pulsing of the Ring. It throbbed in rhythm with his heartbeat, pulsing with the brilliant, fever-yellow coloring of the Light, on the ring finger of his right hand.

Chunks of the dome plummeted to the floor of the Plaza around him, huge slabs of ice breaking free and plunging to the ground without pause.

Cracks radiated across the surface of the dome, huge fissures that reached down thirty and forty meters into the ice. It struck Kennian that they must have presented an absurd sight, some thirty-five Falcons circling the disintegrating dome lazily, like the buzzards that existed around the edges of the Glowing Desert. They had been circling so for two or three minutes when Commander Colonel Tristan's slipship broke over the horizon and established contact with them again.

"Is he down there?"

"His slipship is down there, Commander Colonel," Kennian reported.

"Nobody's gone down?"

"The dome is falling even as we speak, Colonel. It's not safe."

Frustration tinged the Colonel's reply. *"What if he's unable to get out on his own?"*

"Then he's going to die," said Kennian simply. "I'm not going to send a slipship down into that mess, not even for my best friend. Slipships only have room for one person, Tristan. If Orion can't get out by himself, we can't do it for him."

The dome was falling about him in slow, majestic pieces as Orion hit the belly jets to bring the landjacks up and away from contact with the street's surface and turned the slipship about with the attitude jets. He moved forward slowly, afraid to fly too fast lest he not see one of the falling chunks of ice in time to evade it.

Far ahead, nearly a full kilometer away, he could see the distant pale blue gleam of open sky. Ice fell around him like giant-sized snowflakes, struck his ship in chunks ranging from pebble-sized to a small boulder that bounced off the thrusters at the rear of the fuselage. Huge sheets of ice, some even larger than Orion's ship, fell all around him, and he evaded them by chance or design for most of half a kilometer before his nerves finally snapped and he said aloud, "The hell with it," and pulled the throttle back as far as it would go and blasted up and away through the rain of ice like a bat out of hell.

The whoops of joy came audibly despite the distance they had traveled, the long connection from the slipships to the bomber craft and back again to the War Room at Parliament. At first Cain could not make out words in the babble of voices, and then First Temera's voice sounded out with as much excitement as Cain had ever heard in it before. "He's up! Orion is up!"

The applause started slowly and built among the Eastmarchers and the Eagles warriors alike until the walls in the War Room were shaking with it.

In the midst of the rising wave of approval, Cain sat alone. He was aware of Maston Veramorn's glare against the back of his head and thought to himself that there was no gift he would more gladly have surrendered than that of seeing a thing before it had happened. It was the least reliable of his gifts, and certainly the least enjoyed. Never in his life had it told him a single thing he really wanted to know.

When the applause had died down to the point where Cain could be heard, he said quietly, "Bring them home. We will give the surviving Giants terms for surrender at noon tomorrow. Commander Dantes, leave one squadron and bring the rest home for repairs and maintenance." Cain was barely finished with the statement when the ovation began again, thunderous applause that seemed as though it would never end.

Cain could not help but think what a contrast it was with the Twenty Years' War.

Not quite three hours after the launch of Orion's slipship, after losing nearly two thirds of his army, after a single decisive battle on the same day it began, the War with the Giants was won.

· 4 ·

The flight to Parliament should not have taken Orion more than half an hour. They did not hurry, but returned cautiously, flying high above the serene waters of the One Ocean, taking care that their hundreds of crippled slipships were not overstressed. Orion flew with only the tiniest fragment of his attention, Kennian at his left wing and Commander Colonel Tristan in the old, Eagles-built slipship on his right. Orion had switched off his comm channels; he did not wish to argue any longer with Tristan.

Tristan thought himself betrayed, and Orion wondered briefly whether the older man had actually trusted him. Foolish, if so. Surely Tristan had not expected them to publicly broadcast their intentions to recover the Ring.

Had he?

Even now Orion was not prepared to admit that he actually had the Ring in his possession, not over an open comm channel. It was almost as though he could *hear* what Cain was thinking, the desire for silence and secrecy.

He felt drunk, senses swamped with information overload. Colors were unnaturally vivid, sounds had reverberations and chords within them which he had never perceived before. With the new sensitivity the Ring had given him, Orion heard the thought with perfect clarity.

Well? Are you going to come and get me, or not?

Orion ran through his diagnostics carefully. His fuel cells were in good shape. The slipship's lifeplant had sufficient water to keep Orion's air breathable for a full week. He ran a rough trajectory through the slipship's onboard computer; at full acceleration there and back, round-trip travel time was four and a half days. Five gravities spread out over four and a half days; Orion lay in the cocoon, thinking about it. It would have killed an ordinary Worker, he knew that. *But I,* thought Orion, *am not a Worker.*

I am the work of T'Pau Almandar.

Senta's thought came again. *Well? Really, it's **boring** here.*

Perhaps they were right, thought Orion distantly, thinking of the Rulers who had left Earth a decade and a half since. *Perhaps they were right, and we were never meant to live among Workers.*

He brought the nose of his slipship up and kicked the thrusters in, and the One Ocean fell away beneath him.

Okay, Orion thought finally, *I'll be there in a little over two days. You better be worth it.*

He had the feeling he had offended her. *Trust me.*

Kennian did not know how long Orion had been gone before he noticed that the craft was no longer flying thirty meters off his right wing. The closest craft in that direction was Tristan d'Volta's. He hit the map refresh almost without having to pause to think, and suddenly the blip that had shown Orion's craft had jumped on his map display to a spot high above Kennian's current altitude. He keyed open the squadron's private communications channel. "Orion!"

There was no response. "Damn," Kennian Temera muttered to himself, "what does he think he's doing?"

He heard Tristan d'Volta asking much the same question. *"Orion, where are you headed?"*

No reply again.

In the War Room at Parliament the huge holographic display of the North Land vanished for the first time that day and was replaced with a graphic showing the returning fleet of slipships. The ships held to a ragged formation, except for a single slipship that was climbing rapidly into orbit. Another slipship—not a Falcon, from the slow speed at which it was rising—was attempting to follow.

"What's he doing?" demanded Maston Veramorn from the other side of the War Room.

The Warriors in the War Room were watching him. Cain said, slowly, deliberately, "That's an excellent question."

Tristan d'Volta's relayed voice issued from the outspeakers. *"I'm losing him. Orion, this is Tristan. . . . Orion, why don't you answer?"*

"He doesn't answer," Maston snarled into the open circuit, "because he'd rather not waste time talking to a fool. And whatever he's doing, mark this," he shouted across the War Room, "it's because he has the Ring! This day is our victory against the Giants? Or is it merely Cain's victory over us?"

Cain stood slowly and made his way from the War Room, four bodyguards trailing behind him. An Eastmarch Warrior looked a question at him, and he shrugged and said as politely as though to an equal, "I really don't know. Let me know if anything interesting develops. I'm going to go get some sleep." He brushed by Maston Veramorn on the way out without even looking at the man.

Tristan d'Volta swore foully and said, *"Air's too thin. I'm not going to catch him."* They could hear the rage and frustration in the man's voice. *"Abandoning pursuit. I'm coming back."*

Orion lay back in the cockpit of the Falcon as it left Earth's orbit under five gravities of acceleration, thinking calmly to himself, *This is crazy, this is crazy, this is basically really crazy.*

Well, the girl said, *the universe is crazy. Didn't anyone ever tell you?*

The word was slurred by acceleration effects. "No."

He had the impression of a shrug. *Trust me.*

· 5 ·

Two days later, early in the morning, they sat together on the steps leading up to the War Room near the center of the city of Parliament. They were all three of them armed, handguns and variable lasers both. Lisa was carrying a laser rifle. Parliament had become a tense city, with two armies encamped at once.

The discussion they were having made Kennian Temera uneasy. Bellows was clearly confused by everything that had happened, and angry that he had never had a chance to fight against the Giants. Lisa was angry for the same reason and also seemed far too willing, for Kennian's peace of mind, to believe Maston Veramorn's propaganda about both Cain and Orion alike.

"I know they were Maston's Warriors," Lisa said fiercely, "I know that. But why would they lie to Bellows about why they wanted to drown the Workers at the Caverns? Damn it, they were going to kill Bellows anyway!"

Kennian sighed. It was a cold morning, and his breath frosted. "Lisa, would you please try to calm down and think? I know you can when you want to. What happened back at the Caverns breaks down nine different possible ways I can think of—I'll list them if you're interested—and none of them involve orders from Cain." Kennian grinned suddenly, lips moving in a fashion that did not look entirely normal upon him. "You really think that just because they were going to kill Bellows it means they wouldn't lie to him?"

"I think maybe Cain did order it done," said Lisa stubbornly, and then with a flash of anger, "And maybe Orion as well. You trust Orion? Our *friend?* Why didn't *he* tell us we were risking our lives for nothing better than the Ring?" She laughed suddenly, without any real humor. "And now Orion has the Ring and Cain's sitting there wondering where his loyal son has gotten off to. I bet he feels alone now. I hope he feels alone."

Bellows had been fairly quiet most of the morning, but he spoke up now. "I don't have much love for Cain, but let's at least condemn the bastard for the things he's actually done. We went to war against the Giants because they enslaved something like a hundred and forty thousand Workers. Orion risked his life in a slipship without lasers to bring the Shield down—and *then* went to get the Ring." The wind whistled through the bare branches of the ancient trees in the courtyards around them. "I wish Orion had told us myself. . . ." Bellows shrugged. "He may not be my friend any longer, but he's not my enemy."

"Damn it," Lisa exploded, "If Cain didn't order the Workers be kept in the Caverns when the floods came, why doesn't he deny it when Maston accuses him?"

"Maybe," said Kennian evenly, "Cain doesn't think anybody is so stupid as to believe he'd actually kill his own Workers. Maybe he thinks that people will stop to consider that if he'd wanted to kill his own Workers he wouldn't have used Maston's Warriors to do it with when most of his own Warriors are loyal enough to him to do anything he commands." Lisa was flushing, staring down at the step her feet were resting upon. "*Maybe* he thinks that anybody with two brain cells to rub together would wonder why he bothered to engineer a reasonably well-planned evacuation in the first place when he could just as easily have blown the damned fusion generator on Level Four and killed all you stupid shits in the first place before you ever got your shirts wet."

Lisa stared at him as though she'd been slapped. *"Shirts* wet? Do you know how many people *died* in the water?"

"Sixteen hundred and twenty-three as near as the best figures we have indicate, almost half of them children," said Kennian flatly. "On top of that we lost thirty-two hundred and fifty-five Warriors in actual battle. You add them up and it comes to a lot. You know what disturbs me?"

"Why don't you tell us, No-Name?" Bellows leaned back against the wall at the side of the steps, wrapped his jacket tightly against the cold, and closed his eyes as though he were planning to sleep.

"Cain."

Lisa snorted. "No kidding."

Kennian shook his head slowly. "That's not what I mean. He's a brutal man, or can be, we all know that. But he's *smart*, and has been for a long time. Now—he's behaving stupidly, or if there's reason behind the way he's behaving I can't fathom it." He was silent while he ordered his thoughts. "Look. Maston and Tristan d'Volta have been organizing their Warriors, and broadcasting their propaganda to *us* at the same time. General Dantes is keeping discipline up, but he's not handling the situation as well as Cain would, or even Orion, and we all know it." He looked at both of his friends. "So why? He sits there up on the hill in the Chamber and doesn't deny anything, doesn't mobilize his Warriors. . . ." His voice trailed off. "Doesn't make sense." He chuckled suddenly, and Bellows lifted a single eyelid and looked at him in surprise. *A grin and a chuckle both in the same conversation,* Bellows thought with something like amazement. "Must be nice, Lisa, to know the exact truth about everybody like you do. The only thing I know for sure is I don't know too damn much of anything."

Lisa Wanaré sat silently beneath the cold, gray sky. That the air hung heavy with impending rain and snow seemed nothing but appropriate to the thoughts locked in her skull, thoughts that she could not seem to make anybody else understand at all, not Bellows, not even Kennian, who was the smartest person she knew.

The hell of it was, Orion would have understood, if she'd only been able to talk to him.

"It's not nice," she said finally, with a flat desperation in her voice that the other two could not help but hear. "It's terrible."

THE RING

*H*e lay in the cockpit of the Falcon, eyes clenched shut against the twin blazes of Light, from the Ring on his hand and the coldly incandescent surface of the Star. The slipship hung not a quarter of a kilometer above the surface of the glowing asteroid. The reports Orion had read concerning Eastmarch's investigation of the Star's surface, though they were now some fifteen years old, might have been written yesterday. If there had been a significant change in the Star in the fifteen years since that time, it was invisible to Orion.

"Real? What's reality?" the woman asked precisely.

They walked together down the streets of Parliament, through a warm summer day, beneath surreally blue skies. The Ring pulsed on Orion's finger, blazing brighter than the sun, building a brilliant glow within Orion. The only analogy Orion could think of that made any sense at all was that it felt as if he were some brilliantly made machine and the fusion generator that powered it had just come on-line.

The woman who walked at his side could have been his younger sister. Her name was Senta Almandar, and Orion was still not entirely sure she was even alive. Oh, she felt real enough, flesh to his touch; her speech was the warm contralto of a human throat, not the crisp precision that Orion associated with telepathy.

Unfortunately it was not real. Nor was the Parliament through which they walked, nor the pool they had bathed in before that. If it seemed real, Senta said, it was only because, as she put it, "I've had a very long time to practice." Though Orion was only distantly aware of the cockpit of the slipship in which he had journeyed there, of his own body recuperating from the pounding it had taken during better than two days' acceleration and deceleration, that was all that was *real*. The rest of it, everything, was only Senta's thoughts and memories, constructed into a false world for her to inhabit because the Lords of Light had, fifteen years ago, cut her off from the real one.

"And since then," she said softly, "nothing. I've been aware of Loga from time to time, but even he has not been able to break through the bonds they placed upon me. I haven't been able to communicate, not once, not with anyone, not until now." She was silent a moment and then laughed. "Until you came, I did not even know how long I had been here. I'm thirty-two now," she marveled. "Isn't that amazing?"

"I suppose," Orion replied. Parliament was strange. It was Parliament as she remembered it, still clean and maintained, with Rulers and Workers bustling through its streets. The folk in the streets did not seem to be aware of either Orion or Senta; after one attempt that amused Senta, Orion did not try to talk to them. "I spoke to Loga about you. If he had the Ring, I think he could have freed you." Senta nodded, and Orion continued, "I don't have his skills, and now that I'm here I'm not entirely sure what I'm supposed to do."

Senta looked at him in surprise. "You don't have to do anything. I'll free myself."

"Oh?"

The puzzled flavor of the thought must have reached her. Senta looked at him curiously. "Surely it's obvious? I can free myself. All you have to do is give me the Ring."

Orion stared at her. "Not a chance."

"Please?" she said politely.

Orion was distantly aware of his motionless form lying in the cockpit of his slipship, hand closed around the Ring. "I don't think I . . . can."

Senta turned on him and smiled.

The smile was an utterly dazzling thing, a pure and amazingly direct grin that was like nothing Orion had ever seen before. He found himself smiling back without even knowing why. "*I* think you can," she said cheerfully, "and I have had a very, very long time—to think."

In one of the observer's seats in the dark Chamber, high above Parliament, Cain sat alone and watched the sky. His mind was empty of thought. He was not planning, not anticipating.

He was merely waiting.

Sometime around midnight, Loga appeared in the center of the debating floor.

Cain said softly, "Hello, Loga."

"Hello, Cain." The redhead wandered around the edges of the darkened Chamber and finally sat in a chair not far from Cain's. "I've been in the Eastmarch hills recently. Things are pretty bad out there."

Cain nodded. "I know. We've been flying food out to them, but I'm told they're still not eating well. Seventy-seven thousand Workers trying to survive in the hills. . . ." His voice trailed away. "I wish I could help them, but I can't. We've got burn victims to treat at Saerlock. The situation at Saerlock's not quite as bad as it could be, but only because most of them drowned when the Dam was breached. And the entire length of Almandar overflowed its banks. There's hardly a community in this Valley does not need help in some way."

"But they'll have to find it themselves, eh?"

"My engineers are working upon the problems, many of them, where they are solvable. Only two percent of the Great Dam was actually destroyed, you know. It can be rebuilt, my engineers tell me, and the seawater drained again."

"It sounds as though your engineers will be busy. What of you?"

"I'm a dead man, Loga."

Loga said softly, "I have myself, over the course of the centuries, had visions that did not become reality. Haven't you?"

Cain actually smiled at that. "Not yet."

"They need you back at Eastmarch. They'd follow you, if you'd go. Maybe you'll die anyhow, but at least you'll die trying."

Cain simply shook his head. "No. I'm waiting for Orion to return, and after that—I am done, my friend."

"Cain, they need a leader."

"Then lead them."

Loga stared at him. "*Me?* No." He looked legitimately offended. "I won't."

"Okay."

Loga was still staring at him. "Cain, that entire end of the Valley is under water."

Cain smiled again. "My father," he said, "was a fisherman."

Loga blinked.

"You would have liked him."

Loga sat silently with Cain for a long time. They did not speak to each other. Finally Loga said, "Probably I would have." The silence before he spoke again was interminable. "You could have done it, Cain, if you'd only had the nerve." The wind of his passage buffeted Cain, tugged at his clothing.

Cain was not entirely certain Loga would not hear his reply. "I know. It's just that I'm very tired. Good-bye, Loga."

They lay upon the slope of the hill together and looked down upon the imaginary city of Parliament. The sun was very warm, and the scent of the grass sharp and strong. It all left Orion feeling very drowsy, and disinclined to argue with the very remarkable woman whom Senta Almandar was turning out to be.

"I knew so many things then, when they imprisoned me here," Senta said quietly. She lay on her back next to him, hands clasped behind her head. "So very many." She shook her head slowly. "And understood almost none of them. My life went easily because I was a Ruler, because there were Workers to serve me. As, Orion, your life, I think, has gone easily, because there have been Workers to serve you. I do not say that it is wrong that you have been made to lead and others to follow; before T'Pau made us, that was the order of things for all humans, that some outshone the others."

Orion nodded quietly, thinking wordlessly of the friends he was not certain he would ever recover.

Senta sat up suddenly, hugging her knees. "It becomes difficult when there are *many* who are so much better, on the average, than the rest of humanity. We were a good people, Orion," she said suddenly. "I have thought about this, and thought about it. We were a good people. We did far more good than we ever did harm. If there was a crime we were guilty of, it was that we were, truly, *better* than the Workers. Stronger, smarter, with senses that only the best of them—Cain, the rebel Artemis, and the like—could ever hope to equal. Cain came near our level in all ways but the physical. I am told he is not a remarkably strong man." She shrugged. "I did not understand at the time. That was why we left Earth, because the Workers could not compete with us, and it was not fair to make them. We had to leave. Our guidance was not wanted and could not help the Workers. We found peace for ourselves, the harmony—a very real thing, Orion, that one Ruler need not strive against another—but we could not teach it to the Workers. They are only human, and it was not in them to learn."

"It was not in them to learn," Orion repeated softly. "I think you are wrong, in that at least. Certainly they have not learned, but it does not mean they cannot."

Senta chuckled. "It is a strong indication, Orion. We educated Workers for some seven centuries at Academy, and in all that time there was rarely a Worker—even their best—who approached our level, until Cain."

"I could teach them," said Orion after a long pause. "I think I could. They try so very hard, you know. Lisa, and Bellows and No-Name. I'm one of them. They know me."

"Jesus was one of them, also," said Senta quietly. "And see what —" She broke off suddenly. "You do not know the name?"

Orion shook his head. "Should I?"

"Cain knows of it," she said thoughtfully. "But I think, Orion, that there are many things Cain knows that you do not. You tell me he has never taught you the disciplines of the mind. He does know them, Orion, and as Loden's blood—T'Pau's blood—you have the skill to master the Light within you."

Orion laughed at that, suddenly. "Skill? I?" The laughter was real and lasted several moments. Finally he stopped. "Cain has that skill, I know, I've felt it. So does the Ruler Loga. I've felt the power of his thoughts as well. So did the women that night." He broke off and then said swiftly, "Perhaps I could do what they do, but I've no time to learn now."

> Do ye know what silence is,
> My friends, or not?
> This life that faces both ways
> Has marked the human face from within.

The words gentled and slowed, and Orion realized that he was hanging on to them, waiting for more when there could be no more. "That is as nearly true as anything I can tell you," said Senta quietly. "Cain raised you all your life to seek outward, to direct yourself against the barriers of the Giants, to the goal of retrieving the Ring. You have done great things as the world reckons them, Orion." She turned slightly where she was sitting and looked down upon him. "But the world is a fool and a harlequin. I promised your mother I'd come for you, and here you've come for me, all these years later. You're quite correct. I won't teach you the control of the Light in the short time we have together, and therefore, there is only one way for me to be freed. Orion, you are blood of my blood, and I tell you by my name and by my father's name and by T'Pau's name, if there is or ever was any honor to be found in the name of Almandar, *I will give you back the Ring.*"

Orion simply nodded, not wearily, but with a great and very real reluctance.

"But before I can give it back," she said gently, "you must trust me enough to give it to me. Forget the world, Orion, forget the wisdom of the world, for it is not wisdom. Trust me.

"Give me the Ring."

That night there were no clouds in the sky over Parliament. Cain was still sitting in the Chamber, waiting for his fate to reach him, when the light from the Star suddenly flickered, went dim for the merest instant, and then flared like a nova.

When the night sky had faded back to darkness again, the Star, for the first time in fifteen years, was gone.

· 6 ·

Orion orbited Earth, sat through several revolutions above the surface of the planet, looking down upon the blue of the Ocean. He was not certain whether it was his imagination or if his air was actually going bad, but it did not matter.

I stink, Orion thought clinically, *I'm thirsty, and I'm bruised all over.*

At least, he thought with a distant, weary relief, *I'm home.*

He took his slipship out of orbit, down into atmosphere.

Maston paced restlessly across the length of the War Room. There were no Eastmarchers in that room, no longer. They had all withdrawn to the Eastmarch camp at the lower north end of Parliament.

Tristan d'Volta, half drunk, sat at a dead workstation and drank and watched Maston pace. The old man was in fine form, he thought cynically. Bordine's death, and the small and literally symbolic victory that Orion's bizarre behavior had given him over the course of the last five days had, it seemed to Tristan, restored to Maston Veramorn some lost piece of his youth. When the thought came to him, he spoke without censoring his tongue, for he had found that Maston was no longer capable of frightening him. "Orion will be back. I know him that well."

Maston's growl was sheer reflex, as though he were practicing. "Did you know he'd betray us all once he had the Ring? The boy's a Ruler in his blood, and it shows."

"He'll come back," said Tristan coolly, "and I'll discuss the subject with him." Tristan came to his feet carefully and walked out of there without staggering. He carried an aura of frustration and disgust with him like a decoration he had awarded himself, and it left when he did. Maston watched him go with a small portion of his mind. Tristan, he had very nearly decided, was going to have to die soon.

"Lord Maston?"

Maston whirled as though he thought he were under attack; one of his bodyguards began to reach for his weapon.

Commander General Mondàl Dantes smiled at them from the entryway. There were five Eastmarch Warriors, armed with rifles, standing behind him. "My lord Cain," he said formally, almost condescendingly, "requests your presence at the Chamber of Parliament as soon as it is convenient. You are invited to bring your bodyguards; Lord Cain intends a peaceful meeting. As the current situation is intolerable, it is in all our interests to see it resolved. He is awaiting you now."

Dantes did not wait for a reply. He bowed, very slightly indeed, and backed out of the War Room with his men.

Maston made him wait an hour, and then, in one of his own personnel carriers, with twenty of his bodyguards, went up the mountain to the Chamber.

On a ledge of stonesteel high above the refugee camp, Senta stood and drank in the scent of the wind, the beauty of the growing shadows and orange fire of the setting Sun.

Loga's voice drifted to her from a great distance, loud and angry. He was, she could tell, enjoying himself immensely.

". . . no, no, *no*," he shrieked. "Are you all brain-damaged? Just because you never fished before in your lives doesn't mean you *have* to screw it up. It's not like it's an obligation or anything, all right?"

A Worker down there said something that the wind bore away from Senta, or perhaps he was merely not shouting as loudly as the Lord of Light. "Do you think maybe you're going to *catch more fish* by tangling the bloody damned lines together? *What?* I know they're slimy," he screamed at them, "they're supposed to be, they're *worms.*"

Fifteen years of sensory deprivation, though she surely had not enjoyed it, had done wondrous things for her control of the Light; she knew instantly when Orion's slipship entered the atmosphere of Earth. *I'm going,* she said quietly to Loga, and went.

The Workers below had grown almost as blasé about the sight as had the Workers of old Parliament. Nobody even looked up at the sharp crack of thunder that heralded her passage.

The two technicians at the far-radar workstation conferred with each other before approaching the Commander First who was on duty. Finally they reached a consensus, and the senior technician spoke up just as Tristan d'Volta entered the War Room. "Commander? We're picking up a blip on far radar. It was originally coming on an unpowered trajectory; we thought it was meteoritic material at first, because slipships usually don't have such a distant radar signature—"

Tristan interrupted the man. "Spit it out. What is it?"

The Warrior had been directing his words at the Commander First on duty. He turned slightly to face Tristan. "Sir? I can't say for sure, but it's under powered flight, and it's too small to be Giant craft— and coming from the wrong direction as well." The Warrior shrugged. "It's a guess, sir, but a good one. I think it's Commander Captain Orion. His slipship's shiny enough to give this kind of radar signature."

Tristan stared down at the workstation's display. The Warrior technicians on duty could smell the alcohol on the Commander Colonel's breath. "That's him. He's come back." He glared at the senior technician. "Why wasn't I notified of this sooner?"

Half a dozen replies seemed to be fighting for expression; the Warrior said finally, "You weren't here, sir. In addition, Lord Maston told us to inform him if—"

Tristan backhanded the man with his full strength, reached down to where the man lay sprawled on the floor and lifted him back to his feet with one hand. "You tell anyone," he whispered fiercely, "and I'll have you before a firing squad before the day's out." He shoved the Warrior away from him and yelled at the Commander First. "I want a roof of laser fire, Tiers One and Two all at once, the instant he drops below two thousand meters absolute. I *want* him, he's *mine.*"

Commander Colonel Tristan d'Volta did not even wait to see whether they accepted his instructions; he turned and ran.

Tristan took up fifteen slipships with him, the few men in all of Maston Veramorn's service whose loyalty to Tristan d'Volta was, he believed, greater than their fear of Maston Veramorn.

An aide came to Commander General Mondàl Dantes, where he waited in the personnel carrier on the landpad below the Caverns. Though styled as a personnel carrier, it was a deceptive craft. If need be, it was capable of blasting Maston Veramorn's carrier, on the other side of the landpad, halfway to hell without even trying too hard.

"Sir? Fifteen, possibly sixteen slipships just lifted from the south end of Parliament. We're monitoring their communications, but we've heard nothing to indicate why they're doing so."

Dantes considered it briefly and then dismissed it. "If they can harm us with fifteen bloody slips, let 'em."

"Yes, Commander General."

The ships that rose to meet him so swiftly were clearly not Eastmarcher craft. Still Orion did not worry about it; he had not hailed the Parliament War Room on his way down from orbit, and until they had visual contact they might not be certain who he was. He moved stiffly to touch the stud controlling the choice of comm channel and switched it to general hailing frequencies. "This is Commander Captain Orion, Eastmarch; to the ships approaching, hello."

"*Commander Orion, this is Commander Colonel d'Volta. You are in Eagles flight space and you will continue your descent under our escort.*"

"Tristan?"

"Speaking." The slipships continued to rise, coming about to parallel Orion's own course toward Parliament.

"Why the formality, Tristan? I'm perfectly willing to come down with you."

"You'd better be, because you don't have any choice, Ruler."

"Ruler? Tristan, what the hell is that supposed to—"

He was in that instant still better than a hundred meters above the Eagles slipships, but dropping rather faster than they were. The altimeter showed him at just a hair under two kilometers absolute, and the sky immediately above him turned the color of blood. He did not stop to think for even an instant, but merely reacted as years of training took hold, took the slipship over and hit the thrusters at their fullest acceleration, took it straight down and away from the ceiling of laser fire. He was below the level of the Eagles ships within seconds, falling like a stone, and he heard Tristan d'Volta's voice screaming across the open hailing frequencies, *"He's running! Stop him!"*

He realized quickly that there was no way he was going to make Parliament. The predicament he found himself in was one his dead father might have appreciated; though any one of the Eagles ships were no match for his own, fifteen surely were. They herded him slowly toward the Black Mountains, using laser fire and missiles alike with enough indifference that Orion knew within seconds that, though they were not trying to kill him as hard as they might, they did not care if they did.

They were already in the shadows of the mountains when Orion found the first moment when he was safe long enough to switch to Eastmarcher comm channels and broadcast an appeal for help over it. He had no idea if anyone even heard him except for his attackers. Tristan d'Volta, at least, was monitoring on Eastmarch channels, for after Orion's call for help his voice came in on that channel. *"Now I know you better, Ruler, we'll make a fair fight of this."*

"Fair fight? Only fifteen to one?"

"Sixteen, actually. It's fair enough, if you fly the way either of your parents did."

"I wasn't counting that carefully. It hardly *seems* fair, Tristan. I haven't even got any lasers on this craft." They reached the mountains then, and Orion had no more time for speech for several seconds, bringing the ship up into a darkening ravine, into the inner reaches of the Black Mountains.

"Not fair, Orion? Bring the Light, Ruler. You could do that regardless, and you carry the Ring."

Laser fire struck around Orion, growing closer and closer; they were trying to force him down. The chase continued, further and further south, until the Valley was lost to sight behind them. "Tristan, damn it, what's gotten into you? Can't we at least talk about this?"

"This is how I'll talk!" Laser fire actually touched Orion's craft, and he swore, diving even closer to the blurred peaks of the Black Mountains.

"Tristan, is it just the Ring? I'll *give* it to you, I don't even know how to use the damn thing?"

Tristan d'Volta's snort of disbelief came plainly over the comm circuit. *"Sure you will. Rulers are so well known for sharing the secrets of the . . ."*

A deeper blackness in the growing darkness was the only warning Orion had of what was, almost certainly, his only chance. He snapped the slipship over almost on its side, scooped air wildly, and hit the thrusters. The glowing heatwash of the thrusters illuminated the trail of his passage, and then his slipship was entirely inside the blackened gorge, flying far too fast in an inky darkness where only Orion's own thrusters gave any light at all. He had his airscoops at their fullest extension, and it probably saved his life when the tip of his right wing touched an outcrop of rock and sent his ship down into the darkness at several hundred kilometers an hour.

The slipships prowled through murky passages in the heart of the Black Mountains. Their lasers were set for widest dispersion, scarlet red searchlights covering the areas where Orion's ship had vanished, wavering in pure monochrome ruby across snow and stone and occasional patches of pine trees.

They found the ship twenty minutes into their search, a tangled mass of gleaming, fire-scorched wreckage.

One of the Warriors with Tristan whistled at the sight of the smashed craft. "Well, that's the end of him."

Tristan said quietly, "Looks like. I'm going down to check it out."

He set down on a small ledge sixty meters above the crashed ship and took a quarter of an hour covering that sixty meters' distance. He walked around the wreckage of the craft, playing the beam of his hand flash across the ship as though it might give him some clue as to what had happened to Orion. The ship itself had burned fiercely, the fusion cells igniting and slagging the entire rear third of the craft. The carbon threads reinforcing the gleaming silver-tinged hull, which as far as Tristan had ever heard were not supposed to burn at any temperature, were perfectly black where the flames had crawled along their length. The cockpit was blasted beyond recognition. Tristan could not tell for sure whether Orion's body was in the cockpit or not, and the glowing heat of the melted fusion cells convinced him it was perhaps not the best idea in the world to get close enough to check. With an odd feeling in his stomach to which he could not put a name, he climbed back to his slipship.

The blade of the variable laser appeared not two centimeters from his right ear the instant he reached the ledge where his slipship sat. The voice said softly, "If you move, Worker, if you breathe, if you do any of the stupid things you're thinking about, I'm going to cut your damn head clean off your shoulders."

Tristan d'Volta stood very still. Twenty centimeters of the blade extended far enough over his shoulder to see. The fog of Orion's breath was visible to him.

"I'm not sure that'd be such a waste at this point. This is the second time I've had this arm busted, and it's making me cranky. Drop your handgun on the ground, clasp your hands behind your head, take three steps forward and turn around. Take your gun from its holster with your left hand's thumb and little finger. Do it slowly. Do it now."

Tristan d'Volta did exactly as he was bade and, when he was done, found himself looking at the dim form that was Orion. His left arm hung limply, and he was pointing Tristan's own gun at him with the other.

He did not, as nearly as Tristan could see, have the Ring with him. "You offered to give me the Ring," Tristan said slowly, hands still clasped behind his head. "Did you mean that?"

"I did then," said Orion practically.

"Do you even have it?"

"Of course." With the free little finger of his gun hand he pulled the fragment of crystal from a breast pocket on his flight suit, and suddenly a small piece of the sun blazed on the ledge. "Had to put it away when you got here," he said mildly. "Damn thing's like a puppy, some ways. Doesn't know about 'Keep quiet, stupid.'"

Tristan d'Volta stared in amazement at the Ring. It was the first time he had ever seen it, the insignificant thing for which so many men had fought and died, hanging there on the end of Orion's little finger beneath the slick steel of the gun.

"So what do we do now, Tristan? What's it take to have peace between us, or is it even possible? You keep calling me 'Ruler,' as though it's some insult, but I'm not a Ruler. It's just me, Orion. That's the truth."

"Truth?" Tristan laughed harshly. "What's truth, Orion? Now you've got the Ring, and you've always had the power. That's the *truth.*"

"I suppose I could kill you," said Orion quietly, "but we've done a lot of that. I've spent my entire life learning to kill. I'm pretty good at it, it turns out. But we don't *have* to kill. Come down to Parliament with me—you and I. Let's take a shot at peace and see what happens." He smiled wearily. "The worst is we fail and we end up trying to kill each other anyhow—which is what we're doing now."

"It's easy for you talk about peace. You have the Ring. It's bloody damn easy to talk about making peace when you can't be hurt in the first place. Do you *really* think we'd be content to live our lives secure in the warm knowledge that even though you're a Ruler, you'd really never try to enslave the Workers again? Do you think that about any of us? *Of your own damned Eastmarchers?*"

Orion stood pointing the gun at Tristan d'Volta and, slowly, let the gun drop. He said softly, "Not a bad point, that." He stood motionless for a long instant. "Trust has to start somewhere." He dropped the handgun to the ground and said quietly to the staring man. "You're my witness," and threw the Ring toward the dark chasm beneath them.

Tristan d'Volta never even thought about what he was doing. He lunged for the thrown Ring, got a hand on it, felt for an unmeasurable brilliant instant the singing bright contact of the thing against his flesh, and then the contact ended and the icy stone beneath his feet slid away from him, and his fall was quiet and did not last very long.

It all took barely an instant. The Ring glowed serenely on the ground three meters in front of Orion.

Tristan was gone.

From a far place her thoughts touched his, as Orion stood paralyzed staring at the Ring. *It's never easy, Orion.*

I guess not. The feather touch of Senta's thoughts faded, and Orion stepped forward and took the Ring of Light from where it lay on the icy ground.

The negotiations were lengthy, acrimonious on Maston Veramorn's part, and detailed. Cain bargained Eastmarch's side of it alone, without help from any aides except Jimal, or computers, with only three bodyguards behind him. Maston Veramorn, with a half dozen servants and all twenty of his bodyguards present, bargained for Eagles, shivering in the cold open-air Chamber where the Rulers of Earth had once debated among themselves. The stars were visible still, though a solid wall of dark storm clouds was approaching from the north like the promise of Giant retribution. Maston Veramorn had visited the Chamber perhaps ten times in all the years he had held Parliament, and had not ever learned to like it; tonight, when the tension stretched his nerves and the very air stank of ozone, he would rather have been almost anywhere else in all the world.

At one moment, when Cain proposed dividing Parliament and Goldriver evenly, Parliament to be left to Maston and Cain to take over Goldriver, Maston lost his temper entirely and shouted at Cain nonstop for better than a full minute. Cain sat quietly and did not interrupt, though Maston Veramorn's bodyguards were fingering their weapons nervously. When Maston finally ran down, Cain said quietly, almost reflectively, "In Eastmarch I once had a man executed for bad manners. It didn't teach *him* anything but people were real nice to each other for a couple of weeks."

Maston Veramorn stared at Cain for just a moment, and then smirked. "I am sure you did that, once, in Eastmarch," said Maston, voice suddenly silky, "but you are not, Cain of Eastmarch, in Eastmarch any longer. You are in Parliament, alone, without your Ruler son and with only three bodyguards. I've seen your silver-eyes work, Cain, and they are impressive, but twenty handguns at once will, I think, make short work of them."

Cain grinned at Maston Veramorn, black eyes cold as northern ice. "I'm sure that's true. Of course, you'll die first, and probably half your bodyguards with you."

The comment took the fire from Maston's demeanor in a flat instant, though he tried not to let it show. "So I die. I'll die anyway, without the youthbooster you've kept from us all. At least, in Tristan, there is someone to succeed me. Who will succeed you? The Ruler who fled you the instant he had the Ring?"

Cain did not even bother to deny the accusation that Orion had the Ring. "Orion will be back," Cain said mildly.

Down the slope of the mountain Cain caught sight of three fluorescent forms, flickering in and out of sight at the edge of the trees, and suddenly Cain knew what it was that had been haunting the edges of his awareness this last week.

Maston Veramorn simply glared at him and spoke for the benefit of his listening bodyguards. "I doubt it."

Cain shrugged, dismissed the Sisterhood of the Ring from his thoughts, and smiled. Two could play to the masses as well as one. "Only one of us can be right, and based on our respective records, Maston Veramorn, I don't think it's you."

If there was any hurry, Orion was not aware of it. He landed at the south end of Parliament, calling ahead to warn the Flight Commander on duty that he was coming in an Eagles slipship. He had his arm attended to by a field doctor who could barely keep her nose from wrinkling at the smell of him, then showered, drank a full liter of water, and donned a dress uniform appropriate to the negotiations he was informed were taking place at the Chamber of Parliament, high above the city. Dressing, he saw that there were purple bruises everywhere he had had any contact with the slipship's acceleration cocoon.

The news of his return, the news of the Ring he wore upon his hand, spread throughout the Eastmarch ranks at lightspeed, and by the time he was ready to go up to join Cain, the only three friends whom he had in the world were waiting for him at the landpads, waiting wordlessly. He stood for a long silent moment without addressing them, for though he knew what it was they needed to hear he did not know quite how to say it. When the words finally came they were like a wind that used him as its instrument, speaking directly to them, without ornamentation, the words that were in his heart.

To Kennian Temera he said, "You are the best friend I have ever had."

To Bellows he said, "Have faith. I'm the same man I always was."

To Lisa Wanarè he said gently, "I've always loved you."

To them all he said only, "Follow me."

They did, the four slipships moving gently up the mountainside to the landpad where the Eastmarch and Eagles personnel carriers waited.

Cain watched the slipships come up the mountain. There were four, and he knew instantly who they must be, all four of them. One slipship led the other three slightly, and even at that distance the man who had once worn the Ring on his own hand could feel the bright electric pulse of the power coming up the mountain. Maston Veramorn broke off when it became apparent that Cain was not listening to him and followed the path of his gaze.

"What treachery is this, Cain?" Maston demanded instantly.

"No treachery, Maston. It's just my son."

They walked up from the landpad together, four young Warriors. The Ring cast a brilliant light away from itself, and their shadows wavered grotesquely across the landscape. They came up to the Chamber and entered it through the south opening. There was silence as they came and silence when they had arrived, and it was broken only when Orion said softly, "Lord Cain, Lord Maston." He turned to face Maston Veramorn and said gently, for he did not know what sort of affection there might have been between the men, "Lord Maston, Commander Colonel Tristan d'Volta is dead."

There was silence still. Maston did not say a word. Orion moved more fully into the Chamber, the Ring ablaze upon his hand. "Tristan died, Lord Maston, because he could not bear to see the Ring abandoned, because it was in his mind the power he needed to be safe in a universe where one cannot be safe. Living is dangerous, gentlemen, and everyone who lives, dies. I am," he said flatly, speaking now more to Cain than to Maston, "going to see this Ring returned to the place from which you took it."

Maston Veramorn had grown very pale as Orion was speaking. He had to lick his lips before he could bring words forth. "Fine words, Ruler. I believe you no more than I'd have believed Loden or Solan or any of his ilk."

There was a sharp crack, the thunder of her appearance, and Senta Almandar appeared at the edge of the Chamber. The explosion of air, away from the spot of her appearance, cut through the last of his words. Senta Almandar said quietly, "Hello, Maston Veramorn."

Fifteen solid years had passed since the last time any person in that Chamber save Cain had even seen one of the Lords of Light, appearing cloaked in the full power of the Light. Its glow shimmered across Senta's skin, gathered at her eyes and in the hollow of her throat. Its liquid touch never left her as she stood regarding Maston Veramorn. The tableau held, perfectly motionless, for perhaps three seconds. One of Maston's bodyguards moved slightly as though he were considering reaching for his weapon, and Senta stopped him with a single gesture. She observed Maston Veramorn for a long moment and said at last, "Why? You refuse to believe Orion because of an accident of birth which he had no control over?"

There was no one present who missed the twitching of the muscle in Maston's cheek. Cain watched the proceedings with an apparent keen interest, but said nothing. Finally Maston sputtered almost incoherently, "*Believe* him? Cain's child, and a Ruler to boot? *One of you?*"

Orion had not even looked away from Maston Veramorn. He was surely the only person there who had not even turned at the sound of Senta Almandar's appearance. "I will no longer deny who I am, Worker. My father's father was a Ruler, and if blood is everything then I am a Ruler. I am not ashamed of that; they wrought many great things. Except that they were not extended to all, there was nothing *wrong* with the ideals of the Rulers. A belief in peace, that striving together was worth more than striving against one another. A belief that killing is wrong. Are those such terrible things?" He turned to Maston Veramorn's bodyguards and said as directly as though to equals, "We joined hands, Workers, to attack the Giants. I think we must be able to do the same thing for peace. You can do it. We can do it. Who will we attack next?" He turned slowly, gesturing out toward the Valley, toward the world. He laughed suddenly. "Who's bloody *left?*"

Maston Veramorn swore at his own bodyguards. "You'd listen to *him?*" He turned to Orion. "To a Ruler, with the Ring in his clutch?" He took a step forward, closer to Orion, and shouted the words: "If you will have peace, Ruler, then *give me the Ring.* Show us *all* your good faith."

Orion did not hesitate an instant. "Very well." While Maston was still glaring at him in utter disbelief, he took the Ring from his finger, stepped forward and placed the Ring in Maston's open palm. Maston Veramorn grasped his hand, the Ring held between their two palms, stepped forward and in a single motion withdrew the knife tucked at his belt and stabbed Orion in the stomach. Orion left the Ring in Maston's clutch and took two slow steps backward, to where Cain was rising calmly from the seat he had been in all that evening. There was a puzzled expression on his face, and Cain caught him before he could fall. One of Cain's silver-eyes moved in that instant to stop one of Maston Veramorn's bodyguards from taking the shot he was attempting and did in fact split the bodyguard's throat with a throwing knife in the very moment that the man shot Cain of Eastmarch dead between his eyes.

Dusk descended swiftly.

They walked together along the shore of the Ocean as night fell. They spoke of trivial subjects, things of no importance. The things that mattered had largely been said long years since, and now there was no need. Orion became aware of his surroundings but slowly, of the chill touch of the water against his ankles. To his left the beach stretched away into a rocky desolation, and to his right the One Ocean extended out to the far horizon. The surroundings began to puzzle him, and he finally asked Cain where they were.

"We are at the end of a journey, Orion." The man looked at

Orion a moment and said then, "My journey. I think if it was yours, you would see something different. I think you must go back."

"Leave you here alone? Surely you're not serious."

"I am," Cain said slowly. Thoughts came to him with difficulty, and he struggled with them because there it was very important that Orion not follow him where he must go. "Turn," he said quietly. "Go back, son."

"Son?" Orion nodded thoughtfully and looked back the way they had come, at the far-distant gleam of life. He turned slowly and began walking back the way he had come, but after only a few steps he turned back again and saw Cain looking after him. "Cain?"

"Yes, Orion."

"Cain? If it had been given me to choose a father, it would have been you."

"Orion." In the deepening purple twilight, the dark-haired man and the light-haired looked at each other. "Myself, and my master Loukas—while you live, we have not died." Very gently he said, "Go back."

• 7 •

The darkness gathered about his soul.

Standing quietly at the shore of the great dark ocean, Cain wondered whether the kriss had the right of it, that death was only a gateway to another place, another life. Would he see his sisters again? And Jenny, the first woman he had ever loved, and Elli, who was the last? Perhaps he might see his mother, as an adult now, and reconcile their differences; Cain knew that he could, now, bring her to love him as he had always loved her.

Far in the distance, there was a shimmering radiance.

By the Light, maybe he would see Loukas again.

It was growing very cold, and the sound of the waves slapping the shore had all but ceased. A great stillness was descending all about him, until all that was left was the dim, distant Light, and the utter blackness and emptiness; and in the last desperate act of his life Cain reached out with all his soul for the Light which, since his childhood, had always eluded him.

· 8 ·

Orion walked back through the gathering dark.

The cold sucked at his strength, racked his body with shivers. He placed one foot before another, trudging forward without stop. He did not dare slow; it took all the strength that was within him merely to continue forward in the face of the glacial quiet cold.

Their voices called to him, beckoning, the voices of the Sisterhood of the Ring, most of the way back.

At some point in that journey, when all of his reserves had failed him, when he could no longer hear the voices of the three women pulling him back toward reality, after a long stretching silence in which he had nearly given up, her form appeared next to him. Her eyes sought his, and she said quietly, *If you would live, follow me.*

The Light took her, and Senta Almandar vanished.

Orion reached away from himself in some fashion that was unlike anything he had ever known before, and on the shores of that great and immortal emptiness, the power came to him, crept down at his command and bathed him in the liquid heat of the Light.

The glow of the Light touched Orion as he fell, Cain's dead arms still trying to cushion the fall. He never struck the ground at all, but vanished and reappeared standing straight in front of Maston Veramorn. Orion was only distantly aware that the bloodbath he had expected was not taking place, and he was not certain why that was not so, but had no time to think about it. He took a step forward, and Maston Veramorn took a step back and, still clutching the Ring, stumbled back from Orion.

Maston was staring at Orion's glowing form in stark disbelief and then without pause had withdrawn his handgun and began firing. Even at what he must have known was the very end of his life, he did not quite break. Somewhere in the back of his mind Orion's features grew mixed with Solan's, and both of those with the face of Loden Almandar. The bullets struck Orion's glowing form, again and again and again, struck him and did not emerge again. The man's terrible, even step never altered; he came to Maston and slapped the revolver from

Maston Veramorn's hand. With the full blazing power of the Light, for the very first time, he reached forth and put his hand over Maston Veramorn's, over the Ring.

Time stopped.

It seemed that he stood out of time, outside of the tableau where Maston Veramorn and he stood together with the Ring. Every mortal human in the Chamber stood frozen in the moment. The only movement, and even that seemed glacially slow to Orion as he stood with his hand around the Ring, was the gliding motion of the Ruler Loga, who came from nowhere in that critical instant and passed among Maston Veramorn's bodyguards and with a thought or a touch took from them their weapons. Orion saw Loga touch a thrown knife in midair, the knife moving aside from its trajectory just sufficiently that it missed the Warrior at whom the silver-eyes had thrown it and tumbled lazily out into the night.

Even the appearance of the three women, as the Light took the shape of the Sisterhood of the Ring, took a perceptible amount of time. To Orion, the times he had seen Loga do it, it had always seemed an instantaneous thing.

What an astonishing power, he thought clearly. For the first time he understood Cain, understood the drive that had brought him to gamble all to bring the Ring back. With such power one might do anything, enforce peace, bring prosperity back to the scattered Workers of the Valley such as they had never known since the height of the power of the Rulers of Earth.

Will you let us have what is ours?

Orion looked toward the three women with senses made vast and subtle and saw in them a commitment no greater than his own, an understanding that, if it was better than his own in some ways, was no better than that of which he was capable. The Warriors stood frozen, and Orion looked at them all, found them wanting each in their various ways. With the power of the Ring he was able to delve into their minds so fully that he became them in that instant. Loga was, for all his striving, at the very edge of despair himself. His friends, Kennian and Lisa and Bellows, lacked the discipline to enforce the things they *knew* were good, even in their own lives. Jimal was vastly intelligent, but lacked passion, and Maston Veramorn, who had it, cared for nothing in the world but those passions.

And then there was Senta. With the full power of the Ring he reached to encompass her, and met a grave discipline that denied him. He knew instantly that he could break the barrier and have the knowledge of her that he desired. The pulse of the power in his hand was like a drug, seductive and sweet, and made it hard for him to even think.

The Sisterhood repeated the question: *Will you let us have what is ours?*

Senta stood watching him. The thought seemed slowly formed to him, but perfectly clear. *There are things that no one else can do for you. Were Loden himself alive, he could not take this cusp from you. It is your choice, Orion. Not mine, not Cain's; yours.*

"There is so much good I could do." Orion whispered to the women who confronted him, the three and the one. "Do you understand that?"

The shriek of their incipient rage was barely contained. *It is not yours!*

"So it's not." Orion did it before he could think up a reason to stop himself, took his hand away from Maston Veramorn's, and took a step back from the man. Time resumed in that instant, and Orion took another step backward from Maston and said aloud, "Take it from *him.*"

They did.

Maston's screams did not last very long at all.

They buried Cain later that same evening, high above the city of Parliament, in the earth of the Black Mountains not far from the Chamber where a young man of twenty years had once proclaimed that there was some greater power than the power of the Light.

Orion hoped he was right.

The rain came as the earth was thrown over his still form. There was no service, no words were spoken. Those who had come to bury him would never forget him, and as for the man himself he was, after all, dead.

After they had buried him they went back down the mountain together to where the lights of the city glowed, bright against the night.

The Adult

The Year 3018 After the Fire

". . . We were not well, in those days, not any of us; we struggled because it was not in us to quit. But you should not judge us too harshly, children. For all our failures, we created in the end the world you were born in. That's something."

"Loga?" said Innelieu gently. "Are you all right?"

"All the death," the oldest living human in the universe murmured to himself, and turned back to where the children were waiting and together they went down and left the old city in the hands of time, Loga moving quickly as though he were not sure he cared to wait for them. He kept moving, traveling fast, for when he kept busy the memories were not so bad.

T H E   R I N G

A CHRONOLOGY OF EVENTS
(Excerpted from *The Book of Years,*
by Kennian Temera)

●————————————————●

In the year that was, by their calendar, 2002. A.D., five years before the first and worst of the Fire Wars, youthbooster was discovered in the land that in the Old Tongue is called America. The drug was among the major reasons for the destruction of the first world in the Fire Wars. There were, in that time, not millions or even hundreds of millions of humans on the face of the planet, but seven and a half *billion.* A drug that ended death by old age could not help but be a disaster; in this case it was one of the many, many sparks that brought about the Fire.

Armageddon occurred in the year 2007 A.D.; on our calendars it is the Year of the Fire.

A.T.F.

0—The Year of the Fire

8—The fusion-powered ship *Malacar,* a type of vessel called *aircraft carrier* in the Old Tongue, desperately seeking the technical knowledge required to remain operational, rescues a colony of scientists from the northwest coast of America. Among them are T'Pau Almandar and her eighteen-year-old son, John Almandar.

24—T'Pau and her son John Almandar rediscover youthbooster.

27—Birth of Loden Almandar.

41—T'Pau's People, living in a chain of artificial islands off the coast of California, build a clumsy, inefficient rocket that enables them to reach geosynchronous orbit and take over the orbital factories and a fleet of shuttles from before the Fire. Never again do they lack spaceflight capability.

111—Donner Almandar is born.

122—T'Pau's People meet the Sisterhood of the Ring and learn that the Light exists.

134—T'Pau's People go to war with the White Flame Tribe and the barbarian ken Hammel (later called ken Selvren).

165—A six-year-old barbarian child and mutant named Loga is rescued by Donner Almandar from the scene of a battle with the ken Hammel barbarians. Donner Almandar announces that he intends to raise the barbarian mutant as though he were one of T'Pau's People. John Almandar, a firm believer in racial purity, swears that he will kill the child Loga. John's son Loden flickers out of existence in one spot, appears behind his father, and with a blow of his staff crushes John Almandar's skull. The power of the Light has been used by one of T'Pau's People for the first time.

167—T'Pau Almandar injects Loga with a minor transform virus, changing the color of his eyes and skin so that the boy no longer resembles the hated barbarian silver-eyes.

178—The Sisterhood of the Ring condemns the Rulers for their constant warring upon the remaining humans on Earth and leaves Earth entirely.

191—The White Flame Tribe is exterminated after attempting to use thermonuclear weapons upon T'Pau's People. The ken Selvren flee south.

193—T'Pau's People, a term that at that time includes both the genetically altered descendants of T'Pau Almandar and the genetically normal humans who have fought at their side, settle in a huge valley to the north of the Glowing Desert. It is a nearly perfect home, though slightly too cold. A lengthy shoreline provides T'Pau's people with access to the ocean.

199—Rumors of Giants reach the People. They dismiss the rumors as just that, until, across the entirety of the Earth, the weather begins to warm. The ocean rises, threatening to flood the Valley. Three men go north: Loden Almandar; his son Donner; and the barbarian who has learned to use the Light, Loga.

200–206—The War with the Giants.

206—The Giants are conquered in short order. The Giants have set in motion a global warming that they cannot stop. Under threat of destruction by those who have come to call themselves the Rulers of Earth, they begin construction of the Great Dam, to protect the Valley from the rising Ocean.

242—The Great Schism. T'Pau's People learn to regenerate themselves through the use of the Light. In a brief but utterly conclusive war, T'Pau Almandar's descendants, using the power of the Light, seize control of the facilities that produce youthbooster and destroy them. Donner Almandar declares that the decision to refuse youthbooster to those who cannot control the Light is unethical, and a great schism develops among T'Pau's People. The technologists generally end up following Donner Almandar; the antiscience forces remain in the Valley and concentrate upon developing the power of the Light.

Those remaining in the Valley propose, and implement, the Covenant of the Rulers; an agreement whereby those Rulers who choose not to go with Donner Almandar swear that they will follow in all subjects—as Donner did not—the decisions of the Ruling Tribunal. Donner Almandar goes south, to the edge of the Glowing Desert, and in 244 begins construction of the greatest spaceport the world has ever seen: the city of Donnertown. For near three decades Donnertown is engaged in the task of building a great fleet of starships.

255—T'Pav Almandar commits suicide.

271—When the fleet of starships is completed, Donner Almandar and almost half of T'Pau's People, with better than two thirds of the normal human population of North America, lift into orbit, enter their starships, and are never heard from again. Only one of the most brilliant of the engineers who helped Donner Almandar build the fleet of starships in which his followers left Earth does not leave with them; the former barbarian Loga, at the last moment, changes his mind and stays behind, in the Valley, possibly—though this may be apocryphal—at the urging of Loden Almandar.

THE RING

271–1153—Pax Almandar : The Time of Peace

(There are relatively few entries in this chronology for those eight hundred eighty-two years which separate Donner Almandar's exodus from Earth and Artemis of Erebion's rebellion against the Rulers. There was a reason it was called the Time of Peace by historians; simply put, not much happened.)

301—The Chamber at Parliament is built by the Rulers.

526—Academy founded.

1129—Artemis of Erebion is born.

1130—Eric Malachor is born.

1133—Cain's grandfather Garret is born.

1137—Mistress Sandahl is born.

1141—Artemis of Erebion enters the Academy at Parliament.

1149—Artemis leaves Academy after failing the Test.

1150—Garret enters the service of Eric, Lord Malachor.

1153—The Rebellion of Erebion.

1160—Marric is born.

1164—Jenny is born.

1178—Marric learns how to fish through the waterlock overlooking Eastmarch.

1180—Marric and Elena marry.

1181—Cain's elder brother, Misa, is born.

1184—Anton Lusende is born.

1185—Risa Lusende is born.

1187—Winter 8, Cain is born.

1188—Siva is born.

1191—Barra is born.

1193—Winter 22, Marric is killed in a freak storm.

1194—Winter 8, Siva is enrolled in school with Mistress Sandahl.

1195—The rebel Artemis of Erebion, who called himself at that time Loukas of Semalia, comes to teach Cain of Eastmarch.

1201—Cain is sent to Academy.

1202—Loukas leaves Eastmarch.

1207—Spring 1, Cain is sent into the Glowing Desert.

1211—Cain finds Donnertown.

1213—Succeeds in opening youthbooster vault.

1218—Cain succeeds in turning on Donnertown's Shield.

1253—Cain returns from the Exile.

1258—Tristan d'Volta is born.

1261—The genegineer Riabel brings to term the twins Solan and Rea.

1267—The Ruler Senta is born.

1274—Fall 33, Treaty of Eastmarch.

1277—Solan enters the service of Maston Veramorn.

1278—Lisa is born.

1279—Orion is born; also, Kennian Temera (No-Name) and Jackson son of Donal (Bellows) are born.

1284—Abdication of the Rulers; death of Loden Almandar and Solan. The Ruler Senta is imprisoned; Rea is blinded and imprisoned. Orion is taken by Cain to be raised in the Caverns at Eastmarch.

1299—The War for the Ring.

Date and Time Usages
in *The Ring*

•————————————————————•

The calendar used herein is essentially the one proposed by Isaac Asimov in his essay "The Week Excuse," which is collected in his anthology of essays *The Tragedy of the Moon.* The only substantive change I've made in Asimov's proposed World Season Calendar is the retention of the seasons of the years as the names of the year's four quarters. (Asimov's proposal was that the quarters of the year be labeled A, B, C, and D, which I am sure would be sensible and convenient once people got used to it. For the purposes of this story, however, I've chosen to retain the season names, with their clear and immediate meanings.)

This calendar has several advantages over the current hideous mishmash we use to count the passage of a year. Sunday (using our current weekday names) is always the first day of the week; the first, and then the eighth, and then the fifteenth, and so on, so that you can, from the date, tell what day of the week you are dealing with. The four "months" are all of the same length. A calendar for an entire year consists of nothing more than a sheet of paper containing the ninety-one days that comprise any given month, or quarter. Lastly, you don't need an entirely new calendar each year; the year simply repeats itself over again.

Only one quarter, Spring, has more than 91 days. Spring has 92, thus bringing the total count of days in the year to 365. The ninety-second day is not counted as a weekday. Every Leap Year, Fall Quarter also has a ninety-second day, which likewise is not counted as a weekday. The four quarters, in order, are Winter, Spring, Summer and Fall.

CALENDAR MONTH, MODIFIED ASIMOV CALENDAR

ONEDAY	TWOSDAY	THREESDAY	FOURSDAY	FIVESDAY	SIXDAY	SUNDAY
1	2	3	4	5	6	7
8	9	10	11	12	13	14
15	16	17	18	19	20	21
22	23	24	25	26	27	28
29	30	31	32	33	34	35
36	37	38	39	40	41	42
43	44	45	46	47	48	49
50	51	52	53	54	55	56
57	58	59	60	61	62	63
64	65	66	67	68	69	70
71	72	73	74	75	76	77
78	79	80	81	82	83	84
85	86	87	88	89	90	91

The metric day is my own invention. It consists of a day of our current length—though the Earth's rotational speed does slow, it does so only slightly, and over the course of millennia—which has been subdivided into ten metric hours; each metric hour is further subdivided into 100 metric minutes, and each metric minute is subdivided into 100 seconds.

For conversion purposes, the following are the equivalent values in both standard and metric time units:

One metric hour = 2.4 standard hours
One metric minute = 1.44 standard minutes
One metric second = .864 standard seconds

The decimal day (along with a decimal calendar system that is, by comparison with the Asimov World Season Calendar, flawed) was in fact *used* in France, beginning in 1792, and lasted for thirteen years before Napoleon abolished it and replaced it with the date and time system prevalent then and now throughout the rest of the world. Only two centuries later I managed to reinvent it entirely on my own.

—DKM

ABOUT THE AUTHOR

Bantam Spectra published Daniel Keys Moran's highly praised debut novel, *The Armageddon Blues*, in the spring of 1988. His second novel, *Emerald Eyes*, came out in July. The story of Trent Castanaveras, Denice Castanaveras, Emilé Garon, and Mohammed Vance continues in the sequel, which Spectra will publish in the spring of 1989. *The Ring* is Moran's third novel. Moran and his wife, Holly, live in Southern California.

Husband and wife screenwriting team, William Stewart and Joanne Nelsen, have worked nearly ten years toward the film production of *The Ring*. Native Canadians, they now live in Malibu, California.